LIZZIE I

CW00418288

Dark
highland
skies

Lizzie Lamb © Copyright 2023

The right of Lizzie Lamb to be identified as the author of this work has been asserted by her in accordance with the Copyright, Designs and Patents Act 1998.

All rights reserved.

No reproduction, copy or transmission of this publication may be made without express prior written permission.

No paragraph of this publication may be reproduced, copied or transmitted except with express prior written permission or in accordance with the provisions of the Copyright Act 1956 (as amended).

Any person who commits any unauthorised act in relation to this publication may be liable to criminal prosecution and civil claims for damage.

Created by Goldcrest Books International Ltd
www.goldcrestbooks.com
publish@goldcrestbooks.com

ISBN: 979-8-373398-41-1

February 14th 2023
A great day to publish
and to kick start our
Golden Wedding Anniversary year.

We were very lucky to have 'found each other' in 1969 and
to have remained together through thick and thin.

This book is dedicated to the love of my life –
Dave (aka Bongo Man).

Chapter One

Jet lagged and disorientated from driving on the wrong side of the road, Halley Dunbar pulled into a layby above Loch Morar and switched off the engine. Now she wished she'd heeded everyone's advice, stayed overnight in Fort William, completing the last leg of the six-thousand-mile journey from Hawaii to Mallaig tomorrow.

Instead, she'd left Inverness and driven off into the November gloom bracing herself for whatever the weather and terrain threw at her. So far, that had included gusting winds, hailstones as big as golf balls and deep puddles making her car aquaplane.

When her family had seen her off from Honolulu airport three days earlier, warning her to 'look out for haggises, they're fearsome beasts', she'd grinned and blown farewell kisses. There the temperature had been in the low eighties, here in Lochaber, thousands of miles away, the mercury had barely risen above nine degrees Celsius all day.

'Forty-eight degrees,' she groaned, converting it to Fahrenheit. '*Failte gu Alba*: welcome to Scotland. Some welcome.' It seemed as if she'd been travelling forever, sleeping on planes or in airport lounges waiting for connecting flights, drinking strong black coffee to stay awake. Any amusement she'd felt at her family's parting joke had vanished somewhere between Honolulu and Heathrow along with her sense of humour. Now she wished she'd packed warmer clothes; she'd forgotten how cold Scotland could be in November.

In May, too, come to that, if memory served her well.

'This is the land of your fathers, Dunbar. Man up.'

Under normal circumstances her parents, or one of her siblings, would have made the journey and left her to gaze at the cosmos through a multi-million-pound telescope in the observatory at the Haleakalā Observatory, Maui. Instead, she'd stepped up to the mark and volunteered to sort out her late great-uncle Tam's affairs.

Removing the keys from the ignition she struggled into a waterproof jacket bought in the pop-up shop at Heathrow. Then, planting booted feet firmly on the ground she got out of the car, blipped the alarm and gazed into the darkness. Somewhere below, between the layby and the steep incline leading down to the river Morar there were rough steps cut into the bank. She needed to remember their exact location if she was to reach the beach and her great-uncle's bothy without breaking her neck.

A vengeful squall of wind threw rain, sharp as glass into her face, she sucked in her breath at the strength of it.

However, Halley Dunbar was nothing if not determined. Drawing on her last reserves of energy and digging booted heels into the soft earth to slow her descent, she slithered down the bank. The resinous scent of pine needles and dank vegetation greeted her, bringing back memories of holidays in Lochaber when she was younger. Too late, she remembered the torch and walking poles lying on the back seat of the Volvo and let out a *damn*. A stout branch would have to do instead. Once she reached her Uncle Tam's bothy she'd switch on the lights, push back the darkness and breathe a sigh of relief that her journey was at an end. Providing the electricity hadn't been switched off following his death two weeks previously.

She could, she supposed, have rung ahead and let the estate know she was on her way. The factor would have switched on the heat and electricity and made sure a welcome pack of groceries was left for her. However, she wanted to remain incognito for as long as possible. Give herself time to adjust to being back in Scotland, deal with the past in her own way before memories came crowding in, affecting her judgement.

Halley Dunbar prided herself on being logical, hard-headed but that concealed a soft heart which was easily bruised. Picking up the nearest sturdy branch she prodded the ground in front of her and edged forward, forgetting about everything other than reaching the beach without breaking her neck.

Luckily, the moment she set foot on the silver sands, the clouds parted, and the pale light of a gibbous moon showed the way to the old salmon bothy. Straightening, Halley looked across the loch towards the lights on the far shore and despite her earlier resolution, memories crowded in thick and fast. Voices. Laughter. The touch of a hand on her skin. A Judas kiss. Now she could finally admit that putting her uncle's affairs in order wasn't the only reason for making this trip.

She had ghosts to lay.

The word made her shiver and reluctant to cover the last hundred yards to the salmon bothy. Great-uncle Tam had always kept a light burning in the window when she stayed with him during the long summer holidays. Now the house was in darkness and he was in the undertakers in Mallaig waiting for her to bring him home. That weighed heavily on her heart and conscience.

'Forgive me, Uncle Tam, I should have returned sooner.'

She let out a shaky breath, throat tight and tears pricking her eyes. Her breath seemed to blow the clouds back across the moon and darkness descended again. Dismissing the notion as fanciful she made her way over silver sands. Halley Dunbar didn't do whimsical. Right? She was an astrophysicist, an acknowledged expert in the field of exoplanet research and whimsy had no place in her life.

However, this place, so steeped in history and legend, had such an otherworldly feel to it that whimsy won hands down. She paused, listening to the wind whipping through the pine trees and became aware of heavy footsteps moving towards her. She turned, peering into the darkness as, without warning, she was tackled to the ground.

'Got you, you bastard,' a voice growled in her ear.

It had all happened so quickly that, conversely, time seemed to slow down and she was flipped over, pinned onto the sands by an unmistakably male body, her breath crushed out of her lungs. When she opened her mouth to scream all that escaped was a pathetic whimper before her mouth was filled with sand. Everything she'd learned in self-defence classes went out of her head except the need to survive. Wriggling her right shoulder free and twisting her body as far as she was able, she swung her makeshift walking stick upwards and outwards, smacking her assailant squarely on the side of the head.

A sickening crack followed by a loud groan and then his grip slackened.

Adrenaline gave Halley the extra strength needed to roll him off her. Scrambling to her feet, limbs scarcely able to support her weight and gasping for air, she staggered backwards. She'd stunned him, but he was powerfully built and would soon recover and doubtless come after her. Picking up the branch, prepared to hit him a second time if the need arose, Halley regained her courage. Then, deciding that discretion was the better part of valour, she dropped the branch and ran towards her great-uncle's bothy. Reaching the porch, she found the key hidden underneath the stone Skye Terrier as it had always been, locked the door behind her and leaned against it, catching her breath. Then, groping for the panel of light switches to the right of the door she flicked on every one.

A security light, a new addition since she'd last stayed there, showed her assailant out for the count and lying on the sands.

'God help me, I've killed him.' Her grasp of Scottish law was shaky, but surely the worst she could be charged with was justifiable homicide. Or had she watched too many episodes of CSI?

Picking up the telephone with nerveless fingers she dialled 9-1-1. Then, remembering that she was in Scotland, ended the call and dialled 9-9-9 instead. About to press the last 'nine' she glanced over at her assailant. Something about him, the colour of his hair, the set of his shoulders, long legs and athletic build was familiar.

'Oh God,' she breathed replacing the handset on the cradle.

She knew exactly who she'd murdered. No longer fearing for her life so much as the consequence of her actions, she fetched the first aid kit from under the sink and headed back down the beach. Soon she was kneeling beside him, conscious of the trickle of blood running from his temple onto the silver sand.

'Jayzus,' she muttered, waiting for him to regain his senses. 'What have I done?'

Her voice had the desired effect because he groaned, opened his eyes and raised his hand to the gash on his temple. His fingers came away, sticky with blood.

'You,' was all he could manage.

One word, but with the power to push back the years and remind Halley how it felt to stand on this beach twenty years ago, in trouble and with no one to turn to.

Chapter Two

Forgetting for a moment that the man on the sands was her enemy, Halley opened the first aid kit, found an antiseptic wipe and dabbed at his temple. At first glance, it appeared that she'd inflicted no more than a flesh wound. However, because the skin was thin in that area, the wound was bleeding copiously. Deftly, she held a small lint pad over the wound to stem the flow of blood, wrapped a bandage round his head and secured it in place with a criss-cross of antiseptic tape.

'X' marks the spot.

There, all done and it was more than he deserved, more than any Strachan deserved. Her first aid training kicking in she checked for signs of concussion. 'How many fingers am I holding up?' she asked. He knocked her hand away and gave out an ungracious grunt. Ignoring his churlish behaviour, Halley persisted: 'Can you stand?'

'Of course, I can bloody well stand,' he barked.

'Fine.'

She snapped shut the lid of the first aid kit with more force than necessary to show her displeasure, brushed the sand off her knees and waited. Despite his snarky reply, when he stood up, he lurched forward and took several steps before righting himself. He held out his hand as though asking for help and then dropped it to his side.

'Damn and blast.'

In spite of herself, Halley reached out to steady him, only to be shrugged off a second time. Okay – message received loud and clear. Tucking the first aid kit under her arm she started up the beach back towards The Salmon Bothy, hoping that he'd apologise for pinning her to the sand, limp his way home and that'd be the last she'd see of him.

Hector Strachan, never one to do exactly what was expected of him, overtook her and barred her way. Pulling a torch out of his pocket he shone it in her face.

'We wondered who the Dunbars would send over to settle Tam's affairs. You were the last one I -we- expected.'

She pushed the torch aside and sent him a haughty look.

'Is that so? Although, *affairs* is rather a grand word for Tam's worldly goods, isn't it?' Her gesture took in the salmon bothy, rented from the estate, his meagre belongings contained within its four walls and such savings as he'd doubtless put aside to pay for his funeral. 'My parents are in their late seventies, my sister is expecting her second child, my brother is on a research trip and so,' she swept herself from head to toe with a gesture and accompanied it with a mocking curtsy, 'you got, me. I –' She stopped mid-sentence.

'Go on.'

'Nothing.'

'Nothing?' Unconvinced, he walked away, leaning on the branch she'd earlier used to defend herself. After limping a few paces, he stopped and, without turning, asked, 'How long has it been?'

No need for clarification. She knew exactly what he meant.

'Twenty years.'

'Twenty years,' he repeated, his voice fading as he headed up the beach away from her and towards the path leading to *Creag na h-lolaire – Eagles Crag*, his family home. Unlike Halley's descent to the beach that path was clearly defined, each step edged with wooden slats to hold back the shifting sand and illuminated by a single round light. Thick marine rope attached to posts on the edge of each step acted as a banister and at the top of each post a single LED light lit the way. Had the laird, Sir Montgomery Strachan, installed the handrail for her uncle's sake, Halley wondered? They often sat on the bench outside the bothy reminiscing about their army days when Sir Monty had been a young lieutenant and Tam Dunbar the batman appointed to look after him.

Halley remembered Sir Monty fondly, such thoughtfulness would not be out of character. She watched Hector make his way up the steps to the plantation of ancient Scots Pines marking the boundary of the Strachans' land. He held the branch in his right hand, using it as an improvised walking stick while gripping the banister rope with his left. The bough, having been used as a potential murder weapon, apparently decided that enough was enough. Clearly, not up to supporting Strachan's weight it snapped clean in two, suggesting that he'd been leaning on it more heavily than Halley realised. He staggered forward and crashed to his knees. If it hadn't had been for the rope banister, he would have slithered back down the steps and landed at her feet.

Instinctively, Halley rushed forward to help but then stopped. When she'd stayed with Tam, she and the village children had been expressly forbidden to cross the line demarcating the beach and the Strachan estate. Uncle Tam, usually so laid back about such matters, had been most insistent that she did not go up there uninvited, leaving Halley with the lasting impression that she and the village children were beings of a lesser god and not good enough to mix with the Strachans.

Surprised to find that time had not altered that perception or made it any more palatable, Halley put the thought from her and moved closer.

'I can manage,' Hector Strachan growled, staying her with his hand, again without glancing in her direction. However, Halley was no longer eighteen and in awe of him or his family. She had a doctorate in astrophysics, written papers on the likelihood of discovering exoplanets outside the solar system and was in demand on the lecture circuit. There was no place in her life for outmoded notions of hierarchy and privilege. She remembered Tor Strachan only too well and evidently time hadn't improved his demeanour or lowered his high opinion of himself.

He owed her an explanation and an apology for pinning her down on the beach and they were going nowhere until she received it. If he wanted her respect then he'd damn well have to earn it, and the same went for his family.

'Let me see you manage, then.'

Her command caught him off guard and earned her another dark look. Halley countered it with an unruffled one of her own. Men! To emphasise her point, she stood with her arms folded and watched him try, and fail, to scramble up, his boots slithering on ground made sodden by winter rain. Then she frowned; something other than a bang on the side of his head was responsible for his lack of coordination and balance. After an impressive selection of swear words, he held his hand out to her, his fingers curling and uncurling into his palm.

Plainly, asking for help – especially from her, did not please Hector Strachan.

Walking over, Halley gave a loud tut expressing annoyance with men, their egos and false pride. Unwilling to take his outstretched hand – that was a step too far, she grabbed his forearm, manoeuvred her shoulder under his arm pit and helped him to his feet. Tor Strachan was well over six feet and no lightweight. They slithered on the mud, however by edging forward they managed to make it to the top of the steps where the ground was drier. Halley wondered if she should leave him to walk the short distance up through the gardens to the house unaided. However, she felt some responsibility for his condition, even if he had brought it on himself by virtually attacking her on the beach.

There would be a time and a place for him to explain why he'd done that, but this wasn't it. It would be killing him to ask for help, however mutely, and she'd settle for the satisfaction of knowing that.

The Strachans were an ancient clan, their lineage stretching back almost a thousand years. They were proud as Lucifer and just as fiendish in their own way. She reminded herself not to lose sight of that as, joined together like lovers, they made their way through the gardens of *Creag na h-Iolaire* towards the castle.

Chapter Three

The castle's double doors were wide open and powerful security lights sliced through the November darkness unerring as laser beams, stopping just short of where they stood.

Despite its fairy tale appearance: pele tower complete with arrow slits, crenulations, pepper pot turrets covered in dragon-scale tiles, something about the castle made Halley shudder. Dark deeds had been carried out behind its stone walls: kidnapped brides forced into marriage for their dowries, enemies disposed of in the loch or thrown down the deep draw well in the courtyard. There was a saying in Lochaber: *never accept an invitation to dine with the Strachans. It could be your last meal.* Nowadays, it was said in jest, but it underlined the fact that the family were used to getting their own way.

They simply went about it more subtly these days.

As an astrophysicist, Halley spent her life focusing on what could be quantified, measured, calculated. Blood feuds, ancient or modern, had no place in her world. She was here for one reason and one reason only, to lay her beloved great-uncle to rest. Once that had been achieved, she could return to Hawaii and get on with life.

She glanced at the coat of arms above the stone arch leading to the double doors. The crest, a leaping stag with a thistle in its mouth, had lost some definition over the years. However, the motto, cast into relief by the security lights – *Non Timeo Sed Caveo* – *cautious but not afraid,* summed up the Strachans' unassailable belief in themselves.

Time to bring this encounter with Hector Strachan to a close. 'Can you manage on your own?' she asked, her body language making plain that she was keen to return to the bothy

'Not coming in?' He raised an eyebrow and the wry smile indicated he knew the answer. 'Probably not.'

'Probably not,' she affirmed.

Evidently in no hurry for her to leave he tightened his grip on her shoulder. 'Don't you think, having almost killed me, you owe it to me to walk me to the door?' He made it sound like a challenge, something to test her mettle.

'Don't think so.'

'Right.' He shrugged, leaving her to put her own interpretation on the word.

'Don't think I dare?'

'Quite the reverse, I suspect that you've gained in audacity and self-assurance since we last met. You were never – how does the saying go, backwards at coming forwards.' He waited for her to correct him.

'You suspect right,' she said, frowning at the clumsy sentence. To make her point, she wriggled free from his armpit, withdrew the arm curled round his waist and took several steps back. 'There, you can make the short distance to the door unaided, call for a footman, fall over. Whatever. You're not my problem.'

In spite of her words Halley had the feeling that he was very much 'her problem'. Making the most of him dropping his guard she slipped into the shadows, hurried down the steps and was standing on the beach before Tor Strachan realised she was gone.

Standing in the middle of the room which doubled as the salmon bothy's kitchen/sitting room Halley raked her fingers through her dark auburn hair and tried to massage away a burgeoning headache. Catching sight of herself in the mirror over the sink she pulled a face. She looked a wreck – makeup smudged, sand in her hair and mud on her waterproof jacket. When she looked down at her new walking boots caked with a mixture of damp sand and pine needles, they had left a trail from the front door to where she stood.

She'd wanted her first encounter with the Strachans to be on her terms, needed to show them she was all grown up and nobody's fool. She'd failed miserably on both counts.

Some homecoming.

She fancied a long hot bath but the tiny bathroom contained a loo, a sink and a shower tray surrounded by, if she remembered correctly, a slightly mouldy curtain on a curved rail. Baths with candles, tea lights and her Spotify playlist would have to wait until she checked back into the airport hotel at Heathrow in two weeks' time.

'Good job, Dunbar,' she congratulated herself. 'You set foot on Morar and the next thing you know, you've almost killed a man. And that man *would* have to be Hector Strachan, the laird's son and heir.'

Ach dinnae fash yersel', hen, she could hear her uncle's voice in her head. *Tor brought it on himsel'. Always been a hot head. Nothing's changed.*

It saddened her to realise that Tor Strachan had seen more of her uncle over the years than she had. 'Sorry, Uncle Tam, I've stayed away too long,' she said, looking round the sparsely furnished bothy which, at first glance, hadn't received a lick of paint since she'd last stayed here. She glanced over at her uncle's chair, remembering how the Strachans' factor, Frank Bunce, had placed it next to the wood burner, well out of draughts from the front door.

All for Tam's sake.

It looked as if it hadn't moved from that spot during the intervening years.

She recalled Tam laughing when she'd draped a large tartan shawl over it to add a feminine touch. How delighted he'd been when she'd plumped a cushion and placed it at his back with a flourish and said: 'Would Sir like to try it out for size?'

Tam had obliged, declaring: 'That's the boy for me,' before crashing down on it and patting the chair arms in proprietorial fashion.

Then she'd brought the side table closer, made him a cup of strong brown tea in his favourite mug – the one with the faded transfer of Rangers Football Club, placing the mug and a shortbread finger within reach.

Her throat tightened as she glanced at the chair and table, out of date newspaper and a mug of tea with a skin of mould growing over it. How long had Uncle Tam been in his chair before anyone realised he'd passed away? She tried to work up righteous anger against the Strachans for not keeping an eye on him but she knew that wasn't the case. Uncle Tam had his shopping delivered, his laundry taken care of, wood and coal provided by the estate and his utility bills paid by the laird, his old commanding officer, Monty Strachan.

If anyone had let her uncle down it was her family in pursuing their own dreams, forgetting all about Tam and the auld country.

A Victorian wag-at-the-wall clock with a painted face and exposed pendulum chimed nine o'clock. Who was keeping it wound up? It had been her job every other day when she'd stayed here in the summer. Taking her phone out of her pocket she checked the time in Hawaii, eleven am. She hadn't slept a wink last night wondering what was waiting for her in Morar, and it hadn't included being leapt upon and pinned to the beach by Tor Strachan.

Now, standing in the middle of her uncle's bothy the memories came thick and fast, buzzing around her head like flies. If only she could swat them away and hold back the tears so easily.

'Come on, Halley,' she counselled herself, 'Tam would hate to see you like this. Buck up. See if there's anything in the fridge, make yourself a hot drink, check out your bedroom and then go fetch your bags from the car.' She opened the under the counter fridge and saw that someone had left a 'welcome pack' of milk, butter, bread, bacon and coffee. An ironic use of the phrase, given the circumstances, she thought, closing the fridge door. Turning her back on the kitchen she crossed the floor and pushed open the door to what she still thought of as her bedroom.

In the intervening years central heating had been installed and the wee house was warm and, astonishingly, everything just as she'd left it, as though waiting for her return. Books in their rightful place on a small bookcase she and Tam had bought in Fort William and dragged down from the layby where her hire car was currently sitting, a faded astrological chart on the wall, a pebble representation of Morag, the monster said to inhabit the loch. And, on the deep window ledge the Victorian orrery Tam had given her when she'd passed her O levels. Walking over to it she turned the handle and the planets orbited the sun in their pre-ordained path. Then she turned towards her precious brass telescope Tam had bought for her thirteenth birthday. The brass showed signs of having been regularly polished and the lens was free of dust and cobwebs. The only chair in the bedroom was positioned in front of the telescope, perfect for reading the stars through the window which overlooked the beach. How many nights had she and Tam sat here mapping the constellations and looking for meteor showers? A shared hobby which had kick-started her career.

'Uncle Tam,' she whispered, 'I've been a knowing fool.'

Then, throwing herself on the single bed thoughtfully made up for her, she drew the duvet around her shoulders and stared dry eyed out of the small window at such stars as were visible in the dark highland sky, wishing for the tears which refused to come.

The next morning, she made breakfast. In Hawaii, she usually went for a run before heading for the observatory after a light breakfast of fresh fruit and yoghurt but that wouldn't do today. A cold wind was whipping up the fine silver sand and draughts were winnowing through the gaps in the wooden sides of the bothy. Clearly, bacon, eggs, toast and coffee were called for. She paused half way through cooking the meal and stared out over the beach, feeling as though she'd stepped back in time and it should have been Uncle Tam, not her, standing by the stove and asking if she wanted mushrooms or French Toast.

After eating breakfast, she stood by the sink, putting off the moment when she'd have to drive over to Mallaig to sort out the arrangements for Tam's funeral. Little had she thought when she'd left all those years ago that she'd never hear his gruff, loving voice again. Dashing away the tears, she looked out over the windswept sands and steeled herself for the ordeal ahead.

Chapter Four

She parked near the station and stood by her car, aware of how different Mallaig looked in November compared to the summer months when Uncle Tam drove them here in search of the best fish and chips in the world. Or she caught the train to Fort William, Inverness and the road south when her holiday was over. Halley smiled, focusing on that happy memory as she walked towards Ferguson's Funeral Directors where Uncle Tam was waiting to be brought home.

Feeling the tears welling up again, despite her brave resolution, Halley concentrated on noting the transformation Ferguson's Funeral Directors had undergone over the years. New windows, a tasteful arrangement of flowers, examples of monumental masonry and headstones on display and a discreet notice in the window detailing who to contact out of office hours. The signage above the door had changed, too. Then it had read *Robert Ferguson, Funeral Director and Monumental Mason*. Now Auld Rab Ferguson was long gone and the business had been passed on to his daughter, Rowan.

Pushing open the door Halley entered a reception area with a low table, two settees at right angles to each other and a coffee machine. Celtic music played softly in the background and a stone diffuser puffed essential oils into the air. Nothing as crass as a bell over the door announced her arrival, instead a discreet CCTV camera linked the foyer to an office behind the panelled wall.

Closing the door to keep out the winter chill she waited hesitantly until the door in the wall opened and Rowan Ferguson stepped through. 'Halley Dunbar! Is it really you?'

'It's me alright,' Halley grinned, stepping towards her childhood friend. That was all the signal Rowan needed, she rushed forward and wrapped Halley in a warm embrace, almost knocking her off her feet. Neither woman spoke as they hugged each other until, finally pulling apart, they dashed away the tears and exclaimed how the other had grown, become a woman.

'I know we've kept in touch over the years via the internet, but nothing's as good as seeing you in the flesh.'

'You, too,' was Halley's inadequate response. Words failed her as being back in Mallaig with someone who knew and loved her, was overwhelming.

'My word, you look fantastic. Living in Hawaii obviously suits you.'

'You, too. Look fantastic, I mean.'

'Well, hardly,' was Rowan's self-deprecating reply. 'C'mon, give us another hug and then we'll go through.' Halley was only too happy to comply and, when they drew apart, Rowan pulled paper handkerchiefs from the box on the table with professional expertise and handed a bunch to Halley. Rowan laughed. 'Will ye look at us? Anyone would think we hadn't seen each other for almost twenty years. Let me look at you properly.' She took a few steps back and gave Halley a searching look. 'Ye were a stoater, even when you were a teenager. I had the spots and the puppy fat, while you –'

'Stoater,' Halley laughed, 'I haven't heard that word in years. But look at you,' she indicated Rowan's discreet business suit, the collar edged in Ferguson tartan and her blonde hair arranged in a becoming chignon. 'Yer no sae bad yersel' hen.'

'You still speak the patois, then?'

'Aye, though I'm out of practise.'

'We'll soon sort that. Come on, there's someone out back you'll recall from the old days.' Taking Halley by the hand she led her through to the office. A man in his mid-thirties was hunched over a radiator hugging it for warmth and looking very sorry for himself. 'Ye'll remember Halley, James?'

'Aye, I do,' he responded without much enthusiasm, sending her a baleful glance.

'James helps me out from time-to-time, to please my auntie. Although,' she sent her cousin a withering look, 'another cockup like this morning's and he'll be back to gutting herring down at the docks.'

'Aw, gie us a break, Rowan. Everyone's allowed the odd mistake.'

'Let's ask Halley what she thinks.' She passed an iPad showing the obituaries in the local newspaper over to Halley. Halley read the in memoriam notice several times: *Asleep with the angels.*

'What am I missing?' she asked, sending Rowan a puzzled look.

'Look again,' Rowan instructed as James developed a sudden interest in a spot on the wall above his head.

'I see it now. *In loving memory of Auntie Sheila, asleep with the angles.*' She didn't know whether to laugh or cry but sent James a sympathetic look because he looked so wretched.

'I give this eejit a specific task because he said he wanted more responsibility. And, soft-hearted fool that I am, I thought he was ready for it. All he had to do was check the memoriam notices for typos before uploading to the newspaper's website. And this is what happens.' She cuffed her cousin on the shoulder with a rolled-up newspaper. 'Pah,' she let out a snort of indignation. 'Go on, get out of here before I say something I'll regret, ye great numptie.'

'I might've had a couple of bevvies more than I should,' he muttered, sidling past Halley and making for the door.

'You think?' was Rowan's curt reply. 'I'll have to make it up to the family and it'll be coming out of your wages, Jim-Boab.'

He closed the door behind him. Rowan and Halley exchanged a look and then burst out laughing.

'It could've been worse,' Halley mused, wiping her eyes.

'How's that?'

'At least he didn't mention the Jutes or the Saxons.'

'You always were good at history,' Rowan added, the years slipping away until they were, once more, kids playing on the beach outside Tam's bothy. Then the laughter turned into something deeper, more emotional and they hugged each other a second time, lost in memories.

'I'm sorry about Tam.' Rowan said, releasing Halley and signalling that she should follow her through to the living quarters.

'I'm glad that you've looked after him, Rowan. Seriously, I am.'

'Och, well, he was like an honorary grandfather to me. I was pleased when Hector, acting on the laird's instructions, asked me to take charge of his funeral. It was like keeping it in the family.'

'Hector did that?' Halley asked, surprised, taking a seat at the kitchen table when prompted by Rowan.

'He also went down to the bothy, collected Tam's uniform and brought it over to us. Tam told me many times that he wanted to be buried in it.'

'Many times?'

'I saw a lot of Tam over the years. I used to take him some of Mammy's cakes after she'd had a baking session. When she passed, I carried on with the tradition, making them myself. Rather inferior I'm sorry to say. Are you alright? I didn't mean to upset you.'

'It's an emotional time,' Halley said, drawing her sleeve across her eyes. Rowan sent her a sympathetic look, pulled out a few sheets of kitchen roll and passed them across the table. 'Sorry.'

'No need to be sorry, I'm used to it. Tears are good, they're . . . cathartic. Is that the right word?'

'Exactly right.' Halley managed a watery smile and blew her nose. 'Besides, I owe you.'

'You do?'

Rowan went over to a high cupboard, brought out whisky, two glasses and a bottle of Highland Spring water. 'A wee dram? To toast Tam? I know you've driven over but I'll make sure it's a weak one. Or I can get Jim to drive you home, he has his uses.' She rolled her eyes in a comical fashion.

'Go on, just a wee one.' They clinked glasses together. 'Slainte.'

'Ye havenae forgotten your Scottish roots, Miss Dunbar,' Rowan said approvingly. 'To Uncle Tam, friendship and your homecoming, however brief.'

'Tam,' Halley said, sipping the uisge beatha. 'Go on, explain how you owe me.'

'When you stayed with Tam in the summer holidays you always included me in the group of kids who played down by Tam's bothy.

You came back to my house for tea, sat on my bed listening to pop music and went on the train to Fort William with me to help spend my birthday money.'

'That doesn't seem like a big deal.'

'But it was. The other kids, the ones I went to school with, wouldn't come near the house because we lived above the shop. They wouldn't walk through the yard to the backdoor to call for me because that's where my father stacked the half-finished coffins.'

'Really?' Halley's heart squeezed in sympathy for her friend.

'Some of them said that they'd seen ghosts floating around out there.' She mimed a ghost rattling its chains. 'Then, when you stayed over and because of Tam's connection with the laird,' she gave Halley a long look before continuing, 'it suddenly became okay for them to visit, too.'

'Kids, huh? I understand, believe me. I help out at the Mauna Kea Observatories as a volunteer guide and you wouldn't believe some of the behaviour I've witnessed. Or the feedback some parents leave on Trip Advisor if I dare to remonstrate with their little darlings. I much prefer being in front of my telescope staring into the blackness of space. I'd never make the grade as a teacher.'

'Sadly, once you stopped coming to Morar, they reverted back to their default position, calling me Freaky Ferguson. Nice, eh?' She shrugged but it was plain that the hurt was still there. 'You know, I've always wondered why you stayed away.' Having raised the subject, she waited for Halley to fill in the gaps.

'No mystery. I won a fully funded scholarship to MIT – The Massachusetts Institute of Technology, to study astronomy and Dad took up a position as a visiting lecturer. After that, coming home every summer was no longer an option. Then I graduated, secured a position at the observatory in Maui on the exoplanet research team, my family moved to Hawaii to enjoy the climate and to be nearer to me, so it became our home.' That was her stock response to anyone who asked.

Brief, to the point and didn't invite further questions.

'Hawaii or Mallaig?' Rowan held her palms out weighing up the options. 'And the winner is – Hawaii.'

'You should come over and stay with us, my parents would love to see you and you'd hardly recognise my brother and sister. Surely you could shut up shop for a fortnight?'

'I'd love to, but . . . who would run the business in my absence?'

'Good point,' Halley frowned, wondering if there was a way round the problem. 'Okay, time's moving on. Can you let me know how much uncle Tam's funeral is likely to cost? I don't know if he's got insurance to cover it and haven't had time to go through his papers. If not, I'll pay.' *It's the least I can do, Tam,* she swallowed hard.

'Och, no need. It's been taken care of.'

'Really? By whom?'

'Sir Monty, through Tor Strachan.' Tor Strachan, again! 'Are you okay, you look a wee bit put out.'

'Oh, it's not that. I almost killed him last night –'

'What! How?' Succinctly, Halley related what had happened on the beach and instead of being appalled, Rowan burst out laughing. 'Oh, I wouldn't worry, Tor's a grown up; he'll understand you're upset over Tam's death and cut you some slack.' Her indulgent smile suggested that she had a bit of a soft spot for Tor Strachan. Deciding that she'd taken up enough of her old friend's time, Halley got to her feet. However, Rowan stalled her by placing her hand on her arm. 'One last question.'

'Go on.'

'Did you want to see Tam?'

'See him?' Halley asked, bewildered.

'Yes, he's in the Chapel of Rest. However, he stipulated that no one, not even the laird,' again that searching look, 'should see him laid out in his coffin.'

Halley shivered and shook her head, relieved that she'd been spared that ordeal. She wanted to remember Tam as he had been, not as he now was. Rowan looked relieved too, clearly having no desire to countermand Tam's wishes, not even for a dear friend.

'Thank you. I didn't want to insist that Tam's instructions were adhered to. However, sometimes relatives insist on overturning the deceased's wishes. So,' she rubbed her hands together, effectively bringing the discussion to a close. 'I'll come over and see you tomorrow, we have the burial service and the wake to sort out. You should have words with Tor or Sir Monty as I believe they have their own ideas regarding both, especially where Tam will finally be laid to rest. The laird's friendship with Tam was of long standing and very special.' Again, that searching look but Halley, swept along by a tide of emotion, didn't have time to work out what it meant.

Then the phone rang in the office and Rowan 's father's voice came through, not just from the sitting room, but from beyond the grave: *That's another poor bugger, gone.*

'How? What?' Halley asked, bemused. This was turning out to be quite a morning. Then the penny dropped, 'That's not . . .'

'Polly? Yes, it is. Come and say hello.' They walked into the sitting room overlooking the back yard which no longer held a collection of half-finished coffins. In the corner an African Grey parrot sat on a perch cracking a Brazil nut and going through its repertoire. 'We had to move her in here because every time the phone rang . . .well, you heard. She can do Dad, Jim-Boab, and me giving Jim a rollicking when he's got something wrong, which is often. She can even tell Alexa to play Classic FM and to STOP when she's had enough. Eh, Polly?' Walking over she scratched its poll and ruffled its feathers.

'Jim's a numptie,' the parrot said in perfect imitation of Rowan's voice.

'That he is.' They both laughed.

'I remember your father buying her, I think we were about ten at the time. She always looked fearsome on account of her beak. Hello, Polly, remember me?'

'Ach, hold yer wheesht,' Polly responded with an evil cackle.

'Charming,' Halley laughed.

For an encore the unrepentant Polly counted to ten, finishing off with, 'Bingo. Eyes down for a full house.' After shutting the sitting room door, Rowan led the way back to the front office where she gave Halley a hug, kissing her on both cheeks.

'I still can't believe that you're here in person, not after years of talking to you over the internet via Skype, Face Time and now, Zoom. I'll come over the day after tomorrow and finalise things.'

'I'll cook dinner if that suits?'

'Next time maybe. I'll bring over a takeaway and it'll be just like old times. And, Halley,' she added as Halley headed for the front door.

'Yes?'

'Be nice to Tor, he's been through a lot. But I'll leave it up to him to tell you about that.'

Sending a puzzled look Halley left the premises, pulling her collar up against the cold. She couldn't imagine Tor Strachan paying her an uninvited visit and, as soon as Tam was laid to rest, she'd be on her way back to Hawaii and they'd never need to see each other again.

Which would suit her – both of them – just fine.

Chapter Five

Later that morning, Halley was sitting by the wood burning stove nursing a mug of hot chocolate going over her visit to Ferguson's, considering everything Rowan had said. The flames behind the glass door of the stove leapt and danced and she found it strangely comforting, hypnotic even, helping her process everything that had happened since her arrival in Lochaber.

A knock on the door broke through her reverie and she frowned, hoping it wasn't Tor Strachan. She'd decided to keep contact between herself and the Strachans to a minimum and planned to leave Lochaber as soon as feasibly possible. Putting her mug on top of the wood burner she pushed herself out of Tam's chair just as the door opened and an uninvited, not to mention unwanted, guest entered.

On seeing who it was, Halley's heart beat quickened and her mouth was suddenly dry. Swallowing hard and finding her voice, Halley greeted the visitor with an uncompromising: 'Turn round, go straight back to where you've come from. You're not welcome here.'

Undaunted, Lysander Strachan entered the bothy, closed the door and took a couple of steps towards her. Once, his black hair, dark eyes and confident manner had made Halley's teenage heart flutter and she'd thought herself in love. Today, that heady rapture was a distant memory, replaced instead by feelings of dread and unease. Lysander Strachan was bad news and there was no place for him in her life. She had hoped that she wouldn't see him while she was in Lochaber.

Seemed like she'd lucked out.

'Good morning, Halley,' Lysander greeted, confident of a warm welcome. To emphasise that wasn't going to happen, Halley walked round to the far side of the table, putting its bulk between them and glowered at him. To cover the awkward silence Lysander looked around the bothy, suggesting that he hadn't been down here in years, his gaze finally rested on the wood burning stove. This provided him with a new topic of conversation, giving him the 'in' he sought. 'Would you like me to stoke up the wood burner for you?'

'What I'd like you to do is retrace your steps, head back up the hill and go to hell. If that's not too much to ask.' Halley accompanied this with a saccharine sweet smile.

Lysander laughed. 'You always had a sharp tongue, Hal. As I remember.' He shot her a look which spoke of shared history.

'Really? Shame your memory wasn't so good, back then.' was Halley's cool response.

'What do you mean?'

'I mean, conveniently forgetting that you had a girlfriend taking a gap year and you'd be getting engaged when she came home for Christmas.'

'Oh, that,' he shrugged, as though it was of no consequence.

'Yes, *that.*'

'I thought it was understood that we were simply enjoying each other's company and having a bit of fun before settling down. I, heading for Sandhurst in the time-honoured tradition of the Strachans,' a note of bitterness crept into his voice, 'and you to the States where you no doubt covered yourself in academic glory.'

'A bit of a last fling you might say?' Halley's deceptively sweet smile hid that she disliked his patronising manner and how he dismissed her dreams and aspirations.

'Ex-actly.' He clicked his fingers, apparently believing she was in agreement.

Halley folded her arms across her chest and regarded him poker-faced, remembering who she *was*, not who she had been. Young, impressionable, gullible and in love, taken in by his good looks and attentive behaviour. He'd been her first serious boyfriend, they'd spent the summer swimming in the river Morar, lying on silver sands baked hot by the sun and sitting under the stars drinking wine as she'd pointed out the constellations. An idyllic summer during which she'd fallen head over heels in love and thought he felt the same. With no one to guide her, she didn't know that some men said one thing but meant another if it meant getting a woman into bed.

Her parents had already moved to Cambridge, New England where her father had taken up a post at the Massachusetts Institute of Technology. Her mother was busy looking after her two younger siblings and studying part-time towards a doctorate in astrophysics. Sex education hadn't been on her agenda. Besides, it was hardly the type of question she could broach with her mother, whose disapproval would have been loud and vocal.

She couldn't ask Uncle Tam for advice because she knew he'd disapprove of a liaison between his great-niece and the laird's younger son. As for Rowan, the closest thing she had to a best friend, she was barely a year older and had less experience of the world than Halley.

Instead, she'd learned the hard way.

Making the most of the pause, Lysander edged his way round the table.

'Oh, come on, Halley, don't dredge up the past. It was all so long ago and,' he sent her a smile, designed to charm, 'I'm sure you soon forgot about me once you left Lochaber.' He paused, giving her the opportunity to contradict him.

'Well, to be honest, I did,' Halley lied, concealing how scarred she'd been by his deception and the subsequent fallout. 'But that doesn't mean I liked being taken for a fool.'

He waved an airy hand. 'Water under the bridge. Bygones.'

'If you say so.'

'Friends?' He extended his hand and sent her a burning look. Halley ignored the overture and his pathetic attempt to rekindle what had once been quite a flame.

'Which brings me to ask, for a second time, what do you want?'

He had the grace to blush. 'I – well, I thought I'd come down,' he worked his way round the table towards her, 'renew an old friendship and shoot the breeze with you.'

'Shoot the breeze?' Halley laughed. 'Down with the kids, are you? How modern.' Her disparaging tone made it plain that she couldn't believe that she'd imagined herself in love with him. 'The only breeze I'm interested in is the one blowing off the loch and lowering the temperature in here. Make sure you close the door on your way out.'

'You've changed,' he observed, dropping all pretence of friendliness.

'Twenty years is a long time. Then I was a girl; now I'm a woman with a life, career and plans for the future. So, if you don't mind, door?' She gestured towards it and believing that she'd made her point, walked past him.

He lunged for her, catching her off guard and gripping her upper arm tightly, pulling her towards him, his breath hot on her cheek. His aftershave wafted towards her, stirring her senses and making her feel physically sick as she remembered smelling it on his skin and hair all those years ago.

'You weren't always so standoffish. Once you couldn't get enough of me.'

'That was then and this is now.'

'You have no idea,' he hissed, 'how difficult my life has been these last few years. Always playing second fiddle to Tor and . . .'

His sentence was left unfinished as the door was pushed right back on its hinges and Tor Strachan stood on the threshold, as if in saying his name Lysander had conjured his presence. It would have been comical, Halley reflected going over the scene in her head later, if it hadn't been so damning. Like a scene out of a badly scripted Rom Com. Lysander, his cheeks beetroot red, sporting a guilty expression, Tor dark and glowering in the doorway his head still swathed in the dressing she'd applied last night. And herself, leaning as far away from Lysander as possible, in a parody of a lovers' embrace.

'I hope I'm not disturbing you.'

'Do come in,' she said, twisting free of Lysander grip. 'It's open house; I was thinking of installing a turnstile and donating the money to charity.'

Ignoring her snarky rejoinder, Tor addressed his brother. 'Lysander, your wife is looking for you.' Was it Halley's imagination or did he put an extra stress on 'wife'?

'Of – of course, catch you later Halley.'

'Don't bet on it,' was her crushing reply as she turned her back on both of them and carried dishes over to the sink. The skirmish with Lysander, on top of everything else had shaken her more than she cared to admit. She'd spent the last twenty years wondering what she'd say to Lysander Strachan if they ever met again. She hoped that she'd conducted herself with dignity and made plain that theirs was one flame she had no intention of re-igniting. In spite of that, her hands shook as she stacked the crockery on the draining board and her stomach twisted itself into knots.

Aware that Tor Strachan was on the threshold regarding them with antipathy, Halley gained mastery over the situation and leaned back against the sink. She squared up to him as Lysander, making the most of the distraction, exited stage left.

'Is there something I can help you with?' Her tone made it plain that he'd used up his *Get Out of Jail* card when she'd helped him off the beach, patched him up and left him at *Creag na h-Iolaire's* front door last night. However, having knocked him out, she felt a certain degree of courtesy was owed to him, but nothing more. 'Make your mind up: come in or leave, but shut the door. You're letting the cold in.'

She frowned. Lordy, she sounded all of eighty years old and exactly like her Scottish granny.

Deducing that she wasn't in the mood for pleasantries or entertaining unwanted guests, Tor Strachan did as she instructed. He didn't like her tone or the way his brother had looked guilty as hell as he'd sidled past. Something felt 'wrong', but he couldn't put his finger on it.

As far as he was aware Lysander hardly knew Halley Dunbar, and certainly not well enough to pay a call at the salmon bothy on her first day on the estate, let alone grab her by the arm. However, he sensed a connection between them and, given Lysander's track record with the opposite sex, that made him uneasy. He watched as she turned away from him and tidied up the kitchen. Her movements were those of a woman in command of the situation, precise, measured. She made it plain that she had things to do that afternoon and he was in the way.

Trying to lighten the mood he opened with: 'I suppose, I should check you for concealed weapons?' It was meant as a light-hearted aside but came out all wrong.

'No need.' She turned round, drying her hands on a tea towel and tucking it into the waist of her jeans. Somehow, the movement made a shiver run through him, as though she was deliberately drawing attention to her slim waist, flat stomach and those parts of her body her tight jeans emphasised, demanding a response from him. 'Unless you have plans to rugby tackle me to the ground and call me a bastard?'

'About that –'

'Yes?' She folded her arms, making it plain that an explanation was expected and the conversation wouldn't move forward until she'd received it.

'The estate's been plagued by poachers. In the summer they steal eggs out of the nests, empty our red diesel tanks and sell the fuel to anyone willing to buy it, take salmon out of the river and poach our deer. Monty and I believe they've been using the loch and the river for their smuggling enterprises. I thought, seeing you on the beach in the darkness and moving like a shadow, that you were one of their number.'

'Ill met by moonlight, is that it?'

'By security light to be accurate.'

'I see. Coffee?'

Detecting that the atmosphere had thawed somewhat he pushed his luck and sat down at the table. 'Please.' He glanced over at the sink and the wood burner noting that there was only enough crockery for one. Plainly, Lysander hadn't been invited down for lunch. He relaxed, perhaps he'd got her – them – all wrong. He thought back to the last time he'd seen her on the beach. He'd been on leave from the army prior to being posted to Afghanistan and had been struck, not only by her loveliness, but by the fact that Lysander was spending more time down here than was good for either of them.

At the time, he'd wondered if someone should advise Tam not to let her go wandering along the loch and beach on her own. However, in the end he had decided that it was none of his business and left it like that.

He was then distracted by Halley asking: 'Who should I thank for putting on the heating, buying the groceries, making up the bed and so on?'

'Monty,' he said, back in the present. 'Or, at least, the staff following Monty's instructions. He was anxious to ensure you were as comfortable as possible, given the circumstances and the bothy's shortcomings.'

'Thank him for me, would you?'

'You can thank him yourself. That's why I'm here,' he paused, hoping it was plain that he wasn't checking up on her. 'I'm to ask you for the keys to your car. It's probably not a good idea to leave it in the layby, I'll get one of the staff to park it round by the stables. Also, Monty's anxious to see you.'

'I've always liked Monty and, over the years, he's been very kind to Tam. Looking after him while his nearest family was thousands of miles away in Hawaii.'

'Can I ask a favour in that case?'

'Go on.' She glanced over and frowned, clearly uncertain of him and his intentions.

'I didn't tell him about last night, flattening you on the beach and you helping me up to the house. He wouldn't be happy if he found out. My actions didn't exactly show me in my best light.' Her look suggested that she didn't consider that he had a 'best light' or any redeeming qualities. That stung, but he kept his cool. 'In case you wondered, I borrowed one of the estate's Land Rovers and drove myself home. I don't live in the castle.' The look she shot him suggested that it was none of her business where he lived, how he conducted himself or what he did.

'I understand, I won't mention it, but wasn't it a bit foolhardy driving after you'd been knocked out?'

'Possibly, but at the time it seemed a good idea.' He tried a rueful smile but could see that she wasn't impressed.

'What about Lysander? He's just brushed past you on his way out and my handiwork,' she gestured towards the bandage and managed to squeeze out a smile, 'is hard to miss.'

'Ly? He's so wrapped up in himself that he wouldn't notice if I was swathed in bandages like Tutankhamun.' The reference broadened her smile and she sat down at the table, pushing the milk bottle towards him.

'I'll look at your wound, then we're quits.'

Quits? Why did the finality of that word unsettle him? Of course, they'd be quits; he wanted nothing further from her and, seemingly, the feeling was mutual. While he drank his coffee she returned to the sink and retrieved the first aid kit.

'May I?' she asked, walking over and examining the makeshift dressing

'Go ahead.'

'In case you're wondering, I'm not making it up as I go along. I'm designated first aider at the observatory.' Having distracted him, she ripped the antiseptic tape off his temple before he had time to demur, or to wonder what the reference to 'observatory' related to.

'Ouch,' he exclaimed, playing along.

'Don't be such a baby,' she said in no-nonsense tones. 'Although, I think I might have overdone the bandaging last night. Looks more like a field dressing than a patch up job. But I guess you're used to that: field dressings, I mean?'

'What, oh yes.' It was hard to concentrate when cool fingers were trailing along his brow. It seemed eons since anyone had touched him so gently, intimately, or any other way come to that. He felt strangely bereft when she stood back to have a good look at his wound and removed her hand from his brow.

'I won't put another dressing on, best to let the air get to it. Although you should keep an eye on it over the coming days in case infection sets in. I could put a plaster over the wound, if you like, though?' He shook his head and she snapped the first aid tin closed, placed it on the counter top and moved away.

'What does 'at the observatory' mean exactly?' The question was designed to bring her focus back to him.

'It means that I'm one of the exoplanet research team at the observatory in Maui.'

'Exoplanet? Take pity on a poor highlander and explain.' She looked as though she wasn't buying the 'poor heilan' laddie' act for a second but went on to explain in any case.

'An exoplanet is a planet outside the Solar System, the first evidence of which was noted in 1917. However, the first confirmation of the phenomena occurred in 1992 when one was detected by an extremely powerful radio telescope. Now there are almost five thousand confirmed exoplanets with over seven hundred planetary systems having more than one planet.' She recited the information rote fashion, as though she didn't want to invite supplementary questions and prolong his stay in the salmon bothy.

Conversely that piqued his male pride and made him determined to draw her out, make her tell him more. 'You make it sound so exciting,' he observed, straight-faced. 'What will you do if you discover one?'

'Log it, report it to my superiors and hope to gain some recognition for the find.'

'I see. And what got you interested in astronomy in the first place?' She tutted, making no effort to hide her impatience. However, good manners and her enthusiasm for the subject compelled her to answer his question, leaning back against the sink with her arms folded across her chest.

'I was born in March 1986 when Halley's comet last paid a visit to our solar system. My mother was an astrophysicist and . . . do you really want to know all this?

'I do,' he replied, genuinely interested.

'. . .was on standby to go up on the space shuttle, Challenger, to observe Halley's comet at close range, should anyone drop out.'

'Challenger? Isn't that the one which –'

'Exploded during take-off? Yes. Luckily for her, and me, she became pregnant and had to stand down. She was watching the launch on television with my father when the disaster occurred. Two months later I was born and, in honour of the comet and the two female astronauts who perished in the explosion, was christened Halley Crista Judith

Dunbar. That's why, encouraged by my parents – and Tam, I became interested in astrophysics. How could I not with that pedigree?'

'That's quite a tale. But I suspect that you're being modest, I remember Tam telling Monty that you gained your doctorate and have aspirations to become Professor Dunbar.'

'That's so.' Walking over to the pedal bin to dispose of the dressing and glancing pointedly at the wag-at-the-wall clock she made it plain that there was nothing more to add.

Tor realised, as he watched her dispose of the bandage, that there wasn't much between them, age wise. He was forty-four and she was about thirty-eight. That gap seemed nothing now, but back in the day, when they passed each other on the beach it'd felt like a yawning chasm. And, in terms of life experience the same was true. She inhabited the world of academe searching for new planets – safe, warm, protected.

He was trapped in a never-ending nightmare which played through his mind on a loop, like a bad dream: hot desert wind, yellow-red sand stinging his eyes and clogging his throat, constantly being on his guard even when working with so-called friendly Afghan forces. Waiting for his team to be sent out at a moment's notice to defuse a bomb, disarm an IED or make a road safe for civilians.

Until the day when . . .

'It didn't hurt that much, did it?' Halley inquired giving him a strange look. 'You looked pained and miles away.'

He forced a smile on his face. 'No, it didn't hurt.'

He didn't elaborate. He knew, once she'd dealt with her uncle's funeral and sorted out his goods and chattels that she'd be back on the plane to Hawaii. Hasta la Vista, baby. After which, Morar and everything connected with it and the Strachans would be forgotten. Unaccountably, that made him feel . . . well, he couldn't quite put the feeling into words. The best he could manage was *lonely;* sensing that an opportunity to know her better had been missed. Which, considering that they'd only just renewed their acquaintance after a gap of almost two decades, was crazy. Maybe his mother was right, it was best the Strachans kept apart from the villagers.

They had no place in each other's lives.

Time to redraw the lines, remember his responsibilities as heir to the estate. In that moment he recalled the scene which had greeted him upon entering the bothy: Lysander trying to draw an, albeit reluctant, Halley into an embrace. Getting to his feet, he pushed back the kitchen chair and prepared to leave. Reaching the door, he paused briefly, frowning and choosing his words with care.

'Look, don't take this the wrong way but I don't want any trouble between now and when you leave.'

'Trouble?'

'You and Lysander. Their marriage is under a lot of strain. Fertility treatment.' Was it right to let a stranger know that Lysander and Suzie had been trying to start a family for a couple of years without success? He wished he could call the words back. Not only because it felt as though he'd betrayed a confidence, but because it was obvious that she was put out that he'd broached the subject in the first place.

'And you've reached this conclusion, how?'

'When I entered the bothy and saw you together, I thought, well . . . I have a vague recollection of you hanging out together that summer before Ly went up to Sandhurst.' He took a deep breath before continuing, aware that he was digging a pit to fall into. 'I don't mean to offend, but I have no intention of allowing you to be the catalyst which brings down that particular house of cards.' At this, high colour stung her cheeks and her lips pressed together. 'If I've got it all wrong, spoken out of turn then . . .'

'That,' she said, drawing out the words, 'doesn't even come close. I might not live in a castle but, for now, this bothy is my home and I want you out of it. Furthermore, you can tell your family that the Strachans aren't welcome here and shouldn't cross my path unless they want something more substantial than a house of cards to come crashing down on their heads.' She looked as though it would give her the greatest pleasure to find another stout branch and crack him over the head with it.

'Look . . .'

'No, *you*, look. I want nothing from you, any of you. I don't want my car parked near your stables. I don't want to be summoned by your father to come up to the 'big hoose',' she said in an exaggerated Scottish accent. 'I want to respect my great-uncle's memory, see him buried with the honour and dignity he deserves, settle his affairs and then return to Hawaii where the sun shines and the past doesn't matter.'

Getting the message, and acknowledging that his concerns over Lysander's marriage and her potential to be the catalyst which destroyed it had come out wrong, he left. Halley slammed the salmon bothy door behind him and turned the key in the lock.

Plainly he'd screwed up.

Big time.

Chapter Six

Next morning, after she'd had time to reflect on Strachan's offer, Halley decided she couldn't afford to allow false pride to stand in her way. She lived very simply in Hawaii, doctors of astrophysics not being in the supertax bracket. If the hire car was stolen, broken into or damaged she'd lose her deposit. Something she could ill afford.

Against her better nature and eating a large slice of humble pie, she climbed up the embankment to the layby where the car was parked. Calling Tor Strachan everything from a pig to a dog and going through a list of things she'd like to do to him given half a chance, she worked off some of her anger. She held something back for Lysander and used it to power her to the top of the embankment where she ran out of steam.

Reaching the layby, she was relieved to find the car miraculously undamaged, all four wheels intact and the last of her meagre luggage still on the back seat. Strachan had made Lochaber sound like bandit country where lawless poachers held sway and no one was safe. Letting out a long breath she got in the car, fastened her seat belt and turned the engine over. Seemingly unaffected by the damp Scottish air creeping through her thin clothes and seeping into her bones it fired first time.

Small wonder Tam had caught pneumonia, the climate was unforgiving and so unlike Hawaii. Deciding that was a stupid, not to mention pointless observation, Halley returned to venting her anger on Tor Strachan.

'Who did he think he was? Talking to me like that?' she demanded as she slipped the car into gear. Oddly, Tor Strachan's high-handedness had angered her way more than Lysander's pathetic attempt to turn back the clock. 'Argh!' She banged the steering wheel in frustration, making the horn blare. 'Calm down, Dunbar,' she advised herself. 'You'll need your wits about you to make them realise you aren't the inexperienced girl, just out of sixth form, who'd spent her last summer in Lochaber. You're used to dealing with the male of the species and coming out on top. That's what earned you your position at Haleakalā Observatory. Never forget who or what you are and how much you've achieved. Park the car behind their wretched stable block, visit the laird, smile and stare back. If that's what it takes to get through the next week, bring it on.'

Taking a deep breath, she reminded herself that here in the UK people drove on the left-hand side of the road and headed for *Creag na h-Iolaire.*

Jet lag finally caught up with Halley as she drove through the gates of Eagle's Crag. Stifling a yawn she recalled how, once, on the train back from Fort William she'd seen an eagle circling over Lochailort, the tips of its wings spread out like fingers. Then the train had crossed the Glenfinnan Viaduct and her attention had been taken watching the front carriages curve round the viaduct. Was that before it'd gained world renown as the Harry Potter Bridge? Her brain was too tired to remember so she drove round to the stables where Tor had said she could park the car. She'd barely switched off the ignition when a groom approached, opened the door and waited for her to get out.

'Miss Dunbar? The major said you might want to park your car here for the next couple of weeks.'

Did he now? Was he so certain of her falling in with his plans?

'The Major? Oh, yes, Tor.' She'd temporarily forgotten that he'd followed a long line of Strachan ancestors into the army.

'I'll take any belongings you have for you. Do be careful when you go down there later, the steps are treacherous this time of year.' *Tell me about it*, she thought, remembering all that had taken place. 'Can I say how saddened the staff were to learn of your great-uncle's passing? He was a grand old chap and liked nothing more than to come and groom the horses with Sir Monty and feed them mints when no one was looking.'

'Thank you.' Halley passed over the car keys after collecting her handbag from the passenger foot well. Getting in, the groom drove the car round the other side of the stables and out of sight. Halley stood rooted to the spot, uncertain what to do next. Tor had said Sir Monty wanted to see her but she could hardly walk into the castle by the back door. Knocking on the front door didn't seem an option and she certainly didn't want to bump into Lysander, his wife or Lady Strachan.

It was all so complicated. She exhaled a puff of frustration and her breath coalesced before her. However, tired as she was, she decided it was better to visit the laird and then retire to the bothy and have a nap. She pulled a face, a nap? She was thirty-eight, not eighty-eight! Her train of thought was interrupted when a beaten-up Land Rover pulled into the yard. Tor Strachan stepped down from cab rather stiffly and walked over to join her. She noticed that he limped quite badly on his left leg and immediately felt guilty.

Surely that wasn't the result of the ill-fated bang on the head?

He launched straight in with, 'Ah, I'm glad to see that you've taken me up on my offer.'

'Of course. It was very kind of you.'

Tor looked stunned, as though he'd put his head in a tiger's mouth and come away unscathed.

'I – I'm pleased that you think so.'

Feeling that she'd got one over on him and not the other way round, Halley changed the subject. 'A member of staff has driven my car round to the other side of the stables and offered to carry the last of my stuff down to the salmon bothy. Would now be a good time to visit Sir Monty?'

Tor smiled, as though he preferred this biddable, amenable version of Dr Halley Dunbar and was pleased that she was falling in with his wishes. 'Of course. Where did you go yesterday?' He gestured for her to walk ahead of him across the yard and towards the castle.

'To visit Rowan Ferguson in Mallaig,' Halley supplied.

'She's a great girl and has handled Tam's funeral arrangements with tact and compassion. I've come to know her quite well over the years. She's friends with my sister Lexie and a good influence on her.'

Halley nodded, but a dart of something she couldn't quite identify hit her squarely in the chest, catching her off guard. Why should Strachan's regard for Rowan make her feel scratchy, uncomfortable?

Shrugging it off as an anomaly, she continued. 'Yes, about that.'

Tor stopped in his tracks, forcing her to turn round.

'Go on.' He frowned, as if sensing what was coming next.

'It isn't appropriate for the laird to pay Tam's funeral expenses. My family would prefer it if we took care of things.'

'You'll forgive me for saying so, but your family has been conspicuous by their absence these last few years. The last time anyone came to visit Tam was when he was hospitalised with pneumonia about ten years ago.'

'I've already explained, my parents are too old for thousand-mile trips, my sister has a young family to care for and my brother spends most of his time on research trips in remote corners of the world. Which leaves me.' She tapped her chest and continued. 'I'd managed to secure funds for a project I wanted to set up and had to see it through. By the time I was able to come over, Tam rang to say he was being well looked after and not to worry.'

'Surely the planets don't require attention twenty-four seven? I believe a person can always make time for something that's important to them.' His expression implied that Tam wasn't important enough to warrant thousand-mile trips to the Dunbars.

'I –' Halley stopped herself from blurting out the real reason why she'd stayed away. She'd been a moonstruck idiot, allowed herself be taken in by Lysander and almost wrecked a promising academic career. The only way she could cope at the time and for years afterwards was to put distance between herself, Lochaber and the Strachans. Sadly, that had meant putting space between herself and Uncle Tam. 'Things happen, life gets in the way. You should know that. Now, you're in my way so – can we just visit your father and get it over with?'

That came out all wrong but she couldn't, wouldn't, call it back.

'Get it over with? The friendship between Tam and my father was special and of long standing.' The same look Rowan had flashed her in the office yesterday, as though they were reading from the same book but were on different pages, passed between them. 'As father's batman, Tam saved his life not once, but twice, while they were on active service with the Argyll and Sutherland Highlanders in Aden and Northern Ireland.'

'I get all that, but you know nothing about my family or me. It's best that you don't say another word or we won't get through the rest of the day, let alone the next week, without coming to blows.'

'Blows?' He raised an eyebrow and swept her over from tip to toe. He was well over six feet tall, athletically built without a spare inch on him. Halley, on the other hand, was on the slender side and looked as if a strong wind would blow her over. But looks can be deceptive, she was made of tough stuff as many of her colleagues had learned to their cost when they'd tried to devalue her or ignore her opinion.

'You might have knocked me out last night when my guard was down, but . . .'

'I meant verbally,' she explained, sending him a scathing look.

'Fine. In which case, let's try to be pleasant to each other in front of my father. He wants to do this for Tam. Please let him.' Halley nodded, this argument wasn't about the money, it was about his family's belief that the Dunbars had let Tam down. She wouldn't be able to reverse the Strachans' opinion during the short time she'd be in Lochaber, so no point even trying. She simply wanted to see Tam laid to rest with honour and dignity and then head back to Hawaii where she could gaze into the boundless, non-judgemental universe through a telescope and forget Lochaber and the Strachans existed.

Although feeling outmanoeuvred, Halley wasn't prepared to let him have the last word or occupy the moral high ground. 'My family will match every penny the laird spends on Tam's funeral and donate it to

Help for Heroes or the Royal British Legion in Tam's name.' Squaring up to him, chin held high, she extended her hand. 'Deal?'

'Deal.' Her fingers were cold but Tor's hand was firm and, just for an instant, she was warmed by it. Then Tor broke the contact, as though touching her was in some way distasteful. 'Shall we?'

'Of course.' Hiding her anger, Halley followed him into the castle down a narrow passageway whose thick walls ensured that the temperature was almost as cold as outside.

The only time she'd been inside *Creag na h-Iolaire* had been when Lysander, no doubt trying to impress her, had shown her round the ancestral pile while the family were attending the local Highland Games. He'd somewhat ruined the guided tour by jumping out of his skin every time a floorboard creaked or a pipe rattled. Then she'd been too impressed by the castle's splendour to wonder why, now she knew better.

They had no right to be there.

The passageway gave on to a cavernous kitchen where wintery sunshine touched rows of copper pans lining the walls. An ancient pine table, bowed in the middle and scarred from years of use, dominated the room. A fire burned in an ancient grate, more to heat the huge space than to cook on Halley guessed, taking in the massive Aga and modern range cooker. Two Gordon setters, stretched out on either side of the fire with their heads on their paws, looked as if they had no intention of budging that day. However, when they saw Tor, they were immediately alert, stretching out their long legs and walking over to him, tails wagging and smiling in that amusing way dogs have.

Tor clicked his fingers and they came to heel.

'Bet you wish you could do that with humans,' Halley observed as one of the setters nudged her hand, no doubt looking for treats.

'Who says I don't?' came the dry response. Then he turned to a female member of staff drawing a pheasant on the table without a trace of squeamishness. 'Any idea where I might find my father?'

'In the Laird's Smoking Room watching the racing,' she replied, nodding towards the door. 'Will ye be wanting tea brought up Major Strachan? Lady Strachan is taking hers in the drawing room with Mrs Lysander.'

'No, that's fine, I'm sure you have plenty to do so we'll get out of your way.' His use of 'we' made the woman glance at Halley, openly wondering at her identity. Clearly, it wasn't Tor's usual practice to bring guests into the castle via the back door. Maybe even to bring female guests into the castle at all. 'This way,' he said, brushing past and opening a huge door which looked as though it'd been there for years. 'Not you,' he said to the dogs, pointing back at the kitchen and the fire.

Unlike Halley, they obeyed his commands without question.

A short staircase led into the original part of the house where thick pillars supported the immense weight above it. At one end of the hall a wide staircase, laid with carpet in the Strachan tartan, linked Eagle's Crag's medieval pele tower to the seventeenth century wing.

A memory flashed into Halley 's mind – Lysander taking her hand, laughing as he'd whisked her up the staircase towards his bedroom, stopping every fifth step to cover her face in kisses. Imagining herself in love, she'd been as keen as Lysander to take their relationship to the next level. What a trusting fool she'd been, unaware that he regarded her little more than a summer dalliance. The thought of her naivety and how it'd been exploited brought colour to her cheeks and made her stomach churn. Stiffening her back, she vowed to block all recollections of that disastrous summer until she was back on the plane to Hawaii. It was the only way to get through the next ten days.

Leaving behind the ancient structure of the original castle, its thick grey walls concealed behind priceless tapestries, they entered the more modern wing where family portraits adorned the panelling and wide windows gave onto Lady Strachan's precious gardens.

Here, comfort was the order of the day, the rooms more concerned with making the Strachans' lives as untroubled as possible and less with keeping their warlike neighbours at bay. Tor pushed the door open on the Laird's Smoking Room and signalled for Halley to enter ahead of him. The cold November wind was left behind as ancient double radiators, coiled like sleeping serpents, belted out heat and a roaring fire pushed the temperature even higher.

In spite of this, Sir Monty seemingly felt the cold, and wore a shawl in Strachan tartan over his bowed shoulders for extra warmth. He was so immersed in watching the racing from a tweed upholstered club chair drawn up close to the fire that he didn't notice them enter the room. Tor put a hand on Halley's arm and they stood on the Chinese carpet until the race ended and the laird gave a cry of disappointment, scribbling on the pages of the Racing Post with a stubby pencil.

'Backed another three-legged nag, Monty? Looks like you'll be dipping into your army pension to keep the bookies at bay,' Tor quipped, walking further into the room and signalling for Halley to follow.

'Don't tell your mother,' he joked in what obviously was a well-practised routine. Then he spotted Halley, switched off the television via the remote, dropped the paper and pencil on the floor and beckoned for them to come closer. Pushing himself out of the chair he walked over to Halley. 'My dear girl, is it really you? No, don't answer, I can see Tam in you; the same grey eyes, hair and how you hold yourself. Aye, you're a Dunbar alright.'

To Halley's consternation he put his arms around her and held her close, a shuddering sob wracking his thin frame. 'Oh dear, I'm so sorry that my being here has upset you,' was her inadequate response. She patted Monty's back as one might sooth a child, feeling each knobbly vertebrae even through the thick shawl round his shoulders.

She looked over at Tor, mutely appealing for help.

'Pull yourself together, Strachan,' Tor said in mock sergeant major's tone. 'What would Tam say?' Walking over, he disentangled them. 'Where are your manners? Offer the young lady a wee dram.' Thus distracted, his father wiped his eyes on the corner of the shawl, brought a whisky decanter and three glasses out of the court cupboard on the far wall and poured them all a generous tot. Halley hoped that the 'wee dram', combined with jet lag and emotional exhaustion, wouldn't be responsible for her missing her footing on the steps leading to the bothy and ending up face down on the silver sands.

'Tam,' they toasted. The laird and Tor knocked theirs back with a deft flick of the wrist while Halley sipped hers more cautiously. Uncle Tam always kept a bottle of the finest Macallan single malt in the bothy, 'just in case' the laird or one of his British Legion friends dropped by. Knowing the price that a bottle of Macallan commanded, Halley suspected that the laird ensured Tam's supply never ran out.

'Sit, sit.' Sir Monty led Halley over to the matching club chair on the other side of the fireplace. Tor sat down on the wide, squashy, sofa opposite the fire and refused a second glass of whisky. 'I'm driving back to the Airstream once we've settled things. Should I ask Mother to join us?'

Airstream? Surely Tor Strachan didn't live in a caravan? As if sensing her bewilderment, Strachan sent her a look which implied that his life and how he lived was none of her business.

The mention of Lady Strachan brought a deep frown to the laird's brow. 'No, this is strictly between us and the Ferguson lassie. I've been thinking, now Halley's here, we can finalise details and move things along.'

'Of course,' Tor agreed, his look silently begging her to accommodate his father's wishes.

'Such as?' Halley inquired. The Strachans might be paying for Uncle Tam's funeral but Tam Dunbar was family and they'd better not try to make her agree to things Tam wouldn't have liked or wanted.

'Well,' the laird's voice caught in his throat as though the words could only be spoken with difficulty. The tears Halley kept at bay threatened to surface in the face of the laird's obvious distress. 'Tam is to be buried in the Strachan churchyard. That's not up for negotiation, no matter what your mother says.' He sent Tor and then Halley a fierce look. 'I'm the laird and everyone would do well to remember it.'

'I'm certain that Tam wouldn't want any fuss, Father.' Getting up, Tor banked up the fire with peat turves in a clear attempt to move the conversation along.

'I – we, that is, my family assumed that Tam would be laid to rest in the local cemetery in Mallaig.' Halley took a deep breath, sensing her uncle being buried in the Strachans' church yard overlooking the silver sands would open up a whole can of worms.

'Well, he won't be getting buried there or at Our Lady of Perpetual Succour, St Cumin,' the laird asserted. 'No matter how much certain people might wish it.' Clearly the laird's much grander plans for Tam's internment brought attendant problems and undercurrents Halley couldn't quite fathom. 'Tam and I often talked about our funerals.' Then, seeing Halley's expression, laughed. 'Don't look so surprised my dear, it's something people past a certain age do, sitting round the fire on a winter's night. In fact, when we were pinned down in Aden during the Battle of Crater and in Armagh during The Troubles, we would often spend the night talking about how the one left behind, in this case, me, would ensure that the other's wishes were respected.'

Halley couldn't quite imagine her uncle demanding to be buried in the Strachans' graveyard that, clearly, was Sir Monty's wish.

'Very well,' she concurred, 'if that's what Tam wanted.'

'And the other thing,' the laird said, walking over to an oak humidor on a side table and taking out a fat cigar. He lit it defiantly, as though it was a forbidden pleasure and Tor's expression confirmed it.

'I'm holding my breath,' Tor said, almost speaking for Halley. 'No thanks,' he refused the cigar his father proffered and waited until Monty lit a spill from the fire and ignited his cigar.

'The night before the funeral, Tam will be brought from Ferguson's and his coffin laid on the dining room table so his friends can pay their last respects. Halley, I want you to bring his glengarry up to the house and lay it on the coffin. As per my instructions, Rowan has ordered a wreath of white heather twined with red poppies, in remembrance of our time in the army together.'

The laird wiped away a tear and Halley tried to make sense of the family dynamic. One minute Sir Monty was seemed every inch his eighty years, overcome with grief at losing a dear friend. The next he was Brigadier Sir Montgomery Strachan, a decorated soldier who expected folk to stand to attention when addressed and to carry his instructions out to the letter.

And that included his family.

Halley stifled a yawn and then apologised. 'Sorry, Sir Monty, the journey from Hawaii was a long one, full of cancelled flights and holdups. Quite frankly I'm bushed. Would you mind terribly if I returned to the salmon bothy?'

Sir Monty put his cigar to rest on an ashtray.

'How selfish of me, of course. Tor will walk back with you.'

'There's no need,' Halley said, heading for the door before turning. 'I speak for my family when I say that we will go along with your and Tam's wishes. I'll bring the glengarry up, first thing tomorrow. No need for Tor to walk me to the bothy, I can find my own way.'

With that she was out of the door before either of them could say another word.

Chapter Seven

A little of the Strachans went a very long way Halley reflected, heading for the beach.

Reaching the top of the steps, she grasped the rope banister in her right hand and started her descent. The groom was right, the steps were treacherous due to fallen leaves and last night's rain. However, she reached the beach without incident and headed for the bothy.

She was surprised to find a man sitting on Tam's bench as though he had every right to be there. She walked up, a polite smile on her face but delayed entering the bothy because she didn't want to reveal that the key was kept underneath the stone dog. All this talk about poachers was unsettling, maybe it was time to find a safer hiding place? However, old habits, especially those linking her to Tam, die hard.

The stranger got to his feet and smiled in a friendly fashion but moved no closer. That showed he had some sense at least, Halley thought, no woman wants to be approached on a deserted beach by a stranger.

'Hi. You must be Halley,' he greeted her.

'Must I?' she asked, still not in the best humour after her encounter with the Strachans.

'Sorry, I should introduce myself,' he took a step closer. Instinctively, Halley took a step back. 'Geordie Souter, a friend of Tam's. We've spent many a happy hour sitting on this bench, putting the world to rights.' Although he appeared to be in his mid-thirties his turn of phrase seemed to belong to a different generation. 'I live further along the beach in an old caravan.'

What was it with caravans? First Tor and now this stranger.

'Really?' Friendly, but not too friendly.

'With the laird's permission,' Souter added, perhaps detecting the hesitancy in her voice. 'I collect driftwood off the beach and turn it into 'Morags', the Monster of Loch Morar', to sell to tourists in the summer. Seriously, she's out there, and when she surfaces, I'll be ready to capture her on film.'

Halley began to relax; he seemed friendly enough. She'd spent too long behind her telescope, only mixing with a handful of colleagues and was fast losing the knack of exchanging a few words with a stranger. She needed to chill. She gave him a closer look, he was quite good looking in a rough sort of way, hair sticking up at odd angles as though he cut it himself, three day's growth of beard showing more ginger than brown, and his clothes were slightly grubby as though he washed them in the loch.

Ah well, she reflected, we can't all be the heir to a highland estate.

'What are the chances of that?' she asked, referring to his quest.

'Slim I'm afraid but it keeps me busy.' He grinned and shrugged his shoulders. 'I'm not long out of the army and The Brig, Sir Monty, offered me a place on the beach until I find my feet. He helps old soldiers through his connection with the British Legion,' he explained. 'In the winter months I help on the farms hereabouts or with landing the catches in Mallaig.' Smiling, he held out his hand and when Halley smiled but didn't take it, he raked his fingers through his short brown hair, seemingly not in the least put out.

'You'll have to excuse me Mr Souter, I'm very tired – jetlag – and not feeling very sociable,' she explained.

'Aye, and y'er doubtless sad about Tam's passing. So am I.' As he relaxed, his accent thickened and Halley guessed he was from the Central Belt, not the Highlands like her family. 'And it's Geordie, by the way, we don't stand on ceremony here. I just wanted to introduce myself and say how sorry I was to learn of Tam's passing. We were old pals. I did his shopping and the odd bit of DIY for him.'

'When you weren't carving monsters out of driftwood, presumably,' Halley smiled, putting her hand over her mouth to stifle a yawn.

'Aye, very funny; good. I'd spoken to him a day earlier and he seemed fine, I didn't realise anything was wrong until I saw Major Strachan a couple of days later and he told me Tam had passed away. Makes you think, doesn't it?'

'It certainly does.' She drew the conversation to a close, making it clear that she wanted to be left alone.

'Aye, well, nice meeting you. I'll see you at Tam's wake, all his old pals are coming. I just wanted to introduce myself.' He started to walk up the beach and then turned back on his heel. 'If there's anything you need, just call out. I'm often passing this way and it'd be my pleasure to help Tam's great-niece in any way, no matter how small.'

'Thanks.' Halley waited until he was fifty or so yards away from her, bent down and retrieved the key from beneath Grey Friar's Bobby, bought after a trip to Edinburgh with Tam and lugged home on the train. She entered the bothy, closing the door behind her and turning the key in the lock. It'd been quite a few days: meeting Rowan after a gap of almost twenty years, even if they exchanged birthday and Christmas cards and had kept in touch via the internet; discussing funeral arrangements with Sir Monty, not to mention Lysander's unscheduled visit and then walking through the castle, so redolent of memories of her last summer in Lochaber.

Desperate for a hot drink, she walked over to the sink and filled the kettle. What was it with folk round here? You could get a 'wee dram' any time of day but it occurred to no one that what she really wanted, needed, was a cup of strong coffee. As the kettle boiled, she walked over to Uncle Tam's calendar and picked up the stubby pencil dangling from a piece of string. She drew a ring round a date two weeks hence when she'd be driving over to Inverness, returning her hire car, getting on a plane and heading home.

She felt lost, alone and out of kilter with everything and everybody. She couldn't put that down to jet lag alone. She glanced round the bothy and its contents, some of which were valuable. Tam's bagpipes, for example, lying like a drunken, deflated animal on his bed, its 'legs' splayed out at an odd angle. Her brass Victorian telescope, worth a few pennies. The piece of meteorite Tam had discovered before she was even born, tales of its discovery inspiring her interest in astronomy, the antique orrery in her bedroom.

The kettle started to whistle and she dragged herself out of her reverie.

She'd have coffee, hope the internet signal was strong enough to zoom her parents, hiding from them that, as far as she was concerned, she couldn't leave here soon enough.

Next morning Tor Strachan was at his desk in the remodelled caravan he called home. He'd imported the Airstream from a dealer in America and modified it to look less like a caravan and more like a Zeppelin on stilts. He'd erected it on Strachan land where planning permission wasn't too hard to come by, connected it to a septic tank and provided his own electricity via a small wind turbine and a couple of solar panels. It was far enough away from the house to escape the suffocating protectiveness of his mother who wanted to wrap him in cotton wool after he arrived home from Afghanistan with the life-threatening injuries which had effectively ended his military career.

Deep in thought, he swivelled his desk chair from left to right and tapped a pencil against his upper lip, going through the mantra he'd learned at the Defence Medical Rehabilitation Centre at Stanford Hall. Part of the self-help regime which had kick-started his road to recovery after the horrendous injuries he'd received in Afghanistan.

- Get moving
- Mindful breathing
- Take care of your body
- Deal with flashbacks
- Work through survivor guilt
- Create a safe place
- Connect with others

Well, this was his safe place, the home he'd named *Beag air bheag*, meaning *Little by Little* in Scots Gaelic. It was all his own work and he was proud of the result. One of the first improvements he'd carried out was to raise the Airstream well above ground level so there was no risk of flooding. Next, he'd removed both end walls and installed bow-fronted, dragonfly-eye windows where he could sit at his desk and watch stunning sunsets in the summer and the last of the light during the long winter months. A kind of mini observatory from which to observe the sky and northern lights common in Lochaber – and to keep an eye out for poachers and other uninvited guests who trespassed on Strachan land.

He'd kitted out *Beag air bheag* with porthole windows, a wood burning stove, kitchenette, shower room and a raised patio for use in fine weather. He'd insulated it with good Scottish pine and used local materials and building methods wherever possible, there was even a small sitting room with Wi-Fi, laptop and television. In all, a comfortable space for one which could, at a pinch, accommodate two.

Not that he'd ever invited anyone to stay over.

This was his safe place and he didn't welcome visitors.

So, what had happened to the last part of his mantra: *connect with others?*

He'd be the first to confess that he wasn't very good at that. As Major Strachan, leader of his bomb disposal team he didn't have to ask people to do things for him. He gave the orders and his lieutenant and sergeant made sure they were carried out. Life was so much easier in the army, no frills, no gimmicks, no extras. He missed that.

He glanced over at the queen-sized bed, not quite long enough to accommodate his six-foot-three frame. So far, he hadn't found a princess, let alone a queen, with whom he'd care to spend the night. Unbidden, Halley Dunbar's face swam before him. He imagined them together in the too-short bed, limbs tangled, snuggled up against the wind that rocked his house on stilts in the winter months. He shook the thought from his head, best not to go there. Relationships were a complication he could do without. Apart from which she was a bird of passage and would soon be heading home.

Moving his thoughts along he glanced over at the stainless-steel model of a Zeppelin his sister Lexie had found at a car boot and given to him on his last birthday. It was so like *Beag air bheag* that he couldn't help smiling every time he glanced its way. Next to it on the wide Victorian partners' desk was a small telescope on a tripod. And, until the night before last, the telescope was simply that; a device through which he surveyed the land which would one day be his.

He'd forgotten that Tam's great-niece held a doctorate in astrophysics and would doubtless laugh in his face if she saw the telescope on his desk. Not to mention thinking of her, himself and the queen-sized bed in the same sentence. In spite of his earlier resolution, he thought back to their first meeting on the beach. He'd been unforgivably rough and deserved everything he got but, in his defence, he'd thought her a poacher and his military training had kicked in. Had he apologised for his behaviour, explained about why he'd acted as he did? Probably not. Or, if he had, only briefly and a little grudgingly. It hadn't pleased that he'd had to ask her to help him climb the steps up to the castle.

He had some pride left.

Catching her and Lysander in a clinch had made his blood boil. Ly's marriage was in enough trouble and didn't need an unattached, toothsome female in the form of Halley Dunbar to push it over the edge. Was he being entirely fair? He wasn't sure. Putting down the pencil he rubbed his hands over his face and tried to get her out of his head.

Maybe mindful breathing would help?

He planned to visit the bothy this morning and check everything was okay, as he'd promised his father. It would be interesting to see how long they could be in each other's company before another row kicked off. He felt along his jawline and wondered if he could get away without shaving. However, as he was visiting a guest on his father's land and, to a certain extent representing the Strachans, he felt he should make the effort.

After shaving, he collected a beanie, down filled jacket, shepherd's crook and headed for the beach.

No matter how dark his mood, the beach had the power to lift his spirits. In the summer, the sand was pure white and the waters turquoise blue. Now, in early November the sand had been turned over by the high winds and ranged from white to light caramel and all shades in between. It was still damp from recent rain and as he headed for the salmon bothy his heavy boots sank into the sand leaving a deep imprint and making the going hard. Next to his footprints was a round indentation, left by the shepherd's crook which helped keep his balance and took the weight off his injured thigh.

When he had been sent home to recuperate after his operation and rehabilitation at Stanford Hall a walking stick had been suggested. He'd balked at the idea, a combination of male pride and a refusal to accept that his military career was over. It had been his father's suggestion that he rooted through the collection of hats, coats and wellingtons kept by the back door to find a walking stick that, somehow, wasn't a walking stick. In the end, he'd found the cromack, a shepherd's crook almost as tall as himself and with `a handle fashioned from a ram's horn, and decided that'd do.

Deal with flashbacks, he reminded himself as, fifteen minutes later, he reached the bothy, entered its weathered porch and knocked on the door.

Chapter Eight

Uncertain of his welcome he stood back and waited.

The porch had two bench seats, one on either side, and on them was a collection of the flotsam and jetsam which washed up on the shore from time to time. Tam was an avid beachcomber and collected any little thing that amused him – a headless doll, a burst tennis ball, the remains of a toy boat and oddly shaped pieces of driftwood. He wove stories around those objects and shared them with Monty and Tor over a glass of whisky.

Tam's death served to underline Monty's mortality. He was eighty years old and although he was in good health, no one lived forever. Aware of the fact, Tor vowed to visit his father every day and keep an eye on him. Time he forgot about his own problems, considered others and got on with life. The expensive psychologist paid for by his mother would doubtless applaud that sentiment.

Next to the miscellany of objects was an old sign, and on it a name burned into the wood by a hot poker – THE BAT CAVE. He was pondering the significance of that when the door opened and Halley Dunbar stood on the threshold freshly showered, wearing an oversized denim shirt and smelling of something so undefinably feminine that his senses responded instinctively.

Her face dropped when she saw him and she cut straight to the chase. 'Is there something I can help you with?' She might have well as said: *what do you want?*

'Good morning, Miss Dunbar,' he responded with commendable

calm in the face of such hostility. He looked at the flotsam and jetsam and then back at her. 'Having a clear out?' Her face clouded over and he regretted his throwaway remark. Idiot! Of course she was having a clear out, her uncle had just died and ...

'I am. My family won't want any of Tam's stuff, apart from a few mementoes, so I thought I'd sort it into piles and ask Rowan if she knows any local charities who might take it.' She sighed and pushed a long strand of dark auburn hair off her face, her grey eyes troubled.

'Don't you want any of Tam's stuff?' Briefly he felt sorry for her, having to travel thousands of miles to wind up her great-uncle's affairs and draw a line under his life. He chose to forget that the reasons for her staying away these past twenty years were shrouded in mystery. One which had caused her uncle a great deal of pain because he loved her, missed her and couldn't understand her absence.

'I've sorted through a few bits,' she gestured towards the interior of the salmon bothy. 'And, there's this.' Reaching past him she picked up the sign for the Bat Cave. 'But I can take that to Hawaii in my hand luggage.'

'Bat Cave?'

She managed a watery smile as she explained. 'When I stayed for the summer, Rowan Ferguson, her cousins and their friends often came over to play. We learned that Uncle Tam was Sir Monty's batman and, not knowing what that meant, thought it was something to do with Batman, the character from the DC comics.' Her smile broadened as she reminisced. 'Uncle Tam played along and made a sign to hang over the door. When he called me in from the beach for my tea, supper, or whatever, he played the theme from the television series on his bagpipes.'

He sent her a puzzled look and then twigged. 'You mean like: dinner-dinner-dinner-dinner-Batman?'

'Exactly.'

'If he's Batman does that make my father, Robin?' Tor wanted to laugh but didn't dare risk destroying the fragile peace. 'Can't quite see either of them in tights or wearing a cape.'

'Me, neither.' This time they both laughed and the atmosphere lightened a little. 'Come in and I'll show you what I've put to one side.

Time's in short supply and I was going to ask if you or Sir Monty would have these things shipped over to Hawaii after the funeral. My family will pay, of course.' Tor followed her into the bothy noting that her phrase; *my family will pay* showed her continued unwillingness to be beholden to the Strachans.

Laid out on the kitchen table were Tam's bagpipes, regimental glengarry, an orrery and a piece of charred rock. Unable to resist, Tor turned the handle and the planets orbited the sun in pre-ordained fashion.

'To make me laugh, Uncle Tam used to play *Walking on the Moon* on the bagpipes while I made the planets revolve.' She smiled and patted the bagpipes fondly, her expression far away as if remembering happier times.

'What's this?' Tor picked the charred rock off the table. Halley took it out of his hands, not in an unfriendly fashion, but because she obviously considered it too precious to be handled.

'Tam'd always been interested in the stars and he told me about some of the sights he'd seen in the desert when the Argylls were posted to Aden during the Arab Uprising. One night, Uncle Tam and Sir Monty were part of a detachment sent deeper into the desert to flush out any Arab insurgents. Tam was driving the Land Rover with Monty beside him when they saw a meteor shower and Tam asked Monty's permission to go and see where the shower had come to earth.'

'That sounds like Tam, taking a chance, making the most of an opportunity.'

'Exactly. As the story goes, the meteor shower streaked across the sky, headed earthwards and they followed it, not really expecting to find anything. Incredibly, they found a smouldering piece of rock on a sand dune, right in front of them. This is it. The other soldiers in the back of the Land Rover couldn't understand why Tam was so excited over a piece of rock and let him have it.'

'Really?' Tor picked the rock up for a second time.

'Well, it could be a tale spun to amuse me when I was growing up. But Uncle Tam's meteorite and my given name are responsible for kickstarting my career. Well, that's probably enough for one day,' she stated, evidently deciding that she'd revealed too much of herself. 'I plan to give the meteorite to the Kelvin Grove Museum in Glasgow, that being where Tam was born.'

'Glasgow, or the museum?' Tor risked a joke.

'Glasgow,' she laughed. 'I'll donate it in Tam's name, of course. Tam had it assessed many years ago and it was found to be a rare example of carboniferous chondrite. Some meteorites are incredibly valuable and a prime example can fetch forty pounds a gram. Tam's has an estimated worth of tens of thousands of pounds. What, don't you believe me?'

'I do. I'm just surprised that Tam kept something as rare as this under the bed.'

'Under the sink, to be precise. But no one knows its value apart from my family and the laird. So, you see, if push came to shove, we could easily sell the meteorite to pay for Tam's funeral.'

'But push hasn't come to shove, has it? Monty wants to pay for the funeral. I thought we'd settled on that.'

'We have.'

'Well then,' he sensed that the slight thawing in her demeanour was temporary and permafrost was about to descend once more.

'So, will you?'

'Will I, what?'

'Ship these things over to Hawaii?'

'Of course. Is there anything else I can do to help?'

She shook her head. 'Nope. Although, the old wag-at-the-wall clock should go to your father as I believe that he admired it? It's the only object which could be classed as a Dunbar heirloom.'

'I'll ask him.' Tor glanced over at the clock, ticking away as though nothing had changed. He guessed that his mother would take a hammer to it rather than have it in the castle, but kept that to himself.

Halley wrapped her arms around her slender form and shivered. 'I just want to get the funeral over with and ensure that Tam's memory is honoured.'

'I'm sure that's what we all desire.'

She glanced past him and towards the door, making it plain that his time was up. Taking the hint Tor headed back into the porch, picked up his cromack, dragged the beanie out of his pocket and pulled it on. It was then that he noticed footprints in the sand leading away from the bothy, clearly a man's judging by the size. So, she had visitors, did she? Surely not Lysander after the bollocking he'd given him the other morning?

'Man Friday?' he inquired, pointing at the boot print with the end of his crook. The look she shot him implied that it was none of his business, and she was right. But he had to know for certain that it wasn't Lysander.

'I know what you're thinking,' she made a pre-emptive strike, 'FYI it wasn't Lysander. It was Geordie –'

'Souter?'

'Presumably you know him? He seemed nice, friendly.' The opposite to *you*, her look implied. 'He said that he lives along the beach in an old caravan, making driftwood models of the mythical Morag of Loch Morar to sell to the tourists.'

'Father's a sucker for a hard luck story from a former squaddie and gave permission for him to stay a couple of summers ago. In my opinion he's overstayed his welcome.' He didn't add that once Tam's funeral was over, he'd be suggesting to Souter that it was time he moved on. He couldn't prove it but he thought that he was somehow linked to the poaching and petty crime in the area.

'He told me how he used to help Tam out with his shopping and so on. He seemed genuinely upset over Tam's death,' she added, openly taking Souter's side. Sensing that this could soon become a further cause of friction between them he changed the subject.

'I nearly forgot.' Standing on the damp sand he held onto the side of the porch for support, making it appear that he was oh-so-casually examining the flaking paint and not using its framework to steady him. After his long walk up the beach from the Airstream his leg wound was making its presence felt. 'It's short notice I know but you're invited up to the house for dinner tonight. Mother wants to meet you, she says she can't remember you as a child.'

Her face darkened as though her memories did not tie in with his mother's. In an obvious attempt to lighten the atmosphere she made a joke. 'Instantly forgettable,' she said, taking a little self-deprecating bow.

'Maybe when you were ten,' he countered, feeling that he should meet her half way by responding to the joke. 'I remember seeing you a couple of times over the years when I was home on leave. Once, I saw you standing on the rocks, your arms outstretched, face turned up to the sky shouting something I couldn't make out.'

'Oh, that. It was my vain attempt to make Morag the Monster of Loch Morar reveal herself. I was a fanciful child; moongazing, looking for monsters, dreaming of being the princess in the tower.' She gestured towards the castle. Now it was her turn to look embarrassed. 'Is that why you uttered '*You*' when you came round on the beach after I'd knocked you out?'

'Yes. But only partly.'

'Go on.'

'I was seeing stars and couldn't decide if I'd died and gone to heaven, or descended to hell. If you were angel or demon.' This time he laughed, glad that they were beginning to relax in each other's company. Tonight's dinner was going to be a pretty tense affair and he'd been in two minds whether to ask Halley up to the house. His mother's opinion of Tam and his occupancy of the salmon bothy was on record and it wasn't flattering. Better if Halley came up to the house relaxed and in a positive frame of mind, matters were bound to go downhill before the second course.

It was his mother's speciality.

'So?' he prompted.

'Of course, thank you.'

'Any dietary requirements or allergies we should know of?'

'I'm pretty catholic in my tastes and eat most things. Although,' now it was her turn to smile, 'I might turn down Cullen Skink. Although I do like bouillabaisse and most shell fish.' He liked the way her grey eyes sparkled when she laughed, how the wind off the loch whipped colour into her cheeks and her habit of pushing her hair behind her ears, as though she found it troublesome.

He tapped the side of his head twice, making a mental note. 'No Cullen Skink.'

'Oh, what should I bring?'

'Bring?'

'Yes, wine, flowers. I have brought a couple of touristy things from Hawaii to give to Rowan and others as small presents, perhaps your mother would like one? Or, I could drive into Mallaig and –'

'No, don't go to any trouble. Father likes to choose the wines for dinner from the cellar. Just bring yourself.' He didn't add that his mother would turn her nose up at anything homespun or produced for the tourist trade and that would sour the atmosphere. He glanced at his watch, not to check the time but to end the conversation on a positive note. 'Seven thirty for eight suit you?'

'Fine. I've got lots to do.' She seemed eager to get on with packing up the salmon bothy. 'I'm assuming you dress for dinner? I haven't packed much in the way of formal clothes other than what I'll wear to Tam's funeral.' She swallowed hard and looked so forlorn that Tor wished that her mind hadn't returned to that solemn tack. He tried to think of something to say which would ease her pain, make her feel better.

'Come as you are, you have other things to worry over. It'll be dark so I'll make sure that the lights up the steps and through the gardens are switched on. Or, would you prefer a member of staff to come down show you the way?'

'I'll be fine.' Neither of them referred to the incident on the beach or the fact that she'd practically dragged him up the steps the other night. In that moment, they mutely acknowledged that her stay in the salmon bothy would be brief and she'd be on her way to Inverness before they knew it. Best to keep things on an even keel until then.

The thought of her leaving made a shiver run through him closely followed by another sensation, deep in the pit of his stomach. One he couldn't quite identify. Regret? Disappointment? The thought of what might have been? That was crazy. They'd only renewed their acquaintance a few days ago, she was leaving soon and chances were they'd never meet again.

Why did that thought bother him? He straightened his shoulders and repeated his mantra: *work through survivor guilt, connect with others.* Enough of the soul-searching, it was time to draw the conversation to a close. 'Fine. I'll see you then.'

'Seven thirty for eight.' She tipped him a cheeky little salute and went back indoors, closing the door behind her. Tor started up the beach, his trusty shepherd's crook helping him stay upright in the head wind which whipped sand into his face and stung his eyes. Pulling his beanie down lower over his forehead he made for the sanctuary of *Beag air bheag,* anticipating with dread how an evening playing happy families with the Strachans would pan out.

Chapter Nine

It was twenty-five minutes past seven when Halley walked under the stone arch towards *Creag na h-Iolaire's* nail-studded double doors. True to his word, Tor had ensured all the lights were on so there was little danger of her coming a cropper. The wind had dropped and a hoar frost was setting in, sprinkling the castle with glitter. It looked impossibly like a Christmas card but Halley knew she wasn't about to enter a fairy kingdom.

Two nights ago, she'd recalled the saying: *never accept an invitation to dinner from a Strachan. It could be your last meal.* Tonight, she'd be on her guard. How was she supposed to sit opposite Lysander and his wife exchanging pleasantries as though their pasts weren't connected? How could she politely shake hands with Lady Strachan who might deny that they'd ever met but whom she remembered sending the gardeners to chase off herself and the village children because they'd picked a bunch of her precious roses.

She recalled the epithets hurled at them: guttersnipes, trespassers, intruders. A couple of generations back she would have set the dogs on them. Perhaps that's where Tor got his attitude from, rugby tackling folk on to the beach and asking questions later.

As for Brigadier Sir Montgomery Strachan . . . she had only the highest regard for him. He'd paid frequent visits to the salmon bothy during the summer holidays, teasing her and her friends, smuggling treats from the castle kitchens, telling wild stories about their days in the army. Teaching the children how to dance the highland fling over two crossed sticks from the pine plantation while Tam played the pipes.

To the Birdie Song!

Raising the large knocker – complete with stag's head, natch, Halley banged on the door, demanding to be let in. There was nothing timid about her peremptory rat-a-tat-tat. She was Halley Dunbar, deal with it.

The door opened and she walked in. Never having entered the castle via the front door she was curious to see *Creag na h-Iolaire* from the perspective of a guest. She found herself in a round tower topped by a square turret, every architectural feature added to the castle in the last thousand or so years resulting in a hotchpotch of styles. She followed a liveried member of staff into the hall and was beset by memories, good and bad. Yesterday, she'd missed the huge fireplace with its heavy fire irons and the unusual umbrella vaulting supporting the massive weight above it.

It all looked so different by fire and candle light, less forbidding, almost romantic.

She was led up the steps and through the inner hall, past portraits of Strachan ancestors, some distinguished and others frankly villainous. Most were in military uniform, dating back to the late seventeenth century, judging by the men's long hair and peruques. The distaff side of the family was well represented by beautiful ladies in off-the-shoulder gowns, coifed hair and wearing heirloom jewels secure in the knowledge that no one would chase them out of the gardens . . . provided they produced the requisite heir and a couple of spares.

She grimaced at the thought as she was escorted into the Laird's Smoking Room and asked to wait there for 'The Major'. She knew little of Tor Strachan's military career but she bet he'd progressed through the ranks quickly. After all, it couldn't hurt to have Brigadier Strachan as your father.

'Your coat, Madam?' Her escort broke into her thoughts and she handed over coat, scarf, hat, gloves. He bore them away, leaving her standing in the middle of the room. This at least was familiar to her and she spent several minutes examining the exquisite pieces of porcelain on the Adam mantelpiece. She glanced at her watch and frowned; twenty-to-eight. Evidently the Strachans were not great time-keepers. Wasn't there an old saying about punctuality being the politeness of princes? Did the Strachans' punctuality depend on the calibre of their guest?

Walking over to the edge of the carpet she pushed the door slightly ajar and peered into the inner hall. Several rooms led off it and a furious argument was being conducted in one of them. It didn't take a genius to figure out that Uncle Tam was the cause of it. Casting good manners aside Halley crossed the hall, stood outside the half-closed door and listened.

'There is no way that man is lying in state on the Chippendale table, bought by my father's money. The very money, I might add, which rescued the Strachans, *Creag na h-lolaire* and the estate from bankruptcy. Without it, you'd just be another highland laird with a long family history and an inflated sense of his own importance.'

'Mother, don't start.' Tor attempted to interrupt her flow, but to no avail.

'You know very well that my father –'

'Wanted a title for his wee lassie and a bit of Strachan lustre to make everyone forget that the Robinsons' were Glasgow merchants who'd made their money through trade,' Sir Monty cut in. Halley suspected that this was a well-worn argument which came with bitterness and acrimony as a side order.

'Nothing wrong with that,' Lady Strachan snapped.

'Indeed,' Sir Monty agreed, but not in a conciliatory fashion. 'And, by the way, darling, one inherits one's furniture. One doesn't buy it from an auction house, even if it is Chippendale.'

'And, another thing,' Lady Strachan continued, the bit firmly now between her teeth. 'If you think I'm attending the funeral, the internment and the wake for *that man,* you have another think coming. I'm glad that he's dead. I only hope that my years of shame and humiliation die with him.'

'Much better if you stay away,' Monty lobbed back.

'Suits me,' she huffed. 'However, if I'm allowed to make an observation?'

'If you must, but I think you've probably said enough.'

'Perhaps,' Tor tried again to bring the argument to a close, 'you both should –'.

'I want *the niece,* or whatever she is, out of the salmon bothy, it emptied of Tam Dunbar's rubbish and back in Strachan hands before the week's out.'

'That's not yours to decide,' Monty said. 'I'm laird here, however much you might wish it otherwise.'

Lady Strachan would not be silenced. 'She's trouble. Mark my words.'

'How do you work that out?' Tor asked calmly 'You haven't met her.'

'I don't need to, I know the type. She almost killed you the other night –'

'Hardly,' Tor remonstrated. 'And, to be fair, I did leap on her out of the darkness and pin her down on the sands.' Lady Strachan's harrumph implied that any young woman should be honoured to have the heir to Eagle's Crag pin them to the ground.

'And, another thing . . . why *her*? Isn't it her parents' responsibility to see him buried?' It was as if she could hardly bring herself to say Tam's name. 'None of the family need have attended, a simple phone call to Ferguson's in Mallaig would have sufficed and the matter would have been dealt with.'

Throwing caution to the wind, Sir Monty came back with, 'I made it my business to take care of it.'

'Well, that's only to be expected, he's been milking you for years though you couldn't see it. And, doubtless organising a bit of poaching and stealing of birds' eggs on the side. The salmon bothy's perfectly placed for such activities with no one to witness the comings and goings. Then there's the path up to the layby. Anyone could park there at dead of night and load salmon, or whatever, into a van and be off on their toes.'

'That's right; discredit his name and his memory, before he's even cold in his grave,' came Monty's bitter retort.

'I would say that the two of you have managed that without my help.'

'If the gloves are off tonight, let's not forget your peccadilloes and the reminders there for all to see. What about my humiliation? Or doesn't that count?' They were referring to events and people unknown to her and Halley was unable to make sense of the last bitter aside.

Tor, evidently feeling this family head-to-head had gone on long enough, intervened.

'Time out, both of you. If you want to continue this argument, can I suggest that you do so when we haven't got a guest waiting, not to mention dinner being ruined?'

'A guest? Well, that's one word for her. She's here to stir up trouble; you're quite a catch, Tor darling, and I'd lay money on her being aware of that.'

Tor laughed a little bitterly. 'Invalided out of the army with a life-changing injury and a promising career in tatters? Oh yes, I can see that'd get prospective wives queuing up at my door. Added to which, she'll be in Hawaii before we know it and it'll be back to same old, same old.' He seemed to find the thought rather depressing.

'Only without Tam-bloody-Dunbar around,' Lady Strachan said with evident relish.

Halley, scorched by Lady Strachan's words, felt like bursting into the drawing room and stating, for the record, that she had no designs on Hector Strachan. Furthermore, could someone explain why Monty and Tam's friendship had brought shame on the family and what were Lady Strachan's 'peccadilloes' Monty had referred to?

She was just about to retrace her steps to the Laird's Smoking Room before anyone caught her eavesdropping when the door opened and Tor appeared. Mortified, she tripped, lost her footing and stumbled straight into the arms of Lysander Strachan.

Giving a lop-sided grin he held on to her longer than good manners dictated.

'I – I was – I mean,' Halley stammered, 'I didn't mean to eavesdrop.'

'Don't apologise, Halley,' Lysander said. 'It's how one finds out what's going down at *Creag na h-Iolaire*, I've received quite an education listening at keyholes to Ma and Pa's domestics.'

'That's quite enough, Lysander.' Coming forward, Tor rescued Halley from Lysander's arms, carrying out introductions as though nothing untoward had occurred. 'Halley, this is Suzie, Ly's wife. Suzie, Halley Dunbar, Tam's great-niece.'

Halley shook the cold hand of a diminutive blond in her early thirties whose disappointed expression probably had as much to do with being Lysander's wife as their struggle to have a child. More eggshells to navigate, she thought, colour staining her cheeks as she recalled Tor's words in the salmon bothy: *I won't allow you to be the catalyst which brings down that particular house of cards.* She still seethed at his arrogant assumption that she had any interest in Lysander Strachan.

Giving herself a mental shake, she dismissed the thought that she'd left Scotland heartbroken at Lysander's double-dealing. There was enough to get through this week without dredging up the past. A past which couldn't be changed but, like a heavy chain round her ankles, shackled her to a time and events she'd rather forget.

'Shall we?' Tor held out his arm, and Halley regarded it and him askance.

'Shall we, what?'

The answer came in the form of the Strachans' piper who joined them from the floor below to lead them into dinner. Feeling completely out of her comfort zone, Halley was disconcerted to discover that everyone had dressed for dinner, in spite of what Tor had said. The men in dinner jackets and the women wearing cocktail dresses and second-best jewels. The best she could manage was a pair of jeans and a t-shirt emblazoned with: *Connect with the Cosmos.* She shrugged, even if she'd turned out in haute couture and a diamond tiara, nothing would revise Lady Strachan's unflattering opinion of her.

Laying her hand on Tor's arm and feeling slightly ridiculous, she proceeded in to the dining room behind Sir Monty and Lady Strachan with Lysander and Suzie bringing up the rear.

Once in the dining room, a member of staff pulled out Halley's chair and offered to carry off her thick cardigan. Halley shook her head. She didn't think that the logo on the back of her t-shirt: *I don't date outside my species* would go down well tonight. Fortunately, the first course of tomato and courgette timbales with a piquant tomato sauce accompanied by a dry rosé distracted everyone. Lady Strachan sat at one end of the infamous Chippendale table and Sir Monty at the other. Flower arrangements down the centre of the table meant that Halley didn't have to look across at Lysander or his wife. By accident, or design, she found herself on Tor's right hand with Sir Monty adjacent to her.

The second course was *Creag na h-Iolaire* beef tournedos with a whisky and cream sauce, followed by Rose Bavarois with fresh raspberries. Each course had a specially selected wine but Halley sipped hers cautiously, aware of the journey back down to the beach at the end of the evening. Although, judging by the icy looks Lady Strachan directed at her, not everyone would be broken hearted if an accident befell her.

To counterbalance the frosty atmosphere Monty and Tor related scandalous stories of the ancestors hanging on the oak panelled walls, the historical significance of the ornate plaster ceiling and the story behind two silver elephants on the sideboard. They were an amusing and entertaining double act and Halley began to relax and enjoy the excellent food and wine. At last Lady Strachan rose and Suzie, Lysander and Tor followed suit, heading, presumably, for coffee in the drawing room.

Unsure of protocol, Halley rose, too, but Sir Monty placed his hand on hers and detained her. 'Come to the library first, my dear, I have something to give you. Tor, join us in five minutes.'

Only too happy to pass on joining Lady Strachan and the others, Halley followed Sir Monty out of the room.

Chapter Ten

The library was panelled in honey-coloured oak, mellowed with age. Wire-fronted bookcases, writing desks, circular tables piled high with leather bound estate records and mahogany racks holding magazines and periodicals completed the look. A large bay window held a fine writing desk, brass standard lamp and a velour-covered chair overlooking the inner courtyard. Halley bet that the view in daylight was spectacular, not that she'd be given the chance to find out!

As in the other rooms a fire was blazing in the hearth, this time flanked by two beautiful French Bergere armchairs with silk brocade cushions. Sir Monty indicated that Halley should sit in the right-hand chair then went over to one of the bookcases, unlocked it and returned with a tin. He placed it on a table alongside antique snuff boxes and painted miniatures. Halley wondered if Lady Strachan's 'dowry' had funded the level of opulence in the house but had no time to ponder the matter further because Monty sat down in the chair opposite.

'Tam,' he managed to say his name without his voice breaking, 'knew that the bothy was vulnerable and so gave me this box and its contents for safe keeping.'

'Nowhere safer than Eagle's Crag,' Halley smiled, touched by her uncle's thoughtfulness.

'He wanted to give it to you himself, however –' He sent Halley a quizzical look, as if wondering why she'd stayed away. Squirming, Halley quickly moved the conversation along.

'What's in it?'

'I have no idea, apart from his and his great-grandfather's medals which I suggested he didn't want to leave lying around, in view of the poaching and burglaries which have plagued the estate over the last couple of years. Now Tor's home, he'll sort things out, I'm certain of that.' His pride in his son's abilities was evident from his tone of voice.

Halley coughed to clear the catch in her voice and then asked, 'How – how, did he die? We were told it was a heart attack, but we'd always thought him fit as a flea.'

Monty stared into the fire before answering. 'And he was, right up to the end, although he never quite got over that bout of pneumonia ten years ago. Seeing him combing the beach every morning looking for detritus cast up by wind and tide it was easy to forget his age.' He shook himself of the sombre mood. 'We shared many a laugh over some of the objects he displayed in the salmon bothy's porch. I'd say to him: "Tam, get rid of it, for God's sake, it's a highland bothy, not The Natural History Museum." That always made him laugh.' They turned away from each other, looking into the fire as though the flames held the answer to life, death and all the heartache and joy inbetween. 'Then one morning when he didn't ring me as usual, I sent the factor down to check on him. I had just reached the end of the rose gardens when my walkie-talkie burst into life and Frank, the factor, told me he'd found Tam in his chair, stone cold dead.'

Stone. Cold. Dead. Monty's words plunged knives into her heart.

'Poor Tam.' Halley blinked away the tears, trying to reconcile the image of the fit ex-soldier she'd last seen nearly twenty years ago and the frail old man who'd died alone. 'Was – was it quick?' Despite what Monty, or anyone else thought, she loved her great-uncle and the idea of him suffering tore her in two.

'It was a heart attack so we presume – hope – so.' Sir Monty supplied. 'Most likely, sometime the night before.' He drew a large white handkerchief out of his dinner jacket and blew his nose, noisily. Halley retrieved a piece of kitchen roll from the pocket of her cardigan and followed suit, screwing the paper into a ball and throwing it on the fire.

'Thank you, Sir Monty.'

'For what?'

'For looking after Uncle Tam all these years and, well, everything.'

'I could do no other. What am I going to do without him, my dear?'

Words, the ones which society uses to help the bereaved cope with the emptiness which lies ahead, seemed inadequate on this occasion and stuck in Halley's throat. At that moment, feeling Monty's grief more acutely than her own, she knelt at his feet, taking his hands in hers in an attempt to comfort him. She didn't really know him, but in that moment, they were united in grief for someone who meant a great deal to both of them.

'I don't know, Sir Monty. Losing a life-long friend must be the most awful thing. We'll have to help each other get through the next few days. Won't we?'

'Bless you my dear, we will and . . . beyond that, we'll have Tor, Lexie and Rowan Ferguson to help, too.' He clearly knew that Halley had heard every word of Lady Strachan's tirade against Tam and herself, and didn't include his wife in the list of people he could turn to. Same went for Lysander, too, apparently.

This was the tableau which greeted Tor when he entered the library, closing the door quietly behind him.

'Tor,' Halley said, dashing away her tears, sitting back on her heels and feeling foolish and vulnerable. So much for trying to convince everyone that she could cope.

'Brigadier Strachan,' Tor chided, half-jokingly, 'I leave the lassie alone with you for five minutes and you both end up in tears. What'r'you like? The pair of you?' He held his hand out and Halley took it, staggering to her feet as though she was a hundred years old and wiping her eyes with the cuff of her cardigan.

'Here.' Tor retrieved a clean, beautifully laundered handkerchief from his pocket and handed it to her.

'Thank you,' Halley dabbed at her eyes smearing the lawn square with mascara and eyeshadow. 'Oh, God, I'm so sorry. I'll make sure you get it back before I leave.'

'Perfectly laundered and smelling of lavender?'

'Of course,' she managed a weak smile, 'even if I have to bash it between two flat stones on the side of the loch and buy lavender water from the chemist in Mallaig to sprinkle on it.'

'I'll hold you to that. Keep it for now, you might need it.' He didn't add that Tam's lying in state on the dining table, the funeral and the wake were bound to be emotional. He didn't need to; it was a given. Realising that he was still holding her hand, he released it and pulled another chair up to the fire.

'What are the others doing?' Monty asked.

'Drinking coffee and chewing the fat.' He didn't think it politic to reveal what was being discussed but it concerned Tam, Halley and the salmon bothy. The door opened and a member of staff brought in a tray bearing three tots of whisky. Tor passed one over to his father and then Halley, but she shook her head.

'I think I've had enough for one night.'

'Coffee, then?'

'That'd be great, thanks.'

Tor, glad that his arrival had broken the sombre mood, moved the conversation along.

'Has Monty told you that Tam saved his life not once, but twice?'

'No. How did that come about?' Halley asked, turning a shining face on his father. Tor nodded, giving Sir Monty the opportunity to tell the story and take both their minds off missing Tam.

'I wasn't long out of Sandhurst and green as grass,' Monty began. 'I'd received a commission in the Argyll and Sutherland Highlands and Tam was my batman. He was a tough little so-an-so, ready for anything. How he must have loved being saddled with a highland laird who knew as much about soldiering as a heilan' coo! But, if he did, he kept it to himself. Saw me safely through the jungles of Borneo in sixty-three, Aden in sixty-five and the Troubles in Northern Ireland in the early seventies. His favourite expression was: *keep yer head doon Lieutenant Strachan, Su-hr, if ye dinnae want it blown off.'*

Monty imitated Tam's Lowland Scots accent perfectly.

'I came across batmen and NCOs like Tam when I was first out of Sandhurst,' Tor added. 'Complete professionals. It was their task to keep a close eye on rookie officers who, unwittingly, could lead them all to hell and perdition. They might conceal their exasperation behind a veneer of respect but they were quick to let you know if they thought you were taking risks with your men's lives.'

'When we were in Borneo,' Monty put in, sipping his whisky, 'I heard someone calling: *Tommy, Tommy* from deep in the jungle and would have gone to investigate it, if Tam hadn't pulled me back with: *"Lieutenant Strachan, Suhr. You go in the direction of those voices and you'll never be seen again."* He was right, of course. Later, I found out that was a well-worn trick used by the Indonesian rebels to lure soldiers away from their unit.'

'You don't learn stuff like that at Sandhurst,' Tor said. 'That's why every young officer needs an experienced NCO, or batman, by his side until the rough edges are rubbed off.' Tor raised his glass. 'To Tam, and others like him.' Halley and Monty toasted Tam in coffee and whisky respectively. 'Tell Halley about your tour of duty in Northern Ireland during The Troubles.' Tor turned towards Halley and gave a rueful grin. 'If Tam hadn't have acted so quickly Lysander, Alexandra and I, wouldn't be here.'

Halley frowned, clearly trying to make sense of the timeline. 'How do you mean?'

'The Argylls were sent into Northern Ireland on the twenty-eighth of July 1970,' Tor explained.

'Uncle Tam's birthday!' Halley exclaimed, shivering as a ghost walked over her grave.

'Some birthday,' Tor laughed. 'Eh, Monty?'

'Quite. Tam was thirty-five years old and I'd just been promoted to captain but I didn't have time to enjoy the moment, or Tam his birthday. We'd just taken over responsibility for the Police Division H in Armagh and during the first fortnight we had shooting incidents, bombs and eight arson attacks to contend with. We recovered ten weapons, over four-hundred rounds of ammo and more than twenty pounds of explosive.'

As Monty related the story, he came alive and Tor explained the background to Halley. 'The Argylls were there to keep order but were facing civilians who didn't want them there, including school children who lobbed bricks at them and teenagers with petrol bombs.'

Monty added, 'It wasn't for us to question the where and why, we had a job to do and tried to do it to the best of our ability as professional soldiers.' He sipped his whisky and his eyes took on a faraway look as he remembered those dangerous, stirring times.

'How did Tam save your life?' Halley asked.

'We were sent in to clear some derelict houses, believed to be booby trapped. We had to ensure that the rebels didn't re-occupy the houses while we waited for the bomb disposal team to set their devices and blow the houses to kingdom come. I led the men in but it was Tam, ever vigilant, who spotted a tripwire connected to a pile of explosives, dragged me clear and threw us both on the floor while we braced ourselves for the house to collapse around us.'

'They escaped by the skin of their teeth. It was hearing stories like this which made me decide to study computer cybernetics and robotics at Heriot Watt University, Edinburgh. I left with an MSc, went up to Sandhurst, gained a commission in the Scots Guards and the rest is history.'

'Now you know.' Monty concluded the story by sending Halley a severe look, every inch a brigadier. 'It's clear that you loved Tam but, forgive me my dear, why have you stayed away so long? Tam was very hurt when you stopped spending your summers with him.' He raised an eyebrow, giving her a chance to explain.

'Father, please.' Sensing Halley's distress Tor tried to intervene. He had too much respect for his father to tell him to back off but guessed Halley had her reasons for staying away, ones she didn't want to share.

'Goodness, look at the time,' Halley said, glancing at her watch and adroitly changing the subject. 'I'd better get going. And,' standing, she collected her tin off the table and tucked it under her arm, 'there's no mystery, not really. I finished my A levels, moved to Massachusetts where my father had recently taken up a post at MIT. I was lucky enough to win a scholarship and studied astrophysics there. I gained a degree and moved to Hawaii to study at Haleakalā for my MSc. It was a busy time in my life and I simply just couldn't fit in a trip back to Scotland every year.'

'For twenty years?' Monty asked, pressing hard.

'Tam understood,' Halley said, hoping it was true.

Tor decided it was time to step in. 'Maybe we can pursue this another time? It's late and tomorrow's going to be a difficult day. I'll be round in good time to meet Ferguson's people with Tam's coffin, so –'

There was an almighty clatter as Halley dropped the tin and went a whiter shade of pale at the word 'coffin'. Feeling sorry for her, in spite of everything which had passed between them, Tor picked up the tin and handed it to her, sending his father a severe look. Sometimes, Monty forgot that he was no longer Brigadier Strachan whose word was law.

'Thank you. Sorry.' Her face was ashen and there were unshed tears in her eyes.

'No need to apologise, or explain,' Tor said, guiding her to the door. 'We all do what we have to, governed by the circumstances at the time. Come on, I'll walk you to the top of the steps.'

Closing the library door behind them he led the way back to the lower hall.

Halley followed him down the tartan carpeted steps, head bowed and chewing her lip. She liked Monty but was glad she was returning to the salmon bothy. It'd been quite a night, character assassination followed by emotional turmoil and with worse to come: the lying in state, internment and wake. How she longed for the tranquillity of the infinite universe viewed through her telescope. She couldn't wait to get home and tell her family what she'd been through.

If Tor kept his word and oversaw the return of the salmon bothy to the Strachans she might be able to bring her departure closer, even if it meant buying a new ticket and losing money. She couldn't wait to get away from Lochaber. How could she say to Tor, Monty or Rowan: 'The reason I couldn't bring myself to return was because I'd made a complete fool of myself, almost ruined my life and needed to distance myself from Lochaber in order to survive?' How could she tell Tor that his brother was at the root of her problem? That would leave Tor with an even lower opinion of her and let Lysander know that she'd been brooding over their disastrous summer fling for the last twenty years.

He'd love that, wouldn't he?

Their coats were brought round along with Tor's cromack. They walked through Lady Strachan's precious gardens, the wind making conversation impossible. Stopping at the top of the steps, Halley looked down to the beach, the path illuminated by the lights edging each step and turned towards Tor. 'Don't bother walking me to my door,' she tucked the tin securely under her arm. 'I'll be fine.'

'Yes, I'm sure you will. You're quite resourceful, aren't you? Perhaps I should warn any poachers about your prowess with a stout branch.'

She tried to read his expression, however clouds kept scudding across the moon, preventing her. 'I do power yoga; a girl never knows when it'll come in handy.'

They both laughed and then let out a collective pent-up breath which acknowledged that they'd been circling each other like sparring partners. Tor rubbed his chin thoughtfully. 'I know that you heard everything while you were standing in the hall. I want to apologise for my mother, she can be . . .'

'She was protecting her own, in this case, you. For the record, I don't have designs on you even if you are, to use her words, *quite a catch*. Perhaps she was right, we should have asked Rowan Ferguson to handle Tam's affairs and stayed away. But . . .'

'But you couldn't do that?'

'Exactly.'

He swiftly changed the subject. 'I'm not sure what time Rowan's bringing Tam home but once he's in the house, I'll ring you and ask you to come up.'

'Of course.' Halley descended the first step and then turned and glanced back at him over her shoulder. 'Can I just say, for the record, I'm not looking forward to this, any of it?' Her face crumpled and the brave facade she'd maintained all night finally slipped.

'And why should you? Monty and I will be there to help, so don't worry. With a bit of luck Mother will stay with Suzie at her parents and not return until it's all over, the salmon bothy's packed up and you're on your way to Inverness.'

Halley was cheered by the thought that she'd never see Lady Strachan again. She was more than capable of sticking up for herself but, under the present circumstances, wanted to avoid any unpleasantness.

'Good night then, Tor.'

'Good night, Halley.'

He stepped back into the shadows and Halley headed for the salmon bothy. Searching in her bag for the key, she let herself in, switched on every light and locked the door behind her. She placed Tam's tin on the kitchen table but made no attempt to open it. She'd had quite enough emotion for one night and wanted to be in a calmer frame of mind when she examined the contents and thought of her great-uncle.

Perhaps after the funeral would be best?

Chapter Eleven

The next morning Halley returned from her jog along the beach to find two strangers on Tam's bench. Pulling out her ear pods she shoved them in her sweatshirt's kangaroo pocket along with her iPhone. As she drew closer, they got to their feet and approached, smiling.

'I'm Bryce MacPherson. Hi.' Tall, thin and with hair as red as fire the stranger extended his hand and Halley shook it.

'I'm Alexandra Strachan, Lexie to my friends,' the young woman greeted her. 'Tor's sister.'

'I'm Halley Dunbar.'

'We kinda assumed that,' Bryce laughed. 'Tor described you to us in some detail.'

'Did he?' Halley asked, surprised.

'Tor thought you might welcome some company so we've dropped by to see how you're coping with the funeral arrangements and, well, everything,' Lexie gushed. Ignoring Halley's outstretched hand she went straight for a hug, kissing her on both cheeks. Halley was surprised by the effusive greeting but welcomed it. Being in the bothy with all its attendant memories was heavy going and she was ready for some distraction. Bryce watched the exchange and smiled, inferring that Lexie wasn't one to hold back.

Small and dark, she looked nothing like Tor or Sir Monty, but more like Lysander. Her hair, like Bryce's, was cut in a spiky style suggesting she was hairdresser to them both, and possibly the dog sitting at their feet, too. The tips of her hair were turquoise blue and looked as if they'd been dipped in paint. Threads of fuchsia pink were streaked through the remainder and Halley guessed that her personality was as colourful. Their clothes had a homespun, recycled look, leaving Halley with the impression that here were two individuals unfamiliar with the nine-to-five slog to the office, or any other routine for that matter. A pair of New Age Highland Hippies, Halley decided, liking what she saw. They spoke without a hint of highland brogue, implying that they'd been brought up by an ancient nanny and then packed off to boarding school, returning only for the holidays.

Not that Halley was one to talk. In the past, Rowan had commented during one of their many Skype/Zoom calls that years spent living in the USA and Hawaii had not robbed Halley of her English accent, merely tweaked it a little, giving her a definite Mid-Atlantic intonation.

'So, what can we do to help you?'

Focusing, she answered Lexie's question. 'I'm fine, really. Not that I've had much to do, Sir Monty and Rowan Ferguson are taking care of things, ably assisted by Tor.' There. She'd found something nice to say about him. 'Would you like to come in out of the cold?'

'Sure,' Bryce commented. 'Lead the way. Not you,' he told their dog, who resigned itself to staying on the porch.

Halley led them into the salmon bothy, told them to make themselves at home and then switched the kettle on. As she got down mugs and a packet of biscuits Halley noticed that they didn't cast curious looks round the bothy, as if seeing it for the first time. They appeared very much at home, familiar with its layout and were happy to allow her to play hostess.

'I hear you experienced trial by ordeal last night,' Lexie said, stripping off scarf and gloves and laying them on the table. Registering Halley's baffled expression, she explained. 'Dinner up at the castle? Mother on sparkling form?' The way she said 'sparkling' suggested that her mother's autocratic behaviour was nothing out of the ordinary.

'She was,' Halley said, keeping her thoughts to herself. Lexie and Bryce seemed friendly but they were family and she wasn't. In these circumstances blood, as she'd found out to her cost, was always thicker than water.

'We never go up to the Big Hoose, not if we can help it,' Bryce put in, pronouncing *Big Hoose* in an exaggerated highland accent. 'But on certain occasions, Christmas, birthdays, high days and holidays, Lady Strachan operates a three-line whip and we can't get out of it.'

'We're more or less vegan,' Lexie added. 'We use that as an excuse for passing up on most invitations.' She reached out across the table and held Bryce's hand. 'United we stand, eh Bryce?'

'Totally,' he agreed.

'How does that work?' Halley inquired, pouring boiling water into a large brown teapot. Maybe she could try it next time, not that there'd be a next time, of that she was certain!

'We say our diet is *soooo* restrictive we don't like to put Cook to any trouble and use that as an excuse to stay away. Were Ly and Suzie there?' Lexie rolled her eyes, making no secret that the thought of dining en famille held no appeal for her.

'Yes, and your father and Tor.'

'At least you had two allies,' Bryce added, running his thumb along the back of Lexie's hand.

'It wasn't too bad,' Halley said as she handed mugs of tea round. 'I spent most of the night in the library with Sir Monty hearing about his and Tam's military adventures.'

'Did Tor say much? About his time in the army, I mean?' Lexie asked, a worried frown creasing her forehead.

'Just the bare bones: university, Sandhurst, the Scots Guards.' Lexie accepted a biscuit straight from the packet. 'I'm sure there's more but yesterday evening was neither the time nor the place.' She remembered Tor struggling to climb the stairs the first night they'd met and watching him walk down the beach yesterday with his shepherd's crook supporting him against the buffeting wind. There was a story here, but if she was holding back, so was he.

'No, you're quite right. We need to stay focused, give Tam the send-off he deserves. And don't you worry, we will. Tam meant a lot to us, kind've like an honorary grandfather.' Lexie looked at Halley over the rim of her mug as if worried that Halley might not like her appropriating Tam as her own.

'We saw a lot of him, did his shopping, that sort of thing,' Bryce explained. 'We often sat here with Tor, Monty and Tam, sharing the craic during the long winter nights. And the nights are very long in Lochaber in December, believe me.'

Halley smiled but said nothing. Hadn't Souter claimed that he'd done much the same for Tam? She shrugged the thought away, deciding to be grateful that Tam had been well looked after.

'But in the summer,' Lexie added, clasping her hands together as if in prayer. It rarely gets dark, 'so that kinda makes up for it.'

'It's a shame I won't be here to see it,' Halley said.

'I feel I know you,' Lexie gabbled on. 'Tam told us so much about you, your career, your life in Hawaii. He was so very proud of you but we've often wondered why you haven't visited in years.'

'Oh, you know,' she prevaricated. It was the question which wouldn't go away, one which would have to be answered with, if not the truth, then something close to it. Seemingly, everyone thought that she and her family had let Tam down. That hurt. But she wasn't willing to share the truth with people who, in all likelihood, she wouldn't see again after next week.

Lexie bit her lip. 'Aw, your face; I'm sorry, that's none of my business. How tactless, now I've upset you.' She smacked herself on the back of the hand, adding, 'Bad Lexie. There must be more of my mother in me than I realise.'

They all laughed at that.

Putting down her mug she joined Halley over by the sink and put her arms around her. Halley allowed herself to be embraced, welcoming the contact. Her family were thousands of miles away and she missed them. She'd thought herself equal to the task of handling Tam's funeral, now she wondered if she had the necessary courage to see it through. Lexie smelled of the outdoors and growing things, the wind off the loch and, unexpectedly, Chanel 19. The embrace was enough to reduce Halley to tears, again. Taking a deep breath, she reached into her pocket for the handkerchief Tor had given to her. Lexie took the handkerchief from her, dabbed Halley's eyes and mopped the tears running down her cheeks and into the corner of her mouth.

'It's, it's just that –' Halley croaked.

'No, don't say another word. Come on, sit down and let us look after you like we looked after Tam.' She led Halley over to Tam's chair, put the Strachan tartan rug over her knees and handed Halley her mug of tea.

'Really, there's no need,' Halley managed a watery smile.

'Oh, let her,' Bryce put in, 'we'll get no peace until you do, she's a real mother hen. You should see the animals she's rescued; our house is a veritable animal hospital. She's got a big heart and there's always room for someone who's hurting.'

Halley was about to deny that she was a bird with a broken wing but Bryce meant it kindly and so she sniffed and did as he suggested. Lexie folded the handkerchief over and handed it back to Halley. As she did so she spotted familiar initials embroidered in the corner: HSS. Her raised eyebrow suggested that Hector Strachan was not in the habit of handing handkerchiefs over to females in distress, or otherwise.

'Hector's, eh?' she grinned, putting two and two together and getting five.

'Last night in the library my paper towel handkerchief disintegrated under the emotional strain. 'Tor offered me his, I must remember to return it before I leave.' With all the subtlety of a sledge hammer Lexie indicated to Bryce, via a sideways jerk of her head, that he should make himself scarce and leave them to it.

'Good old, Hector,' Bryce said with no apparent ill will. 'Okay, I'm walking home via the top road to check for road kill and will take the dog with me. I take it you'll be meeting Tor and Rowan up at the castle?'

Before Halley had a chance to answer his question or to query *road kill,* he was out of the door.

'Road kill?'

'That's how Bryce makes his money and supports the animals we rescue.'

'Go on, I'm intrigued.'

'Like me, Bryce is on the run from parents who want to control our lives. His would rather he'd attended university, got a degree in estate management or went into business in Edinburgh or, worse still,

London. That's so not Bryce. He loves Lochaber and the outdoor life, as do I. His family own a humongous hunting, shooting, fishing estate and he could have joined his brothers managing it. However, he can't see the point of breeding animals just to have them slaughtered by city slickers playing highland laird for the weekend. At the end of which, those birds which can't be sold for profit, sent south to restaurants or given to his family's tenants, are burned on huge bonfires. So cruel and such a waste.'

She took a deep slug of tea and looking all hot and bothered moved over to the window. When she turned back, she'd regained her good humour.

'Wow,' was all Halley could manage.

'It's all hypocrisy of course.'

'It is?'

'Bryce and I live on my family's estate, rent free. He draws money from a trust set up by his great-aunt and I'm subsidised by my father who wants me to be happy.' She blew a kiss in the direction of *Creag na h-Iolaire*.

'Isn't that what all parents want for their children?' Halley asked, curling her legs beneath her and snuggling down under the tartan blanket.

'Yes, it is. Not being heir to *Creag na h-Iolaire* means I can follow my star.'

'Which is?'

'Yes, please,' she held out her mug for a top up. 'To help Bryce establish and develop *MacPherson's Wild Sporrans*.' Being unsure exactly what a wild sporran was Halley kept her features neutral. She liked Lexie and Bryce and didn't want to fall out on first meeting over the contentious subject of killing wild animals for pleasure or profit. She thought of the poor animals she'd seen mounted on walls or in display cases in museums, although she noticed not in *Creag na h-Iolaire*. She shuddered and Lexie went on to explain. 'Oh, it isn't what you think. Bryce finds dead animals on the roadside or is given them by folk and turns them into something new. He sees it as his way of honouring the spirit of the animal, of giving them a second life. Rather like our ancestors recording the image of animals they hunted on cave walls, although Bryce wouldn't hurt a living creature. Nor would I.'

'I see.' High colour tinged Lexie's cheeks, an indication of how passionately she felt about the subject.

'Bryce studied taxidermy after leaving school, not quite the career his parents had planned for him. He sees himself as a kind of shaman, if that's not too fanciful, giving animals a second life and honouring their beauty which otherwise would have been wasted. You must come over for dinner before you leave and let Bryce explain. He does it so much better than I do.'

'You're pretty eloquent,' Halley observed, smiling.

'Oh, and don't worry, Bryce keeps his business separate from the cottage on the estate where we live. You won't find a dead badger or fox in the freezer next to the fish fingers. That came out wrong,' Lexie laughed and Halley joined in. 'Tell me about your career.'

Taking a large swig of her cooling tea, Halley explained. 'I'm one of a team of astrophysicists at the Haleakala Observatories on Maui and Mauna Kea researching the existence of exoplanets.'

'What are those when they're at home?'

'Planets on the far edges of our solar system which may or may not sustain life.'

'Wow. To boldly go where no one has gone before? Do you think that's possible?'

'Anything's possible. If I wasn't so interested in exoplanets, I might have segued into studying whether or not time travel is possible. That comes under the banner of astrophysics, too.'

'Like Doctor Who?'

Halley suppressed a smile. 'I guess. However, I'm more concerned with following in my mother's footsteps but she's a tough act to follow. As a student in the sixties at Cambridge she worked alongside Jocelyn Bell Burnell who discovered radio pulsars.'

'Cool.' Lexie left the table and curled up on the sagging sofa near to Halley.

'Sadly, not cool. The Nobel prize for the discovery went to Burnell's male supervisors.'

'Wh-aat?'

'I know. I like to think that it wouldn't happen these days, but I'm not so sure. Physics is littered with female researchers who've been overlooked and haven't received the recognition they deserve: Lene Hau, Vera Rubin, Chien-Shuing Wu, Lise Meitner to name but four. I have to work extra hard to ensure that everything I discover is logged and recorded, no man's going to appropriate my research or destroy my hopes and dreams.'

She zoned out for a moment, thinking how close that had come to happening when she'd fallen for Lysander Strachan's lies and false promises. Her career over before it'd begun. Her stomach gave a sick lurch. Even after all this time, how close she'd come to losing everything still haunted her.

Now, nothing mattered more than surpassing her parents' expectations and, one day, becoming Professor Halley Dunbar.

'Time travel? If you could go back in time and change one thing, what would it be?' Lexie asked, breaking into her thoughts.

'Good question,' Halley prevaricated, knowing the answer but not prepared to elaborate. 'One would have to be careful of not creating a paradox where one small change could change the present. How about you?'

'Easy, I'd go back to the moments before the device which ruined Tor's career and changed his life forever, exploded.' Halley wanted to ask more but Lexie looked so forlorn that she didn't push it. And, to be fair, if she wasn't prepared to share her thoughts with Lexie, she could hardly ask her for more information. She changed the subject, drawing them back to the story of those female pioneers she tried to emulate. 'The story has a happy ending. Professor Burnell was awarded the two-point- three million *Breakthrough* prize which she used to create a fund to counter unconscious bias in physics.'

'Now, that is cool. Right?'

'Yes. Super cool,' Halley smiled at Lexie who, sitting on the sofa and curling her hair round her finger seemed younger than her years.

'I'm neither clever nor ambitious, I simply want to be happy and Bryce makes me happy.' She looked so glum that Halley felt compelled to say something encouraging.

'Nothing wrong in that,' she avowed. 'We all have to follow our star.'

'Is that an astrophysics joke?' Lexie asked, brightening.

'If it isn't, it ought to be.'

'I must be the only child who was happier at boarding school and cried when the end of term arrived and Monty and Tam came to fetch me home. During the long holiday I'd stand at the top of the steps to the beach and watch you, Rowan Ferguson and village children playing beach cricket, taking part in Tam's scavenger hunts and swimming, desperate to join in. But mother wouldn't allow it. I'm not sure why she thought playing with the village children would harm me. The only time I went anywhere was when I was decked out in my best clothes and taken over to our cousins or friends of mothers. Poor little rich kid, huh?'

'Seems a shame. She wasn't so particular with Lysander, then?' Halley asked, dredging up the past in spite of her earlier resolution.

'Once he got to his late teens Mother wasn't able to control him. He was desperate to break free, which is ironic.'

'Ironic, how?'

'Lysander soon discovered how harsh life can be outside the walls of *Creag na h-Iolaire*. Added to which he's bone idle, scraped through uni and flunked Sandhurst, citing his asthma as the reason he didn't pass the fitness tests. He came running back to the estate and here he's stayed, even after marrying Suzie.'

'Really?' Halley let Lexie fill in the gaps in Lysander Strachan's timeline.

'When Tor returned from his first tour of Afghanistan tanned, with sun bleached hair and covered in glory we nicknamed him *Lawrence* of Arabia. When Ly flunked officer training, the cousins and I took to calling him *Florence* of Arabia until Mother made us stop. She always sticks up for her darling boy.'

'Ouch,' Halley commented. Was it wrong to feel pleased that Lysander's life hadn't been plain sailing? Human nature, she decided, cutting herself some slack. 'I guess that the age difference in those days would have meant we would have had little in common.'

'You're right. I'm thirty and you're . . .'

'Almost thirty-eight. Practically geriatric.'

'You look pretty amazing for a geriatric, Miss Dunbar. A seven-year gap doesn't seem huge now but back then it was a yawning chasm. Bryce had a similarly dysfunctional childhood but I won't bore you with the details. We're happy now and that's all that matters. Life has looked up since Tor left the army for good and returned to manage the estate, even if under circumstances none of us would have wanted.'

Then, evidently thinking that she'd taken up enough of Halley's time, Lexie uncurled from the sofa and stood up. Halley walked her to the door and watched as she left the porch, turned right and strode up the beach, head down against the buffeting wind.

With plenty of food for thought, Halley went back in to the salmon bothy to wait for Hector Strachan to ring her to announce the arrival of Tam's coffin up at the castle. Then she would walk up there, place his glengarry on top of the coffin and prepare to say a final farewell.

Her last chance to apologise for letting him down and hope that, somehow, that he would understand.

Chapter Twelve

It was almost two o'clock when Tor knocked on the salmon bothy's door and Halley opened it with a surprised: 'Oh.'

'I know I was supposed to ring and let you know when Tam arrived.' There was a pause as he realised how crass and insensitive that sounded. If she thought so too, she didn't show it. In a vain attempt to lighten the atmosphere and in deference to her scientific background he made a feeble joke. 'Houston – we have a problem.'

'I see. You'd better come in.' She pushed the door open, stood to one side and allowed him to brush past and enter. The lintel was so low that he had to duck to clear it and, in doing so, inadvertently nudged shoulders with her.

'Sorry,' he mumbled.

She waved her hand to indicate that the accidental touch was of no consequence and that he should sit at the kitchen table. She pulled out a chair opposite him. She looked less stressed than when they'd last met, her cheeks had a tinge of colour and eyes were no longer heavy-lidded from jet lag and her long, dark auburn hair fell in glossy waves about her face.

They had been getting on okay and he hoped this meeting would be less fraught.

'A problem?' she prompted.

He cut to the chase. 'It's been quite a morning. The hearse pulled up in the stable yard and Monty and I came down to talk to Rowan Ferguson. Once Monty saw Tam's coffin, the reality of the situation struck home and he went to pieces, refusing to be consoled. I've tried, believe me, but he keeps brushing me off.'

'I'm not looking forward to it myself. My hands have been shaking since I woke, although Lexie and Bryce's visit helped a little. I've tried to kid myself it's because I'm cold, but really, I'm apprehensive because I've never been to a funeral, let alone one for someone I loved and where I'll be representing our family. I don't know what to expect.' She held out her hands to show they were shaking and, possibly without meaning to, sent him a beseeching look. 'I expect you're used to dealing with this sort of thing? Being an ex-soldier, I mean.'

Tor flinched. His career was well and truly over and he'd accepted that. However, memories of the day his life changed forever came crowding in before he had time to employ his seven-point mantra. In answer to her question, he reached out and captured her hands to stop them trembling, that seemed simpler somehow.

'Your hands are cold and shaking due to stress. That's not uncommon. And, in answer to your question, yes, I've seen things during my time in the army that would turn your hair grey. However, nothing prepares you for the death of a loved one, I know that. Don't be too hard on yourself.'

'I have led a sheltered life, almost cloistered you could say. I spend so much of my time behind a telescope or in front of a computer and hosting zoom seminars that I've almost forgotten how to interact with people and cope with the ups and downs of everyday life. But that doesn't mean that I can't cope when I have to. I just need to get my head round what's expected of me and then I'll be okay.'

Nodding, he released her hands, hadn't he seen her resilience for himself when he'd flattened her on the beach? She was a tough cookie and had an inner strength. He was gratified that she was prepared to open up to him, on this subject at least.

'As I said, we – Monty, Rowan and I, have a problem and we need your help to overcome it. Sorry about the 'Houston' joke.'

She smiled. 'How can I help?'

'Mother's thrown a strop worthy of a toddler. Said she'll bar the door to the castle and order the staff to raise the portcullis if Tam's coffin comes within three feet of *Creag na h-lolaire*. Furthermore, she refuses to allow the coffin to rest on her fu . . . bloody Chippendale table.' He stopped himself from using a stronger adjective.

'I see,' she frowned, sending him a direct look. 'But, isn't your father laird? I'd've thought his word was law.'

'And it is. Usually. However, when Mother gets one on her she really lets rip. I fear for her blood pressure and Father, at the end of the day, always lets her have the last word, because . . .' He paused, unsure how far to take this conversation. Luckily, she didn't appear to notice the pause.

'Yet, you're so calm and Lexie seems such a sweet soul.'

'Military training m'dear,' he said in the bluff tones of an ancient colonel. 'As for Lexie, she's living the life she's always wanted with a man who adores her.' He was about to bring Lysander into the conversation, however, remembering finding them in a clinch on her first morning in the bothy and unsure of the exact nature of their relationship, decided against it.

That was a can of worms best left unopened.

Plainly she was trying to process the information as she bit her bottom lip before continuing. 'Okay, I understand that for some reason, Lady Strachan hates Tam. What I don't get is *why* she hates him. Is it because he and Monty were so close? Or because she wants the salmon bothy returned to the estate and has been thwarted in achieving that for the last thirty years or so?'

Tor looked at her, wondering that she hadn't grasped that the bond between his father and her great-uncle went beyond mere friendship. But today wasn't the time for revealing the exact nature of their relationship or allowing skeletons to come rattling out of the family armoire. She'd be on the plane back to Hawaii in just over a week, Tam would be laid to rest in the family graveyard waiting for Monty to join him and life would go on. If Tam hadn't revealed his and Monty's relationship to his family it wasn't his place to do so.

Instead, he said, 'Tam's going to spend the night in the family church and be carried to his grave from there. As you remarked earlier, Tam wasn't religious and he made it known to Monty that he wanted a graveside ceremony conducted by the local minister not a full church service. Then, the funeral party will return to the bothy for the wake.'

'That sounds like Tam, alright.' Halley gave a weak smile.

Glad that she was accepting the alternative arrangements without fuss, Tor continued. 'Rowan and I have been thrashing out the practicalities and, to be honest, it might work out better if the coffin didn't enter the castle. It'd please Mother at any rate. I've informed Father of the alternative arrangements and he's okay-ed them. That just leaves you.'

Halley released a long sigh. 'I suppose, Tam being your father's former batman it's only to be expected that would present a problem for your mother. My family would have been quite happy to see Tam laid to rest in the local cemetery in Mallaig, but your father was adamant that wasn't going to happen.'

'It's father's intention to visit the grave every day, weather permitting, and to talk to Tam as he has always done. They'd discussed their respective funerals many times over a glass or two of malt.' Now it was his turn to dredge up a weak smile as he edged his way forward, unsure of what her reaction to the alternative plan was likely to be. 'I gather it's something old folk do.'

'Very practical,' Halley nodded her approval. 'However, theirs is a long and enduring friendship, tomorrow isn't going to be easy for Monty.'

'Or you for that matter.' He decided to leave it there. 'I haven't only come down to tell you about the change in arrangements, I want to drive you up to the church. It isn't far but I thought that you might welcome someone to walk into the church with you? Or would you rather do so alone? Rowan, Lexie and Bryce are waiting there for us. Tomorrow, Rowan will be here with her staff to ensure that everything runs like clockwork.'

'You and Rowan have taken much of the weight off my shoulders. As I said, Tam wasn't religious, that particular gene seems to have passed my family by.' A faint smile lit her features and she sent him a direct look. 'The Dunbars deal in facts, figures and the world according to scientific principles. Best to keep everything plain, simple and as unemotional as possible, that's what Tam would have wanted.' Her voice snagged, demonstrating that she wasn't finding this easy. 'I'll get my coat.'

With that she headed for the bedroom giving Tor the opportunity to glance round the salmon bothy. The tin which his father had given to her last night was on the worktop and he nodded towards it when she re-entered the room.

'Have you opened the tin?' he inquired.

'No, I'm sticking to my original plan of opening it once everything's over and I'm alone. Things are going to be difficult enough tomorrow and I don't want to add to that by discovering mementoes in the box which will take me back to childhood, or . . . I did think of taking it back to Hawaii unopened, but I might get stopped at customs and I'm not sure what it contains, other than Tam's medals. Once I've examined the contents, would you be kind enough to send it on with the things I mentioned the other day?'

'Of course. It'll make things easier if you're travelling light.' He helped her on with her coat and this time she didn't flinch when their bodies touched. She smiled and gave him an oblique look. One which implied that it wasn't only possessions which weighed a person down, sometimes memories were the heaviest weight of all.

He nodded, completely understanding and wanting to say more. However, he collected his shepherd's crook from the front door, and asked: 'Shall we?'

'After you. I'll lock up.'

'Tam's glengarry?' he reminded her.

Tutting at her forgetfulness, Halley headed back into Tam's bedroom and returned with it, tucking it into her large tote bag. Tor headed for the Land Rover musing that until recently he would have said it was safe to leave the salmon bothy unlocked. But now? Given the incidence of poaching which was on the increase, the unusual lights seen round the loch in the winter darkness, locking the door was probably a good idea.

Chapter Thirteen

Sitting next to Hector Strachan in the Land Rover was intimate and strangely unsettling. Halley frowned; she couldn't remember when she'd last been so close to a member of the opposite sex in a confined space, physically let alone emotionally. At least, a member of the opposite sex not wearing a lab coat! She shivered, recalling how a certain male colleague, one of the exoplanet team, liked to approach her while she was at her desk, deeply engrossed in her work. He'd look over her shoulder, ostensibly to see what line of research she was following, but more often than not use his professional connection as an excuse to get up close and *way* too personal.

Halley shuddered. If he only knew how much she hated her personal space being invaded by his cheap aftershave or body odour because his lab coat hadn't been in the laundry for weeks. Should anyone wonder why she found the idea of dating him or anyone like him repellent, the answer was right under their noses.

Then there was his pathetic attempt to discover the line of research she was pursuing, possibly with the intention of appropriating her work. Her mother had warned her all about that. It was a shame that she hadn't been more specific with the advice given to Halley regarding the opposite sex when she was teenager. If she had, then maybe she wouldn't have made such a fool of herself over Lysander Strachan.

One thing was certain, no man would ever make a fool of her again.

'You, okay?' Hector asked as she gave out a huff of annoyance.

'Sorry, just thinking about my job and wondering how everything's going in my absence.'

'You're keen to get back, then?'

'You could say that.' Turning, she smiled, attempting to make plain that it wasn't anything personal, simply that here, in Lochaber, she was a fish out of water. Sure, she had memories of happy summer holidays playing on the beach until she'd been forced to grow up and discovered that life was no fairy tale.

Now the life she led thousands of miles away was calling to her and . . .

'I get it. You feel displaced, out of kilter. No need to explain.'

Tor drove along the beach without another word, leading Halley to think that he was no stranger to feelings of dislocation.

They headed along the beach and then up a concrete slipway onto a wide, rough path overlaid with hardcore and gravel; a makeshift roadway. Soon the ancient graveyard with lopsided headstones and whitewashed church hove into view.

As a child, Halley had never dared trespass on the consecrated ground where generations of Strachans had been buried. Monty and the other Strachans went to church every Sunday as befitted the laird and his family. However, Tam had stayed resolutely away. Together, they'd spend the Sabbath wandering the shore or going into Mallaig to see the boats take the tourists whale watching. When she was old enough, they'd pass on cooking Sunday lunch and go to The Strachan Arms instead.

It was a standing joke that one day Lady Strachan would invite them up to the castle for fore rib of Aberdeen Angus beef with all the trimmings and they'd sit round her precious Chippendale table, pinkies extended as they sipped a fine Chablis from crystal glasses.

'You're very quiet,' Tor commented, turning to look at her.

'Thinking about the past.' Halley concealed her negative thoughts about his family. 'I'm a little apprehensive, but fine.'

'You won't be alone. I promise you that.'

'I know. Thank you.' She assumed that being responsible for the welfare of the men in his unit, Tor was used to thinking about others and ensuring things ran smoothly. Halley smiled at him for his thoughtfulness although, concentrating on driving down the rough track, he didn't see her smile. 'The others are waiting. Look.'

Rowan, Lexie and Bryce were sheltering in the tiny porch of the church, their collars turned up against the wind. When they saw Tor's Land Rover they stepped forward. There was no sign of a hearse and for that Halley was glad. Neither was there any sign of Sir Monty and she was glad of that, too. If, as Tor had indicated, he was in an emotional state, she preferred him to stay away until tomorrow. Coping with her own feelings of grief and guilt was bad enough. Tor and Lexie could support their father.

Tor cast her an oblique look as if trying to guess what was going through her mind. However, she kept her face shuttered, her expression neutral. That way she could cope with whatever the day threw at her.

'Halley,' Lexie came forward, opened Halley's door and practically dragged her out of the Land Rover before enfolding her in a warm embrace. 'Tor,' she greeted her brother in similar fashion and he resigned himself to her effusive kisses before shaking hands with Bryce.

'Rowan. How can I thank you? You've made everything so much easier for us all, especially for Monty.' Rowan stepped forward and Tor kissed her lightly on both cheeks. Even on this grim occasion it amused Halley to see Rowan's face turn bright red at the warmth of Tor's greeting.

'Well, it's what I do,' Rowan said, lowering her head modestly. 'I loved Tam and I want to ensure he gets the send-off he deserves and Monty expects.' Tor patted her on the shoulder and then Halley came forward and greeted them all in turn. To her surprise, Bryce followed Rowan's example and kissed her on both cheeks. In that moment she forgot all about not belonging here, basking instead in the warmth of their friendship.

'Shall we?' Tor asked, leading the way to the church.

Out of the corner of her eye Halley saw a freshly dug grave, sides lined with green tarpaulin, a pile of excavated earth covered in plastic close by and planks of wood holding it in place, preventing the winter rains from washing everything away.

'I –' She started to speak but her tongue cleaved to the roof of her mouth and the words wouldn't come.

Lexie interrupted, 'Ach, dinnae fash, hen, all will be well.'

Her attempt at a lowland accent made Rowan laugh and roll her eyes. 'She's right, you know. Nothing for you to worry about. Tam made sure of that.' She gave Halley's arm a comforting squeeze. 'His instructions for tomorrow are quite precise. Mind you, I'd expect nothing less of Monty's batman.'

Halley squeezed her eyes shut in a valiant attempt to hold back the tears, took a deep breath and announced: 'Ready.'

Tor stepped forward, opened the heavy church door, switched on the lights and indicated that they should precede him into the church. Detaching herself from Rowan and Lexie, Halley entered the church.

The interior was cool and smelt of dust, candlewax and hymn books. Once the door was closed to keep out the biting wind, it took on the appearance of a dimly lit cave, the last of the autumn sun slanting in through the windows. The ancient church was simply decorated, no stained glass, high altar or lectern with a brass eagle for holding the bible, just two carved family pews on either side of the aisle and wooden benches for the other worshippers. On the walls, faded lozenges in wood, plaster and brass recorded that Strachans had been buried here for as long as anyone could remember. Strangely, it didn't seem to bother Tor or Lexie that one day they would be laid to rest in the churchyard or in the family vault alongside their ancestors.

Dismissing such gloomy and depressing thoughts, Halley concentrated on how many mourners would attend Tam's funeral and if she should be helping with arrangements instead of leaving everything to Rowan.

As if telepathic, Rowan put her mind at rest.

'Apart from the immediate family and friends there will be about fifty mourners, mostly from the British Legion in Mallaig and other branches round about. That's the number I've catered for. Tam's old pals wouldn't pass up on the opportunity to give him a good send-off or to enjoy the laird's hospitality. As per Tam's wishes, there won't be a service as such, the mourners will just gather here out of the wind before heading out to the graveside for the internment.'

'The minister will say a few words,' Tor added, 'those who wish to, can join in with the Lord's Prayer and then it's back to Tam's bothy where his life will be commemorated by those who knew him best. We,' he looked round at Bryce, Lexie and Rowan, 'want it to be as joyous an occasion as possible. Tam lived a long and eventful life and I'm sure there will be many a tale for his ex-service pals to share over a wee drap o' the swally.'

He grinned and the others nodded.

'Swally?' Halley asked.

'Whisky, wine, beer,' Bryce explained, 'alcohol. That's down to Monty.'

'I don't know what to say,' Halley stammered.

'You won't have to say anything, unless you want to. Monty will give the eulogy at the wake and we'll toast Tam's memory,' Tor reassured her.

'Just be there, be yourself and remember a lovely, lovely man in your own way.' Lexie put her arm round Halley's waist and gave another reassuring hug.

'Here he is,' Tor said, gently disentangling Halley from his sister's embrace. For one, disconcerting moment, Halley's confused brain thought that Tam hadn't died and was about to join them, laughing at their long faces. Giving her a moment to compose herself, Tor turned her to face Tam's coffin which was resting on a simple table which looked as though it usually held hymn books. The coffin was invisible beneath a blue and white saltire and all that could be seen were the legs of the table the casket rested on. Somehow, that was more fitting than Lady Strachan's Chippendale dining table. Halley straightened her shoulders and gritted her teeth. She knew exactly what her uncle's reaction would have been to all the hullabaloo and the choice swear words he would have used.

Words more suited to the barracks than her ladyship's delicate ears.

'The wreath was Monty's choice,' Lexie explained, taking Halley's hand and guiding her over to the coffin. 'And will be the only flowers tomorrow. Tam's request.' Halley looked at the tight posy of white roses intertwined with heather and poppies and nodded. 'Have you brought Tam's glengarry?'

'Here.' Taking her cue from the others and no longer quite so apprehensive, Halley brought Tam's glengarry out of her tote bag. Wintery sunlight shafting through the lancet window touched the cap badge; the boar's head, prancing cat, crown and thistle insignia standing out against the square of black ribbon it was pinned to. Halley put her hands inside the hat in an attempt to open the brim wide enough to make the glengarry stand upright on the coffin, but had to settle for it lying flat on top of the flag.

'Here, let me,' Tor stepped forward, positioning the glengarry so the two ribbon tails hanging down the back were splayed out and the red pompom, or toorie, which identified the glengarry as belonging to a regimental piper were displayed to their best advantage.

'Thank you,' Halley said quietly. Their hands touched as he put the final touches to the glengarry and Halley moved the garland further to the right. If she hadn't been so focused on the task in hand, she would have seen Rowan and Lexie exchange a significant look.

Bryce broke the silence. 'Is that everything? Rowan?'

'What? Oh, yes. I'll head back to Mallaig and see you all tomorrow at ten o'clock. Can I give anyone a lift?'

'No, we're fine, a walk along the beach will give us an appetite for dinner. Care to join us Tor, Halley?'

'Thank you, Bryce, some other time. I'd like to be alone with my thoughts, if that's okay?' Halley replied.

'We'll leave you to it, then.'

Bryce, Lexie and Rowan left the church closing the door behind them. Tor walked up to the box pew just to the right of the coffin and pushed the door open. 'Sit in here, although you might find the draft round your ankles uncomfortable after a few minutes. Take your farewell of Tam but don't stay too long. Night descends very quickly this time of year and you'll be walking back to the salmon bothy over unfamiliar, uneven ground at dusk, unless you want me to wait for you?'

'No, I'll be fine, thank you.'

'I'll see you tomorrow then, in fact I'll come and fetch you. No –' he held up his hand to forestall Halley's protests. 'No one expects you to walk to the church on your own. My father would think it remiss of me *not* to fetch you and Tam would expect nothing less.'

'Put like that, how can I refuse?'

'You can't.' Tor grinned, seemingly taken aback at her caving so easily. Then he closed the pew door, disappearing from view. Halley stood up and peered over the top of the pew, watching in silence as Tor drew himself up to his full height and saluted the coffin. 'Goodbye old friend. *Cruachan!*' He raised his fist into the air, giving the war cry of Clan Campbell and the Argyll and Sutherland Highlanders before turning, picking up his cromack and leaving the church.

Chapter Fourteen

Sitting back in the pew Halley pulled her coat more tightly around her, dragged hat and gloves out of her bag and put them on. She recalled Tam's retelling of the regiment's history and the list of battle honours they'd won. How the Argyll and Sutherland Highlanders had fought bravely at the battle of Balaklava and that each pony mascot was called Cruachan, after the first of the name. As she sat in contemplation, the afternoon headed towards dusk and the chill rose up from the church floor, despite the pew being carpeted with an offcut of tartan rug.

It was time to take her leave of her great-uncle, ask his forgiveness for everything and put that chapter behind her. Returning to Lochaber wasn't only about seeing her great-uncle laid to rest. It was about closure, about shutting the door on that distant summer and the resultant fallout. However, she was a scientist and part of her regarded 'closure' as nothing more than psychobabble, but she knew that before she could move on with her life, she had to confront her demons and conquer them.

As she was about to get to her feet the church door opened. She thought it might be Tor returning in an attempt to make her change her mind about a lift back to the Salmon bothy. However, when she peered over the top of the pew it was Sir Monty, making his way up the aisle towards Tam's coffin.

Not wishing to intrude upon his last farewell to his dear friend Halley sat back down, hoping he was unaware of her presence. She heard him move closer before stopping before Tams' coffin. It was strange to be sitting there in the family pew, the light fading as evening approached, her beloved uncle lying within touching distance but with so much left unsaid.

'Tam,' Sir Monty cleared his throat, his voice echoing in the empty church. 'Dear Tam, what am I to do without you? My family don't need me, the estate runs better without my intervention, my wife hates me for what I – we've done to her, and any hope of a grandchild to carry on the line are fading fast. Lysander's having no luck, Tor seems disinclined to marry but maybe Alexandra will come through for me, which wouldn't really help because the estate is entailed away from the female line. You were all that stood between me, loneliness and despair, and now you're gone. That isn't how we planned it, is it? I don't know if I'll be able to stand at the graveside tomorrow and watch as they lower you into the cold earth, but I will. It's my duty to ensure you have a fitting burial, a soldier's funeral. It's what you deserve.' There was a pause as he pulled his handkerchief out of his pocket, blew his nose and a shuddering sob escaped him.

Listening to his leave taking, Halley swallowed hard and brushed a tear away with a gloved forefinger. Monty cleared his throat and continued more steadily. 'I've become re-acquainted with your great-niece, a bonnie lassie if ever there was. I've tried to get her to divulge why she stayed away all these years but to no avail. Maybe you were right, something *did* happen between her and Lysander that summer. I was never very good at that sort of thing, always too wrapped up in myself to notice what's going on under my nose. You were always much better at reading people, of getting to the root of things.'

Halley put her hand over her mouth. Hadn't Lysander said the other night that listening at keyholes was how you found out what was going down at *Creagh na h-Iolaire*? Sitting quietly, she listened while Sir Monty blew his nose a second time before continuing. 'If something did happen between them, then shame on Lysander. He should have known better; engaged and about to go up to Sandhurst, it was wrong for him to have dallied with your great-niece.'

Dallied? Halley whispered. Oh, what happened between them went beyond mere dalliance.

She rarely allowed herself the extravagance of remembering that fateful summer because she found the recollection painful. However, in this chapel with just the three of them, it felt like a confessional. It was as if she'd been granted a chance to go over it one last time. Forgive herself for being a naive teenager unversed in the ways of the world, not knowing that men could profess love but mean something else entirely.

She remembered sitting in the airport lounge on her way back to Massachusetts, ticking off the days in her diary until her A-level results arrived, hopefully with good enough grades to allow her to take up her place at MIT to study astrophysics. She was feeling emotionally battered and bruised because she'd just discovered that Lysander had a fiancée whom everyone expected him to marry. It was then that she'd noticed other dates. Ones which had passed by unannounced, unheralded and, in the throes of first love, she hadn't noticed.

No! She couldn't be.

She was as regular as the comet she'd been named after, returning to earth every seventy years or so. It was the stress of studying which had knocked her cycle out of kilter. Yes, that was it. Her hands had started to shake and her stomach churned with apprehension. Cheeks flushed and feeling hot and sick she'd snapped the diary closed and stuffed it into her rucksack. There was one way to find out. Grim faced she'd marched into the pharmacy and bought a pregnancy test, staring down the assistant who'd looked at her questioningly. Although she was eighteen, almost nineteen years old, with her long hair and slim figure she looked much younger. Then she'd rammed the test into her rucksack almost in the same moment her flight was announced . . .

Monty spoke, breaking into her corrosive memories. 'I keep thinking back to the day you were assigned as my batman. A wet nurse to polish my kit and keep me out of trouble until I learned how to be a soldier. You must have thought me a right eejit, all the questions I asked you, damn stupid some of them, but you hid it well. Just as we hid our feelings from each other in the beginning and everyone else in the end.'

Halley sank lower in the pew, pushing her own memories aside and trying to make sense of what she'd just heard. The church door opened and footsteps walked up the narrow aisle, the accompanying tap of the cromack every other step marked the mourner as Hector Strachan.

'Monty, what are you doing here? Okay, stupid question. What are you doing here alone? I would happily have –'

'I know you would, Tor. You're a good son, better than I deserve.'

'Now, we both know that isn't true. Only you and Tam understood what I went through when I was flown home from Afghanistan and spent months in rehabilitation, having to accept my career was over.'

'Tam was like a second father to you, wasn't he?' Monty's voice cracked as he sought assurance.

'The best,' Tor confirmed. 'Two fathers for the price of one.'

'Made up for the damned mess your mother and I made of things. I should never have married her, but noblesse oblige. I should have let the title and the estate pass to my cousin, but pride got in the way. The estate needed money, she had it by the bucket load, wanted a title and, well, it seemed a fair exchange. Strachans, as you know, make better soldiers than lairds. In the end I made us both unhappy.' His deep sigh reverberated around the church. 'You're the only good thing to have come from this hell of a marriage. Damn it.' In her hidey-hole, Halley heard his groan of pain undercut with frustration and annoyance at how life had worked out.

Wait – the *only* thing? What about Lexie and Lysander? Didn't they count?

'Come on, Monty, buck up. Tam would give you a good talking to if he were here. Tomorrow, we'll give him a send-off worthy of a five-star general.'

'Not that he'd want it,' Monty put in. 'He could have been a regimental sergeant major, a colour sergeant or a pipe major but he wouldn't leave my side. Loyalty was his watchword.'

Then he started crying and it was heart-rending to hear his sobs. Tor allowed his father's tears to flow unchecked for a minute or so and then, evidently deciding that enough was enough, called a halt to them. 'Come on, Monty, save all that for tomorrow. Recount the story of Tam and you at the Battle of the Crater, how the Argylls defeated the Arab insurrectionists and retrieved the bodies of their fallen comrades.'

'Och,' his father managed a laugh, 'no one wants to hear that old story.' The wistful edge to his voice begged Tor to contradict him.

'Well, I do for one and I'm guessing that Halley and Tam's old friends from the British Legion wouldn't balk at hearing it again. Now, shall I drive you home or do you want to go on alone?'

'Alone. Your mother and Suzie are spending the weekend with some friend or other, so it'll just be me and Lysander for dinner tonight. I don't suppose you'd consider staying over. No? That's fine. I'll see you in church at 10 am tomorrow. Don't be late.'

'When am I ever late?'

'Never. You and Tam are – were – sticklers for punctuality. I'm the one who's always kept everyone waiting. Tam said I'd be late for my own funeral.' Another large sniff, followed by further nose blowing.

'Aye, ye would that, Brigadier Strachan,' Tor mimicked Tam, making his father laugh. 'Come on, I'll walk you to the door and then return to light the candle and lock up.' He came closer, as if wanting to check that they were alone, glanced over the top of the pew and looked down on Halley sitting there, quiet as a wee mouse. He caught her gaze but said nothing. After walking his father to the door and closing it behind him he returned and opened the door of the pew.

'You heard.'

'I heard.'

'Thanks for staying silent.'

'It's important that Monty could have this last conversation with Tam.'

'You really didn't know that Tam was the love of my father's life?'

She shook her head. 'I've guessed as much from things which have been said since I arrived in Lochaber. But it wasn't my place to comment or interfere. I was little more than a child when I came up for the summer holidays. Such matters were outside my limited life experience and beyond my ken. All that mattered to me was that Tam loved me like a daughter and Monty was always kind.' She shut Lysander out of her mind. 'They found a lifelong love in one another, nothing else matters.'

'You aren't shocked?'

'Surprised, yes. Shocked no. We live in different times. Everyone deserves a chance at happiness, don't you think?'

'Yes.' Tor was most emphatic. 'And what about you?'

'What about me?' she asked, stepping out of the pew and closing the door behind her.

'Have you found lifelong love?'

'Hardly,' she retorted. 'There hasn't been time. Not that I'm looking for it, I have other things on my mind.

'Such as?'

'You really want to know? It's quite boring.'

'So, bore me.'

'I have aspirations to make it to the top of my field.'

'Go on.'

'Become Professor Dunbar and, who knows, get taken on by NASA.'

'Not quite the answer I was expecting,' he grinned, before becoming serious. 'And that's what matters to you?'

'It is. Does that make me sound selfish? Nothing less is expected of me by my family and, to be honest, I expect nothing less of myself.'

'Focused, yes. Selfish, no.' Moving away, he walked over to a tall church candle skewered on a wrought iron stand. Pulling an electronic candle lighter out of his pocket, he handed it to her and bent the candlestick towards her. 'I think you should do the honours.'

It took several seconds before she realised what he meant. 'Of course.' Standing on tiptoe she clicked the candle lighter and carefully lit the wick. Tor stood the candlestick upright, took the lighter from her and returned it to his pocket.

'We should go. I'll wait for you in the porch and leave you to take your farewell of your uncle.'

'Oh.' The sound escaped Halley as she hadn't expected such consideration from a man she'd knocked out only a few days previously. She turned back towards the saltire draped coffin and put her hand on Tam's glengarry, beset, not by sorrow and grief – although that would come, but by the knowledge that she'd played him false, letting him down by not being honest and open with him. Monty was right, Tam valued loyalty over everything. Had she explained, he would have understood and doubtless have punched Lysander on the nose, laird's son or no. That's who he was.

As for the baby she'd lost . . . she'd blocked that out of her mind, kept it her secret – as she had for the past twenty years.

'Bye, Tam. I love you; I've always loved you. Forgive me,' her voice was hardly more than a whisper. Night was closing in fast and the light of the solitary candle did little to dispel the gloom. Turning on her heel she straightened her shoulders.

This time when she left Lochaber it would be the last.

She walked towards Tor Strachan, waiting for her by the church door. Illogically, she wondered how it would feel to walk down the aisle of this tiny highland church, a harpist plucking out a tune as the congregation turned to look at her and her new husband, their faces soft and sentimental as they remembered their own wedding day. But she knew, as certain as the stars that wheeled above her that she'd never walk down the aisle with any man, get married in a drunken haze at the Little Pink Chapel in Vegas, or run away to Gretna Green.

Events had ruined that dream for her. And she should consider herself lucky that she'd been able to hold onto her secret and live the life of a successful academic with no one any the wiser. Except . . . she didn't feel lucky, she felt absolutely wretched, and unravelled. Reaching Tor's side she shook the thought from her head, forgot the trauma of her miscarriage, how she'd concealed it from her parents by telling them she was staying with a friend before joining them in New England, had sorted it all out on her own.

And had pretty much organised her life along those lines ever since: independent, self-determining, autonomous.

'So, what about you?'

'Me?' He gestured for her to precede him out of the church. 'I'll get married and raise a fine brood of sons and daughters to look after *Creagh na h-Iolaire* when I'm gone. As expected, but not yet.'

'That sounds depressingly unromantic. And why "not yet?"' she queried as the wind whipped long strands of hair across her face.

'The Strachans are known for their longevity. I wasn't born until my father was in his forties. So, there's no rush.'

Now, Halley understood the reason for Monty's late marriage. He'd married for practical reasons which, at the time, had appeared to suit both parties. The tape in her mind rewound to Monty's earlier remark about Tor being the only good thing to come from the marriage. So, where did that leave Lexie and Lysander? And what were Lady Strachan's peccadilloes? She sighed; it was nothing to do with her. She'd chosen not to reveal what had happened all those summers ago and could hardly expect the Strachans to release skeletons from their family cupboard and make them dance a highland fling at her command.

That made her smile. Inappropriate? She wasn't sure. She looked over her shoulder towards Tam's coffin and the candle one last time.

'Let's get you home.' Tor locked the church door behind them, laid his hand lightly on her back and guided her towards the Land Rover. Her mind in turmoil, Halley hardly said a word as they drove back to the bothy where she leapt down from the vehicle, turned her back on Tor and made it plain she was in no mood for company.

Chapter Fifteen

Next morning, Halley checked herself in the cracked mirror above the kitchen sink and sighed. Her mother had insisted she wear black to Tam's funeral. Or, as she put it, 'didn't let the side down by not showing proper respect for Tam and the occasion.'

Halley frowned, trying to remember the last time she'd let anyone down.

Sometimes her mother forgot that she wasn't sixteen any longer. If anyone let the side down today it wouldn't be her, she assured her mother, as though capable of projecting thoughts across thousands of miles of ocean.

She wondered if her parents knew the true extent of Tam and Monty's friendship. Or, had Tam and Monty hidden it so skilfully that even they didn't guess? Not that they would have been shocked, or surprised. Times had changed, moved on. Like her, they would have been glad to learn that Tam had loved and been loved.

To be honest, the secret she'd kept for the last twenty years would have shocked them more. She glanced back at her reflection, wondering if she should add more blusher to her cheeks. She looked pale, worried about how the day would unfold. Turning, she saw the beach through the small front window, crossed her fingers and prayed it didn't rain. Hawaii was sun, light and dazzling colours and any funerals she'd attended there concentrated on celebrating someone's life in song, dance and wild tales. Not shivering in a cold north-east wind as rain clouds scudded towards them, the mourners wondering when they could go indoors for the wake.

She was still in front of the mirror when an authoritative rat-a-tat-tat on the door announced Tor Strachan's arrival. Unlike previous visits, he didn't wait for permission to enter but walked straight in, bringing bright November sunshine with him but, mercifully, little evidence of yesterday's biting wind.

Really, she was becoming obsessed with the weather, like everyone else who lived here!

Tor jangled his car keys and gave her a critical once-over. 'Ready?'

'Will I pass muster?' she asked, suddenly anxious.

'You'll do,' was his wry observation. You look,' he swallowed hard, searching for the right words, knowing she was quick to take offence.

'Too funereal? Over the top? I don't know what's acceptable in this part of the world.'

'*This part of the world*? Doesn't Scottish blood beat thickly in your veins. Don't you feel as though part of you belongs here?'

Thinking of all that had happened since she'd left Lochaber and her less than enthusiastic welcome by certain members of the family, Halley shook her head. ''Fraid not.' Tor stopped in his tracks and frowned, clearly put out by her reply. Halley derived a certain perverse pleasure from being able to rile him. Like an insistent highland midge after blood. She smiled inwardly, amused by the metaphor. God knows there would be little enough to smile at today.

She waited for him to precede her into the porch and locked the door behind her.

'Why, you're wearing a kilt,' she observed, putting the key safely in her bag.

'What did you expect, a grass skirt? This is Lochaber not Honolulu. Brace yourself, Doctor Dunbar, I won't be the only one kilted-up today. Monty, Bryce, some of Tam's old comrades and other mourners will be wearing plaid, as a sign of respect.' Tor hoisted himself into the driver's seat of a battered Land Rover using the grab handle above the door to help him climb in. The pleats of his kilt swung to one side and Halley saw the long red gash running from thigh to knee on his left leg. Tor was quick to sit down and rearrange the kilt, as prim as a maiden aunt, so that the scar was hidden. Then he concentrated on slipping the car into gear and edging forward across the sands.

'I take it, that your kilt is in Strachan colours?' Halley said to cover the awkward moment.

'It is. A full eight yards of wool has gone into its making, not to mention a good tailor in Edinburgh. It's one of Monty's, the Strachans were recycling before it became fashionable.'

'Very commendable,' she replied, taking his lead and not mentioning the scar.

'I see you're wearing one of Tam's old scarves in Dunbar tartan. Perhaps, by the end of the day, you'll find that part of your DNA you seem keen to deny and will wear it with pride?'

'I –' Halley wanted to say that it wasn't her Scottishness she was at pains to deny, it was everything that had happened all those years ago. She was about to ask him to cut her some slack and to repeat the question at the end of her stay. However, she suspected that Hector Strachan wasn't the kind of man who granted quarter to anyone, least of all himself.

She sensed that in denying her roots she'd somehow disappointed and offended him. She wasn't sure why that mattered to her, but it did. Fastening her seat belt and settling her tote bag on her lap she pretended to look out of the window. Who was he to tell her what to think, how to behave? Didn't he realise that it was only by maintaining a wall of aloofness and detachment that she'd be able to get through the day.

Tor Strachan's sharp words on the day of her beloved uncle's funeral made her heart splinter into a thousand tiny, jagged pieces. Pieces which would never fit back together again. Tears pricked her eyes and her throat and chest became constricted as she surreptitiously dashed away the tears and slipped on her sunglasses.

The mourners were gathered in front of the church and Halley let out an involuntary *oh God,* when she saw them. There appeared closer to seventy than the fifty Rowan had mentioned yesterday. Most were male and, as Tor had predicted, were sporting kilts a little tight across the stomach or too long in the leg. The former soldiers not being as tall and straight as they had been when they'd served with Tam and Monty.

'Are you okay?' Tor inquired, pulling on the handbrake and slipping the car into gear to stop it rolling down the hill and into the loch. 'You haven't said a word for at least five minutes.' He made that seem like an unusual occurrence.

'F – fine.' But she wasn't fine. She'd thought herself capable of handling Tam's funeral without the support of her family. However, the years were slipping away with each passing minute, leaving the green girl who'd once viewed the world through rose-tinted spectacles lost and adrift.

Jumping down from the Land Rover as nimbly as his injured leg would allow, Tor came round and opened her door. Their earlier exchange seemingly forgotten, he helped her down, his dry smile intimating that he knew she didn't need – or want – any man's help.

Regretting her earlier snarky comments Halley accepted the chivalrous gesture but was glad when he released her hand, stood back and allowed her to gather her thoughts. Momentarily she found herself transfixed by the way the low winter sun picked out the red highlights in his blond hair, accentuating his blue eyes. He pulled on his beret, adjusting it so that the regimental badge caught the wintery sunlight and the trance was broken. Halley was appalled that such an inconsequential thought should pop into her head, today of all days. Then he removed his cromack from the back seat and, possibly to cover how much he relied on it, used it to prod the ground in front of them in experimental fashion.

'It's boggy underfoot, take care.'

'Tor, I –' Halley wasn't given the chance to explain or apologise for her early cutting remarks as Lexie rushed forward and wedged herself between them. Dressed in predictably eccentric fashion: short kilt over thick dark leggings, Doc Martens, a belted tweed jacket which looked like it'd been languishing in the Strachans' attic since her grandfather's time and a highland bonnet complete with eagle feather, she gave them both a hug.

'Halley, you poor darling. What a day.' Lexie led her away from Tor and across the graveyard to the church porch where Sir Monty in kilt, blazer, regimental tie and wearing his medals greeted her.

'Ready?' he asked.

As ready as she'd ever be, Halley nodded. Monty raised his hand and a piper sheltering in the porch stepped forward, blew air into his bagpipes and played the regimental funeral salute, "Lochaber no More". The rest of the mourners took that as their cue to line up on either side of the path. The minister and Rowan emerged from the church followed by four pall bearers carrying Tam's coffin on their shoulders. Monty and Halley took their place behind the coffin with Tor, Lexie and Bryce and the other mourners falling in step with the three/four beat of the lament.

Feeling as if she was in a waking dream, Halley took Monty's arm and followed the minister over to the freshly dug grave she'd observed yesterday. There, the pall bearers paused with the coffin on their shoulders while the other mourners caught up. Once everyone had taken their place around the grave the minister intoned the words of the Committal.

'In sure and certain hope of the resurrection to eternal life through our Lord Jesus Christ, we commend to the Almighty God our brother Thomas and we commit his body to the ground; earth to earth, ashes to ashes, dust to dust. The Lord bless him and keep him, the Lord make his face to shine upon him and be gracious to him, the Lord lift up his countenance upon him and give him inner peace. Amen.'

Inner peace

The words stayed with Halley after the final amen faded and Tam had been lowered into the ground. Significant moments in her and Tam's lives played through her head as the pall bearers released the ribbons supporting the coffin's weight and let them fall into the grave. Times only they had shared: Tam meeting her at Inverness airport and driving her over to Lochaber the first time she'd come to stay, trips to Skye to see the fairy pools and discover where Gavin Maxwell had written *Ring of Bright Water*, stargazing on the beach, collecting flotsam and jetsam, firewood for the stove, shopping trips to Mallaig, the long drive to John O'Groats to have her photograph taken beneath the signpost pointing to the faraway places she longed to visit.

She was still lost in memories, scarcely believing that this day had finally arrived when Rowan walked over carrying six long stemmed white roses. She gave one to each of Tam's surrogate family, keeping one back for herself and indicated that Halley should drop hers on top of Tam's coffin. This she did after kissing it and whispering: *Goodbye, Uncle Tam, I'm sorry for letting you down. For everything. I've been a bloody fool.*

The mourners stood respectfully as the other roses followed Halley's into the grave. She was so deep in thought that she didn't register Tor's hand resting lightly on her lower back, as though he understood her conflicting emotions and knew instinctively that she needed support and succour at that moment.

'Look.' He pointed skywards to where a golden eagle was circling above them, its wing tips spread open like fingers, yellow talons tucked neatly into its body. It turned its head and looked down on them, as if demanding to know what they were doing on its land. Its high chirruping cry cut through the bright, still air, drawing everyone's gaze away from the coffin and heavenward.

'It's a sign that Tam is ready to leave us and that all will be well,' Tor murmured, bending his head close so only Halley could hear. 'My ancestors built *Creag na h-Iolaire* on this very spot because a golden eagle circled them when they defeated their enemies the MacDonalds in battle and they took it as a sign.' She looked up at him with a puzzled smile. She wouldn't have put him down as someone who believed in signs, omens and portents. However, highland DNA evidently ran through his blood, which was hardly surprising considering that the Strachans had lived here for almost a thousand years. She'd only ever been an interloper, a summer visitor like the ospreys, no matter what he said about blood line or DNA.

This wasn't some trumped-up modern version of *Brigadoon*. This –

the land and its people were real and meant something to Tor. Now she understood why he'd been so displeased at her denying her highland blood and pretending that none of it mattered in this day and age. That was unforgivably crass of her.

There was little time for further thought as Monty nodded to the piper who struck up a jaunty tune while the pall bearers folded the saltire and handed it and Tam's glengarry to Rowan. Lexie slipped her arm through her father's and they moved away from the grave and onto the path leading to the entrance of the graveyard. Tor, his hand still resting lightly on Halley's lower back, indicated that they should follow. Still dazed with the emotion of the moment and memories which wouldn't let her be, Halley allowed him to guide her back to the Land Rover.

'Where are we going?' she asked when it became apparent that the funeral party wasn't heading for the salmon bothy.

'There's been a change of plan.' Sending her a slightly anxious look, Tor explained. 'Monty spent most of last night crying and drinking whisky. Then, according to Lysander, around about midnight he put down his glass, stood up, wiped his eyes and rang Rowan changing the venue of the wake to the castle's kitchen. Rowan's catering team, aided and abetted by our staff, has been working flat out since first light to get everything ready.'

'Knowing Rowan, I guess she took it all in her stride?'

'Exactly. And, to be fair, it makes better sense to hold it there now we've seen the number of mourners who've turned up. Added to which, some of the old soldiers might find the walk down to the salmon bothy rather challenging. We didn't want to bother you with the details, figuring you've got enough to think about today so we went ahead without your permission.'

'Oh.' Halley could think of nothing to say. It made perfect sense, of course, and also explained why no caterers had showed up at the salmon bothy as Rowan had promised. She'd been too concerned thinking about Uncle Tam that it hadn't occurred to her to ask pertinent questions. So unlike her. Stopping on the path, she turned and smiled at Tor.

'Won't there be all hell to pay when your mother learns of Monty's decision?'

'Most likely,' he frowned. 'But Monty is adept at handling Mother's strops. I don't want to sound disloyal but sometimes Mother needs reminding who is laird round here.'

Halley adopted an unconvinced expression. 'If you say so. To be honest, it's probably what Tam would have wanted but wouldn't have expected. If it makes Monty happy, I'm happy, too. Mind you, I should probably ring my parents and run it past them to see if they're in agreement. If not, we'll have to carry all the food and drink down to the bothy.'

'You're joking me,' Tor exclaimed, openly horrified at the idea.

Light-hearted and feeling a sense of release which was probably totally inappropriate, Halley blew her nose one last time and grinned. 'Of course I am, your face. Anything Monty, you or Rowan think fitting is okay by me.'

Tor looked relieved as he opened the car door and Halley climbed in. Then he turned and addressed Rowan who was still on the path. 'Rowan, do you want to come with us?'

'Yes, if that's okay. I should like to get there ahead of the mourners to check that everything's ready.' Once Rowan was seated, Tor tipped the piper the nod and he struck up with *The Campbells Are Coming* and everyone headed for the castle in time to the rousing marching tune.

Tor positioned himself by the *Creag na h-Iolaire's* kitchen door ready to welcome mourners. Most of them he knew from his involvement with the local branch of the Royal British Legion. When the mourners drew level with him, they saluted or, if they hadn't served in the military, shook his hand. When he glanced over at Halley who was stationed at Monty's side, he was relieved to see that his father had temporarily cast off his air of bereavement and was, for today at least, Brigadier Sir Montgomery Strachan.

When the old soldiers drew level with Monty, they pulled themselves up to their full height and saluted, full of pride. Monty responded with a salute of his own. Halley, from what Tor could make out, seemed moved to hear Tam referred to as a 'guid man' and a 'grand sodjer' as the mourners shook hands or patted her on the shoulder.

Now Tor regretted the tone he'd used earlier, berating her for refusing to acknowledge her Scottish roots. What right had he to do that? He might have commanded a battalion of men, earned glory in the bomb disposal team and was heir to a vast estate but that's where it ended. Halley hadn't been in Lochaber for years and could hardly be expected to feel the same degree of attachment that he, Monty and Tam felt for the people and the place.

'How Tam would have loved this.' Rowan was at Tor's side keeping an eye on staff handing out drinks and making sure everyone was looked after. At first, the old soldiers and Tam's other friends from Morar and Mallaig stood around talking in awed whispers. It wasn't every day they were invited up the Big Hoose to sup with the laird, albeit in his kitchen. Tor smiled at Rowan and then turned his attention to Lexie and Bryce who were making sure no one felt overawed or out of their depth, pointing them towards the buffet.

It might be inappropriate, but Tor felt that he was attending a farewell party rather than a wake. And in a way he was bidding a last goodbye to an old friend and fellow soldier.

'Yes, Tam would have loved this. The sad irony is that your wake is probably the best party you'll never attend.' Rowan sent him a sympathetic look and then walked away, conscious she had duties to perform. Tor glanced over at Halley looking so very formal and proper in her black trouser and jacket combo. In many ways he was glad that she didn't know the history behind the injury which had ended his military career. People meant well but he detected an air of compassion and sympathy when they looked at him. It wasn't like that with Halley Dunbar, she'd made plain her dislike of him right from the start.

Better that than pity.

He thought of the six men in his unit who'd been brought home from Afghanistan in the belly of a military aircraft in Union Jack draped coffins. No more celebrations of any kind for them. He ran that awful day through his head, thinking what he would do differently if he had it to do over. He should have followed his gut instinct which told him something wasn't right, been less accepting of the intel provided by their local interpreter, curbed the enthusiasm of an inexperienced second lieutenant who'd rushed in without waiting for their 'Vallon Man' to sweep the ground ahead.

The jagged scar down the inside of his thigh gave a sympathetic pulse as he relived the moment the IED had exploded in their faces. If he'd been alone, he would have rubbed the wound, maybe warmed a hot pad in the microwave and laid it on the scar, alternating it with a cold compress. As it was, he was lucky to be alive and had to live with the pain and the guilty knowledge of a job badly done. One which had resulted in men's deaths and a long spell in a field hospital until he was well enough to travel home to the UK for a series of life-altering operations.

'You okay, Tor?' Rowan asked.

'Yes. Yes, of course,' he shook himself free of the haunting memory of sand, blood, limbs and screams of pain. As always, he fixed a smile on his face, straightened his shoulders and tried to lighten up. Today wasn't about him. 'Just wondering where Lysander is. Monty won't think much to his not being here. I know that Tam had little time for him, but even so, Lysander is a member of the family and . . . talk of the devil.' The door leading from the small flight of stairs down from the inner hall opened and Lysander stepped in with Frank Bunce, *Creag na h-Iolaire's* factor. 'Birds of a feather.' Tor muttered, focusing on greeting the last of the mourners entering the kitchen.

'I'll check everything's okay and then ask Monty when he wants to say a few words,' Rowan said, leaving his side.

'Of course, thank you,' he answered absent-mindedly, frowning as Lysander homed in on Halley with the accuracy of a heat-seeking missile. Taking her by the elbow Lysander drew her away from Monty and whispered something in her ear. Clearly displeased, she shook him off, turned her back and moved over to talk to Rowan. A lesser man would have got the message – however Lysander, thick-skinned and full of himself as per usual, followed Halley round the kitchen. Rowan, evidently sensing the vibe, gave Halley a task which, judging by her expression, she was only too happy to carry out. She moved as far away from Lysander as she could. Lysander, catching Tor's inimical stare, sidled over to Frank Bunce and engaged him in conversation.

Just as he was about to relax, Tor caught sight of Geordie Souter sloping into the kitchen unannounced and helping himself to a plateful of food from the buffet and a generous peg of Monty's best malt. Catching Tor's eye, he raised his glass in sarcastic salute. Tor didn't know where best to direct his attention: Souter whom he openly distrusted, Lysander who would probably approach Halley and carry on with the conversation interrupted in the salmon bothy a couple of days ago; or Monty, who was holding up for the moment but who would need his support when he delivered Tam's eulogy.

Emitting a deep sigh he walked over to his father, took him to one side. 'Everything okay, Monty?' he asked.

'As good as it can be in the circumstances. Cast your eye over Tam's eulogy, would you?' He pulled a sheet of A4 paper, folded over so many times that it resembled a crumpled piece of origami, out of his sporran and handed it to Tor. Tor frowned but bit back the tut of irritation before it left him. For the past week he'd been asking Monty to let him cast an eye over the eulogy. Not because he didn't trust him to say the right thing, as a former brigadier he knew how to conduct himself and to address a gathering with dignity and authority, but because he wanted to be free to keep his eye on things. It would only take a few seconds for Lysander, Souter and – yes, even Frank Bunce to turn a solemn occasion into a farce. Judging by the empty bottles of whisky Rowan's staff were putting in the recycling bin, drink was flowing freely and that, too, could present a problem.

Then there was Halley . . .

There being nothing else for it, Tor parked himself on the corner of the large zinc topped table and read the eulogy, his father looking on anxiously but with a mulish expression, his eyebrows drawn together as though he expected Tor to insist on some last-minute changes. When Tor glanced up, Halley was nowhere to be seen and Lysander was missing, too.

Chapter Sixteen

Halley was pleased Rowan asked her to go to the store room on the other side of the kitchen to fetch a couple of bottles of champagne. So typical of Rowan to provide her with a brief escape, a chance to gather herself before delivering Tam's eulogy. Halley felt sick with nerves, which was a first. She was used to addressing colleagues and fellow scientists at conferences, but this was different. Emotions were involved: remorse, guilt, bereavement and she wasn't sure she could keep it together once she started talking about her great-uncle.

The store room lay at the far end of a long, dark passageway, the entrance guarded by a yett gate – a hinged portcullis designed to provide a barrier should invaders find their way into the castle. The corridor was lit by bare electric bulbs strung along a thick cable and had the air of a place where dreadful deeds had been carried out by order of the Strachans. Halley shivered at the thought of what those deeds might be as she pushed open the heavy door and entered the cellar.

Drawing her phone from her bag she switched on the torch to illuminate the darkness. The beam did little to push back the blackness, merely highlighting walls carved out of grey stone some twelve feet thick and glistening with damp. It picked out the original castle well, built to withstand a siege and the space above it where food could be raised or lowered from the hall upstairs; dark corners where anything could be hiding.

'Get a grip, Dunbar. This might once have been a dungeon but now it houses nothing more dangerous than the laird's wine collection and some rather large mouse traps.' Her voice bounced off the walls and she glanced at the floor. 'Make that rat traps.'

Finding the light switch, she returned her phone to her pocket, picked up two bottles of champagne and headed for the door, anxious to return to the warmth and light of the kitchen. When she opened the door Lysander Strachan was standing there, blocking her exit.

'What do you want?' She made no secret of her annoyance at his unscheduled appearance.

'To pick up where we left off the other morning.'

Really. Did the man have no sense of timing? 'I don't think so, Tor will . . .'

He affected an air of insouciance but glanced down the corridor, anxiously. 'Relax. Major Strachan,' he sneered, 'has wrested control of the wake from Rowan Ferguson. She's had a soft spot for him for years and would throw herself off the battlements, should he ask her.'

'A bit unlikely I would have thought,' Halley replied.

'I don't get it. You ladies,' he said, disparagingly, 'love Tor. But then I guess, being heir to Monty's land and Mother's money does make him a rather irresistible package.'

'It has nothing to do with either of those things,' she said.

'Ah, is it the whole 'wounded hero' thing?'

'What do you want, Lysander?' she asked, sighing heavily.

'A chance to catch up and discover what you've been doing with yourself all these years.'

'I – I really don't think –' Halley tried to sidestep him.

'Relax. We won't be missed and we won't be disturbed.'

His words sent a shiver down Halley's spine which had nothing to do with dungeons or rat traps. She *wanted* to be disturbed; she *wanted* Tor to come along and hoik Lysander out of the cellar by the collar of his Paul Smith shirt. She wasn't in the mood for a self-pitying tête-à-tête and if Lysander wasn't so self-obsessed, he would have realised that. Plainly in no hurry to leave, he stepped over the threshold, closing the door behind him. With an ease which suggested he was no stranger to raiding the laird's wine cellar he switched on extra lights.

'There. All the better to see you with. And, can I say that you're more beautiful than I remember?'

'No, you cannot,' was Halley's crushing reply. Grasping the bottles of champagne like a pair of Indian clubs she made it plain that she felt like braining rather than embracing him. 'We have nothing to say to each other.'

'I disagree. Put the bottles down and listen to me.' He grabbed her arm as she attempted to push past and sent her a pleading look. 'Please, Hal?' For a moment he was the Lysander she remembered, the man she'd fallen in love with: tender, thoughtful, considerate. But it was all a veneer, a mask concealing his true character: inconsiderate, thoughtless, self-centred.

'Listen to you? I don't think so.' She dragged her arm free, almost dropping the bottles in her haste to escape. 'Say what you have to say and then get out of my way or, God help me, I'll . . .' She raised the bottles to waist height, demonstrating that she wouldn't think twice about using them to protect herself. Lysander appeared to find her fighting spirit amusing. Giving an exaggerated sigh he perched on the large sherry cask to the left of the door and sent her a reproachful look.

'Quite the firebrand, aren't you? Relax, I mean you no harm. I simply want to set the record straight, put right the past.'

It was on the tip of Halley's tongue to say that the harm done all those years ago could not be put right with a few beguiling words. However, sensing that she wouldn't be allowed to leave the cellar until he'd said his piece, she put down the champagne, took two steps back and swept the space in an expansive gesture.

'You have the floor. Say what you have to say and then get out of my way. In case you'd forgotten, this is my great-uncle's wake and I have things to attend to.' Her scathing look made it plain that chewing over the fat with him wasn't one of them. 'Monty, Tor and Rowan will be looking for me,' she added.

He gave a harrumph of annoyance. 'As if I care about any of them.' Then, holding up his hands in a mock gesture of self-defence he fielded her inimical look. 'Okay, cards on the table. Tell me, is your refusal to see or speak to me, anything to do with what happened between us?'

'And what, in your considered opinion, happened between us?'

'A summer romance which *you* brought to an abrupt end. One

day you were there and then – pouf – you vanished without so much as a *haste ye back tae Bonnie Scotland*. When you didn't turn up at our usual meeting place I took my life in my hands, went down to the salmon bothy and asked Tam where you were. I'd always suspected that Tam kept a sgian dubh tucked down the side of his sock, a hangover from his time in the army, and was waiting for an excuse to tickle my ribs with it.'

'Now you're being ridiculous.'

Although she regarded him boot-faced, Halley smiled inwardly. Tam thought Lysander a complete waste of space and, although he had been sad to see Halley cut her holiday short, he'd been more than happy to take her to Inverness airport and away from Lysander's malign influence.

Lysander shifted position on the sherry barrel, making himself more comfortable. 'Either he was unaware of your reason for cutting your holiday short or wasn't prepared to share it with me.'

Halley remembered it all only too well, her sobbing on her bed, refusing to be consoled as she'd stammered out to her great-uncle how she'd been taken in by Lysander, what a fool she'd been to trust him. Naturally, she hadn't told Tam *everything*, that would have been too shaming, but he'd caught the gist of it and understood why she wanted to return to her parents in Massachusetts and put the whole sorry episode behind her.

Time for her to lay a false trail and put Lysander off the scent. 'You know why I cut my holiday short, don't you?'

'I imagine because you'd listened to whispers, got the wrong end of the stick about my girlfriend? Thought it more serious than it was, and –'

Halley cut across him, annoyed that he was presenting a sanitised version of the past by demoting his then-fiancée to 'girlfriend'. 'Don't flatter yourself, it was nothing to do with that. To be blunt, I was bored with Lochaber, the midges and you; not necessarily in that order.' Lysander looked unconvinced, as though the idea of any female not finding him irresistible was preposterous.

'Really?'

'Really.'

'Nothing to do with you finding out that I would be getting married once my girlfriend –'

'Fiancée –'

'–whatever, returned from Operation Raleigh and I finished officer training at Sandhurst?'

'Not in the least,' she lied, straight-faced. 'As you said the other day, it was a bit of a fling. Once I started my freshman year, I was too busy to think about you. So, if you don't mind, I'll be getting back.' Lysander watched intently as Halley bent down and picked up the champagne bottles.

'You know, no one has ever held a candle to you, Hal.'

Halley gave an exasperated sigh, keen to draw this conversation to a close. She dared not put the bottles back on the floor knowing he'd take it as a sign she was falling for his lies a second time.

'Is that so?'

'Yes. You ruined me for other women, Hal. No, don't look at me like that, it's the truth. Seeing you now, after all these years reminds me what I passed up on, what I've missed.' Now it was Halley's turn to give a harrumph, but of disbelief.

'To put the record straight, Lysander, you didn't 'pass up' on me. I was never yours. Now stand back, otherwise when I swing the door open, I might accidently break your aristocratic nose.'

He placed his hand against the door so she couldn't open it. 'To put the record straight, as you phrase it, Mother put her foot down and insisted that I marry Suzie or she'd cut me off. Without-a-penny. And, believe me, she would've too, she can be a very hard woman.' Fleetingly, he looked as though he lived in fear of the formidable Lady Strachan. 'I lead a truly miserable and pointless existence.'

Halley burst out laughing. 'I must say that you look well on it.' One swift, critical look took in his beautifully cut hair, unseasonable tan and smart clothes. 'I'm guessing that you don't work for a living. Have your own apartments in the castle. Spend most of your time huntin', shootin' and fishin', that's when you're not abroad catching a few rays?' She raised a questioning eyebrow.

'Some of that might be true,' he admitted. 'Until Tor was invalided out of the army, I at least had a role, accompanying father on the few official visits he carries out as Brigadier Strachan. But that's about it. Now my raison d'etre is to provide the next Strachan heir as Tor shows no inclination to find a woman and settle down and do what's expected of him.' Now on a roll Lysander's feelings of resentment and bitterness came pouring out. 'We – that is, Suzie and I, have been trying for almost five years to start a family. At first, we thought it was just bad luck but after a while Mother insisted that we embark on fertility treatment; paid for by her, natch. But still zilch; nada.'

'Lysander, I –'

An involuntary shudder of disgust ran through Halley. Only Lysander could apply such unfeeling adjectives to his and Suzie's childless state. She knew he was capable of fathering a child, of course she did. However, she'd kept her miscarriage secret and wasn't about to blurt it out now. In a week's time she'd back in the observatory and this conversation would seem like a bad dream.

Wrapped-up in himself, Lysander didn't register Halley's half-finished sentence or reactive shudder. 'I think we must be cursed. Barren. Not,' he added, almost to himself, 'that the rest of my family is in any position to judge me.' He raised his head and gave a bitter laugh. 'Father's relationship with your late uncle is common knowledge, Mother has allowed herself more than a few compensations for a loveless marriage. Lexi is a total flake; an upper-class dippy hippy selling dead animal heads at the roadside with that ginger geek Bryce. And, as for the Galloping Major . . . how can I compete? Everyone loves Tor, don't they?'

It was as if he wanted her to deny the fact.

'Maybe you don't have to compete.' In that moment, Halley found it in her heart to feel sorry for him. Perhaps this was the closure she'd been searching for all these years and Lysander Strachan was the one to grant it?

'What do you mean?' In the blink of an eye his dejected look vanished, he sat upright and sent her an engaging, lop-sided grin.

'I simply meant that you should be yourself and –'

'You always had a kind heart, Hal, that much I do remember. Maybe,' he paused, biting his lower lip, choosing his next words with care. 'Maybe you'd have dinner with me before you leave and we could discuss this further? While Suzie's staying at her mother's, perhaps?' Halley had no chance to show how incensed she was by his suggestion as the door was flung back on its hinges and Tor entered the cellar.

'Ah, there you are. I was worried you might have become lost in *Creag na h-Iolaire's* labyrinthine corridors.'

Remembering Tor's reaction the last time he'd found them together, Halley brushed away his concern with a feeble joke. 'No, I'm fine and the minotaur appears to have been given the day off.' She stopped Tor from walking further into the cellar by handing him the champagne bottles. Fortunately, Lysander and the sherry barrel he was perched on, were behind the door and out of sight.

'I'll switch off the lights and follow you if you take these to the kitchen,' she suggested. His hands full of champagne, Tor had little choice but to agree. Reaching to the right of the door, Halley found the switch and plunged the cellar into darkness. Closing the door behind her, she followed Tor's kilted figure along the vaulted passageway.

Her hands were shaking when she reached the kitchen, hoping that everyone would put her flushed face and strained expression down to performance nerves and the realisation that her darling great-uncle had left her. Rowan and Lexie came to join her as she searched in her handbag for the eulogy she'd written.

'Monty's up first,' Lexie whispered, passing Halley tissues in anticipation of more tears, then led her over to the large kitchen sink to wait her turn.

Chapter Seventeen

There was no need to call the gathering to order. As soon as Monty walked over to the Aga, leaned back against it to warm his buttocks and straightened his notes, the room fell silent. Tor and Lexie offered chairs to some of the older ex-servicemen but most regarded it as a point of honour to remain standing throughout Tam's eulogy.

Monty opened with: 'This isn't a history lesson. It's a chance to give Tam the send-off he deserves and for us to remember a dangerous, exciting time when we served with the Argyll and Sutherland Highlanders under Lieutenant Colonel Colin Mitchel.' Those in close proximity to the kitchen table brought their whisky glasses down on its surface and echoed Monty's sentiments with: *Aye. Aye.*

Lexie whispered in Halley's ear, 'I know this is a sad occasion but Monty's loving it.' She squeezed her hand and then sniffed loudly into a tissue. 'It's his chance to say farewell to the love of his life and to remember a time when he was happiest.' Judging by the conversation overheard before dinner the other night, Halley judged that Monty's days of wine and roses were over. Lady Strachan plainly had other plans for his declining years.

'The Arab Police Mutiny and the Argyll's part in it is well documented. Many of you here today fought alongside Tam and I, and I'm proud to remember that service. For the youngsters present, I'll simply say that our job was to enter the Crater district of Aden and retrieve our comrades who'd been ambushed by the insurgents, murdered and their bodies mutilated – sorry, ladies.'

He nodded towards Halley and other women attending the wake. Tam had recounted this story so many times that Halley didn't feel the need to reach for the smelling salts. Apart from which, she loved to hear his and Monty's tales of bravery in the face of the enemy. She raised her hand to signify that she wouldn't drop in a dead faint hearing them again. Was it her imagination or did she detect a nod of approval from Tor Strachan in her direction?

'I was a newly fledged second-lieutenant, wet behind the ears and green as grass. Tam was appointed as my batman to keep me safe and turn me into a soldier. I'll be the first admit that he had quite a job ahead of him. However, he was a tough son-of-gun and always *had my back*, as I believe the current expression has it.'

'Monty's down with the kids,' Lexie laughed but was shushed by several of the old soldiers, anxious to hear every word of Monty's eulogy. She mouthed: *sorry*, at them.

'We landed at Strah Island in an RN helicopter and joined the main part of the Battalion at the South Gate.' Monty went on. 'Leading the battalion was Pipe Major Kenneth Robson playing *Monymusk*, the Regimental charge, ably supported by Tam who, like his counterpart, carried on playing even when under machine-gun fire.'

He paused to take a nip of whisky and Halley could just picture her great-uncle playing his pipes in defiance of the Arab insurrectionists. Not only was he a tough son-of-a-gun as Monty had said, he was also stubborn and determined and she hoped some of that bloody-mindedness had passed down to her.

'Funny how the bagpipes have the power to strike fear into the heart of the enemy, and to rouse the troops,' Bryce reflected, letting out a long breath. 'I don't know if I'd have the courage to fight in a skirmish, let alone a war.'

'Let's hope that you're never put to the test,' Lexie said, moving away from Halley and snuggling up to him. This time they were shushed by Tor as Monty took up the story.

'Tam's greatest worry was having a bullet rip through his bagpipes and him not be able to play and bolster the men's courage.' They all laughed, knowing Tam only too well. 'My only regret, as the fighting continued, was watching Brigade Major Downward drive up the Queen Arbour Road in his Land Rover with his batman riding shotgun. God, how I wanted that for Tam and I.' At that point, emotion got the better of him.

Overcome, he turned away and blew his nose on a paisley-patterned handkerchief. Tor walked over and continued the eulogy, giving his father breathing space.

'If it wasn't for Tam's quick thinking, I wouldn't be here. He more than had my father's back, he saved his life in the opening days of The Troubles when the regiment was sent to Armagh. Ever alert, he prevented Monty from catching his foot on a trip wire and triggering an explosion which would have blown them, and the reconnaissance party, to kingdom come.'

Something in his speech, niggled away at the back of Halley's mind but she had more important things to worry about, concentrating instead on how she could follow Monty's eulogy without boring everyone rigid. If she'd learned anything from the lecture circuit it was to keep your presentation short, to the point and to leave your audience wanting more. However, her talks involved facts and figures and speculation about there being exoplanets at the far edge of the universe.

This was different. This was real.

She had no stories of derring-do, all she had were tales of childhood holidays in Lochaber, her family's regret that they couldn't visit Tam as often as they would have liked and that she hadn't taken her leave of him properly. Not that she'd mention the last part, that was for her to mull over on the journey back home.

Tor, evidently sensing that Monty had nothing more to say without becoming emotional, led him away from the Aga to sit on a large Windsor chair at the head of the table. Taking a deep breath, Halley readied herself to deliver her tribute. Tor raised his glass, toasted Tam, and everyone followed suit. Then he turned, smiled at Halley and led her forward with the same gentle guidance as he had at the graveside.

'Now it's the turn of Tam's great-niece, Halley, to say a few words on her family's behalf in celebration of her uncle's life.'

'Thank you, Tor.' Halley walked over to the Aga and leaned against its comforting bulk as Monty had done. All eyes were on her and she flushed under their appraisal, not from nerves but from an eagerness to do her uncle's memory justice. 'Sir Monty mentioned Northern Ireland and Tam's time there. That seems like a good place to start as the Dunbars originally hailed from Ulster.'

Tor considered that he knew most stories chronicling Monty and Tam's life. He didn't focus on the content of Halley's eulogy, rather on how she delivered it. The husky timbre of her voice, the way she glanced at her notes from time to time as she spoke confidently but movingly about her uncle. Her soft smile of remembrance which drew the mourners' gaze to her flushed face. His breathing slowed and he became absorbed by how her grey eyes misted over as she mentioned Tam's name or shared some personal recollection. The way her breasts rose and fell beneath her silk camisole and the delicate flush spreading across her collar bones and décolletage.

Tam's contemporaries seemed similarly transfixed as she delivered her eulogy and made plain her love for her great-uncle.

Or, was it more than that? Perhaps they, like him, were waiting for her to explain her absence from Lochaber. It soon became clear however, when Halley folded up her notes and smiled to signify she had finished speaking, that was one story they wouldn't be hearing today. She glanced over at Tor almost as if seeking his approval, so he pulled himself together, raised his glass and evoked Tam's name a second time and the guests followed suit.

'You are all welcome to stay until the last sausage roll has been eaten and the Brigadier's cellar's drained dry.' They laughed and raised their glass in Monty's direction, mutely acknowledging the connection between him and Tam. 'In a couple of hours, the piper will play *Monymusk* in Tam and the Argylls' honour and transport will be available for those who require it. Enjoy yourselves my friends and, please, stay as long as you wish.'

There was a round of applause and loud 'thank youse' as the mourners turned the wake into a party, just as Tam would have liked. Tor wanted to have a word with Halley but she was surrounded by Tam's old pals, so he stood back. Time for that, later. He was just congratulating Rowan on how well she'd organised everything when the kitchen door opened and Lysander sauntered in. Tor frowned, displeased that his brother had missed the burial service and the eulogy and, adding insult to injury, was wearing neither kilt nor black tie as tradition demanded. Although, why should he be surprised? Lysander only had time for himself or his circle of friends who, like him, were younger sons who didn't know quite what to do with their lives.

Lysander leaned against the kitchen door to Halley's right. Frowning, she glanced between them, as though sensing Tor's displeasure and then turned her attention to the other mourners.

Tor wondered what wasn't quite right with the picture, then the penny dropped. Of course, Lysander hadn't been in the corridor when he'd gone to fetch Halley and, as far as he was aware, hadn't been in the kitchen when Monty had started his eulogy. Which could only mean one thing. He must have been in the cellar, hiding behind the door until Halley left and the coast was clear.

Typical Lysander. He knew his feelings about him renewing his friendship with Halley. His wife visiting her parents for the weekend, presented him with the ideal opportunity to play away from home. He frowned, hoping that Halley had more sense than to get involved with his brother. Lysander accepted a glass of whisky from one of Rowan's staff and walked over to stand beside Frank Bunce, the estate factor, and Souter the ex-soldier. Souter, seeing that Tor was keeping an eye on them, raised his glass in ironic salute and then turned back to talk to Bunce. Tor controlled his anger but promised himself that, once Monty's mourning period was over, Souter would be told that his presence on the estate was no longer required.

'You a'right, hen?' Rowan asked in a faux Glaswegian accent.

'I'm a'right, thanks doll,' Halley responded, smiling as she remembered how Rowan had taught her to speak with a Scottish accent when they were children.

'You got the tone of the eulogy spot on.' Rowan signalled a member of staff to bring them over a cup of tea with a finger of shortbread in the saucer.

'I am used to *peeblic spooking*,' Halley joked, glowing under Rowan's approval.

'I could see that Tor was impressed, and he's a hard one to please.'

'I'd say that he is equally impressed by the way you've handled Tam's funeral and wake, especially with Monty's last-minute change of venue.' Now it was Rowan's turn to blush as she sipped her tea and cast a covert glance in Tor's direction. 'I wonder what Lady Strachan's reaction will be when she returns home and finds out?'

'You won't have to wonder; you'll probably hear their raised voices down in the bothy. Their 'domestics' are legendary and they don't care who witnesses them. Poor Tor, small wonder he's in no rush to get married if that's the example his parents have set. I think he finds their behaviour quite embarrassing. Who wouldn't?'

'Is that why he's chosen to live in his converted Airstream and Lexie elsewhere on the estate?'

'You've got it in one.'

'As for Lysander . . .'

'Typical Lysander,' Rowan said, scornfully. 'Always taking the easy way out.'

They glanced over at Lysander and Lexie who were standing on either side of Frank Bunce. Although she'd never been formally introduced to him, there was something about Bunce which struck Halley as familiar. She wrinkled her forehead, trying to figure out what it was. Following Halley's gaze, Rowan was only too happy to supply the answer.

'Frank Bunce, Lochaber's answer to Sean Connery. He does rather work the image, don't you think?' Rowan laughed. 'Another glass of Dom Perignon, Pushy?' she said, mimicking 007's habit of replacing 's' with 'sh'. 'They say that his hair plugs have been paid for by a certain lady.' Halley's sip of tea went down the wrong way, making her cough and splutter. Rowan rubbed her back and patted her shoulder. 'Glad I've made you laugh, Hal, on a day like today.'

'You always could make me laugh,' Halley replied, giving her a fond hug. 'And Tam would have approved, he had a wicked sense of humour.'

'And didn't like Bunce. Not many folks do. He does rather regard himself as the unofficial laird of Glen Annanacross.' Then, evidently deciding that she'd said too much, Rowan drank the last of her tea and handed the cup to a member of staff. 'Okay, tea break over, I'd better go and supervise the guests. One or two are getting a wee bit too tipsy on the laird's *swally*.' Still smiling, she walked over to the table where the buffet was laid out and instructed her staff to start tidying up – subtly, mind – otherwise the wake would carry on until morning.

Halley, although grateful to Rowan for providing much needed distraction, was pleased to snatch a few moments on her own. Something Tor had said during the eulogy about Tam saving Monty's life in Northern Ireland stuck in Halley's mind. *'If it wasn't for Tam's quick thinking, I wouldn't be here,'* Surely, he should've said: 'If it wasn't for Tam, we wouldn't be here?'

Tor, Bunce, Lexie and Lysander sauntered over to Monty's side. Tor, a head taller than the others and fair like the Vikings who'd once marauded these shores, put his arm round his father's shoulders and kissed his cheek. Standing side by side their likeness was obvious. Even in his early eighties, Monty had the blond good looks evident in the photos of him in uniform scattered around the salmon bothy. Tor's siblings on the other hand resembled Lady Strachan with thick dark hair, pale skin and eyes as brown as chocolate drops beneath straight, dark brows.

Lady Strachan and . . . to be blunt, Frank Bunce.

Halley looked at them as a dawning realisation struck her. Each of the Strachans was handsome in their own way but the tableau they presented was like the pieces of a mismatched puzzle. She remembered the furious argument she'd overheard the night she'd joined the Strachans for dinner. Then, Sir Monty had said to Lady Strachan: *Let's not forget your peccadilloes and the reminders for all to see.* And Lysander's bitter aside in the cellar just now: *Mother has allowed herself more than a few compensations for a loveless marriage.*

Tor glanced over and she caught his look and then turned away, embarrassed. He must have realised that she was regarding the Strachans intently, putting two and two together and making five. Deciding that it really wasn't her business who'd fathered who and that none of it mattered because she'd soon be heading back to her research, blue skies and warm breezes. Rolling up her sleeves she set about helping Rowan collect empty plates and glasses, which was much safer than trying to sort out family dynamics.

The piper played *Monymusk* as the last of the guests were helped into Land Rovers and driven home by estate staff. The same member of staff would deliver their cars to their homes tomorrow, Tor having declared that he and Monty didn't want any accidents to mar today's event. However, getting the old soldiers into the Land Rovers was easier said than done. Some of them decided to dance an impromptu highland fling to the regimental marching tune, accompanied by wild whoops and *hooch-yas*. It took all of Tor's powers of persuasion to get them to leave the castle grounds.

'Aye, yer a bonnie lassie and a scientific doctor, too? Tam would be proud of you,' the last guest declared, draping himself around Halley's neck and having to be physically removed. 'Awful bonnie,' he repeated, patting her cheek as the piper finished his tune, tucked his pipes under his arm and headed for his own car. Rowan caught up with Halley by the steps leading down to the salmon bothy.

'Go and put your feet up, you look all in. I'll see you on Sunday, if not before.'

'You will?'

'It's Remembrance Day and we'll all be at the war memorial for the laying of poppy wreaths. Tor said that you'd probably go along with the group from the castle.'

'I –' Halley wasn't given the chance to ask another question as Rowan headed back to Mallaig with the catering staff. Turning, Halley checked that the lights had been switched on and it was safe for her to start her descent to the beach. The LED lights at the edge of each step led the way to an enchanted world of sand, river and large outcrops of limestone which resembled the humped backs of half-buried creatures. The loch was like a mirror, reflecting the lights on the opposite shore. Unbidden, memories of summer nights lying on sun-baked sands with Lysander came to mind and she brushed them away.

Unlike Lysander, she had no intention of resurrecting the past.

No, it was Tor's face which pushed itself into her consciousness. He'd been so kind and generous, making sure everything ran smoothly. She'd noticed, as time passed that his limp had become more pronounced and she guessed he'd be glad to drive back to the Airstream for a hot shower to help ease the pain.

The thought of Tor Strachan naked in the shower sent a shiver through her, taking her by surprise. It'd been years since any man had caused such wanton thoughts to flit through a mind usually filled with statistics and scientific data. Such thoughts were dangerous. Hadn't she spent years suppressing such feelings as unwanted and potentially dangerous?

Whistling *Monymusk* and smiling, she descended to the beach holding onto the thick rope and remembering the night she'd brained Tor Strachan and laid him out on the sand. *That's* what she should have done to Lysander when she'd found out he had a fiancée waiting in the wings. Not run off like a startled deer. Grimacing at the analogy, she pulled her door key out of her pocket and let herself in.

After switching all the lights on she entered her bedroom, fetched the tin Monty had given her the other night and steeled herself to deal with whatever she found inside.

Chapter Eighteen

The tin was large and deep and had once held biscuits for cheese. Tam had loved cheese in its many forms, the stronger the better. He'd introduced her to *crowdie,* a soft white cheese traditionally made by crofters with origins dating back to the Vikings. They'd eaten it with rough oatcakes, sharing the craic over a glass of dry white wine. Part of her didn't want to take the lid off the tin because of what she might find inside.

However, needs must . . .

Prizing the lid off and almost breaking a nail in the process Halley placed the lid on the table and began sifting through the contents. The first thing she came across was a collection of brooches, each one representing Halley's Comet as a star with a fiery tail. Tam, despite his gruff exterior, had loved mooching round charity shops and car boot sales looking for the holy grail – a Carl Faberge brooch created to commemorate the 2010 sighting of the comet. He hadn't found it, but the brooches Halley laid on the table showed a fine eye for detail and some of the better pieces contained semi-precious stones.

Next, she removed Dunbar family photographs from the tin, the oldest showing her 'three times' great grandparents who'd left Belfast in the late nineteenth century and moved to Scotland. Seated in front of the sham backcloth of a highland landscape they stared glassy-eyed into the camera lens, stiff and formal. She turned the photograph over and read the address of a studio in Belfast. Clearly her ancestors had wanted to mark leaving Ulster for a new life in Scotland working the shipyards of the Clyde and this photograph was their record. By all accounts her great-great-great granny had been quite a beauty with grey eyes, porcelain skin and delicate bones, however, bearing eight children in as many years had robbed her of her bloom. Halley looked at the photograph searching for a family resemblance but couldn't find one except, perhaps, in the shape of her nose and the colour of her eyes. She'd often wished that she'd inherited her granny's strawberry-blond locks, but her Dunbar genes had decided otherwise and the only trace was an auburn sheen when the light touched her hair.

Tam had recounted tales of their Ulster ancestors who were always up for a fight. He'd made her laugh when he'd revealed how, before they acquired the surname *Dunbar*, they'd gone by the name of Peacock and had been teased in the school playground with the rhyme:

Peacock,

Straw cock,

No cock at all,

Cock.

They'd often arrived home from school with a bloody nose or a black eye. Not exactly Peaky Blinders but it'd felt quite racy when he'd shared tales of the old days and she wasn't entirely sure that her parents approved. That was the best part of having a great-uncle who treated her as an almost-a-grown-up. She started to relax, nothing in the tin was going to upset her or send her on a guilt trip . . . no birthday cards he hadn't posted after she'd left that fateful summer, unopened presents, or little notes addressed to her in his distinctive handwriting.

Tam wouldn't have done anything to distress her or make her sad, which made the way she'd behaved and how she'd treated *him* even more unforgivable.

All for the sake of Lysander-bloody-Strachan.

She exhaled an exasperated breath and then walked over to the fridge and poured a glass of wine. Should she continue going through the biscuit-tin-time-capsule or leave it until tomorrow? Squaring her shoulders, she switched off the too-bright overhead lights, returned to the table and continued.

Next, she came across a battered Observer's Book of Astronomy minus its dust jacket, published in 1962. It had belonged to Tam, but he'd crossed out his name and written hers on the frontispiece instead. The book, the story of how he and Monty had found the meteorite in the desert and his knowledge of the stars had sparked her love of astronomy. She kissed the book as reverently as she would a bible and placed it on the table.

She found Tam's service medals wrapped in a yellow duster and she spread them out. How she'd love fastening them to her cardigan and marching round the kitchen with an old broom as a makeshift rifle while Tam played marching tunes on his pipes. Beneath them in the tin, protected by a teased-out wad of cotton wool were more military medals stretching back to the Boer War. What stories could they tell she wondered, polishing the medals with the cloth. Tam had been a natural story teller and she'd never grown tired of hearing the tales attached to the campaigns and battles the Dunbar men had fought in. The medals would be going back to Hawaii with her. Her parents could decide what to do with them.

Taking another sip of wine, she pulled a long envelope out of the tin. Inside were two airline tickets and hotel reservations purchased the summer of her twenty-first birthday. The date she and Tam had planned to visit the Scrovengi Chapel in Padua to see Giotto's Adoration of the Magi. Academics and scientists believed that the appearance of Halley's Comet in 1301 had inspired Giotto to represent the Star of Bethlehem as a long-tailed fiery comet in the fresco.

Her comet. Her namesake.

'Oh Tam,' she breathed. That summer she'd told Tam she was too busy to fly over to Scotland. In reality she'd been too ashamed to admit what had happened between her and Lysander and was still coming to terms with the baby she'd conceived and lost.

Her secret. Her loss.

'I've been a fool. A bloody fool.'

If anyone would have understood what she'd gone through, it would have been Tam. But she'd never given him the chance. Now it was too late for regrets or too late to ask for forgiveness. Fat tears ran down her cheeks and plopped onto the tickets and great, tearing sobs wracked her lungs, making her throat ache and burn. She brushed away her tears with the heel of her hand and dried her face with the sleeve of her funeral suit. Then she sat back in her chair wondering if she dared open the last document in the tin.

Deciding that if she left it until tomorrow, she wouldn't be able to sleep, she pulled out a thick, cream A5 envelope and, reading the contents, let out a shuddering gasp.

Tor was concerned for Halley's welfare.

It'd been an emotional day and he'd been impressed at how she'd conducted herself. Not that he'd say as much to her, she might find his praise unwelcome and patronising. However, as his father's representative and Tam's friend it was incumbent upon him to look in on her before heading up the beach to his Airstream. Part of his duties as an army major had been looking after the welfare of his men and that, seemingly, was ingrained in his nature.

He gave a derisive snort, who was he kidding?

Despite his reservations over her links with his brother, the fact that she'd be heading home soon and her thinly veiled antipathy towards him, he was drawn to Halley Dunbar. Dress it up how he liked: concern for her wellbeing, offering moral support and a listening ear on an emotional day, the truth was less noble.

God help him, he couldn't stay away.

Here he was outside the bothy wondering if it was too late to come calling. He should be in his Airstream, applying hot and cold packs to the wasted muscles of his inner thigh which had contracted during the long hours of the funeral and the wake, most of which he'd spent standing. Going for broke he parked close to the porch, switched off the engine and swung himself out of the Land Rover.

'Christ,' he muttered as his feet touched the hard-packed sand

and a burning pain travelled the length of his leg from knee to groin. Grimacing, he walked over to the front door and knocked three times. Receiving no reply, he repeated the action and was about to head back to the Land Rover when a heart-wrenching cry, almost a keening sound, half sob, half moan, overcame his restraint. He walked in, uninvited, and the sight before him made his blood run cold. Halley, still in her funeral clothes, was seated at the kitchen table, blotting her tears with a yellow duster. Her shoulders were hunched and she looked totally dejected and disconsolate. In front of her on the table, laid out with care and attention was a collection of brooches, military medals, a little blue book and, as far he could make out, a document printed on thick cream paper.

The type of stationery beloved by bank managers, solicitors and estate agents.

'Halley. Are you okay?' Stupid question, but all he had in his arsenal. Halley took several seconds to register his presence, then raised her head and sent him a bleak look. That, allied to the fact that she didn't ask: *what the hell are you doing here at this time of night,* or showed him the door, unnerved him.

Walking over to her he repeated his question. She looked at him as though he'd asked the most stupid question in the history of stupid questions. That was more like it! He let out a relieved breath.

'As it happens, I'm not.' Picking up the sheaf of papers, she handed them over to him. 'Read this.'

He dragged a kitchen chair out from under the table, crashed down on it and stretched his injured leg out in front of him, not bothering to hide that he was in pain. Leaving him to read through the paperwork, Halley went over to the sink and made a cafetiere of coffee. In the time it took her to pour out two cups of strong coffee and put a milk bottle and a bag of sugar on the table he'd read the document through twice.

He let out a long, slow whistle.

'Did you know that Monty had signed the bothy over to Tam?' she demanded.

'I did not.' Tor looked through the document a second time, noting the date when the bothy had passed from his family to her great-uncle. 'I was in Afghanistan and Monty certainly didn't inform me, or anyone else, of his intentions. Being laird and a former brigadier gave him the belief that he could act as he pleased. Perhaps he thought I'd never return from Helmand Province and wanted to ensure that Tam was provided for in the event of his own death.'

Neither of them spoke, each trying to get their heads around the fact that the bothy had passed from his family to hers. Correction – not to the Dunbars, to her. Curling a long strand of hair round her finger Halley spoke quietly, thoughtfully.

'Tam has lived here for as long as I can remember. Forgive my bluntness, but if Monty pre-deceased him who would want to evict him from what is, in essence, a glorified beach shack? Oh, of course.' Realisation dawning, she wiped away the last of her tears and straightened her back as it evidently occurred to her that she might have a fight on her hands. 'Of course – your mother. Lysander.'

Tor was gratified that she didn't include Monty, himself or Lexie in the list. 'I would have looked after Tam. Old soldiers stick together.' He managed a weak smile, which required a response from Halley.

'You make it sound as if you served in the Boer War and was at the siege of Mafeking.'

'I wasn't as a matter of fact, but my regiment was.' Tor laughed, glad to see her relaxing. Her ownership of Tam's bothy was something to sort out tomorrow. For now, he'd take her mind off it and these medals provided him with the perfect distraction. 'Looking at the decorations on the table I can see that you have two very rare examples connected to that campaign, the Queen's South Africa medal and Kimberley Star. 'May I?'

'Go ahead.' Halley moved everything else to one side. Reaching over, Tor picked up two individual honours attached to ribbons of alternating cinnamon, orange and black stripes. On the ribbons were medal clasps commemorating the battles Halley's ancestors had fought in: Defence of Mafeking, Transvaal, Driefontein and Belmont.

'Tam was right to give these to Monty for safekeeping, any collector would give their eye teeth to look at them, let alone own them. These photographs of Tam's great-grandfather wearing them, however cracked and faded, gives them provenance and doubles their value. Look, round the edge of the medal, and you'll find your,' he did the maths, 'three times great-grandfather's name: *Pte Peacock* and his regiment *Scots Gds* inscribed on it. I served in the Scotch Guards until . . . well, never mind all that. Highlanders make the best soldiers,' he said, proud to be part of that long tradition of service and duty.

Halley looked impressed. 'As they say on *Antiques Roadshow*: "We won't be selling them". Obviously, I can't possibly accept Tam's bequest. What would I do with a wee bothy on a beach, thousands of miles away from Hawaii? I should talk this over with Monty as soon as possible. Will you meet me at the castle tomorrow morning? I think it might take our combined efforts to convince Monty that, as much as I value Tam's home and all the memories connected with it, I really can't accept the bequest.'

Tor was gratified that she should ask for his help but hid it behind a casual shrug.

'Sure. If you think it'd help.'

'I do.'

'So, what else did you find in Pandora's Box?' He picked up his coffee cup and took a long swig of the cooling liquid.

'Oh, this and that. I'll tell you about them tomorrow.'

Tor read the message loud and clear. It was time he left. He pushed his chair back and stood up. Holding on to the edge of the table for support he winced. 'Leave it with me, I'll have words with Monty and ring to let you know when you should come up to the castle. As you say, it's probably best that we meet in the morning, before Mother arrives home.'

He didn't need to say any more, the look they exchanged showed Halley understood. She walked him to the door and stood there as he made his way back to the Land Rover. It was a point of honour that he walked as straight as he could, hiding the extent of his disability. When he reached the sands, he turned and looked at her, backlit by the bothy's lights.

'Goodnight, Halley.'

'Goodnight, Tor – and thanks for everything you've done today. I'm in your debt.'

'Think nothing of it.' He dismissed her gratitude with a casual wave of his hand, hiding how moved he was by her thanks. 'Get a good night's sleep, we're going to need all our powers of persuasion to convince Monty that returning the bothy to him is the right thing to do.'

Halley nodded and then gave an extravagant yawn. They both laughed and then Tor climbed back into the Land Rover, gunned it and shot forward over the silver sands and towards his home with the incoming tide lapping at the car's wheels. When he next looked in his rear-view mirror Halley was in the doorway and remained there until he rounded the bend and she was lost from view.

Chapter Nineteen

The following morning a shivering Lexie Strachan pushed the bothy door open and stepped inside. Halley liked Lexie but wished she'd chosen another time to visit as she had the pressing business of Tam's bequest to sort out before Lady Strachan returned. However, good manners won the day and she greeted Lexie with a welcoming smile.

'Lexie. Nice to see you, come in.'

'This isn't a social visit,' Lexie cut in, seemingly reading her mind. 'Tor's tried ringing you but the phone signal's non-existent this morning. Atmospherics. So, he's sent me to fetch you instead. The brown stuff's about to hit the fan.'

'Brown stuff?' Halley questioned, still half-asleep after a night spent tossing and turning, coming to terms with yesterday's events *and* the contents of the biscuit tin. Lexie grabbed her coat off the peg and shoved her into it, dressing her as though she was a toddler.

'Yes. Brown stuff.' She fastened up Halley's coat and added a scarf and hat to the ensemble. 'She-who-must-be-obeyed has returned early, having been tipped off that Tam's wake was held in the castle kitchens.'

Brown Stuff? Wake? Of course!

'Tipped off? It could hardly be kept a secret,' Halley suggested, gathering her wits and locating handbag and phone while Lexie waited impatiently by the door.

'Quite. Cook – who adores Tor, informed him that Mother was on the warpath and a battle royal is imminent. The important thing is we get up there and present a united front before she arrives. Monty will need all our support. I've been sent to fetch you while Tor heads for the Laird's Smoking Room. This morning's confrontation will make the Battle of the Crater look like a walk in the park.' She stepped onto the porch and waited while Halley locked the door.

Once standing on the hard-packed sand in the biting wind, Halley's brain kicked up a gear. If things were bad now, what would Lady Strachan's reaction be when she found out that *she* – Halley Dunbar – was now the owner of the bothy? She pulled a face; more of the brown stuff heading for the fan, that much was certain. She was glad Tor would be fighting her, and Monty's, corner and she wouldn't have to face Lady Strachan alone. Not that she wasn't capable of sticking up for herself, working in a male dominated world had helped her to develop a carapace as hard as one of the leatherback turtles native to Hawaii.

Lexie grabbed her arm, giving her a gentle shake. 'Come on, Halley, time for dreaming later. We need to be firing on all cylinders. Let's use the steps, much quicker than bringing the car round,' she said, leading the way. Living an outdoor life kept Lexie at the peak of physical condition while desk-bound Halley could only trot at her heels. 'We have to defuse the situation. Monty's had enough to deal with over the last couple of weeks without Mother adding to his woes.' Reaching the top step, she turned and regarded Halley with an expression so fierce that Halley almost lost her footing and slithered back down to the beach.

'I get it. Okay? How – how did your mother find out? About the wake, I mean?' Halley asked, following Lexie through the rose gardens and up to the castle.

'Easy. She has a network of toadies and spies. I wouldn't go as far as to say that she pays for information but nothing escapes her. Monty leaves the domestic side of running the castle to her and she does so with military efficiency. She loves to make it plain that being a soldier, even a former brigadier who's risked his life for Queen and country, is a breeze compared to organising the day-to-day running of an ancient castle. Although,' she paused again and spun round, 'Tor might have a different take on that. As far as I'm aware, no one was ever blown-up whilst making Sunday Lunch or organising tours of a castle with afternoon tea thrown in.'

This was a different Lexie. More daughter-of-the-house of ancient lineage and less the dippy hippy Lysander had disparaged in the cellar yesterday.

'I see,' was all Halley could manage. If Lady Strachan was on the warpath over the wake, what would her reaction be upon learning Tam's bothy had passed out of Strachan hands? Halley wondered how much Lexie knew as, presumably, Tor had kept the bequest between him and Monty.

They soon reached the rear of the castle, stopping beneath the arch where Halley had abandoned an injured Tor the night of her arrival. Now, knowing his history and what he'd been through, she felt really bad about that. No time for regrets, however . . .

Lexie broke into her thoughts. 'The main suspects are Lysander and Frank Bunce. Only they would dare to ring Mother at Suzie's parents.'

'The factor?' Halley recalled how the scales had fallen from her eyes seeing the younger Strachans and Bunce standing together at Tam's wake. Peas in a pod, without a doubt.

'Yes. You see, he – he,' she was about to say more but stopped herself. 'Time for that later.' They entered the castle by the back entrance where they were met by a member of staff. 'Thomas, would you take Miss Dunbar's things and then show her to the Laird's Smoking Room?'

'Certainly Miss Lexie.'

'Wait.' Now it was Halley's turn to grab Lexie by the arm. 'Aren't you coming?'

Lexie gave her a long look. 'Tor said I'm to keep out of it – whatever 'it' is. He'll explain later, apparently. I'm guessing that it's something other than Father holding the wake in the kitchens?' She raised an inquiring eyebrow but curbed her curiosity for the time being.

'You could say that.' Aware that Thomas was waiting close by and maintaining a neutral expression Halley said no more. She wasn't sure how one behaved towards staff but she guessed it was a case of not being overly friendly and keeping family matters strictly within the circle of trust. Dismissing the irrelevant thought, she followed Thomas up the steps and through the inner hall, handing over her outdoor things before they climbed the stairs.

When they reached the Laird's Smoking Room, Thomas knocked on the door, pushed it open and announced Halley. Entering, she saw Tor standing by the fire warming his hands, cheeks stung red by the frost and looking very outdoorsy in a padded jacket, Hunter wellingtons and wearing a highland bonnet, tilted at a dashing angle. Unaccountably, her heart beat faster at the sight of him but she filed that thought away for later dissection and looked over at Monty. He was seated in his favourite chair and wearing a mutinous expression which hinted he was spoiling for a fight.

'Ah, Halley, good.' Tor took a couple of steps towards her and their eyes met. Remembering how kind he'd been last night, Halley sent him a cautious smile. He returned it with a crooked grin and a nod, acknowledging they were co-conspirators. Tor indicated she should move over to the fire and sit opposite Monty. 'I'm sorry I couldn't come and fetch you as arranged –'

'No worries. Lexie explained everything on the way up from the beach.' Suddenly, she felt a hostage to fortune, embroiled in a situation which was none of her making. She hoped it could all be sorted out this morning but she doubted it. If Monty was spoiling for a fight, she guessed that Lady Strachan would be, too. Deciding that she couldn't allow the Strachans to call all the shots she adopted a composed expression to let them know she couldn't – wouldn't – be pushed around. 'Monty, I'm sorry if holding Tam's wake in the kitchen has caused you trouble.' She didn't mention Tam's bequest, time for that once Lady Strachan had been dealt with. 'I –'

She was about to say more but the door burst open and Lady Strachan stood in the doorway in the pose of a Shakespearian actress about to play Lady Macbeth.

Dressed to the nines in a Chanel suit, hair immaculate and fully made up at – Halley glanced at her watch – eight thirty in the morning, she was clearly up for a confrontation with her husband and anyone foolish enough to get in the way. Walking into the room she closed the door behind her, stripped off her leather gloves, placing them and her Birkin bag on a side table.

'A collection of conspirators, I might have known. Tor, I really thought better of you.'

'Good morning, Mother,' Tor responded, seemingly used to his mother's tactic of trying to drive a wedge between him and his father. 'Let's keep your reaction to the fact that Monty held Tam's wake in the kitchen in proportion. It would have been disrespectful of him to do otherwise. Tam was a friend of long-standing and –'

'Well, that's one word for their relationship,' she snorted. Hoping to defuse the situation, Halley offered her chair to Lady Strachan. However, Sadie Strachan, apparently aware of the advantage of being higher than Halley, brushed her aside. 'What's done is done, but I find your conduct very underhand, Monty.'

'And why do you think that might be?' he asked, sarcastically. 'I'm not allowed to be master in my own house. Haven't been for years. I've had enough of it and you. I'm thinking of spending the winter with cousin Fergus in Miami, there's nothing here to keep me.'

'That might not be a bad idea,' Sadie conceded, suddenly all smiles and graciousness. 'We could do with a break from each other and Frank Bunce is capable of running the estate in your absence. To be fair, he has been doing so for years,' she added, sending him a bitter-sweet smile.

'Not the only thing he's been running,' Monty observed. 'However, should I decide to go down that road I want you to understand that Bunce will refer everything to Tor in my absence. *Creag na h-Iolaire* will be his one day and nothing you do can change that.'

'So it would appear,' Lady Strachan conceded. Halley wondered if Lady Strachan would prefer Lysander to inherit instead of Tor. However, even with limited knowledge of estate management, she knew that would be a disaster for the estate, the family and their tenants. She glanced over at Tor to see how he reacted to being practically threatened with disinheritance by his own mother. He seemed quite unruffled, leading Halley to assume that this conversation had taken place many times before.

Halley, brought up in the bosom of a loving and supportive family, had never experienced the rancour and bitterness which lay at the core of the Strachans' marriage.

'Why don't you sit down Mother and let me ring for coffee. There are other matters to discuss this morning.'

'Oh?' On the back foot, Sadie frowned, as if wondering what intelligence her moles had failed to pass on. 'Of course.' This time she accepted the chair which Halley vacated, crossing her legs at the ankles in an elegant pose Halley would never be able to emulate, not in a thousand years. Instead, she crossed the room and stood at Tor's side, exchanging the same half-smile they had when she'd first entered the room. A smile which declared them allies. Lady Strachan, never one to miss a nuance, picked up on it and addressed Halley, her eyes sharp and calculating. 'No doubt Miss Dunbar will be keen to get back to family in Hawaii.'

'Naturally,' Halley smiled back.

'Glad to hear it,' Sadie responded. Tor paused, his hand half-raised towards the embroidered bell pull, as though Halley's answer, while not unexpected, was not entirely to his liking. Lady Strachan, looking pleased with herself smiled up at Tor. As far as she was concerned the morning's business was over, her enemy vanquished and his great-niece heading home. Once Halley left, the Dunbars' connection with Lochaber would be severed forever.

Halley could almost find it in her heart to feel sorry for Lady Strachan. She'd entered into a marriage with a man who could never love her but who needed her father's money in order for his estate to survive. In return, she got the title her father craved, had become mistress of a large highland estate and, after producing an heir, had been allowed to do as she pleased, leaving Monty and Tam in peace. In the beginning, the arrangement must have seemed ideal. Monty would be away most of the year carrying out his duties as Brigadier with Tam, his faithful batman at his side, keeping their love a closely guarded secret as exposure would have resulted in court-martial, disgrace and worse. Who could blame Sadie Strachan for turning to Frank Bunce – Lochaber's very own Sean Connery, for comfort and companionship?

Except . . .

Lady Strachan, was unaware of the bombshell about to be delivered along with the coffee. Halley wondered if it wouldn't be better to leave the matter for another time when it was just Tor, Monty and herself.

The door opened and a member of staff brought in a coffee tray, placing it on the table in front of the window. No one spoke as the coffee was poured, the atmosphere becoming frostier as Lady Strachan glanced between the co-conspirators and seemingly picked up that there was more to come. Tor handed a cup to his parents and then offered one to Halley but she shook her head, anxious to get the business over and done with.

Taking her courage in both hands she moved the conversation along. 'Naturally, all those things: my research, consolidating my doctorate, gaining tenure and of course, my family, means the world to me. However, in view of Tam's bequest I –'

'Bequest?' Lady Strachan's head whipped round and she sent Tor a fierce look as though he'd been keeping secrets from her. 'What *is* she blethering about?'

She? So much for manners!

'I believe,' Sir Monty said, stubbing out his cheroot and sipping his coffee with slow deliberation, 'that Halley is referring to the fact that I signed the bothy over to Tam roughly, oh,' he acted out a mime of searching his mind for the date, 'twenty years ago. And he, as is his prerogative, has bequeathed it to Halley. Even when she does leave Lochaber, that won't be the end of the connection between the Dunbars and the Strachans. No matter how fervently you might wish it, my dear.'

Lady Strachan's hand shook and coffee spilled over the edge of the cup, dripping on to the skirt of her Chanel suit. Tor handed her a napkin but she slapped his hand away. 'Did you know about this, Hector?'

'Not until last night when Halley went through the tin held in safekeeping for Tam.'

'Tin? What tin? Who had it in their keeping? Let me guess; Monty! Why do I feel that I'm reading a novel with several of the pages ripped out?' Halley felt sorry for Sadie Strachan – outmanoeuvred, outgunned and unhappy despite the trappings of wealth surrounding her. 'What else is in this – this tin?'

'Nothing you need worry about, Sadie,' Monty replied, relishing every moment of her discomfort.

'I'll be the judge of that,' she snapped back. 'Who else knows about this bequest?'

'No one,' Tor replied. 'As I said, we only discovered Tam's will in the tin last night.'

'Might I ask who you mean by 'we'?' Lady Strachan glared at him.

'Halley and I,' Tor replied, sending a direct look across to his father. 'I can't speak for anyone else.'

'In case you're wondering, I didn't know what was in the tin. Tam asked me to have it for safekeeping and to give it to Halley – or which ever member of his family returned to Lochaber after his d-death.' His voice shook as he stumbled over the last word. 'I assumed that Tam had left his will with our solicitors, as directed, and not in a biscuit tin.'

'Directed? By whom?' Lady Strachan asked.

'Why, me, of course,' Monty returned.

'I see.' Regaining her poise and dignity Lady Strachan stood up and faced Halley. 'Might I ask what you plan to do with the bothy? I can't see you returning to Lochaber once you leave. There's nothing here for you. If it lies empty it'll soon be vandalised, encourage squatters, free campers and the like. I'm sure that's the last thing Tam would have wanted.' She looked as though it pained her to say his name, then she turned back to her husband. 'You really didn't think this through, did you Montgomery?'

'Au contrair my love, Tam and I discussed it at great length. It might interest you all to know that Tam tried to talk me out of signing the bothy over to him. But I wasn't for turning.'

That didn't mollify Lady Strachan one bit.

'I had hoped we'd be rid of him now he's dead. Seems I was wrong. I'll never be free of him.' Tears of frustration made her eyes appear large and luminous. However, Sadie Strachan wasn't one to stay at a loss for long. She shoulder-barged her way between Halley and Tor, driving them apart, then picking up her gloves, drew them on with slow deliberation and hooked her Birkin bag over her arm. Upon reaching the door she stood tapping her foot, waiting for Tor to open it. This he did with such deliberation that Lexie, who'd plainly been listening on the other side, fell through the threshold and onto her knees. 'Rest assured, Miss Dunbar, I will be seeking legal advice on this matter –'

'What matter?' Lexie demanded as Tor helped her to her feet.

'I wouldn't bother if I were you, Tam's will is watertight. I made sure of that. The bothy now belongs to Halley and there's nothing you can do about it.'

'I wouldn't be too sure about that, Monty.' She rounded on Halley, 'And, as for you Miss Dunbar, I hope you have more sense than to accept this bequest, it's a poisoned chalice and will bring nothing but trouble. Mark my words. However, I'm sure you have your own reasons for prolonging your visit.'

'Meaning?' Halley asked in a quiet voice.

'You stay away for years and then return, ostensibly to manage your uncle's affairs, but in reality, to snare yourself a highland laird. *This* highland laird, perhaps?' She touched her son lightly on the arm. 'I'd forget that if I were you. Tor's future wife has already been chosen.'

'First I've heard of it,' the prospective bridegroom muttered under his breath, clearly not wishing to raise his mother's blood pressure any higher.

Lexie, not one to stay quiet for long, waded in. 'Much as I love Tor and *Creag na h-Iolaire*, why would Halley give up her career, sun-drenched Hawaii and a loving family to move to a place where you have to wear three pairs of tights half the year to stay warm and cover yourself in Skin So Soft the other half, to ward off the midges. Not to mention belonging to a family so dysfunctional it makes the Lannisters look loving by comparison.'

Not being a fan of Game of Thrones, Lady Strachan was temporality foxed by the reference. However, she soon regained her poise. 'That's quite enough Alexandra,' she glared at her daughter 'You have no part in this discussion, so I suggest you stay out of it.'

Looking as though she was about to burst into tears Lexie linked an arm through Tor's and Halley's, pulling them close. 'You have no idea,' she began, 'how awful it is to be a Strachan. Everyone knows our business and what they don't know they make up. I would imagine the staff have heard every word of this discussion and are discussing it in the castle kitchens, laughing at us behind their hands. It'll be all round Mallaig by lunch time; Tam's shack has passed to his great-niece and

Lady Strachan has had another meltdown as a result. I, for one, hope Halley leaves and never returns.'

'Oh,' Halley let out a gasp of dismay.

'Oh, sweetie, not for the reasons you imagine.' She unhooked her arm and stood in front of Halley. 'I long to visit Hawaii and stay with you. Get away from this place. And if Bryce doesn't want to come, he can stay at home with his road kill specimens until I return, shouting: *Clachnaben*.'

Halley guessed that *Clachnaben* was the Strachan war cry but didn't think that now was the time to ask questions about the finer points of clan history. She felt desperately sorry for Lexie whom everyone regarded as a bit of an eccentric, flaky to say the least. Clearly, she had family issues which needed addressing if she was to live her life in any meaningful way. Perhaps Tor going through Sandhurst and entering the Scots Guards was his way of escaping the toxic atmosphere.

'And you will be very welcome to come stay with us in Hawaii, any time,' she said soothingly, embracing Lexie. Tor patted his sister on the head and, clearly thinking he was unobserved, glared at his father for putting them all in this situation. Monty appeared unabashed leading Halley to deduce that, much as he wanted the Dunbars to return to Lochaber and keeping Tam's memory alive, signing the bothy over to Tam gave him a further excuse to antagonise his wife.

Lady Strachan left the room, head held high and slammed the door behind her. Tor disentangled his sister from Halley's embrace, holding her at arms' length and looking into her face with loving concern. 'Okay, Lex?' he asked. 'That was quite a –'

She nodded and sniffed. Halley handed her a screwed-up piece of kitchen roll from her pocket in lieu of a handkerchief. Tor looked over Lexie's head at Halley and raised an eyebrow. Halley knew instinctively what he meant: this discussion wasn't over but would be better conducted without Lexie being involved.

'You know,' Lexie continued, 'I would have liked to go to university, got myself a degree and taken up a profession. But I was never given the chance. I've had the stuffing knocked out of me by my parents' constant bickering, the gossip and inuendo which is part of everyday life. Only

Tor – and Bryce – have ever believed that I could amount to more than this, achieve my dreams.'

'It's never too late to make those dreams a reality,' Halley said. 'If I can help you, I will.'

'Will you? Will you really?' Lexie asked, brightening up.

'Of course. Once I'm back home, zoom me and we'll talk through the options available to you.'

Halley glanced at Tor who was looking fondly at his sister. 'Thank you,' he mouthed, sending her a warm look. 'Tell you what, Lexie, why don't you invite Halley, Rowan and I to your cottage this evening? I could ring an order through to 'Sunset' in Morar and Rowan could pick it up on her way over?'

'I could cook,' Lexie suggested half-heartedly.

'Thanks for the offer but I'm in the mood for Thai food and I know that you and Bryce love it, too. Leave it with me,' he said, gently guiding her towards the door. He kissed the top of her head, very much her big brother in that moment, and returned to the room closing the door behind him. 'Now, Monty, I think you owe Halley and I a full explanation. Don't you?'

Chapter Twenty

Tor walked Halley to the top of the steps leading to Tam's – now her – bothy and paused. The tide was in and the wind brought the scent of the shoreline, the pine plantation below the rose garden and the tang of damp, growing things towards them. Since leaving the castle they'd remained silent, each lost in their own thoughts. The discussion with Monty hadn't really got anywhere. As far as he was concerned the bothy belonged to Halley. End of. What she decided to do with it didn't appear to concern him unduly. Tam, the love of his life, was gone and nothing else mattered.

Feeling that enough had been said on the subject for now and having endured his parents' full-blown 'domestic' before the sun had risen about the oak trees, Tor decided a change of subject was necessary.

'I think, after this morning's discussion and Lexie's meltdown we all need time out to get our heads round your ownership of Tam's bothy and plan a way forward. Don't you agree?'

'I do, but time is the one thing I don't have. Not in abundance, anyway. Even supposing I can change my ticket and extend my stay, I have to get back to the observatory. There are things there which need my attention.' Without warning, Tor experienced a sharp pang of regret that she'd be leaving. He quashed it, telling himself to get a grip. Of course, she had to return home, that was a given. However, since their encounter on the beach a few nights ago, even though she'd knocked him out, the fog in his brain had temporarily lifted and a feeling of – well, not optimism exactly, but something akin to it, had made it worth getting up this morning.

That hadn't happened in a long time.

On top of that, he'd enjoyed helping at Tam's funeral. It gave him a chance to return all the kindness Tam had shown him since the accident and served to remind him of the man he'd been before the explosion. Professional, decisive, a leader – not this shadow of a man who flinched at loud noises, flashes and bangs.

Such a small thing, but he was worried that once Halley left Lochaber the feelings of guilt, depression and trauma would return.

'I have a career there,' Halley continued, fiddling with the tassel at the end of her scarf. 'Commitments to meet and lectures to deliver. People seem to think that my post at the observatory involves nothing more than looking at the vastness of space and jotting down anything unusual. A glorified hobby which comes with the right to call myself Doctor Dunbar. It's hard to convince them that I worked long hours for the privilege of adding those three letters – PhD – after my name. If I want tenure, a larger teaching role and the right, one day, to describe myself as a professor of astrophysics, being away from my desk for almost three weeks is the wrong way to go about it.'

Tor felt immediately guilty. The last time he'd seen her, albeit from a distance, she'd been barely eighteen years old. Had he given the impression he still viewed her as such?

'I hope I'm not one of them.'

Halley was quick to reassure. 'No. You're not like that. Apart from flattening me on the beach and the coruscating discussion about Lysander my first morning in Lochaber.' She pulled a face and looked up at him, grey eyes wide and serious but with a glimmer of humour. 'You were a great support yesterday and this morning, too, thank you.'

'No need to thank me, I was impressed with how you handled mother. Most people quell before her when she's on her high horse. Which is often.' Now it was his turn to adopt a sardonic expression and Halley laughed.

'I'm used to dealing with people, it's one of the skillsets I've acquired over the years. Stroppy undergrads, professors with too high an opinion of themselves and members of the public who think I'm an *astrologer* and can guess their star sign and predict their future.' She waved her hands in front of her as though she was scanning a crystal ball and said in a quavering voice: 'You will meet a tall, dark stranger and win the lottery.'

'Tall, dark stranger, eh? Well, that rules me out.' He pulled off his beanie and ruffled his blond hair before pulling it back on, adopting a rueful expression, his eyes bright. 'Mind you, if you can predict this week's lottery numbers, I'm prepared to share my winnings with you.'

'That's magnanimous of you.'

'I am nothing if not generous,' he laughed. 'Go on, tell me more.'

'I have to maintain my game face in order to do my job and be taken seriously. It makes me appear dull and buttoned-up, but I'm okay with that, because that's not the real me. On the other hand, I'm a brilliant poker player and my understanding of numbers and statistics means that I'm ace at roulette and chemin de fer.' Another half-smile, one which made her eyes sparkle. 'Last year, some of the other members of the faculty and I flew to Vegas for a long weekend. Our plan was to return to Hawaii, if not richer than when we left, then certainly not out of pocket.'

'How did that work out for you?'

'Good. I know to quit while I'm ahead. I made enough to pay for my next trip away, while some of my colleagues had to work overtime to make up for their losses.'

Tor was intrigued to discover this side to her and what lay behind the poker face and the serious mien which seemingly hid the true Halley Dunbar. What had made her the person she was? They'd only become reacquainted over the last couple of days and under circumstances neither of them would have wished. Hardly surprising that he knew very little about her.

As if reading his thoughts, Halley continued. 'FYI, I'm not someone who finds it easy to chill out; kick back. There's always an endless list of things to do at the observatory, at home. But here, in spite of everything, I've been at my most relaxed, which probably sounds odd given that I'm really, really missing Uncle Tam. I keep forgetting that he's,' she gulped, 'not here anymore. I turn round to ask him something, to share a joke, only to find that the room is empty and . . .' She shook her head, seemingly to dismiss the depressing thought. Then she looked over at him and smiled. 'Being here, albeit sorting out Tam's affairs, has felt almost like a holiday.'

'Almost?'

'You don't know what an admission that is for me.' She laughed, moving towards the top step where she stopped, picked at strands of the marine rope banister and continued the conversation without looking at him. 'Perhaps that's what Tam intended when he left the bothy to me. He knew I needed a hideaway, a bolthole where every-day cares and worries can't find me.'

'I'm sensing a *but,* in that sentence. What's stopping you from accepting the bequest?'

'The pa–' She stopped, openly terrified she'd revealed too much. 'There are things to be resolved before I leave. Things which, if they're left hanging, will mean I can never return.' She shrugged, dismissing the root of her anxiety as nothing of consequence and certainly nothing she would ever share with him.

pa–?

Had she been about to say *past?* He sensed this wasn't to do with her professional life, she pretty much had that covered. No, there *was* something else. She took a couple of steps down towards the beach as though reluctant to leave. When she glanced back, her brow was puckered and the shutters were drawn. Evidently, she felt she'd said enough. Perhaps they both had.

'Wait.' He reached out and then dropped his hand, aware that he'd allowed feelings he hadn't experienced in a long time to get the better of him. One thing was certain, he didn't want her to return to Hawaii – at least, not yet. 'Please wait,' he said, making it sound less like a command and more a request as he placed a hand on her arm.

'Yes?' Halley paused, looked at his hand and then raised her head, her breathing irregular and her pupils dilating, as though something significant had passed between them. For all his time in the army, the risks he'd taken, Tor found standing before this woman the most dangerous of all.

'Allergies. Do you have any allergies or can I pretty much order anything from the menu?' He pulled a wry face, of all the daft things to come up with . . . he felt like kicking himself.

'I'm quite tough. Years eating at my desk or the computer has given me a cast iron constitution.' She patted her stomach and took another step towards the beach. 'What I don't like the look of, I'll leave.' Now she was standing on the sand. 'One thing, though . . .'

'Go ahead.'

'I have no idea where Lexie and Bryce live. Should I ask Rowan to fetch me, or –' She looked at him, expectantly.

'I'll pick you up,' he said, almost too eagerly, covering it up by explaining, 'the bothy is out of Rowan's way. Shall we say about seven?'

'It's a date,' she said, then coloured and lowered her head. 'No; not a date, just a gathering of friends. I don't want you to think, I . . .'

'Yes?' This time he allowed himself to grin at her discomfiture.

'Okay,' she raised her hand to her mouth. 'I'm digging a hole here, so I'll shut up. Seven o'clock it is.'

'Seven o'clock. Leave the security light on, it'll be pitch black and I'll be driving through waves as the tide won't have turned. I don't want to overshoot landing and end up in Tam's woodshed.'

'Roger that,' she saluted, grinning.

'We don't want any slip ups,' he said, stretching the conversation beyond its limits, reluctant for it to end.

'I imagine that you make very few slip ups,' she said. 'Seven o'clock. *A hui kaua.*'

'Which means?'

'Hawaiian for: until we meet again.'

'*Beannachadh airson a-nis,*' he responded in Gaelic. 'Goodbye for now.'

Halley smiled, climbed down to the beach and disappeared from sight.

Tor stood still, slowly becoming aware of the cold wind whipping up the sand, the call of the seabirds and the rumble of traffic on its way to Mallaig. Halley had managed the impossible, she'd made him forget, albeit it temporarily, images which haunted him.

The rookie second lieutenant who believed that coming from a family of soldiers more illustrious than the Strachans, gave him the right to use his initiative and not follow orders to the letter. A false confidence and arrogance which resulted in him leading his men across a field mined with a daisy chain of IED's. Tor knew he should have pulled him up sooner, given him a bollocking that would have left him in no doubt as to his place in the order of things.

However, he hadn't and that was something he had to live with.

Even on a cold morning like this he could feel the heat from the blast, remember the colour of the smoke, the ringing in his ears and the smell of the IED's crude explosives. He shook his head free of the images as though they were part of a bad dream, a recurring nightmare and remembered instead some elements of the seven steps designed to help him reach acceptance.

- Deal with flashbacks
- Work through survivor guilt
- Connect with others

Turning on his heel he made his way back through the rose gardens and towards the stable yard where he'd parked his battered old Land Rover. He glanced at his wrist watch, ten o'clock. It was going to be a long day until he drove over to pick Halley up and drive her to his sister's cottage.

But something told him it would be worth the wait.

Chapter Twenty-one

Halley had no sooner let herself into the bothy than there was a knock on the door. Not bothering to take off her coat and scarf she put her handbag down and opened the door. She was surprised to find Geordie Souter standing there blowing on his hands to warm them.

'Morning Halley,' he greeted her, stamping his feet and flapping his arms around his skinny frame as he glanced past her into the warm bothy.

'Hi,' Halley replied, ignoring his elaborate mime.

'Bluddy cold, isn't it?' he prompted, taking a step closer.

'You could say that,' she responded.

'You've been out bright and early. I saw you coming down the steps from the castle and I thought I'd just drop by to see if you were alright after the funeral and,' he paused fractionally, 'everything.'

No chance of pretending that she was just on her way out, then. Suppressing a tut of annoyance she opened the door wider. 'You'd better come in out of the cold.'

'Thanks, I'm frozen to the marrow.' Halley took in what he was wearing – tattered combat trousers, a thin bomber jacket over a t-shirt and faded All Star baseball boots. Catching her swift once-over he gave a sardonic smile. 'My tailor in Edinburgh is working on a tweed suit but it won't be ready for another week.'

Feeling that she was being mean and remembering what she said to Tor earlier about having to deal with all kinds of people in the course of her work she adopted her polite, professional face, suppressing her dislike of Souter. It was nothing to do with him being down on his luck, having limited funds and living in a caravan on the beach. Whatever her other failings, she wasn't a snob. There was just something about him which put her on edge, made her feel uneasy, as though he wasn't to be trusted. To counter her lack of enthusiasm at finding him on her doorstep she ushered him over to sit in Tam's favourite chair and stripped off her outdoor things.

Her father's words on her first day at the observatory echoed in her head.

Remember, Halley, not everyone has had your education or your opportunities

'Coffee?' she asked.

'Aye, that'd be rare,' Souter replied, rubbing his hands together. Halley walked over to the sink, observing Souter via the mirror where Tam had shaved every morning. Thinking he was unobserved he scanned the room with slow deliberation, as though making an inventory of its contents. Now Halley wondered if she'd done the right thing by inviting him in. Maybe he had never made it past Tam's bench where she'd first met him a few days ago. Had he been waiting for her, even then?

'Help yourself to sugar and milk and there's biscuits in the tin. No, not that one,' she said, scooping up the medals and airline tickets and replacing them in the tin before placing it on the kitchen worktop. She pushed a packet of shortbread petticoat tails across to him. 'I saw you at the wake yesterday, although not at the funeral, unless I missed you. I was rather preoccupied.' Souter broke off a 'tail' and dunked it in his coffee.

'Dinnae apologise, I get it. I was carrying out a wee job for Frank, the factor. You were busy and the last thing on your mind was to check who wis or wisnae at Tam's funeral. Especially old Geordie Souter. I just wanted to see if you're a'right this morning.'

'I'm as fine as I can be. I've had plenty of help from the laird, Tor, Lexie and Rowan Ferguson. There's nothing else I need, really, but thanks for dropping by.' She hoped he'd take the hint, finish his coffee and go.

'Nae bother,' he said. Pouring himself another coffee from the cafetiere he got up and walked round the room, hands cupped around the mug. 'I see you've got a lot of clearing out to do.'

'It's all in hand, Tor and Rowan are helping out.'

He pushed open her bedroom door and Halley had to grit her teeth as he poked his head in. The first thing he spotted was the brass telescope. He turned, grinning. 'I bet that's worth a pretty penny. If you and the Major want help sorting your stuff, I'm your man. I know folk who would take it off your hands and give ye a guid price.'

She bet he did!

'That's very kind of you. However, as I said, it's all in hand. Now, if you'll excuse me, I'm expecting a zoom call from my parents in five minutes and I need to get my laptop fired up.' She reached over, took the coffee mug from him and closed her bedroom door.

'They live in Hawaii, don't they? I'd love to go there, sunshine and lots of ladies in grass skirts.' He let the thought hang in the air as if expecting her to say: *sure, come on over for a holiday and stay with me.* There was a distinct chance that hell would freeze over and the camels come skating home before that happened. Walking to the front door she opened it. 'How kind of you to swing by; I'll bear your offer of help in mind and, should I need it, I know where to find you.'

'Bye for now,' he said.

His tone implied that he'd be returning for another visit in the not-too-distant future. Halley kept her fixed smile in place until she closed the door behind him and locked it. Not because she thought he posed a threat but more because she needed to feel safe and secure after the coruscating episode with Monty and Lady Strachan.

'Oh, Tam, what were you thinking?' she asked his photograph on the dresser.

Sighing, she set her laptop up on the kitchen table. The pending zoom call was a white lie, Hawaii was ten hours behind the UK which made it one o'clock in the morning. Thank goodness Souter didn't know that or she'd never have got rid of him. However, she needed to bring her parents up to speed regarding the funeral, wake and Tam's bequest. She'd call them before Tor picked her up and took her over to Lexie's. The thought of an evening of uncomplicated company cheered her up and she cleared away the coffee things with a lighter heart.

Then she found the pack of post-its she'd bought in Mallaig and started to make an inventory of what she would be leaving behind when she left Lochaber.

Tor acted as Halley's Uber for the night.

Although she had her hire car, local knowledge was definitely required to negotiate the path along the shore. Tonight, the tide was high and she didn't know where the obstacles lay or how to avoid them. On top of which, she didn't want to damage the hire car and have to pay a premium when she handed the keys back in Inverness. The temperature had dropped to below freezing, forcing her to search out the warmest clothes in her meagre wardrobe. She guessed that Lexie and Bryce didn't dress for dinner so there would be no need for jewels or a second-best tiara. That thought made her smile as she envisaged herself in Lexie's cottage kitchen, the detritus of everyday life temporarily pushed to one side as they all mucked in setting the table with mismatched cutlery and a harlequin collection of plates and glasses.

Smiling, she sprayed herself with her favourite perfume and sat down at her brass telescope – a birthday present from Tam – to pass the time before Tor arrived. Light pollution was low in Morar Bay, making it an ideal spot for stargazing. Earlier, bang on schedule, the International Space Station had passed overhead as bright as a star or planet.

Looking through her telescope she located three star groups with the ease of someone treading a familiar path: Andromeda, Cassiopeia and Pisces. Pisces, her star sign was always hardest to find but she knew exactly where to look for the giant 'V' shaped like a fish's tail, adjacent to the Square of Pegasus. This was her job, what she was good at and sitting here at her telescope reminded her of what she loved and was missing by prolonging her stay in Lochaber. She was just about to cover up her telescope when something caught her attention, lights on the far side of the bay and the sound of a dinghy engine. The lights flashed again and there was a corresponding signal from her side of the bay. Fishermen? Hardly, given the temperature. She swung her telescope to the left and then up and down, searching for clues as to who might be signalling at this time of night, but found nothing.

Eventually the sound of the outboard motor died away and all was quiet.

There was no time for further thought as Tor drew up in his Land Rover and tooted the horn. Her stomach flipped over as though she was a teenager on a first date. She shook her head at the preposterous idea but her heart gave a glad leap. She let herself out of the salmon bothy, locking the door behind her, checking that the security light was on and the other lights were burning behind the curtains, making it appear she was home.

She frowned, not quite sure why she considered that important. In the past, when she'd stayed with Tam, they'd never locked the door. However, times had changed and Souter's impromptu visit had made her realise that there were items of value in the bothy: the telescope, the Boer War medals and the meteorite under the sink. Although, the latter looked just like a lump of stone to the untrained eye.

She thought about taking the meteorite back to Hawaii but decided that her original idea of donating it to The Kelvin Grove Museum in Tam's name made better sense. Chastising herself for thinking too far ahead she walked towards the Land Rover. Having seen how difficult it was for Tor to climb in and out of the vehicle she didn't want him to come over all chivalrous and attempt to open the passenger door for her. Instead, she hauled herself in and attempted to fasten the seat belt.

However, the mechanism was well and truly jammed. 'Here. Let me.' Tor joined in the tug of war, reaching across and pulling the slack out from the side wall. It was a tricky manoeuvre and, as he tugged, his hand slipped and grazed Halley's breast.

'Oh,' she exclaimed, not in pain but in shock at the unintended contact.

'God – I'm so sorry. Here, let me . . .'

Surely, he wasn't going to suggest that he rubbed it better!

God help her, where had that thought come from?

There was an awkward moment as hands, fingers and flesh collided. The seatbelt was given one last yank and then it was free. Halley sucked in a shaky breath, glad that Tor couldn't see the stain of colour working its way from her neck to her forehead, nor register her shiver of awareness. Butterflies performed flick-flaps in her stomach; the sensation woke memories long considered dead and buried, reminding her how it felt to be young and in love.

'There!' Having freed the belt, Tor ran his hand along the length of it until he found the buckle. 'I'm not used to having a passenger on board,' he explained, fastening her in.

'And I'm not used to being looked after quite so,' she struggled to find the right word, 'proficiently?'

'I was going to suggest that we dispensed with the seat belt but the terrain will be bumpy and uneven.'

'Better safe than sorry, huh?'

'Exactly.' The trite phrase appeared to transport Tor to another time and place. Miles away from Lochaber. He gave a reactive shudder as though a ghost had indeed walked over his grave. Placing his hands on the steering wheel he stared into the darkness, an uneasy silence descending.

Halley laid a gentle hand on his arm and he gave a start, as though her touch had woken him from a bad dream. 'Shall we?'

'Hmm? Yes. Of course.' He slipped the car into gear and they moved forward.

In an attempt to break the mood, he drove through the waves at the edge of the shore and water sprayed up the side of the vehicle and over the bonnet. He switched the headlights on to full beam and flicked on the windscreen wipers. 'Lexie used to love me driving through the waves when she was younger, always demanding to ride shotgun, banishing Lysander and any of her little friends to the back seat. Urging me to go faster, faster and to make the waves splash higher.'

'That doesn't surprise me. She's quite a girl.'

'I was going to say, remember that when you sample her cooking tonight, then I remembered that Rowan is bringing a takeaway. Praise be to God.' They laughed and the dark moment vanished. 'She really likes you and I'm glad of it, sometimes I think she leads too isolated an existence. Just herself, Bryce, their dogs and the wild sporran business.'

'I like her too. She said something that made me think.'

'What was that?'

'About longing to hang out with me, Rowan and the village kids back in the day. Sadly, I wasn't really aware of her at that time – the age gap I suppose. Plus, Tam had drummed it into me to keep to his stretch of the beach and not trespass on Strachan land.' Not wanting to bring his mother into the conversation and ruin tonight's impromptu dinner, Halley changed the subject. 'Well, we can all be friends tonight and enjoy the moment before I start packing.'

'Of course,' Tor replied, then silence descended once more.

'You know,' Halley said, waving her hand to take in the beach, 'this is an ideal spot for stargazing. There's virtually no light pollution, the constellations really stand out and even an amateur stargazer could pick out the ISS when it passes over. If you wanted to capitalise on it, you could get someone to organise and conduct Dark Sky stargazing events.'

'Not you?' He turned his head to look at her.

'Be a bit tricky commuting from Hawaii to Lochaber,' she laughed. 'If I lived here permanently then, sure, it's something I could take on and make a success of.' She didn't want to sound like she was bragging, but she knew her strengths and how to play to them. 'Tam's bothy –'

'Your bothy,' he corrected.

'*The salmon bothy*,' she emphasised, 'would make a great centre for stargazing and maybe raise funds for your favourite charities.' She guessed that the Strachans didn't need extra income, not in that sense, but hoped that she hadn't spoken out of turn.

'I do my best to raise funds for Help for Heroes and other forces charities, especially those designed to help veterans deal with PTSD.' He drove them away from the beach and onto an uneven path which led through a wooded area thick with oak trees. Halley remembered it from her childhood as a place she and the other children spent many happy hours hunting for fallen acorns.

She sent him an oblique look. She didn't know the full details of his injuries or why he chose to live alone, but she guessed it was to do with his service in Afghanistan. She didn't say more because it was none of her business and besides, once she left Lochaber she would never return; no point in opening cans of worms to see if they wriggled.

The dark sky, diamond bright stars and constellations encouraged introspection and they travelled in silence for the rest of the journey. Halley wished she had the skill to draw Tor out of the bleakness which appeared to descend upon him without warning. Or knew how to encourage more of the light-hearted moments they'd enjoyed during their brief acquaintance.

'Here we are,' Tor said, drawing up before a substantial stone-built house with a blue slate roof. Light shone out from every window, pushing back the darkness and welcoming them in.

'Oh, I thought . . .'

'What did you think?' he asked, teasing her.

'I thought Lexie's cottage would be like the bothy only on a slightly larger scale. I didn't expect anything as grand as this.'

'Well, yes, I can see how it would appear quite grand.' He didn't add – *to someone unused to how Highland aristocrats live*. He didn't need to. 'And, to be fair, Lexie only has it on loan.'

'On loan?'

'Yes. It's the Dower House, the place where mother will – or at least, should – decamp to when father passes on.' He remained at the wheel looking at the brightly lit house. 'Only . . .'

'Only you can't see her giving up living in a castle for life in a Dower House, no matter how palatial.'

'Correct.' Quickly losing interest on where Lady Strachan would live once Monty joined Tam on the great Parade Ground in the Sky, he opened his door and climbed out of the Land Rover. Only a half-muttered oath and the way he clung to the overhead handle demonstrated how difficult he found this simple manoeuvre.

Then, Dower Houses, Dark Sky Parks and what the future held were pushed aside as Lexie came rushing out, dogs in tow, and threw herself at Halley and Tor. Her delight at having her beloved brother and her new best friend Halley in her house was evident. Halley and Tor exchanged a look but remained straight-faced as Lexie kissed first one then the other.

Bryce came out of the house at a more sedate pace and put his arm round Lexie's shoulders as if to calm her down. Tor sent Halley a humorous look, as if apologising for his sister's effusive welcome. It was such a perfect moment of friendship and camaraderie that Halley let out a contented sigh, glanced wordlessly at Tor over her shoulder and followed the other two into the Dower House.

Chapter Twenty-two

'Halley, Tor, welcome.' Bryce greeted them, pushing Lexie into the house in diplomatic fashion. 'Rowan's already here and the meal's keeping warm in the oven.' He kissed Halley on both cheeks and shook Tor's hand. 'I've been looking forward to us all getting together and hearing more about Tam's bequest.'

Halley suppressed a sigh. Did she really have to think about it this evening?

Evidently picking up the vibe, Tor spoke for her. 'I wouldn't say the topic is off limits tonight, but I think that Halley needs some time to get used to the idea of being a highland landowner.' He smiled to show that he was talking in jest.

'Sorry, Halley. It's just that Lexie and I –'

'Bryce,' Tor growled out a friendly warning.

'Okay. Roger that, Major Strachan.'

Saluting, he and Lexie led them into a square, panelled hall where a Scots Pine fireplace, flanked by two massive baskets of seasoned wood and dried peat turves burned brightly. The wooden floor was covered by beautiful, if faded, kilim rugs and wall lights cast soft shadows on a velvet porter's chair with a hooded back designed to protect a night watchman from draughts.

'What an amazing room,' Halley commented, feeling immediately at home and not in the least intimidated by her surroundings.

'There's more to come,' Bryce said, 'follow us in to the kitchen.'

Tor laid a guiding hand on Halley's lower back, much as he had at the graveside yesterday. His touch was light, non-threatening and,

Halley guessed, designed to be gently reassuring. She didn't shy away from it or shrug him off as she might have other men. In fact, in view of everything that had happened over the last few days, she welcomed it. She smiled at Tor to show the accidental contact in the Land Rover with the seat belt was forgotten.

Common sense told her that Hector Strachan didn't want – or need – to force himself on any woman.

'Halley!' Rowan walked forward, meeting them in the middle of a large kitchen fitted out with a scrubbed table on a stone-flagged floor surrounded by an assortment of chairs as old as the Dower House itself. The paintwork was a soft, chalky green, doubtless mixed by an expert hand to blend in with copper pans and kettles on shelves above a range cooker. A Scots pine dresser held a collection of cookery books and a Delft rail, running round all four walls, displayed antique serving platters. Plainly, the Dower House was a comfortable place for the laird's widow to live in.

Reading Halley's expression, Lexie laughed. 'The Strachans don't do Ikea. Or, at least, mother doesn't. She's spent a considerable amount of money turning the Dower House into a mega-comfortable place to live in once Monty's passed.' Momentarily she looked glum as she contemplated his passing, then she brightened. Lexie, Halley had come to realise, never stayed in a dark place for long. 'Although I can't see her taking up residence here and leaving Tor's future bride to lord it over her in the castle.'

'That's enough, Lexie. Halley doesn't need, or want, a crash course in how primogeniture works amongst highland gentry. I might never marry and then Lysander and his children would inherit and, knowing mother, she'd relegate them to the Dower House while *she* remained in the castle,' said Tor.

'Doesn't bear thinking about.' Lexie shivered while the others laughed. Then, tiring of the subject she changed it. 'Have you fully recovered from this morning's bruising encounter? I was telling Rowan that mother was on top form. They probably heard her shriek of outrage in Fort William.'

'The staff certainly did, at any rate,' Tor put in, walking over to the freezer and removing a bottle of champagne.

'Oh yes, I'm quite okay,' Halley responded. 'I spent most of the day grouping Tam's possessions into some kind of order and making an inventory of what I would like to have shipped home. Once that's done, I'll be taking Rowan up on her kind offer to sort out the rest. My parents didn't seem too surprised to learn that Tam had left the bothy to me. In fact, I'd lay even money on him having discussed it with them. As they quite rightly said, it's down to me to decide what to do with it. But not tonight, right?'

'Quite right. Take a seat at the table while Bryce and I dish up the food. Halley, you sit there, next to Tor. Rowan, you're in your usual place; Bryce and I will sit at either end which makes it easier us for us to serve.'

Usual place? That suggested that Rowan having dinner with Lexie and Bryce was a regular occurrence. Halley was glad of it; she didn't like to think of Rowan having only the swearing parrot and dim-witted cousin for companionship. All conversation ground to a halt while dishes were laid out down the centre of the table and Tor popped open the bottle of champagne, filling everyone's glass. It amused Halley to think that Lexie and Bryce probably considered themselves as living in reduced circumstances at Lady Strachan's pleasure while they ate off bone china plates and drank champagne out of crystal glasses, courtesy of Monty's cellar.

At the thought of the cellar and her encounter with Lysander she went quiet while the others chatted around her. Had Tor walked in to the cellar and found Lysander behind the door sitting on the beer barrel his reaction would have been only too predictable. Halley shivered in spite of the warmth blasting out from the open oven door as Rowan removed the takeaway.

'Dig in everyone,' Bryce said, gesturing at the food. 'You first, Halley as you are guest of honour tonight.' He handed Halley a heavy, monogrammed serving spoon bearing the Strachan coat of arms, and she did just that.

Tor watched Halley interacting with the others. She had an honest and unaffected manner and he liked that. He realised that *this* was the real Halley. It had taken her a few days to get over their first bruising encounter and the contentious meeting in the bothy the following morning when he'd discovered Lysander there. He knew now that he was wrong to suspect her of anything underhand. He should have known that his brother couldn't resist hitting on an attractive woman, even one who'd travelled thousands of miles to organise her great-uncle's funeral. She'd be heading home soon and who could blame her for preferring a place where the sun always shone, she had a loving family and a bright future ahead of her?

A rundown former salmon bothy on the shores of Morar Bay, although romantically picturesque, couldn't compete.

His future looked less bright. The next couple of years would involve intense physio to repair his shattered leg and therapy sessions to help him come to terms with what he'd seen first-hand in Helmand province. He frowned. He'd been ducking out of those sessions, preferring to offload to Tam and Monty who'd experienced the horror and exhilaration of war and understood how he felt. However, with Tam gone and Monty weighed down with grief, maybe it was time to seek professional help once more?

Living in safe, peaceful Lochaber among people who didn't understand what he'd been through, felt untenable some days. The days when Post Traumatic Stress Disorder made getting out of bed and the most basic tasks impossible. It had only been the last couple of days, ever since Halley Dunbar had breezed into his life like a *force majeure,* that he'd caught flashes of his old self. The optimism, joie de vivre and up-for-anything attitude which had made him the officer everyone wanted to serve under.

Major Hector Strachan, the man ready to take on the world.

He sighed inwardly; that was then and this is now.

Like Halley, he'd perfected his 'stage face', a mask for when people asked: *how are you?* It was kindly meant, but he always felt like countering with: trust me, you don't want to know. Thanks to his injuries, he could never return to his regiment. It was time he got on with his life, accepting the hand fate had dealt him. He couldn't hide away in the converted Airstream or dodge his mother's match-making schemes forever. He didn't see himself the prize his mother and the other local matrons thought him. To be honest, he didn't envy the woman game enough, or mad enough, to take him on. However, as an ex-soldier he knew he had to do his duty and produce an heir to carry on the Strachan line. That involved marriage, there could be no doubting the legitimacy of *his* children.

He glanced over at Lexie whom he loved dearly and wondered if Halley had worked out that Monty wasn't her or Lysander's father. He'd seen her studying them covertly during the wake when they'd been standing alongside Frank Bunce. It didn't take a genius to work out that the dark haired, brown eyed younger Strachans looked nothing like himself or Monty.

Of course, he *could* cite his father as an example for not rushing into marriage. Monty had been well into his forties before he'd tied the knot. Luckily, he'd had his military career as an excuse for not settling down and for staying away from Lochaber once married. Sadly, that particular escape route had now been denied him and, unlike his father, he hadn't met the love of his life when he was twenty-two years old, just out of Sandhurst and green as grass.

He wished that Lysander and Suzie would have a child of their own. It would make them happier, prop up the foundations of their shaky marriage and take the pressure off him. Producing an heir and a spare was the last thing on his mind and he'd wondered how much longer he could go on avoiding the eligible females his mother paraded before him, hoping one of them would catch his attention; be *the one*.

At that moment, he and Lexie locked eyes and it was as if she could read his mind. Although he hoped not, his thoughts ran dark and deep and she was his baby sister and, as such, had to be sheltered from sombre thoughts. He loved her dearly and would never do anything to hurt or distress her.

'Cake. We need cake,' Lexie said, clapping her hands excitedly as though a well-baked pudding had the power to release Tor from his torment. Still, he knew the drill and went along with it; smile, put on a good act, don't reveal your true mental state.

'Pudding? Why not?'

'Here's one I didn't produce earlier.' Walking over to the double fridge Lexie reached in and removed a cheesecake.

'That looks amazing,' Halley said as Lexie set it down in the middle of the table, fetched clean plates and cutlery. 'You've been hard at work.'

'Someone has,' Tor remarked, grinning over at his sister. 'Mrs Richardson?' he guessed, naming the cook.

'The Mary Berry of the Highlands. Who else?' Laughing, she turned to Halley. 'I have no shame. This morning, after you and Tor headed for the beach, I threw myself on Mrs Richardson's mercy and asked if she could rustle us up a vegan pudding. As soon as I mentioned Tor,' she rolled her eyes, 'she produced this baby from the fridge and made me promise not to be caught leaving the castle with it. I barely managed to bring it home in one piece because it kept sliding around on the passenger seat. Bryce has been begging to try it all afternoon but I wanted you to see it in all its glory. The strawberries have come from our hothouses, not Egypt, quite a treat in mid-November.'

'It looks incredible,' Halley agreed.

'You do the honours, Bryce,' Lexie said, handing over a cake slice.

'Of course,' he said, 'how big a piece would everyone like?'

'Humongous,' Rowan answered, eyes bright.

'Make that two,' Lexie interjected.

Bryce paused: 'Halley, Tor?'

'Same here,' they said simultaneously.

'You know what you have to do when you say the same words, in the same moment?' Lexie asked.

'I don't,' Tor said, in full big brother mode, 'but I'm guessing you do and can't wait to share.'

'Okay, you have to link pinkies, and . . .'

'Really?' Halley and Tor chorused a second time.

'That's twice in a row. Now you must do as Lexie says, or you'll have seven years bad luck,' Rowan said, entering the spirit of the thing.

'I thought that was when you broke a mirror,' Bryce put in, earning himself a glare from Lexie and Rowan. 'Okay, backing off. Clearly, as a mere male I know nothing about such matters.' He returned to slicing up the cheesecake with a comical, resigned air.

'Exactly. Now, Tor, link your pinkie with Halley's. They obeyed, though Tor's heavy gold signet ring made linking fingers together rather difficult. 'Now, take turns to repeat after me. *Needles*.'

'Needles,' Halley repeated gamely.

'*Pins*. Come on Tor, don't be a party pooper.'

'Pins,' he repeated, pretending to be annoyed.

'*Triplets, twins*.'

'Triplets, twins. Oh, this is embarrassing,' Halley blushed but didn't release Tor's pinkie or break the link.

'*If we marry, our trouble begins*.'

'Ha, that's a good one,' Rowan laughed. 'No getting out of it, either of you.'

Tor looked into Halley's wide-spaced grey eyes and wondered if she felt as embarrassed as he did, or was she experiencing other feelings – pleasurable ones, even? Perhaps remembering his hand brushing against her breast when they'd tussled with the seat belt. And . . .

Get a grip Strachan, he counselled himself.

'*If we marry our trouble begins*,' Lexie repeated, thoroughly in role. 'Pay attention Hector Strachan and say the words.'

Considering that he'd been thinking about his mother's plans for finding him a wife, and how he could avoid them, Tor wondered if this game was his punishment. Laughing, he dismissed the thought and copied Lexie, word for word. 'I don't remember you being this bossy, poor Bryce, you have years of this ahead.'

'I'll live,' Bryce said. He grabbed Lexie in a bear hug, dipped her over his knee and kissed her. She shrugged him off, patently taking the game far too seriously to be distracted. Now it was Halley's turn and Lexie had no intention of letting her off the hook.

'*What goes up a chimney?*'

'What goes up the chimney?' Halley mis-quoted but was forgiven.

'*Smoke*.'

'Smoke,' Tor repeated, considering he'd got off lightly.

'*May your wish and my wish* . . . Halley, your turn.'

'May your wish and my wish . . .'

'*Never be broke*. Repeat it together.'

'It's grammatically incorrect,' Tor said, his face poker straight. 'I don't think I should.'

'T-o-r,' Lexie said, taking a menacing step towards him with a serving spoon full of left-over Thai food.

He grinned over at Halley and nodded, as though counting her in. 'Never be broke,' they said in perfect harmony.

Lexie moved closer and put her hands over theirs, like a minister officiating at a wedding. 'Now kiss.'

Bryce, perhaps sensing that Lexie had gone too far and that Halley might be feeling uncomfortable, broke in. 'I think she's just made that last bit up.'

Rowan took a step closer to Tor and Halley, supporting Lexie. 'No, that's how it goes. Seven years bad luck if you don't do it properly. It's worth a kiss to avert disaster, isn't it?'

'I'd say so,' Tor said, feeling that enough disasters had befallen him. Bending his head, he kissed Halley lightly on the lips. His heart missed a beat as, for one second, he thought she was going to pull back and make him look ridiculous. However, she entered in to the spirit of the game and not only returned the kiss, but deepened it.

Removing her hand, Lexie gurgled, 'Those whom Lexie hath joined together, let no man put asunder.'

'Now it really is time for cake,' Bryce said, sending Lexie a stern look.

Totally unabashed, she walked towards a complicated-looking coffee machine on the counter top. 'You guys take your cake through into the sitting room and Rowan, Bryce and I will make the coffee.'

Doing as instructed by Lexie-the-ringmaster, Tor led the way through a door at the far end of the kitchen and Halley followed. He paused, ensuring they were out of earshot.

'I'm sorry about that. Lexie is incorrigible, she's sees everything through rose-tinted glasses. I hope you weren't too embarrassed.'

Halley laughed. 'No, it was a bit of harmless fun. I can't remember the last time I indulged in that.'

'Me, neither.' He led her over to one of two squashy sofas flanking a massive fireplace where a fire sent out waves of heat. Tor explained, 'Lexie feels the cold, so Bryce is on permanent call as chief stoker, keeping the fire here and the one in the hall going.'

'Doesn't the Dower House have central heating? If I lived permanently in Scotland, I'd probably have it switched on, twenty-four-seven from round about – 'She appeared to be giving the matter serious thought. 'Oh, I don't know, mid-July onwards?' She looked at him as if waiting for enlightenment and then giggled. 'Just kidding. Although, I know that Tam was grateful to Monty for installing central heating and a functioning wood burner after he'd had pneumonia.'

'The least we could do. There's wood and peat in abundance on the estate so, in theory, running fires doesn't cost us a bean. The environment probably takes a hit but we try to offset our carbon footprint by new planting schemes. Frank Bunce,' he tried not to curl his lip at the mention of his name, 'has asked us not to burn peat which is a precious resource and natural habitat for many creatures. So, this could be the last load.'

'That's admirable of him.'

'Yes. Monty's lost interest in the estate, although to be fair, doing more than riding around in the Land Rover has been beyond him for the last couple of years.'

'Tam riding shotgun, I bet.' Halley laughed.

'Always. They were quite a pair and instantly recognisable, Monty in his flat cap and Tam wearing his second-best glengarry. They spent most of their day chewing the fat with any locals or tenants they encountered en route. Or calling in for a swift half at the Strachan Arms.'

'I guess they'd earned that right.'

'Totally. They often dropped by *Beag air bheag*, my home, and we'd spent hours talking about our military adventures, remembering the glory days.' Familiar feelings of bleakness and despondency returned, threatening to ruin the moment but he shrugged them off and held on to how it'd felt when Halley had kissed him. He smiled. 'I'm trying to learn all I can about estate management for when I take over.' He didn't add: *then Bunce can pack his bags and make alternative living arrangements. Mother can take it or leave it.*

'I can't wait to return home,' Halley said, changing the topic. 'November, the first month of the winter season, is known as 'Hooilo'. The daytime temperature is eighty degrees and the night time temperature barely drops below seventy. My star sign is Pisces and I love swimming, especially when the ocean is a balmy seventy-nine degrees.' She looked wistful, as though talking about Hawaii made her homesick.

She would be leaving Lochaber soon and Tor suspected she wouldn't return. The pang of regret he'd experienced at the top of the steps to the beach this morning returned. 'Do you have much free time?'

'I'm on a rota which requires my being on duty for eight-hour stretches, with breaks, obviously,' she smiled, as if to indicate that she wasn't a slave to her work. 'If there's an emergency at the observatory, I have to drop everything and head for the hills, quite literally. The observatory is built on the summit of Haleakalā, which is about three thousand metres in altitude and,' she screwed up her face in concentration, 'above one third of the earth's troposphere. It has excellent astronomical viewing conditions.' She bowed her head over her plate, pushing the cheesecake round her plate with her fork. 'That makes it sound like I don't have a life, but I do.'

Brushing that aside, Tor asked: 'What would constitute an emergency?'

'Well, nothing like the disaster movies on TV where a comet is hurtling toward earth and only a brave astrophysicist can save the world.' Putting her plate on a side table she stood up and adopted a heroic pose – hands on hips and with her face in noble profile. Then she sent him a coquettish look over her shoulder. 'That'd be me, in case you're wondering.'

He laughed. 'All you need is the cape!'

'I could use this tartan throw,' she dragged it off the back of the sofa and draped it over her shoulders before replacing it. 'Perhaps not.'

They both laughed at the thought of her flying through the atmosphere on a mission to save the earth draped in a tartan. Tor wanted to prolong their light-hearted banter. 'You've reminded me of a tattered old Ladybird book Lexie demanded to have read to her every night before bedtime. She knew it word for word and if I left anything out, she'd make me go back to the beginning and start over. Something about a hen rushing round telling everyone the sky was falling in?'

'Chicken Licken! I loved that book. Perhaps that's why I became an astrophysicist? And all this time I thought it was Tam discovering the meteorite in the desert and giving me his prized Observer Book of Astronomy. I rediscovered the book in the tin Monty had for safe keeping.' She looked suddenly thoughtful, as though weighing her words with care. 'You know, you could come visit, my family would be delighted to see you. Lexie and Bryce. Rowan, too.'

But not Lysander or Lady Strachan. The omission was noticeable.

'I'd like that,' was his noncommittal reply. 'When will you be flying home?'

'November 13th. I want to be here for Remembrance Sunday and to stand at the war memorial while the piper plays *Flowers of the Forest,* lay the wreath Rowan's had made for my family and remember Tam.'

Briefly, she looked bereft, then gave herself a shake.

'That leaves you about –' he did a rough calculation, 'ten days to sort out which of Tam's things you'd like us to ship over to Hawaii. By 'us,' I mean Rowan, Lexie, Bryce and myself. The estate staff will help with the heavier items and take anything else to the charity shop.' His spirits lifted, it felt good to be in command again, however briefly. It reminded him how things had been and, hopefully, would be again, although in a different capacity managing the estate.

Being with Halley this evening had raised his spirits and, just as he was enjoying this moment of clear-headedness and uncomplicated conversation, the others joined them in the sitting room with the coffee tray.

'Did I hear you mention Remembrance Sunday?' Lexie asked, plumping herself on the sofa next to Halley.

'Yes, I'm returning home on the thirteenth. That's the plan anyway. It'd cost me a small fortune to change my ticket so I guess I'll be sticking to my schedule.' She pronounced it 'skedual', unconsciously reminding them all that although Scottish by birth and blood, she'd been educated at Massachusetts Institute of Technology and worked in America's fifty-first state for more than half her life.

Some of it was bound to stick.

'Oh, that's too bad. We've hardly had time to get reacquainted.'

'I've just been saying to Tor, you could come visit. There's plenty of room and I'd love to show you round the island.'

'And your telescope?'

'Unfortunately, the observatory is off-limits to members of the public.'

Tor hid that it stung to be relegated to the rank of tourist. 'It sounds idyllic, but I don't know that a dour Scot, such as I, could live there.' The last was pronounced in a thick, highland accent to show he was kidding.

'Oh,' Halley's face dropped as it apparently occurred to her that maybe she'd been laying the ideal living conditions on Hawaii a bit thick. 'No. No, you'd feel right at home because it does rain. Although, mostly at night, unless it's the rainy season.'

'Just like *Camelot*,' Tor said. When she and the others looked puzzled, he explained. 'In the song, doesn't it say that the rain is forbidden until after sundown?'

She responded with an uncertain smile. 'Not sure about that.'

'Don't look so surprised. You don't think an army veteran can have a secret penchant for musicals?'

'N – not at all,' she stammered. Then, meeting his gaze and realising that he was teasing her, she threw a cushion at him which he caught with an easy deftness, 'Why, you, beast!'

'He's such a tease,' Lexie said, linking her arm through Halley's and pulling her closer. Bryce coughed in a meaningful fashion and sent Lexie a long look. 'Oh yes, Bryce wants to show his showroom to you. Don't worry, not the guts and blood side of his workshop, simply the showroom where customers come to buy his Wild Sporrans. Tor, Rowan, you wanna come, too?'

'No, thanks. We've seen them. You guys enjoy yourselves while Tor and I enjoy the roaring fire and finish off our cheesecake.'

'Okay. Help yourselves to a sticky. There's quite a selection on the court cupboard.'

It was plain that Halley had no idea what a 'sticky' was. Rowan quickly enlightened her. 'She means an after-dinner liqueur. I won't have one as I'm driving but I might have another coffee. Tor?'

'Same goes for me.'

Although he answered Rowan, his gaze followed Halley as she left, taking light and happiness with her. Time was running out, so he'd better make the most of it. Then, remembering his manners, he turned to Rowan and started discussing Remembrance Sunday when Rowan would be joining them at the local memorial with her brownie pack.

Chapter Twenty-three

Bryce unlocked a brick building a little way from the house and switched on the lights. Halley braced herself for what she might find there. However, much to her relief there were no carcasses laid out on marble slabs dripping blood. Instead, there was an impressive collection of pristine sporrans hanging from deer antlers fastened to the workshop's pine cladded walls.

Lexie took Halley's hand and squeezed it reassuringly.

'Not quite what you were expecting?' Bryce asked. The effort of addressing Halley and seeking her opinion of what was clearly his passion made his cheeks flush almost as red as his hair. Sidling over to Bryce's side, Lexie smiled as if, like Bryce, she'd been worried that Halley would fail to be less than impressed by their cottage industry.

Wandering over to a beautifully crafted badger head sporran lying on a side bench Halley picked it up, opening the flap. 'I've seen these in books, most impressive.'

Openly pleased by Halley's reaction, Bryce and Lexie relaxed, leaving Halley to assume that in the past they'd borne the brunt of negative comments about their means of supporting themselves.

'There are portraits in the Long Gallery of Strachans in full military uniform sporting badger head sporrans. I'll give you a tour of my illustrious ancestors before you leave,' Lexie promised.

'I'd like that,' Halley assured her.

Lexie gave Bryce another affectionate squeeze. 'Bryce gives each animal a unique expression and tries to make them look individual. I usually choose the eyes.' Moving away, she opened a drawer in a tall cabinet to show Halley a selection of glass eyes.

'You're a great team,' Halley said, meaning every word.

Finding his confidence, Bryce moved from behind the counter and expanded on Lexie's brief introduction. 'Sporrans were originally made of seal skin but when that became hard to come by, craftsmen had to improvise. It takes me roughly six weeks to make a sporran and I have a waiting list for some of the rarer examples.' He glanced over at Lexie who gave him the thumbs up.

'As vegetarians and animal lovers we would never kill an animal for its skin,' Lexie explained, her expression serious. 'The skins we use are ethically sourced and the animals have either died a natural death or are road kill. Some are left over from the game and farming industries or are re-used from old bags people donate. Originally, we called the business Road Kill Sporrans but that gave *quite* the wrong impression.'

'Now we call our business, *MacPherson's Wild Sporrans*. You see,' Bryce's passion became more evident as his confidence grew, 'if I didn't make use of these skins the animals would be thrown into a ditch and their natural beauty wasted. Naturally, protected species, even dead ones, need the required license. Should anyone find a dead animal and be unsure if it requires a licence to handle it or not, they bring it over to us and I do the rest. I have contacts within the various departments at Scottish Natural Heritage in Inverness who are happy to help out.'

'I'm impressed,' Halley commented, wandering round the showroom and stroking the muzzle of a fox head sporran. 'How much does each sporran sell for?'

'It depends on the species. Usually, a badger or fox sporran would sell for two hundred and fifty pounds. Once, I was lucky enough to be given a mink pelt and was able to sell that sporran for four hundred and fifty pounds.'

'Well done for turning your passion for wild life into a profitable business.' Halley was all the more impressed because she gathered that they had money in trust left by their grandparents and didn't need to work. Unlike Lysander they'd chosen to make something of their lives. Putting him from her mind she turned back to Lexie. 'I'd love to see the portraits in the Long Gallery before I leave. But only if –' she bit her lip.

'Only if mother is somewhere else?'

'Exactly.'

'I can arrange that.'

Lexie signalled for Bryce to skedaddle into his workshop. Grinning, he complied after rooting in a drawer and producing a couple of business cards. 'I can't see sporrans fitting in with grass skirts. But you never know.'

'Thanks,' Halley responded with an amused grin, putting the cards in her handbag. Once Bryce was in the next room, Lexie launched herself at Halley and embraced her.

'What's this in aid of?' she asked.

Although by now she realised that Lexie was a force of nature and hugs and kisses came with the territory. Hugs and kisses she hadn't received as a child, perhaps? Lady Strachan didn't strike her as the maternal type and Halley guessed that Little Lexie had pretty much been left to fend for herself before being packed off to boarding school.

'Just to say thanks, for what you've done for Tor.'

'Why . . . what exactly do you think I've done?'

'I haven't seen Tor so relaxed in months, not since leaving the Rehabilitation Centre at Stanford Hall and coming home to recuperate. He's got a long way to go – physically and mentally but tonight I caught flashes of the old Tor. That's down to you, Halley. Somehow, you've managed to bring him out of the dark place he's occupied since he was wounded.'

'I didn't do anything out of the ordinary,' Halley confessed. 'And since we met, I've acted naturally – if knocking him out on the beach and arguing with him every time we meet can be regarded as acting naturally. Take some credit yourself, Lexie, the business with '*needles and pins*' was an icebreaker.'

'I couldn't believe it when Tor kissed you. Normally to get him to do anything like that would be like leading him to the gallows.'

Halley shook her head and laughed. 'Well, I hope it wasn't too unpleasant,' she joked.

'You both kind've looked like you were enjoying yourselves,' Lexie sent her a teasing look.

'But no more. Okay?'

'Okay.' Lexie's brown eyes twinkled in a manner which suggested that she wouldn't be able to keep her promise.

'Whatever you've done – braining him, kissing him, arguing with him, has helped in some small way to bring him back to us and towards, hopefully one day, leading a semi-normal life. One where he can stop reliving, in horrific technicolour, the moment when the IEDs went off. One where he can stop blaming himself for not keeping a tighter rein on an inexperienced, second lieutenant who led the men into a death trap. Each step forward, however small, is progress.'

This was a Lexie she'd never seen before – serious, thoughtful and concerned about her brother. She'd only been in Lochaber eight days but so much had happened that it seemed as if she'd lived here forever. 'You seem to know a lot about veterans suffering from PTSD,' she said to Lexie.

'I've made it my business to find out. The Strachans are a military family first and foremost, being highland landowners come second. When I show you the portraits in the Long Gallery, you'll understand. I want to help Tor and other veterans as much as I can. That goes for Bryce, too. In fact, we give some of our profits each month to Help for Heroes.' Releasing Halley from her embrace she walked over to the door. 'Shall we return to the house?'

'Of course.' Halley frowned, feeling a bit of a phoney.

She'd simply been herself and had joined in with Lexie's game in the spirit intended and without dying of embarrassment. Due to the circumstances which brought her to Lochaber she hadn't really been able to relax, be herself. Anyone who didn't know her must think her another dull, buttoned-up scientist who didn't have a life. As for Lysander, he simply saw her as an opportunity to escape the constrains of married life, fertility treatment and relive the past.

She owed as much to Tor as he did to her. He'd helped her through the funeral and wake, shielded her from his mother's wrath over Tam's bequest and told his father to stop questioning her reasons for staying away from Lochaber. If he would only accept there was nothing between her and Lysander they could truly relax in each other's company and, who knows, even shake hands when she left.

That was a big ask.

Putting that thought aside, she followed Lexie out of the workshop and back to the Dower House.

Rowan and Tor were seated opposite each other on the matching sofas, laughing over a shared memory of Tam and Monty. Both looked very relaxed and at ease in each other's company. Halley was glad she and Rowan had remained friends, she would be able to get updates on the Strachans, especially Tor's rehabilitation, during monthly zoom calls.

'I was wondering,' she began, speaking to Lexie. 'I'd love to order a sporran for my father. But I'm not sure of the import regulations covering such things.'

'Bryce can help you there,' Lexie offered.

'That'd be great. Thanks.'

'Would he have much use for it?' Tor inquired.

Halley grinned. 'He would. Don't laugh; there's a Caledonian Society in Hawaii. My father is an active member, raising funds for the Scottish Education Research Grant which awards bursaries to young people for study related to Scotland.'

'Such as?' Tor asked, looking very interested.

'Organic farming, a study of Gaelic at a college in Scotland and, my personal favourite, a re-creation of the route taken by David Balfour in Robert Louis Stevenson's novel Kidnapped.'

'Of course, I'd forgotten that Robert Louis Stevenson and Captain Cook visited the islands,' Rowan added. 'Halley's father usually hosts a Burns Night Supper at their house overlooking the ocean . . .'

'. . . complete with kilts, haggis and bagpipes. Father recites lines from Tam O'Shanter, much to everyone's amusement as he really hams it up and lays on his Scottish accent. There's also a soup supper, movie night, or a ceilidh organised throughout the year to remind us of Alba.

I'm guessing that when I return, I'll be invited to bring everyone up to date on my visit and Tam's highland funeral.'

She glanced over at Tor remembering that, only yesterday, she'd taken great pains to deny her Scottishness and his angry reaction – *Doesn't Scottish blood beat thickly in your veins. Don't you feel as though part of you belongs here?* She lowered her gaze, not wanting him to guess her reason for denying her inheritance.

'Perhaps we could sponsor a young islander to come over for the summer to learn how farming works on the estate,' Lexie suggested. 'Even make a donation to the Society?' She looked at Tor for confirmation.

'I think that's a great idea,' he responded. 'Maybe Halley could liaise with members of the Society?'

'My father would be delighted to work with you on that project now he's retired. I'm afraid my time is pretty much taken up with my work at the observatory.'

'What exactly do you do there?' Lexie asked, sitting on the arm of the sofa next to Rowan.

'I spend most of my time looking beyond our solar system for planets capable of sustaining life. It's a standing joke among female astrophysicists that finding an exoplanet is a cinch compared with finding the one-in-a-billion man capable of making us happy.'

'Oh, that seems a wee bit cynical, Halley,' Lexie said in a sad tone, flicking a glance at Tor, and Halley knew she'd dropped a clanger.

Female astrophysicists needed a thick skin and a well-developed, wry sense of humour to stay ahead in the profession. It helped keep them upbeat in a male-dominated world where they were passed over and often patronised. She needed to remember she was in mixed company and had no axe to grind with Tor or Bryce. Quite the opposite.

Time to mend fences.

'Bryce is your exoplanet, Lexie. You're one of the lucky ones.'

Rowan, obviously sensing the chill in the air, changed the subject. 'I meant to ask, is Tor planning a firework display for November the Fifth?'

'I am.'

'Can I bring my brownie pack?'

'Of course.' He smiled, showing that he was relaxed in her company.

'And,' Rowan half-turned to speak to Halley who was standing by the door. 'If it's not too much trouble, could I bring my pack along an hour or so earlier? I've checked the weather forecast and November the Fifth should be cold and frosty with clear skies. Identifying constellations is one element towards gaining their Space badge.'

'I'd love to. Let me check what time the International Space Station passes overhead and we can combine the two activities.'

'Make those three activities,' Lexie said. 'Bryce and I usually make hotdogs for everyone and your brownies and their parents would be welcome, too.'

'Better let Mrs Richardson know in advance and she'll help.' Plainly, Tor knew the limits of Lexie's culinary and organisation powers.

'The girls will love it,' Rowan said, enthusiastically.

'That's settled then.' Tor put his hands on his knees, pushing himself off the sofa. 'Time Halley and I headed for the hills. Thanks for a great evening, Lexie, parlour games included.' Laughing he glanced at Halley as if to assess that she hadn't taken offence at Lexie's game. She grinned back to show that she was a good sport.

And not in the least offended

In fact, the way Tor linked their names together – *Halley and I*, had without warning, made her acutely aware of him. His height, the breadth of his shoulders, how his thick blond hair touched the collar of his shirt. When his eyes briefly met hers, a frisson of reaction travelled through her. The quiver, unexpected and unasked for, alarmed her with its intensity. She looked away and was glad when Lexie collected their coats from the hall.

'T– thanks,' was all she could manage. Picking up her handbag she pretended to root around in it and hoped that no one had noticed her reaction.

'Will you be okay?' Lexie whispered to Tor as he wrapped a long, striped scarf around his neck and pulled it up over his chin.

'I'd better be, hadn't I?' was his grim reply.

From the tenor of their voices Halley guessed that they weren't referring to him driving her home.

'Trial by fire?' Lexie asked.

'Something like that,' was Tor's response as he bent his head and kissed her. Then he opened the front door, letting in the cold, still November air and indicated that Rowan should precede him out of the Dower House. 'Thanks for picking up the takeaway, Ro. Has Lexie settled up with you?'

Rowan blushed to the roots of her hair at being the focus of his attention.

'It's my treat. You can pay next time.' Tor kissed her on both cheeks, walked her to her car and waved her off.

'Me next,' Halley joked, giving Lexie a hug. 'Don't forget to mention my dad's sporran to Bryce. I know he'd love a fox head one in time for next year's Burns Night Supper, if Bryce can sort out the customs duties. Yes, I'm ready,' she said to Tor who was waiting at the door. She was anxious to climb into the Land Rover unaided, there'd been enough physical contact between them tonight.

Tor reached the Land Rover and opened the passenger door. He had a brief tussle with the seat belt to make sure it wouldn't snag this time. They buckled up and drove through the waves at the end of the shore, commenting that the tide was on the turn. Halley put her hands in her pockets to keep them warm and curled her fingers round the keys to the Salmon Bothy.

'Quite a day,' he added, 'however you choose to look at it.'

'I agree. A lot to think about.'

'I hope you enjoyed yourself?'

'Oh yes, Lexie is a real sweetie. It was kind of you to include Rowan, I know she sometimes feels lonely. I wish she could find someone to settle down with. Someone who would share the burden of her work, too, but that's a big ask.'

Tor laughed. 'The extremely rare exoplanet-boyfriend who fancies being an undertaker?'

'Now you're teasing me, but yes.'

'I hope the same for her. She's a great girl, or should I say woman?'

'I still think of us both as the girls we once were.' She frowned at the clumsy sentence.

'I wish I could remember more about you and what you were like back in the day. But then, it all seems so long ago . . .'

'There's nothing to remember. Really. You were posted abroad, I was about to take up my place at MIT and spent most of the summer on the beach getting a tan.'

'Still . . .' He gave the matter some thought and then dismissed it from his mind. 'So, what does tomorrow hold for you?'

'Packing,' she sighed. 'Labelling. More packing. I'm glad I'll have the brownies to give me something to do. I'll prepare some fun worksheets and have them photocopied in Mallaig.'

'No need. There's a copier in the estate office. When you're ready, give me a bell or drop them off and I'll have them photocopied for you. I think we can probably stretch to putting them in a folder and including a couple of pens with the estate logo on them for the brownies to keep.'

'Thanks, that'll be great.' She didn't add – let me know when the coast is clear and I can avoid another confrontation with your mother. His oblique look suggested that he knew exactly what she was thinking.

'Here we are,' he said as the salmon bothy hove into view.

'No need to get out, I can manage from here. Goodnight.'

'Goodnight, Halley. Don't forget about the photocopying.'

'I won't.'

She climbed down out of the vehicle and retrieved the keys of the bothy from her pocket. He waited until she'd opened the door and stepped inside then he revved up the engine and with a sharp toot on the horn drove off. Closing the door behind her and locking it, Halley wondered if she should have told him about the lights on the beach and the outboard motors she'd heard earlier. She shrugged off the notion, deciding it was probably night fishermen and not worth mentioning.

Nevertheless, she walked back to the door to double check that she'd locked it. She was a woman living on her own and it was sensible to take all necessary precautions.

Chapter Twenty-four

Two days later on Sunday morning, Rowan and Lexie rocked up at the bothy. Halley had spent the days in between packing and labelling Tam's belongings. It was unusually clement for November and she had a long walk along the shore planned, taking photos to post on Instagram. However, finding she was in the mood for easy company she welcomed Lexie and Rowan with open arms.

'Come away in,' she said, opening the door wider.

'*Come away in?* Did ye hear that, Rowan, she's beginning to speak like a native. Mebe we willnae let her leave on the thirteenth, we'll keep her prisoner and burn her return ticket to Hawaii.'

'Not a bad idea,' Rowan agreed, entering the bothy and casting an approving eye over Halley's thorough packing. The central kitchen-cum-sitting room looked bare and Tam's clothing, bedlinen and other personal belongings were arranged neatly on his bed ready for the charity shop or to be sent on to Hawaii. His best uniform hung on the outside of the wardrobe because Halley wasn't quite sure what to do with it. Should she send it home to her father as a family heirloom – if that wasn't too grand a notion, or give it to Monty? 'You certainly look ready to move on,' Rowan commented, trying to remain cheerful in the face of losing her dear friend again.

'I am,' Halley said, mirroring her expression. 'Nothing else for it.'

'Agreed. However, this all looks final and very sad.' Lexie added.

Halley had stacked everything that wasn't needed between now and when she left at the far end of the kitchen counter, leaving just enough room to cook breakfast or prepare a light meal. Typically, as a last act for his old friend and lover, Monty had insisted on covering all the shipping expenses.

Rowan walked over to Tam's collection of battered pots and pans. 'I can just picture Tam standing by the stove using this frying pan to cook slap up breakfasts on cold winter days. Once, I got into major trouble for washing it with soap and water.'

'Same here,' Halley smiled. 'Tam said it destroyed the pan's finish. It was a combination of salt and vegetable oil to clean it or nothing.'

Lexie wandered round the room touching things. 'Have you noticed how echo-y it sounds? How empty? As though Tam has finally moved on.' In that moment, every inch the fey highlander who believed in an afterlife, she pulled Halley and Rowan into a group hug. They stood in silence in the middle of the bothy, each remembering Tam in their own way.

Unbidden, a great sob rose in Halley's throat. There was unfinished business between her and her great-uncle, things she should have told him. Instead, she'd played the coward and would have to live with that knowledge; that was her punishment. Perhaps that was why her father had sent her over in his stead, knowing she had to achieve closure. Breaking free of Lexie's embrace she walked over to the wag-at-the-wall clock, ostensibly to check the label attached to it but in reality to gather herself together.

'*For Monty*,' she read, her voice thick with emotion. 'I was kinda hoping that Monty might find a place for it in the Laird's Smoking Room.'

'Isn't it a Dunbar heirloom?' Rowan asked, joining her by the clock. 'Tam used to tell us stories of when his family lived in Belfast.' That he should have shared those stories with them and not her, only made Halley feel more wretched. 'He would pull the kitchen chair over to the clock so I, or Lexie, could stand on it. Then he'd show us how to wind it up.' Feeling behind the clock she retrieved a key hanging from a length of hairy string. 'Good; it's still there.'

'If I remember the story correctly, Tam's great-grandfather, my four times great-grandfather, brought it over from Belfast when the Peacocks set up home in Glasgow. Heirloom? Probably not. Precious? Most certainly. I think Tam would want Monty to have it,'

'I only hope mother doesn't knock it off the wall, accidently-on-purpose, when she dusts the room,' Lexie said, pulling a face. 'Not that she'd know one end of a duster from another, or what a can of furniture polish looks like. I can't imagine she'll relish having anything of Tam's in the castle.'

'I suppose not,' Halley said.

'It'll work out fine, Monty's no pushover. What's this?' Rowan asked, picking several worksheets up from the table in an obvious attempt to distract them. Halley guessed that she was used to dealing with bereaved relatives and knew that distraction generally worked.

'Colouring sheets and a fun quiz for your brownies to complete after we return from the beach. I've worked out that the International Space Station will pass overhead well before the barbeque and fireworks. We can fine-tune everything before you leave today, Rowan. Tor said that if I drop the worksheets off at the estate office, he'd ask one of the secretaries to put together a little stationery pack for each brownie.'

'You can never have too many felt tip pens,' Lexie grinned.

Halley smiled, but was lost in her own thoughts. She'd half-expected Tor to drop by the morning after the meal at the Dower House, however, he'd been a no-show. He was probably busy, she reasoned, yet . . .

Was it crazy to feel let down after they'd been getting on so well? He'd said that when the worksheets were ready to 'give him a bell' and he'd do the rest. However, she hadn't done that, preferring to revert to default position of not being beholden to anyone, not even the heir to *Creag na h-Iolaire*. If the three of them dropped the worksheets off at the estate office it looked less obvious.

She thought back to the game they'd played in the Dower House. *Those whom Lexie has joined together let no man put asunder?* That's all it'd been – a game. In spite of that she'd spent two sleepless nights remembering the touch of his lips, the feather of desire which had uncurled in the pit of her stomach and how she'd kissed him back without a second thought.

What had she been thinking?

Unquestionably there'd been a slight thawing in the permafrost since she'd knocked him out on the beach and she'd be eternally grateful for the support he'd given her afterwards at Tam's funeral. However, she was leaving soon and the burgeoning relationship she'd spent the last two days over-thinking, would disappear like scotch mist.

Which was a good thing, right?

'You okay, Halley. You seem,' Rowan sent her a concerned look, 'preoccupied.'

'I'm fine. Got a lot on my mind, packing up Tam's life has been quite emotional.'

Rowan was immediately contrite. 'Stupid comment. Of course, it's only to be expected, he's lived here for the last thirty years, give or take. You're not only packing up his belongings, you're dismantling his life and that can be very upsetting.'

'We would have been around to help, but Tor said that you'd probably want – need – time on your own. But we're here to help now so tell us what we can do.'

'He was right, actually.' Halley quickly put their minds at rest.

'He generally is.' Lexie grinned over at Rowan for confirmation and she nodded. 'Bloody annoying, to be fair. Come on, let's head over to the estate office.'

Then Lexie fetched Halley's coat off the hook on the back of the door and held it up so she could slip into it. With that, restless spirits, family heirlooms and sadness engendered by the passing of a beloved uncle were, for the moment, put aside.

Frank Bunce was in the estate office pouring over accounts with one of the secretaries when they swept in. He put down his pen, stood up and put on a welcoming smile, although clearly annoyed at being interrupted. 'Good morning, ladies, I wasn't expecting visitors this morning.' He straightened his tie and ran his right hand through his hair, checking his reflection in the window.

Lexie took the worksheets off Halley and passed them over to Bunce. 'Can you make,' she glanced over at Rowan, 'fifteen copies of these?'

'Twelve will be enough,' Rowan replied. 'Could you also reserve and mark one set as the master copy so I can use them in subsequent years? I don't see Halley returning annually on November the Fifth bonfire for a stargazing session.'

'More's the pity,' Lexie added.

Bunce gave Halley a swift once-over and smiled, but the smile didn't quite convince. Perhaps he didn't like Lexie and Rowan telling him what to do. Or, maybe the thought of Halley making an annual pilgrimage to take the brownies stargazing held no appeal. 'Of course,' he executed an ironic little bow. 'Tor explained everything before he left for church with Sir Monty and Lady Strachan. Jane here,' he indicated the woman seated at the large partners' desk, 'has made up a pack for the wee ones.'

'Major Strachan's instructions were pretty specific,' she added, getting up and walking over to a table by the window where folders, felt tip pens, pencils and individual clipboards were set out. Now Halley felt that she'd misjudged him and gave herself a mental ticking-off.

'That's really kind of Tor, of you all,' she smiled.

'My brownie pack will be really excited to receive these things and go star gazing.' Rowan removed the worksheets from Halley and handed them over to Jane.

'We're going up to the castle. Any chance everything will be ready by the time we return in, say, an hour?' Lexie inquired. 'Rowan's parked in the stable yard so she can put everything straight into her car.'

'Of course,' Jane replied. 'I wouldn't normally be here on a Sunday but I had some paperwork to catch up on. So, it's worked out perfectly.'

'Sir Monty and Lady Strachan are going straight from church to the MacKinnon's for lunch. I mention it, in case you wanted them for anything.' Bunce's tone was over-officious as though he didn't think Lexie and her friends should be wandering round the castle when the laird and his wife were absent.

'No, that's fine. There's something I want to show Halley and it'll be easier without Mother being there.' It was plain that Lexie didn't like his tone and didn't bother to hide it.

'Anything I can help with?' Bunce asked. Lexie shook her head and Halley frowned. Had she got the relationship between Bunce and Lexie, wrong? Was he her biological father? If so, she seemed keen to keep him at arm's length whereas the times she'd observed Lexie with Monty, a teasing, loving relationship was apparent. Perhaps Lexie preferred to think of herself as the laird's daughter and not the result of a scandalous liaison between Lady Strachan and the factor.

It was all too D.H. Lawrence for words.

Ah, well – families, schm-amilies, Halley mused, then replied: 'No, thank you.'

'Very well, I'll leave you girls to it.'

His use of 'girls' was clearly designed to patronise and remind them of their – his – place in the pecking order: *Creag na h-lolaire's* factor, Lady Strachan's lover and the biological father to her two youngest children. A man biding his time until . . . Halley's brow creased – until? Monty died and Tor tried to run the estate and found it too much for a man with mental and physical scars? Would Bunce, aided and abetted by Lady Strachan who clearly had no desire to live in the Dower House, take over the running of the estate, set themselves up in the castle while Tor lived in his Airstream on the side of the loch?

There was no time for further thought as Lexie turned on her heel and marched out of the estate office, leaving Halley and Rowan with little choice but to follow.

She led them across the stable yard to *Creag's* stone keep, pausing at the foot of a stone staircase seemingly carved out of the wall, each step worn down by the tread of feet over hundreds of years. The staircase ended half way up the wall and to the left there was a large, nail-studded door. Lexie climbed the staircase with aplomb, suggesting that she'd done so countless times, signalling for them to follow. This they did, taking great care as the steps were shallow and there was no banister to hold on to. Once at the top, Lexie indicated that each person should stand on a separate step to give her room. Then, producing a large key, unlocked the door and invited them in to the castle.

Once inside, she ushered them down a vaulted corridor carved out of the body of the keep, stopped by a box bed carved into the wall and laughed. 'For the night porter, to make sure undesirables didn't enter the castle uninvited. Although, we just have! Come on.' They passed under several arches until Lexie stopped by a yett gate, similar to the one separating the kitchen from the cellars and stores. Unlocking it, she gestured for them to go ahead and then re-locked it from their side.

Eyes wide, taking in every fascinating architectural detail of the oldest part of the castle, Halley and Rowan crossed a landing high above ground level, went through another door and found themselves in the Long Gallery.

'Welcome to the Hall of Ancestors,' Lexie said with a dramatic flourish. 'Or as Tor and I refer to it: *Rogues' Gallery.*'

'Did someone take my name in vain?' Tor appeared through a door at the other end of the gallery.

'Tor! Yay.' Lexie threw herself at her brother with her usual enthusiasm.

'Tell me that I didn't just see you leading Halley and Rowan up the steps of the keep?'

'You didn't just see me leading Halley and Rowan up the steps of the keep,' Lexie mimicked with a cheeky grin.

'Key,' he commanded, holding out his hand.

'Tor . . .'

'Lexie . . .' Tor responded, though he looked over her head and winked at the others to show this was a time-honoured routine. Sighing, Lexie handed over the key and he put it in the pocket of his waxed jacket. Intuition told Halley that Lexie would soon have it in her possession again, once Tor's guard was down.

'What – apart from trying to break your necks by climbing that dangerous staircase, are you ladies doing here on a Sunday afternoon when you could be out having fun?'

'I wanted to show Halley our ancestors and to answer a question she posed to me the other day.'

'Which was?' Walking over to one of the window embrasures overlooking the front of the castle Tor perched on top of a radiator, folded his arms and waited for Lexie's reply.

'Why Lysander has a Greek name when we're all Scottish through and through. Like a stick of Portobello rock.' Tor glanced over at Halley and frowned, as though her continued interest in Lysander bothered him. Halley sent him back an answering straight look which warned: don't go there. Evidently catching this exchange and picking up the vibe even if she didn't understand the reason behind it, Lexie was quick to explain. 'I mentioned that our three names: Hector, Lysander and Alexandra come from the song – The British Grenadiers. You know: *Some talk of Alexander and some of Hercules, of Hector and Lysander and such great names as these,*' she sang and then giggled. 'Monty chose our names; I'm just glad that he didn't decide to call me Hercules.'

Tor laughed, his good humour seemingly restored. 'I seem to remember Monty had an evil cat called Hercules, who liked to bite guests' ankles under the dinner table. As for my name, one of our more remote ancestors was Hector the Red. That's him.' Pushing himself to his feet he walked over to an ancient, one-dimensional portrait of a shifty looking character whose eyes sloped down at the corners. His pasty, yellowing skin and wispy ginger beard did him no favours. 'Not much of a looker, is he? However, we owe everything to him and the unfortunate heiress forced to marry him. She brought the money into the family while he received the charter for the land and the castle from Robert the Bruce, allegedly as a reward for fighting alongside him in the Scottish Wars of Independence.'

Halley shivered. 'No disrespect to your ancestors but I would have hated to live in those times. Women were regarded as chattels to be used and disposed of as their lord and master saw fit.'

Lexie clasped her hands together. 'Do you remember telling me about the poor wee Maid of Norway, the legitimate heir to the Scottish throne who died of seasickness when they shipped her over from Norway to marry Edward the First's son? She was only seven years old,' she explained to Halley and Rowan, looking so upset as though it had happened only yesterday.

'I remember you crying for days on end and my receiving a roasting from Mother for telling you the story. Lexie has such a kind heart,' he ruffled her hair as they stood by the portrait of Red Hector. 'I hope you don't detect a family resemblance?' he asked the other two, turning his head to the left and showing his profile.

'Now you come to mention it,' Rowan quipped, straight-faced, 'I wondered where I'd seen him before.' It was all nonsense, of course. Tor Strachan was tall, blond and, apart from his leg injury the perfect example of a Heilan' Laddie. Whereas his ancestor looked as though a bout of winter flu would carry him off.

'Red Hector was granted the power of 'pit and gallows' by The Bruce. Which meant he could drown or hang local wrongdoers without worrying too much about the consequences.'

'Happy days,' was Halley's dry response. 'I suppose the 'red' referred to him having blood on his hands?'

'It could simply mean that he had red hair. Although, legend has it that he was a fearsome warrior, setting the tone for Strachan men who, through the ages, have been better soldiers than lairds.' He walked along the length of the gallery pointing out various ancestors in the uniforms of their regiments, including his ancestor who joined the Sutherland Regiment in 1794. He paused by the last but one portrait, a magnificent oil of Monty in uniform sitting in a large chair with Tam, as his batman, holding his 'feathered bonnet', the regiment's version of a bearskin, in his hands.

Both looked immensely proud of their achievements as soldiers.

'May I?' Retrieving her iPhone Halley took a couple of snaps. 'My family has never seen this portrait and they'd love a copy.'

'Be my guest,' Tor replied, moving on.

Halley snapped away then put her phone back in her bag. She could only imagine how the portrait must grate with Lady Strachan and experienced a glimmer of sympathy for her. Then her attention was drawn to a block canvas of two soldiers leaning back against the massive wheels of an army vehicle, sitting on ochre sand with their legs stretched out in front, smiling. This wasn't an oil painting like the others in the gallery, but a photograph turned into a canvas and made to look like a painting.

The soldier in the forefront was Hector Strachan looking tanned and healthy, his hair bleached almost white by the sun. His eyes were startlingly blue in his tanned face, giving him the confident air of a man at ease in a difficult and hazardous environment. A man who relished danger because it tested him and helped him discover the limits of his courage; who he was.

Halley retrieved her phone from her bag and took another photo. There was something very personal about taking the snap of this Hector; a Hector she had never known. It quite literally took her breath away and her hand was shaking as she slipped the phone into her pocket.

'I love this photo of Tor.' Lexie put her arm around her brother's waist and laid her head on his arm. 'It was taken in Helmand Province, that's his sergeant sitting alongside him. I like to think of it as a modern take on Monty and Tam's portrait. Tor sent the photo in an email and I had it enlarged and made into this canvas for his thirtieth birthday. He won't let the family commission a portrait in oils of him in the Strachan tradition because . . .'

'. . . because this one is totally authentic, captures a moment in time and doesn't need to be embellished.' Tor finished Lexie's sentence, kissing the top of her head to show that he was simply stating a fact, nothing more. Halley moved over to the canvas and studied it more closely. Had Tor added, *'it shows a time when I was happy, really happy,'* she would have understood.

'Where were you twelve years ago?' he asked Halley, moving on and deflecting her interest away from the canvas.

She turned to face him. 'Twelve years ago? Let me think. I'd finished my degree and decided to stay on at MIT and study for a PhD, encouraged by my parents, naturally. They were in no hurry to see me settle down, get married and have a f-family.' She tripped over the word, swallowed and continued. 'They knew I was, still am, ambitious and wanted me to go as far as I could.'

'Then what?' He appeared genuinely interested and not simply framing questions to lead to the million-dollar jackpot, the big tamale: why *have* you stayed away so long?

'Then my parents decided it was time to retire and they moved to Hawaii. I was lucky enough to secure a position at the Haleakalā Observatory on the exoplanet programme and the rest is history. They give guest lectures from time to time but feel that they've earned the right to retire to a beautiful place where . . .'

'. . . it never rains until after the sun goes down and the water temperature is something only wild swimmers can dream of?'

'Got it in one.' She laughed, happy that the photograph hadn't drawn him back to a time when it seemed his army career would go all the way and he'd achieve the rank of brigadier, just like Monty. After one last look at the canvas, she turned to face them. 'Before I leave, you must all promise to come and stay with the Dunbars. My parents would expect nothing less. I will accept nothing less.'

'It's a bit tricky for someone in my line of work to take time off,' Rowan pulled a rueful face. 'However, with forward planning and calling in a few favours, I think I could manage it.'

'Good,' Halley replied. Seemingly that wasn't enough for Lexie as she took Tor's hand, laid it over Halley's and then put her and Rowan's hand on top.

'Let's make a pact. A promise to get together next summer, come hell or high water.' There was a murmur of agreement, if no definite commitment, however she seemed happy to settle for that. She removed her hand from Rowan's who, in turn, removed hers from Tor's and they both took a step back.

Halley looked down at their hands, Tor's signet ring catching the light. She recalled the kiss which, although engineered by Lexie, had felt so natural. Fleetingly, it seemed as if she was in a dream world, suspended in the moment, acutely aware that her time in Lochaber was running out.

She wasn't sure if any of them would meet again; that saddened her and cast the present into sharp relief. Snapping out of her reverie, she realised Tor still had his hand over hers and appeared in no hurry to remove it . . .

Until, that is, the door opened and Lysander slithered into the Long Gallery.

Chapter Twenty-five

'I guess my invitation's in the post,' Lysander commented, closing the door behind him.

'Nothing as formal as that, simply an impromptu gathering,' Tor said calmly, suggesting he was used to pacifying his brother. He removed his hand from Halley's and slipped it into his pocket. Halley wasn't sure if that was for her, or Lysander's, benefit.

'Not that it's got anything to do with you.' Lexie butted in. 'I simply wanted Halley to see the painting of Monty and Tam.'

Ignoring her, Lysander rounded on Halley. 'I expect you're wondering why I'm not featured on the Wonder Wall.'

'Wonder Wall? Oh, you mean the portraits? To be honest, it hadn't crossed my mind.' Lysander looked as though he was spoiling for a fight and she didn't want to give him an excuse. 'I notice that Lexie isn't there, either.'

Lysander regarded her as though she was simple-minded. ''Course she isn't, she's female; spinster of this parish. Unless Bryce,' he curled his lip, 'can put his taxidermy to one side long enough to marry her. Look round, you'll see only male Strachans featured on these hallowed walls.'

Lexie, apparently smarting from his last remark, came back with, 'What he should have said, is that only Strachans who've fought for their country are hung on these walls. Lysander didn't finish officer training at Sandhurst.'

He swatted her comment away as though it was of no importance 'And, as you can see, Tor-zan has taken up the last space on the wall.'

'T-Torzan?' Halley unintentionally fed Lysander his next line.

'Yes. Hector the Hero, our homegrown all-round Action Man.' He gave a derisive snort. 'This gallery is a tad too *Game of Thrones* for me, as I'm sure you'll agree, Halley? Actually, I'd welcome your opinion as an outsider.'

Halley wasn't too pleased to be described as an outsider, no matter how true it was. Lysander was in a vile mood and she wondered how she'd ever imagined herself in love with him. Then she cut herself some slack, all that happened a long time ago and . . .

Tor, clearly deciding this had gone on long enough, joined the conversation.

'Have you been drinking, Lysander? I can smell the fumes from here.' Pushing back the sleeve of his waxed jacket he glanced at his watch. 'It can't be communion wine as you've haven't been to church, so I'm guessing you've been making inroads on Monty's whisky.'

'For your information, we have our own whisky in our wing of the castle. Anyway, back off. Halley has no need of you riding to her rescue. We are old friends; right, Hal?'

Halley glanced at the other three. Lexie looked as if she was hearing this news for the first time. Rowan seemed embarrassed on Halley's behalf and Tor looked displeased by Lysander's use of 'Hal' which hinted at a relationship.

Deciding that returning to the previous conversation was safer, Halley continued. 'In answer to your original question, Lysander, I don't find the portraits in the least over the top. Or, *too* Game of Thrones. If your portrait hung there, I'm sure you'd feel differently.'

'Fat chance of that,' was his response. 'The last space, as I pointed out, was reserved for Hector the Hero.'

Rowan joined in the conversation in an obvious attempt to keep the peace. 'I think the portrait gallery is a great way to remember Strachans over the centuries.'

'You'll be reminding me next that ancestor worship is a religion in certain cultures. What do you think, Halley?' Striking a belligerent pose he put Halley on the spot.

'Not my area of expertise. I'm an astrophysicist, not an historian.'

'Of course, I'd forgotten, you're Doctor Dunbar now, aren't you?

Major Strachan and Doctor Dunbar – how will the rest of us survive without a title and a guaranteed place in the pecking order?'

Tor, evidently thinking that this conversation had gone on long enough broke up the party. 'I promised Monty I'd walk the dogs after church. I assume you all have things to attend to?' He addressed them as a group but focused primarily on Lysander who sent him a nasty smile.

'Thanks for the reminder. I've offered to help Frank and the ground staff get the fireworks ready for Bonfire Night. It occurred to us that expecting you to be involved with the pyrotechnics might be too much to ask? All those flashes, bangs and explosives might set your rehabilitation back months and reawaken memories of Afghanistan. Helping the ladies with the brownies' stargazing activities and the barbeque might be more up your street.'

Rowan, cheeks flamed and she looked mortified, as if asking Halley to help the brownies attain their Space Badge was making trouble for Tor. His riposte to his brother, however, showed he was more than capable of defending himself and Lysander's words had no more impact than a gnat's sting.

'You and Bunce can help on the evening but overall control of the fireworks will be down to me. If you want to help with the brownies and the barbeque, just say.' He smiled over at the women, their appalled expressions leaving him in little doubt that Lysander's help was unwanted. 'That's sorted,' he said, rubbing his hands together to signal that this impromptu gathering was over. 'I'll leave you all to it. Ladies. Lysander.' Turning on his heel, he left the Long Gallery.

'Come on, let's head to my old bedroom and I'll sort out those clothes I've promised Rowan for the brownies bring-and-buy sale. We can go down to the kitchens and rustle up some lunch afterwards.'

'Sounds like a plan,' Rowan said

'Yes, let's do that,' Halley said and all three women strode out of the Long Gallery, leaving Lysander alone with his corrosive thoughts.

Lexie led them through the castle, stopping at a spiral staircase in the oldest part, the Drum Tower. It had whitewashed walls, a rope banister looped through iron rings fastened to the wall and steps which curved round the corner out of sight. The stone treads were old, worn and appeared wet and glistening.

'Don't worry, it's the type of stone used which makes it look wet,' Lexie explained. 'No fear of slipping and coming a cropper.' At the bottom of the staircase was a small table and on it was a handbell. 'Go on, Rowan, I know how much you like ringing the bell.'

Laughing, Rowan obliged and the echo bounced off the walls and drifted up the staircase. 'We ring the bell to let anyone at the top of the staircase know we are at the bottom and intending on coming up,' she explained to Halley.

'If there's an answering ring, we let whoever's at the top of the stairs come down first, then we ascend,' Lexie added. 'Up you go, Halley.'

'Really?' she asked, delighted in having the opportunity to further explore the ancient castle. 'I'm so going to miss all this when I return home.'

'Not the only thing you'll miss, I hope,' Lexie put in.

'No, of course not.' Halley was beginning to realise that, for all her bravado and can-do attitude, Lexie lacked confidence and needed constant reassurance that she was loved.

'It goes without saying that we'll miss you, too,' Rowan said, close on her heels. 'Now, as you climb, tell us if you notice anything unusual about the design of the staircase.'

Halley climbed the staircase holding on to the rope banister. She frowned; something felt 'wrong', but she couldn't put her finger on it. Reaching the top, she walked on to the landing and sat in a low window embrasure waiting for the others to catch up.

Lexie was first. 'This window has glass in it now and has been widened, but originally it had loopholes where the defenders of *Creag na h-Iolaire* would wait until attackers came into range and fire their crossbows at them.'

'Not to mention dropping boiling oil and animal entrails on their heads,' Rowan said with relish.

'Ah, the good old days,' Halley said, laughing.

'Indeed. Go on Halley, what did you notice about the staircase?' Lexie prompted.

'Sorry, you've got me there. It felt odd, but I couldn't say why.'

'A clue is in *left-handedness*, or as they say in old Scots, *corry-fisted*. The trait has run through the Strachan line down through the ages. Does that help?' She and Rowan looked at Halley expectantly, waiting for her answer.

'Not really.' Halley stood at the top and looked down as far as she could to the first bend in the staircase. 'Nope. Give in.'

'This is a reverse spiral staircase, specially constructed for the Strachans who were left-handed. If the enemy gained entry to the tower, the anti-clockwise curve offered an advantage and confused our enemies. See?'

'Yes, I can see it now. But I'm not sure how that'll work to your advantage.'

'That design of the staircase meant that the Strachans' right-handed enemies couldn't wield their swords,' Rowan added. 'In Scotland, left-handedness is also called Kerr-handed, after the Kerr family who had reverse staircases built into their castle for defence.'

'They were left-handed too,' Lexie added, in case Halley had missed the point.

'Got it. I must photograph everything for my father, he loves all kinds of historic and scientific oddities. Knowing him, he'll probably make a PowerPoint of my snaps and present it to the Caledonian Society next time they meet and I'll be roped in to provide the commentary.' Laughing, she reached into her bag for her phone.

While she snapped away, Lexie watched from the window embrasure, restlessly twiddling with her belt.

'Tor is corry-handed, but neither I nor Lysander inherited the trait.' She waited for Halley to stop taking photographs and sent her an oblique look. Evidently that was her way of confirming what Halley already suspected, that Monty was Tor's father whereas she and Lysander were Frank Bunce's children.

Rowan walked over, put her arm round Lexie's slim frame and gave her a reassuring hug. 'These things don't matter,' she said. 'Not in this day and age. Not really.'

'It matters to me,' was Lexie's poignant response.

'I see . . .' Halley sought for some reassuring words because Lexie looked so cast down.

Dragging her pashmina off her shoulders, Rowan wrapped it round her head as if she was an ancient crone. In an obvious attempt to cheer Lexie up, she recited a piece of doggerel with an exaggerated highland accent. 'The Strachans were aye the deadliest foes/ That mony an Englishmen has known/ For they were all left-handed men/ And defence agin them was there none.'

Lexie smiled. 'Oh, I'd forgotten that old rhyme. We should write it down and Halley can recite it to the Caledonian Society when she's back in Hawaii.'

'Ah dinnae ken if ah can do the accent,' Halley giggled.

'Not bad,' Rowan said, approvingly and then took Lexie's hand and pulled her off the window seat. 'Come on, Lexie. Let's head for your bedroom and show Halley round.

Recognising a distraction tactic when she saw one, Halley joined in. 'I'd love to see your bedroom; lead on.' Abandoning her melancholy mood, Lexie led them down another of *Creag na h-Iolaire*'s long, thin passageways. It widened onto a landing with two doors leading off it. Lexie opened the left-hand door and then stood back, indicating that Halley should precede her into the room.

The term 'Lexie's Bedroom' conjured up all sorts of images for Halley. A nursery where Lexie had spent her formative years being looked after by Nanny before being packed off to boarding school. A space where toys, dolls and the like were scattered about, Beatrix Potter plates and bowls on shelves, maybe even a Victorian doll's house and a rocking horse over by the window. Instead, she found a room where, in place of the remnants of a Victorian childhood, there was a silver and giltwood bedhead topped by a coronet-shaped canopy and bed hangings which matched the curtains and the draped skirt of a kidney-shaped dressing table. Fine linen sheets bearing the Strachan crest and a large square pillow embroidered 'Lexie' were neatly arranged on the bed which looked as if no one had slept in it for ages. Needlepoint stools and tasteful watercolours completed the look, but the room had a sad, unused feel to it.

Unable to think of anything more original Halley said, 'It's gorgeous,'

'It's phoney-baloney,' Lexie replied. 'Mother has spent a fortune on the castle, bringing it up to date, repairing and decorating it in the style of her choosing. Unfortunately, her preferred style is that of a five-star hotel, not a castle almost eight hundred years old.'

'I think it looks gorgeous,' Rowan put in, closing the door behind them. 'But good luck convincing Lexie that this a room any girl would love to call her own.'

'I'm sorry if I sound like a spoiled brat but you see, Mother was so against me and Bryce moving in to the Dower House that she had this room decorated to within an inch of its life in an attempt to persuade me to stay. Just as Ly and Suzie have done. Tor, on the other hand, has sensibly set up his own quarters on the far side of the river.'

'I hope you get a chance to see what he's done. It's amazing,' Rowan put in.

'I had to leave. I couldn't face Mother and Monty sniping over everything, Suzie moping because she can't get pregnant, Lysander sucking up to mother and F-Frank Bunce, so that he need never leave the castle, get a job and stand on his own two feet. Not to mention running Tor down when he gets the chance. When Tor was away in the army, I was lost and alone. If it hadn't had been for Rowan and Tam . . .' Her voice trailed off.

'You've been a good friend to me, too, Lex. As I explained to Halley a few days ago, hanging out with the local undertaker isn't everyone's idea of fun.' She turned and directed her next remarks to Halley. 'I was asked by Monty to arrange the funeral of one of his long-standing tenants, Lexie attended the funeral, we became re-acquainted and we've been friends ever since.'

'Fast forward to when Bryce and I met and he rescued – quite literally, the maiden in the tower.' Looking slightly more cheerful she threw herself on the canopied bed, picking up the embroidered cushion and held it in front of her as a child might a teddy bear. 'I often lie awake at night wondering what would have happened to me, to us all, if Tor had been killed in Helmand Province.' Her eyes filled with tears and her bottom lip quivered.

'But he wasn't, was he?' Rowan said, using a kind, firm tone. Most likely the one she used when comforting bereaved relatives. 'Blown up, I mean.'

'No, you're right. I'm just feeling sorry for myself.' Putting the cushion to one side, Lexie made room for Halley to sit on the edge of the bed. 'Tor is the only one who knows how to handle Mother. She loves Tor, although she's very good at hiding it. Not simply because he's the heir to the estate and her first born but because we nearly lost him. What about you, Halley?' Reaching out, she captured Halley's hands and gripped them tightly.

'What about me?' Lexie's hands were cold as ice, despite two oil-fired radiators in the room blasting out heat.

'Do you love Tor, too, Halley? Just a little?'

'Love him? Why, I –'

Rowan rode to Halley's rescue. 'We all love him, right? I mean, who could resist our very own Tor-zan of Lochaber? Especially when the alternative is Florence of Arabia.' She attempted to lighten the mood but Lexie didn't laugh.

'Halley?'

'That's a leading question,' she replied, keen to deflect Lexie's interest.

'To be fair, Lexie, Halley hardly knows him.'

'I know. But, *could* you love him?'

'Lexie . . .' Halley sighed, seeking an answer which wouldn't hurt her feelings. 'I'm leaving in a week's time. I think I'd need to know Tor, any man, a little better before I answer such a leading question.' Smiling, she gave Lexie's knee a reassuring pat. 'I flattened him on the beach not so many nights ago and we've argued over certain things.' She didn't want to bring Lysander into the conversation. 'I like him, and he seems like a good man to have on your side. Let's leave it there.' She looked over at Rowan, mouthing: 'help'.

Rowan got the message.

'Come on, Lex, you've shown Halley your room. Let's sort out the clothes you mentioned, return to the bothy, ring Bryce and ask him to join us. En route you could persuade the kitchen staff to wrap up a slice or two of cake for us to have over coffee.'

'Great idea,' Halley seconded Rowan's suggestion.

Lexie, momentarily distracted, did as Rowan suggested and there was no more mention of Halley, Tor and their regard for each other. Rowan shared a look with Halley which acknowledged Lexie's messed up relationship with her parents, Lysander and her obvious love for Tor.

Let that be enough for now.

Chapter Twenty-six

'Here it comes,' Halley exclaimed as the International Space Station passed overhead. 'Wave your torches,' she instructed the brownie pack who were screaming with delight. Their parents, invited along for the event, barbeque and bonfire afterwards, seemed excited too. The ISS looked like a fast-moving plane and everyone craned their necks to follow its progress across the night sky.

Much to Tor's surprise, the combination of Halley's enthusiasm and the Brownies' reaction to it was infectious. Drawing his eyes away from the dark highland sky, lit by a thousand stars and constellations he focused on Halley. She was a natural, not that he should be surprised. In the short time of their acquaintance, he'd come to realise that Halley Dunbar only allowed people to see what she wanted them to see: astrophysicist, teacher, friend, acquaintance, bereaved great-niece. Everything else was kept under wraps. Tonight, he was being allowed to see another facet of her personality, a scientist who believed passionately in inspiring the next generation.

'The ISS appears to be slow moving, but in fact it is moving at roughly five miles per second and circles the earth every ninety minutes. Travelling at that speed it could make a round trip to the moon in a day,' she told them. The delighted brownies gathered round and followed Halley's pointing finger. 'When you want to find it by yourself and complete the worksheets I've made for you, remember that it's the third brightest object in the sky after the Moon and Venus. Oops, now I've answered the first question for you,' she laughed, and the children giggled, too.

Rowan intervened. 'Careful girls, you'll knock Doctor Dunbar over.'

'Major Strachan, you're on,' Halley turned a shining face to him. 'Come over to the porch, everyone, I have something to show you. Something my great-uncle Tam and the laird, Sir Monty, found in the desert years before you were born. Years before I was born, to be honest. It's come from somewhere out there, in our galaxy.' She pointed above their heads. 'Can you see the streak of paler sky above us? That's the Milky Way. Beyond that are galaxies and stars, just waiting to be discovered. I spend my day looking for them at the research facility in Hawaii.'

'Hawaii?' the brownies gasped and Rowan entered the conversation.

'Halley's observatory is on a mountain thousands of feet above the earth, far away from pollution. She has a clear view of the sky through her million-dollar telescope.' A chorus of 'wows' met this information, and not just from the children.

'It's the observatory's telescope,' Halley explained, laughing. 'Although sometimes I forget that. I've brought my small telescope onto the beach tonight. One of the questions on your worksheet can be answered by looking through it. Brown Owl will organise that while Major Strachan and I get the next part of the evening ready.' As prearranged, Tor walked up to the security light and twisted it round so it shone on the porch. Then he went inside and returned with the meteorite which he positioned on the table Halley had placed in the porch.

When the girls finished looking through her telescope, they gathered before her. Rowan looked over their heads and gave Halley the thumbs up to signify that her pack was having the time of their lives.

'Let's look at the meteorite,' Halley began. 'Major Strachan will tell you how heavy it is.'

'Very heavy.' He feigned his knees buckling under him.

Halley addressed the giggling pack. 'Would you like to know more about where my uncle found it?'

'Ye-ss,' they clamoured.

'One night, my great-uncle and Brigadier Strachan were on patrol in the desert, in a part of the world we now call Yemen. While they were on patrol, they saw a spectacular meteor storm. Just as they were about to return to camp, a fireball streaked across the sky. This was followed by a loud bang known as a sonic boom. My great-uncle was an amateur astronomer and wanted to find out where the meteorite had come to earth. Although that's notoriously difficult without computers and other instruments which weren't so freely available in the nineteen-sixties.'

Tor took up the story. 'Of course, they shouldn't have gone wandering off into the desert, but we're glad that they did. They found this piece of rock and brought it back to their camp. As my father tells the story, it was still hot when they picked it up and wrapped it in a tarpaulin.'

Now Rowan joined in. 'It's a rare example of carboniferous chondrite. Did I say that right, Halley?'

'Spot on. It looks like a chunk of old rock, so when they brought it back to the camp none of the other soldiers showed any interest in it.'

'There are five thousand known meteorites on Earth, but only 51 are carbonaceous chondrites; this is one of them.' Tor looked over at Halley to check that he'd got his facts correct. She nodded her approval and he was unaccountably heartened by it. It made him feel that the three of them were a team. He wasn't quite sure why that should matter, but it did.

One of the girls raised her hand to ask a question. Halley nodded at her. 'Why are these meteorites so important?'

'Well, think about where it has come from – the far reaches of our solar system. Contained within the rock is a mixture of organic compounds and minerals, including the building blocks of life. And . . .' At that point, a member of the castle's staff joined them and whispered something in Tor's ear.

'Sorry, everyone, I have to go. Miss Ferguson and Doctor Dunbar will bring you up to the castle for the fireworks and barbeque.' At the mention of the treats in store, the brownies' enthusiasm for a piece of rock, however rare, began to wane.

Tor grinned and mouthed: *sorry* at Halley and Rowan before heading towards the castle.

'After you've examined the meteorite, I'll tell you all about Halley's comet which came from the far reaches of the solar system and orbited the sun the year I was born, 1986. It will return in 2061 when you will be older than your parents are now.' There was a collective wrinkling of brows as the brownies tried to get their heads round that. 'When it does return, will you do me a favour?'

'Yes,' they chorused.

'Remember this night. This place. Us.'

'Simple,' Rowan responded.

Tor paused a few metres away and exchanged a significant look with Halley, mutely telling her that he would remember this evening, always. Time was running out and she'd be heading home before they knew it. The thought depressed him but he had to stay focused, he had a task to perform and he was determined not to let himself down. Then the last thing he heard was Rowan clapping her hands to get the brownies' attention before sending them over to stand by their parents while she and Halley packed everything away.

Frank Bunce and Lysander were in the stable yard standing by three large oil drums cut through lengthways to create makeshift barbeques. The smell of barbequing food hung in the air as *Creag na h-Iolaire*'s staff arranged plates, cutlery and glassware on trestle tables. Tor smiled as Lexie bossed Lysander, Bryce and Bunce around until she was satisfied that everything was as it should be. The bonfire party was one of the main events in *Creag na h-Iolaire*'s calendar and everyone looked forward to it.

There was one departure tonight, however. Tor was to light the first rocket which signalled the start of the firework display. Usually, Monty performed that task but had made it plain that without Tam alongside him, he couldn't face it. And, in a subtle fashion, tonight symbolised a change in the hierarchy of the estate and reminded everyone that Tor would, one day, be their laird.

The back door of the castle opened and Monty and Lady Strachan stepped out and walked over to Lexie, double checking that everything was running according to plan. Monty might not be lighting the first firework but he was still laird. He was keen to ensure that the brownies and their parents were shown a good time, because he wanted to repay Rowan for the sensitive manner in which she'd handled Tam's funeral.

Lady Strachan glanced over at Tor and smiled, but he held back from joining his family over by the barbeque. Sadie Strachan had a tendency to cluck around him like a mother hen on steroids in case something, however small, would take him back to the seconds before the IEDs exploded. She was constantly on alert in case he retreated within himself and never returned. Tor loved her because she was his mother and had hired the best psychologists and therapists experienced in dealing with PTSD to ensure he got his life back. She didn't seem to realise that it wasn't that easy and the man he had once been was gone forever.

That was his burden and he had to deal with it. It frustrated him that she couldn't see that her attitude towards Halley, the change in ownership of the bothy and her wilful dishonouring of Tam's memory was responsible for some of the angst he had to deal with. Glancing towards the rose gardens and the path Halley and the others would take up from the beach he was seized with impatience. *Others?* Who was he kidding? He was only interested in Halley Dunbar and was glad that the stargazing, bonfire and barbeque gave him a perfect excuse to spend more time with her.

One step in his seven-step rehabilitation plan was: *Deal with others.* In Halley's case, that became easier with every passing day. By his reckoning there was just over a week left to them. A week during which they could . . . well, what *could* they do? Get to know each other better before parting as friends and agree to meet up sometime in the future? Sometime. Never. Eventually, everything would quickly return to how it had been before Halley had breezed into his life turning it upside down and making it better. Then he'd be faced with the daily struggle to recover from his wounds, and be tutored in how to run the estate by Frank Bunce. God, how that rankled. It was an open secret that his mother had sought solace and comfort from Bunce because of her unhappy marriage. Tor understood that and had great sympathy for her, however it didn't make him like Bunce any better.

In fact . . . he glanced over at Bunce and Lysander who had their heads together, thick as thieves. He had never been able to accept Lysander as his half-sibling, not in the way he had Lexie. That was down to Bunce and his over familiar manner with his mother and, since he'd left the army, Bunce's patronising attitude towards himself.

More guests arrived, forcing him to abandon his introspection and to concentrate on playing his part as the heir to Eagle's Crag.

'They're here,' Lexie exclaimed, running over to the rose gardens. 'Let's get this party going. That's down to you, Tor, light the blue touch paper and stand well back.' The last was said jokingly but no one understood, not even Lexie, that this was the part of the evening he'd been dreading: fire, explosions, smoke, the smell of gunpowder. The perfect storm which would take him back to the moment before the IED's exploded.

He could've handed the responsibility for the display over to Lysander or Bunce. However, pride and the knowledge of how much they would relish that, prevented him. He had even considered ordering noiseless fireworks, citing regard for wildlife as his reason, but that would fool no one. Least of all Lysander and Frank Bunce.

Time to stiffen his resolve and remember the Strachan motto – *Non Timeo Sed Caveo* – *cautious but not afraid*. Making his hands into fists he shoved them deep in the pockets of his down jacket and drew upon all his reserves of courage and resolution. Head high, refusing to let down the men who'd served under him, he walked over to the bonfire. His hand was shaking as the pyrotechnician, hired to organise the firework display, handed him a slow-burning taper to light the first rocket and start off the evening's festivities.

He paused and looked around. Saw the expectant faces of the tenants, estate workers, guests, the brownies with their families. His proud parents who, despite their differences, loved him. This was it. Taking a deep breath, he moved closer to a huge rocket.

Suddenly, Halley appeared by his side.

'You can do this,' she whispered, placing an encouraging hand on the small of his back. 'I know you can.' Her light touch was the spur he needed to *light the blue touch paper and stand well back*, as Lexie had jokily put it. She put her hand on his forearm to steady it and the slow burning match touched the fuse. It spluttered and was alight, the rocket shot into the night sky high above their heads with a noisy *whoosh*, followed by a bang and an explosion of light and colour.

The job done, he gave a sigh of relief and turned to thank Halley for her understanding and support. However, he was thwarted in that because, as soon as the first rocket shot into the sky, he was surrounded by friends and relatives congratulating him and wishing him well. When he next looked, she was nowhere to be seen.

'You okay, bro?' Lexie appeared by his side. 'I – we – weren't sure if you could . . .'

'I'm fine, thanks, Lex.' He brushed away her concern and searched instead for Halley. 'Have you seen Halley?' The urgency in his voice was unmistakable.

'I saw her come up from the beach and then walk over to you. I don't know where she went after that. Everything okay?' She laid a hand on his arm.

'What? Oh, yes, yes, everything's okay.'

'How did the thing with the space station go?'

'Hmm? Oh, great; she was really great.' Distractedly looking around for her one last time he pulled himself together. In command of himself, he answered in a more considered fashion. 'She knows her stuff. Didn't overwhelm the kids with technical information and kept everything light and fun. It got me wondering . . .'

'Go on,'

'Why hasn't she married and had children of her own?' He flushed; where had that thought come from? This was hardly a conversation to be having with his baby sister.

'I could ask the same of you,' Lexie laughed. 'But it's a no brainer.

You're both driven personalities with little time for romance or the stuff we ordinary mortals consider the norm: marriage, children, a house in the suburbs. Okay, forget the house in the suburbs.' Laughing, she pointed towards the castle's bulk silhouetted against the dark night sky with every new pyrotechnic effect. 'You've had the trauma of losing your team and I suspect Halley has her own reasons for deciding that all of the above isn't for her.'

'Such as?' Tor looked at his sister, wondering when she'd grown up and developed the canny knack of observing people and looking into their hearts and souls.

Lexie shrugged. 'I don't know. Something in the past, maybe? Go ask her yourself, she's over there and looking as though she suspects we're talking about her.'

Tor's look suggested that she didn't know what a big ask that was. 'Think I'll pass,' he said with his usual wry humour, shaking his head. Tucking her hands under her armpits Lexie made two wings with her arms.

'Chicken,' she squawked and then walked away, laughing.

Left alone, Tor thought about what she'd said. He had secrets of his own, things he wouldn't share with a living soul. He guessed that Halley was the same. Tonight, was the first time that the bangs, flashes and the sulphurous smell of gunpowder hadn't taken him back to the worst day of his life. He had Halley Dunbar's gentle, encouraging touch to thank for that.

Glancing over at the heads of the revellers he spotted his mother bearing down on him with the daughter of one of the nearby landowners. Her purposeful stride left him in no doubt that she was in full on, match-making mode. He groaned; when it came to finding a potential bride for him and carrying on the Strachan line, his mother was quite ruthless.

Pretending that he hadn't seen her, he turned on his heel and saw Halley sitting on a bench watching the fireworks, deep in thought. Picking up two glasses of mulled wine he walked over and joined her. 'You look cold. One of these might help,' He handed her a glass and then sat beside her on the bench. Thwarted, his mother led the potential daughter-in-law off in another direction.

'I'm fine,' she smiled up at him. 'I'm glad that you were able to light the first rocket. I would have hated to see Lysander and the factor get one over on you.'

He was pleased that she understood the politics of tonight's festivities.

'Thanks, your hand on my back gave me just the push I needed. No pun intended.'

'You did much the same for me at Tam's funeral and when you took my side over your mother's when the news broke that I'd been left the bothy. I reckon that makes us even.'

Her words had a ring of finality about them that alarmed him. He didn't want them to be even, he wanted them to be . . . He struggled to find the words. 'Quid pro quo? Is that how you see it?'

'Perhaps.' She sent him a straight look. 'You conquered your fear, I simply helped a little.' It was clear that she didn't want thanking so he changed the subject.

'I was impressed at how well you handled the brownies down on the beach.'

She giggled and deciding that he liked the sound, he smiled back at her. 'You make them sound like a pack of ravening beasts. They're sweeties and Rowan keeps them under control.'

Now it was his turn to make light of how much she'd helped him. 'I wouldn't expect anything less of you, either.'

'Thanks, although it is kinda my job?' Tilting her head, she sent him a searching look. The inflection at the end of her sentence reminded him that she'd lived in the USA for almost half her life. Maybe the clues to her reluctance to settle down and to stay away from Lochaber lay there.

Lexie was right, he was too chicken to probe further.

Instead, he made a joke. 'Handling ravening beasts, is that in your job description?'

'No, I –' Evidently realising that she was being teased, she took another sip of the mulled wine and gave him one of her straight looks over the rim of the glass before continuing. 'Ravening beasts aside, it's something I'd like to do more of. Part of my role involves education, working with the public and helping them to understand the wonders of the cosmos.' Laughing, she tailed off. 'Okay, I'm even boring myself. Here endeth the lesson.' Putting her glass down on the bench she placed her gloved hands together as if praying.

'Not boring at all although I imagine that you're keen to get back?' He was fishing, but hoped it wasn't too obvious.

'Yes and no.'

'Explain.' While she sought for the words he beckoned over a member of staff and asked for two burgers to be brought over to them.

'Right away Major Strachan.'

'What? Why are you looking at me like that?' he asked, returning her grin.

'You, giving staff orders, like it's second nature.'

'As you said only a few moments ago: *it's kinda my job.* My time in the army and the knowledge that all this,' he took in the castle and the surrounding land with a sweeping gesture, 'will one day be mine, gives me a certain authority. Even if it's only for ordering burgers.' They laughed and Halley's brow wrinkled, as though she was considering his words. 'How about you?'

'Me? Well, as I've climbed up the greasy pole of astrophysics, I've been given more responsibility. But I'm still way down in the pecking order. However, I dare say I could ask someone in the faculty to fetch me a coffee but only under extreme circumstances.'

'Such as?'

'My being glued to my telescope or computer charting the path of a particularly difficult comet.'

'Have you ever done that?'

'I've certainly recorded a new comet but I've never dared to ask someone to bring me a coffee. Unless they were a friend and on the way to the coffee machine.' He recalled Lexie calling him 'chicken' and smiled. 'What?'

'Nothing. Just something Lexie said has turned out to be true.'

'She's a smart cookie, your sister.'

'She has a kind heart and that means more.

'It's clear that she adores you.'

'It's good to know someone does.'

'I think your fan club is bigger than you realise.'

He stopped himself from asking if she was a paid-up member. That was too personal, and what if she said no? He glanced over at Lysander and Bunce and adopted a wry expression. 'I'm guessing I still have to win those two over?'

'Why bother? You wouldn't want to belong to any club which has those two as members.'

'You're right.' She had a sense of humour and he liked that. They'd hardly spent any time together and when they had it'd been in the company of others. He sensed a missed opportunity which time wouldn't allow him to put right. 'Ah, our burgers. Thanks Malcolm.' Taking the burgers, he held on to Halley's until she stripped off her gloves.

They ate the burgers in a companionable silence, watching the fireworks arcing into the sky and plummeting to earth in a shower of glittering colour. He wondered why he'd been so worried about the display triggering bad memories, tonight he'd faced his demons and come through. It was hardly the end to all his problems, but it was a start.

Halley screwed up the napkin and moved forward to the end of the bench, signalling that she was on the move. Standing she smiled and then put her napkin inside her empty glass.

'I'd better go. I've got a long drive ahead tomorrow.'

This was news to him. 'Really?' His heart plummeted down to his boots and his pulse began to race as an all too familiar wave of anxiety washed over him.

'Dundee,' she replied. 'I'm presenting a couple of lectures at the Space Technology Centre at the University. Ordinarily, it's something I would enjoy. However, I have more than enough on my plate at the moment and this visit will eat into the time I have left in Lochaber.'

'We'll have to make the days count then, won't we?' He could have kicked himself for being so obvious but she seemed not to have noticed. Or, at least, didn't mind. She smiled as she fished her gloves out of her pocket and put them on. Adjusting the jaunty angle of her beret she prepared to leave and make her way back to down to the beach. 'I'll walk you to the top of the steps although, ordinarily, I'd walk you all the way home.'

'Ravening beasts and all that?'

'Something tells me you would give any ravening beast a run for their money.' They both laughed.

'Go. You have duties to perform; noblesse oblige and all that. Apart from which, Lady Strachan has been glancing over at us for the last ten minutes with the look of a woman on a mission.'

'Trouble is, I know exactly what that mission is,' he said.

Halley laughed. 'I have a feeling I do, too.' A giggle escaped her. 'Good luck,' she held out her hand and he took it in both of his. 'All being well I'll see you all in a couple of days.' Not 'you', but 'you all', he noticed. Keeping everything light and measured.

With that she left him and despite the fireworks cascading to earth in front of him, it was as if the light had gone out of his life. There being nothing else for it, he walked towards his mother and the young woman she had in tow, like a lamb to the slaughter.

Chapter Twenty-seven

For the first time in her professional life Halley derived no pleasure from introducing the public to the world of astronomy or talking to her peers about the groundbreaking work she and her colleagues at the Haleakalā Observatory had undertaken in exoplanet research. All she could think of during the long drive from Dundee to Mallaig was getting home to her bothy. Is that what Uncle Tam had hoped for when he'd bequeathed it her? That she'd come to regard it as 'home'?

A big ask, given the circumstances.

Something else had occupied her thoughts on the long drive home. Or, should that be, some*one*? For the last few days, despite all her efforts to keep Hector Strachan out of her head, he'd managed to find his way in. Everything had happened so quickly since the moment they'd collided on the beach: becoming re-acquainted with the Strachans, the funeral, wake, pinkie-to-pinkie and Lexie's stage-managed kiss, the developing connection between them. At least at the firework display she'd been given the chance to support Tor and repay him for the many kindnesses he'd shown her.

It was strange how sitting on a bench and sharing a burger over a glass of mulled wine had changed their relationship. Moved it on to a different footing. Not that it mattered, she was leaving soon and . . . she crunched the gears at a particularly tight bend in the road; time to focus on navigating these narrow roads . . .

The university had been so impressed by her willingness to deliver the lectures at a difficult time in her life – not that she'd been given much choice – that they'd approved a few days extra leave and reimbursed her for having to change her airline ticket.

She groaned as she parked in *Creag na h-Iolaire*'s stable yard, bowing her head over the steering wheel. Their generosity had caused more problems, however. She was beginning to love Lochaber, the location and its people and, apart from missing her family, she was in no hurry to return home. On top of which, yesterday, an email had dropped into her inbox informing her that she'd been seconded to NASA in Baltimore to join the team monitoring the James Webb telescope.

It would be career suicide to turn down the opportunity in the hope that her relationship with Tor Strachan developed into something more. Then there was the ever-present fear of him discovering the real reason she'd stayed away from Lochaber.

He'd be sure to despise her, wouldn't he?

Another groan, then she straightened her back and climbed out of the car. Was it her imagination or could she really smell the tang of wet sand and hear the whoosh of the incoming tide? Was she becoming more attuned, re-acquainted with a place she had once loved? She wasn't allowed time for further thought as a member of staff took her keys to park the car in line with others in the yard. She searched for Tor's Land Rover and quashed a twinge of disappointment when she realised it wasn't there.

She was eager to share the news and didn't have to wait long as Lexie and Bryce came out of the castle and enveloped her in a 'welcome home' embrace.

After releasing her, Bryce brought her holdall and a carrier bag containing presents she'd bought in the V and A giftshop in Dundee out of the car boot. Taking a step forward, Lexie squeezed Halley's hands, full of anxiety.

'Oh, Halley . . .'

'Lexie,' Bryce said, warningly, 'remember what Tor said.'

'Wh-what's happened?' Halley's breath caught in her throat, her mouth suddenly dry. 'Not Tor?'

'He's waiting for you in the bothy.'

'I don't understand. Why do you look so worried?' Halley's euphoria at having good news to share evaporated as Lexie took her overnight bag from Bryce and walked her to the steps leading down to the beach.

'Tor will explain everything.'

Worried, and with a sense of foreboding, Halley took the steps two at a time and was soon on the beach. When she reached the bothy, the security light and all the indoor lights were on, despite it being a sunny November afternoon. The sand in front of the bothy had been churned up by many feet and the door was open to the elements. She walked in and found Tor by the wood burner warming his hands.

Banking down feelings of disquiet she quickly surveyed the room, taking in the cafetiere of coffee, dirty mugs and a half-eaten plate of biscuits on the kitchen table. If Tor had been entertaining guests, surely that meant nothing bad had happened?

Her brow furrowed. Wait. Why he was entertaining in *her bothy* without her being there?

'Tor. What's going on?'

He leapt to his feet and crossed the floor towards her. 'Halley. Here, let me.' He carried her luggage through to her bedroom, placing everything on the bed.

Returning to the sitting room he cut to the chase.

'While you were away, the bothy was broken into. Look.' He gestured towards the outside door which had been jemmied. 'I'm not sure what's been taken, I've been waiting for your return so we can draw up a quick inventory for the police.'

'Police?' she gasped. Was it really that bad? Shaking her head, Halley focused on searching for the most precious items. 'The meteorite!' She rushed over to the sink and checked under it.

'It's safe, don't worry.'

'My telescope.' Pirouetting away from the sink she dashed into the bedroom before breathing a sigh of relief, finding the telescope exactly where she'd left it. 'I don't understand, why didn't the thieves take that, too? It's antique and quite valuable.'

'It's heavy and clearly isn't what they were after.'

'Which was?'

'The only other thing I can think of is the tin containing the Boer

War medals, your family documents and photos you showed me the other night. Maybe you should check they're safe?'

Halley rushed into Tam's room and opened the top drawer of the tallboy where she'd stowed the tin under some bedlinen. Her heart sank when she realised it was missing. Feeling dazed and shaken, she returned to the sitting room as if sleepwalking, looking at Tor as though he had all the answers.

'Gone?' he asked.

'Gone.' The only word she felt capable of uttering.

Tor's face darkened, making plain what he would do to the thieves should he ever encounter them. 'I'm assuming the deeds to the bothy and your passport were in there, too?'

Trembling, with fingers which had turned into clumsy thumbs, Halley opened her shoulder bag and placed her passport and the deeds on the table. The same sixth sense which had made her hide the orrery had told her that they were too precious to leave lying around.

'Wh-who would want such things?' Halley asked, crashing down on the chair recently occupied by Tor.

'The medals are worth a fair bit on the black market. Whoever broke in, knew what they were looking for.' Tor kept his voice level in a clear attempt to reassure her, even if the reality was distressing.

'Okay, I get that the medals must have been worth the risk of breaking into my house.' She paused, acknowledging that it was the first time she'd referred to Tam's old shack as her 'house'. 'But why on earth would they want my passport and the deeds to the bothy? Presumably Tam's solicitors have copies?'

'I would imagine so. Tam was nothing if not thorough. As for your passport, I'm assuming you have American citizenship?' She nodded. 'An American passport is worth a great deal on the open market.'

'Oh, boy,' she said. 'Have the police been informed? Sorry – you've already mentioned that.' She rubbed her face with her hands and then looked up at Tor.

'What is it?'

'I've just realised, Tam's service medals were in the box. They were in my safekeeping and now they're gone.' The realisation that she'd let Tam down a second time struck home. Turning away to hide her distress she focused on the flames dancing behind the glass of the wood burner. When they shimmered and went out of focus, she realised she was crying.

She dashed the tears away with the back of her hand, but not before Tor caught the movement. 'Hey.' Holding on to the side of her chair for support he hunkered down in front of her although it caused him considerable pain.

'Sorry. Sorry. It's just that . . .'

She searched up the sleeve of her coat for a tissue and blew her nose

'You know, Tam always maintained that the only things worth hanging on to are memories, good and bad. Remembrances are all we have when worldly possessions have gone.'

'He – you're right, of course.' Sensing that Tor was finding it difficult to maintain a hunkered down position Halley stood up, instinctively holding out her hand to help him to his feet. Tor hesitated, seemingly adopting his default position of accepting help from no one. Then, much to Halley's surprise, he took her hand and hoisted himself to his feet, holding on for longer than necessary.

'Don't cry, mo chridhe, we'll sort this.'

The concern etched on his face, his gentle tone and the unfamiliar Gaelic words only made things worse. Her bottom lip quivered and the tears she'd thought she had under control returned with a vengeance. She glanced over at the photograph of Tam and Monty in pride of place on the dresser. It had been taken during their tour of duty in Aden, around the time they'd found the meteorite. Tor was right, Tam wouldn't have given a damn about the missing medals. However, he would have given everything to be in this room with them, right now, and not lying in the cold earth waiting for Monty to join him.

Halley hoped that thought would shore up her resolve but it only served to make her more wretched. Instinctively, she took two steps closer to Tor, turned her head sideways and pressed her hot, damp cheek against his chest. She knew it was wrong, foolhardy even, but in that moment, she craved human contact and comfort.

Instinct told her that Major Hector Strachan was the man to provide it.

How long they stood there she couldn't really say. Seconds turned into minutes, measured against the rise and fall of her breasts and the echo of Tor's heartbeat in her ear. Feeling calmer, she raised her head and took a couple of steps back.

'One last thing to check,' she croaked.

'Go on.'

'Before I left for Dundee, I moved the orrery from my bedroom windowsill and stowed it in the back of my wardrobe.'

'Why did you do that?' he asked, following her as far as the bedroom door and watching her rummage around in the back of an ancient mahogany wardrobe.

'I don't know; instinct perhaps, and because the orrery was the easiest to pick up and move.

'Well?' Tor asked when she turned back to face him.

'Safe and sound. Sorry.' She smiled up at him to show that her emotions were under control. 'I've wet the front of your shirt,' she said with a shaky laugh. Walking over to the sink she fetched a clean towel and returned to dab at the damp patch. Tor stopped her, placing his hand over hers and pressing it against his chest. Then he removed the towel, letting it fall to the floor and drew her so close that only seconds separated them from danger and madness.

'Tell me I've got this wrong,' he said, tilting her face and bringing his mouth tantalisingly close to hers. Halley's heart kicked up a gear and she took a shuddering breath before answering.

'Not wrong, exactly, but –'

Their lips touched, rendering conversation impossible. Halley sighed. Tor, seemingly taking that for encouragement, increased the gentle pressure of his lips on hers, tenderly exploring her mouth with his tongue and curling his hand round her waist to draw her close. Alarm bells rang in Halley's head. Past and present collided and she was forced to concede that Tor was right, it was insanity for them to kiss.

At that moment Lexie, who had obviously had enough of being kept out in the cold, crashed into the porch, kicking over a couple of plant pots in the process. Tor released Halley, picked the towel off the floor and moved over to the sink. Halley took a couple of shaky steps, righted herself, adjusted her clothing and prepared to welcome Lexie as though nothing had happened.

'Oh Migod, Migod, the door frame. Poor Halley. Good thing Tor's here.' Gabbling, Lexie launched herself at Halley and hugged her. Tor and Halley exchanged a look over Lexie's head, doing their best to pretend the kiss hadn't happened. 'Why are you still wearing your coat, Halley?'

'Am I? I haven't had time to remove it.' She and Tor exchanged a look.

'Tor said that I was to allow you at least half an hour to get your head around what has happened before I came down. But I couldn't wait that long. Of course, the estate carpenters will fix the door but, until then, you are very welcome to stay with Bryce and me in the Dower House.'

'Thanks for the offer, Lexie. However, this is my house and I'm staying put. I'm guessing that they found what they were looking for and won't be returning any time soon.'

'You're being very brave but you don't know that for sure,' a worried Lexie put in. 'What if they do return? In the dead of night?' Halley laughed; Lexie had a strange way of calming her fears!

'If that happens, Halley won't be alone,' Tor said.

'She won't?' Her head spinning, Halley referred to herself in the third person.

'No, I'm staying here tonight and every night until I feel it's safe.' Tor spoke with such authority that Halley was rendered speechless. 'As Lexie has correctly stated, the estate carpenters will fix the door tomorrow, hanging a new one if necessary. Until then, I need to make sure you're safe and that they won't return.'

'But, I –' Halley started to protest but Lexie dismissed her protests.

'I think it's a great idea. Much, much better than staying with us in the boring old Dower House.' In full matchmaking mode, the one characteristic she did share with her mother, Lexie turned her back on Tor. Then she winked extravagantly and gave Halley the thumbs up. Halley groaned inwardly wishing that Lexie was less obvious. Remembering the kiss, a tell-tale blush swept over her cheeks and she used the distraction of removing her coat to cover it. 'Well, I'll be off, then. Lots to do; lots to do. See you both tomorrow. Play nicely, children,' Lexie added, skipping out of the bothy and along the beach in the direction of the Dower House.

'Sorry about that,' Tor said, nodding towards his sister's departing figure.

'Pure Lexie, par for the course.' Halley smiled, making plain that Lexie was a one-off and she'd grown to love her.

'Not sorry about the other thing, though,' he added.

Halley's cheeks burned a brighter red. She knew what he meant; he didn't need to spell it out.

'It's no big deal,' she dismissed the kiss with a wave of her hand.

'I thought you needed comforting and I got a little . . . carried away.' He rubbed the length of his nose with his forefinger, a sure sign of discomfiture. 'Sorry.'

'Oh.' Halley was wrong-footed. No man she'd come across had ever apologised for kissing her. 'You acted instinctively and I responded in kind. It was a moment, nothing more. Let's change the subject.'

He frowned, making it plain that that wasn't quite what he meant or the response he wanted. 'Very well.' Walking over to the fire he sat down again.

'Moving rapidly on,' Halley said, attempting to dismiss the new awkwardness. 'Regarding the burglary, I should have mentioned that, on several occasions, I've seen lights and heard outboard motors on the river after dark. I thought it was fishermen, but now . . .'

Taking her lead, he came back with, 'There has been a spate of poaching, smuggling and burglary in the district although the police have yet to make an arrest. The night I leapt on you in the dark,' again the tell-tale trail of his finger along his nose, 'I thought you were part of it. Most of the thieving has been opportunist and poaching of our fish and game is nothing new. However, this,' he waved his hand towards the jemmied door, 'bears the hallmark of people who knew exactly what they were looking for.' Halley shivered and Tor picked up the slight tremor. 'I'm an idiot, I'm scaring you.'

'No, really, you're not. I simply need to get used to the idea that someone made the most of my being in Dundee to break in. Someone who knew my movements. That would suggest local knowledge.'

'You're right.' He looked suddenly pensive and it was evident that the tentative kiss had been temporarily forgotten. By accident or design Halley couldn't say, all she knew with any degree of certainty was that, as far as gentle kisses went, she'd never been kissed so thoroughly.

'Don't worry about me, I'm tougher than I look.' There. That put everything into perspective and established that she wasn't the kind of woman who went weak at the knees because she'd been kissed by someone who knew how to do it properly.

'I can attest to that.' He grinned, touching the faint red mark on his temple where she'd brained him with the branch two weeks ago. 'However, it makes sense for me to stay the night. I'll sleep in Tam's room, no worries on that score and no need to make up the bed.' He sent her a straight look, as if to reassure her that the kiss was a one-off and he would act the perfect gentleman from now on. 'Once the door's mended I'll take the meteorite, orrery and telescope over to the Dower House. The house has a burglar alarm which Bryce sets in case anyone tries to steal one of his sporrans.'

That made her giggle. 'There's a sentence you don't hear every day.'

Tor relaxed and smiled, too. 'We'll be very happy to ship them over to Hawaii, or whatever you decide is best. How does that sound?'

'I have no objections,' she said, touched by his concern. 'Thank you.' There was no one in the whole of Lochaber she'd rather trust with those precious objects. 'What? Why are you looking at me like that?'

'Such docility, Miss Dunbar, seems out of character.'

'That's because you don't really know me. Or I, you.'

'Touché.' The remark appeared to sadden him and his smile vanished, then he became more business-like. 'Now, while you unpack, I'll ring up to the castle and ask the kitchens to send down something for dinner.'

'Dinner?'

'My version of Deliveroo,' he joked. 'You've driven from one side of Scotland to the other, on a good day that would take over four hours. I gather there were roadworks on the A830 which lengthened your journey? I don't think you need the added pressure of cooking dinner tonight.'

'Hardly a pressure, I enjoy cooking.'

'But not tonight,' he responded with gentle firmness. 'Go. Unpack. Shower. Leave the rest to me.'

Feeling unexpectedly light-hearted, despite everything that had happened, she saluted and uttered the battle cry of the US Marines: '*Oo-rah.*'

He laughed and then adopted a mock stern expression. 'Might I remind you, Doctor Dunbar, that this is Scotland and you are addressing a former major in the Royal Scots Guards? *Oo-rah* doesn't quite cut it here.' The banked-down humour in his eyes showed he was teasing.

'Sorry, it's what we say in the observatory when we have a eureka moment.'

'Do you have many of those?'

'More than you might imagine. So, what should I say?'

'The motto of the Royal Scots Guards: *Nemo Me Impune Lacessit.* Not quite as snappy, I'll admit.'

'Which means?' She had a good command of Latin but pretended ignorance in order to keep him talking. In spite of everything that had happened, he was the most relaxed she'd ever seen him.

Was it the kiss or a result of being in charge once more?

'It means, *No one provokes me with immunity.*'

'A great motto for a soldier but not exactly a snappy response to have in reserve in case one makes a major scientific breakthrough.'

'But a timely warning to anyone who oversteps the mark, wouldn't you say?'

'I'll bear it in mind.' She mimed plucking the words out of the air and tucking them away in her pocket.

'Shower,' he reminded her.

'Okay, going.' She paused at the door and turned, her hand on the old ceramic knob. 'Are you sure this isn't too much to ask? Dinner and protection?'

'Highland hospitality demands as much.'

Walking into her room she closed the door and leaned against it, wondering why she felt irrationally put out by the realisation that he was helping from a sense of obligation and tradition and for no other reason.

It wasn't like her to think and act so illogically. Clearly, a hot shower and a good dinner were needed. Everything would fall back into place after that.

Wouldn't it?

Chapter Twenty-eight

Next morning, Tor and Halley were having breakfast when there was a knock at the door. Frank Bunce entered accompanied by Geordie Souter and a carpenter with the tools of his trade. They paused on the threshold of the damaged doorway and took stock of the situation. Obviously, they hadn't expected to find Tor having breakfast with Halley. It was a dark November morning and it didn't take a genius to work out that they'd spent the night together.

Bunce walked over to the kitchen table and greeted them with a knowing smile.

'Good morning, Doctor Dunbar. I hope that you slept well after the trauma of finding you'd been burgled.' He glanced down at the remains of their breakfast and then over to the cafetiere on the stove. Ignoring the hint that he would like a cup of coffee and quite possibly The Full Scottish, Halley and Tor regarded him boot-faced.

'I'm fine, thanks.'

'I didn't expect to find you here, Tor.'

'You didn't?' Tor's reply was cool and succinct, making plain that his whereabouts had nothing to do with *Creag na h-lolaire's* factor.

'No, I didn't.' Bunce glanced past them towards the bedrooms, obviously trying to figure out who'd slept where, and with whom. It was a no-brainer that he'd be rushing back to the castle to inform Tor's mother of their sleeping arrangements, and anyone else who cared to listen.

'I suppose,' Souter added, evidently sensing the tension in the room and trying to defuse it, 'that Halley needed protection after being burgled,'

Then he added, in case Tor had taken his comment the wrong way, 'There's no one better than a *so-dger* of the Scots Guards for that job.'

'Not that I need protection,' Halley said. She put her knife and fork together on her plate to signify that she'd finished her breakfast and that she found their presence aggravating. 'In case anyone's wondering.'

'Aye, aye,' Souter nodded his head, anxious to please. 'Ah can see that.'

Tor stood up and moved away from the table, indicating that he'd had enough of double talk and innuendo. 'I assume that you've come down to make the bothy safe, Frank?' The comment was designed to remind Bunce of his place in the order of things, despite his relationship with Lady Strachan.

'We have. And to carry out any other repairs that Doctor Dunbar might deem necessary. The Brigadier and Lady Strachan are upset that a guest has been burgled. Lady Strachan, in particular, will be relieved to learn that you stayed the night to ensure Halley's safety.' In spite of his show of concern, they both knew that he would take great delight in breaking the news to Sadie Strachan, putting a spin on it and causing trouble.

'Aye, that's Tor – ever the gentleman,' Souter added with an ingratiating smile. Halley was not taken in and neither was Tor. The look the three men exchanged showed there was no love lost between them.

'I can hardly be called a guest,' Halley said, getting to her feet and carrying their plates over to the sink. 'I own the bothy and the land it stands on. You knew that, right?' Her direct look told Bunce that she wasn't fazed by his threat to tell tales out of school. 'As you said earlier, Tor: *No one provokes me with immunity.*' Thanks to Tam's bequest, the Strachans couldn't touch her and Bunce's mock concern and sleazy inuendo could wash over her.

'Of course. No secrets at *Creag na h-Iolaire,* eh Geordie?' This time his smile included Souter, possibly to let Halley know that her ownership of Tam's bothy was the juiciest piece of gossip round the estate in many a long year.

'Yer own wee bit o' Scotland,' Souter commented, placing his right hand over his heart, a true patriot. He really was a creep with his wispy ginger hair and skinny frame, Halley decided. However, Bunce wasn't far behind with his superior air and the knowledge that, as Lady Strachan's lover, he was fireproof.

'Naturally, I know all about Tam's bequest, Lady Strachan informed me a couple of days ago. You can imagine how shocked we all were when Lexie reported that your bothy had been broken into.'

'Ah, so it was Lexie who spotted the forced entry?' Halley asked.

'Yes,' Bunce pulled up a chair at the table and, without waiting to be asked, sat down. Much to Halley's annoyance, Souter followed his lead. 'She was taking the dogs for a run along the beach and saw the damaged door. She came straight up to the castle to find me.'

His last word hung in the air reminding Tor and Halley of his kinship with Lexie. Seemingly this didn't please Tor as he came right back with, 'The ink's hardly dry on the document. I didn't expect anyone outside of the immediate family to be aware of the transfer of ownership.' His comment made plain that he didn't regard Bunce as part of the family, immediate or otherwise.

There was a bit of a Mexican standoff as the men glared at each other. Then the carpenter, who'd been jiggling nervously from foot to foot, dropped his bag of tools onto the wooden floor breaking the spell and making them jump.

'Sorry,' he said and began examining the damaged door. Probably glad to be outside the war zone over by the table and not part of the family.

'Well, not many people are aware of the change in ownership.' Halley said, making it pretty obvious that she didn't trust Bunce or Souter further than she could throw them. 'I only found out less than a week ago, as Tor has intimated.'

The word made Bunce and Souter glance past her and towards the bedrooms.

'Was there something else?' Tor inquired. 'Apart from your obvious concern for Doctor Dunbar's welfare?'

'What? Oh, yes; The Brig wants to know what, if anything, has been taken.'

'I'll see my father later and bring him up to speed.' Tor looked over at Halley who was standing at the sink, hands gripping the edge, anxious about breaking the news about Tam's medals to Monty. 'No need for you to become involved, Bunce. I'm sure there are matters on the estate which require your attention.'

'Aye, there are. But I need to let Constable Frazer know when it will be convenient for him to call and take a statement from Doctor Dunbar.'

'Again, no need for you to concern yourself. Refer Frazer to me. I'll be dealing with matters regarding the break in, on Doctor Dunbar's behalf.'

Halley wanted to say that she didn't want or need anyone to do anything on her behalf, but kept silent. That was a discussion for her and Tor to have once everyone had departed. Things were bad enough between him and Bunce without her making them worse. She felt as if she was watching two stags locking horns during the rutting season to decide who would emerge leader of the herd. All it needed was a couple of deep bellows from either man to complete the image. As for Souter, he was a jackal, waiting to pick up the pieces.

There was a stage cough over by the door and the carpenter entered the conversation. His face was a study as he tried to work out who he should address his remarks to. In the end he plumped for the alpha male with the largest antlers: Tor Strachan.

'I'm sorry, Major Tor, but I cannae fix the door. Too much damage has been done. The best I can do is to make the bothy secure while I order a new door. But it could be weeks before it arrives. Is it possible for the young lady to move somewhere else in the meantime?'

'Weeks! I'll be long gone by then. Can't you order a door from Fort William, or wherever?'

'Sorry Miss,' the carpenter explained. 'This bothy is a listed building and we cannae just stick any old door on it.'

A listed building? Halley looked at Tor for confirmation.

'Of course, I'd forgotten that. There are so many historic buildings on the estate that it's hard to keep tabs on them.' His face a study in concentration, he turned to Bunce. 'I take it that you've brought a vehicle down with you? Good. I want you to take Halley's brass telescope and orrery over to the Dower House for safekeeping. I'll check them later. You might as well take the wag-at-the-wall clock over to Monty while you're at it. You'll find both items in Halley's bedroom and the clock is on the wall. I think that about covers it, so I'll let you get on with it.'

He stood there, an immovable force, giving Bunce and Souter no alternative but to do his bidding. No one spoke as the telescope and orrery were taken out of the bothy and Bunce returned for the clock.

'Is there anything else I can do for you, Major Strachan; Doctor Dunbar?' he asked, snarkily.

'I think we can deal with the rest.'

Now in a thoroughly bad mood Bunce took the clock off the wall, making the pendulum clang. His face was scarlet with suppressed rage and, after sending them a death stare, he prepared to leave. Tor and Halley were sensible enough to know, however, that this wasn't the end of the matter. Just as Bunce was squeezing past the carpenter, Tor fired a parting shot. 'Should anyone inquire about Halley's whereabouts, refer them to me.'

Halley opened her mouth to protest but held her counsel knowing they had to present a united front. It wouldn't do to argue in front of the estate carpenter either. Although he'd said very little, Halley was sure he'd be telling anyone who cared to listen what had gone down that morning.

'Very well, Major Strachan.' Bunce was about to say more but seemingly changed his mind and left with an angry snort; minutes later his vehicle was roaring along the beach.

'Tor, I think that –' Tor cut Halley short with a nod towards the carpenter.

'You go and pack a few things while I wash up the breakfast plates and sort things out with Mikey. I think it's best if you move into the Airstream with me for a couple of days, or at least until we're sure that the burglars won't be returning. Everything else can wait.'

Halley did as she was asked, but the look she shot him suggested that he was skating on the thinnest of ice and had better watch out lest it gave way under him!

The carpenter managed a temporary repair to the door by inserting a metal strip along the jemmied edge. Following Tor's instructions, he checked all the windows and made sure that the catches were fit for purpose and then picked up his bag ready to leave.

'Thanks, Mikey.' Halley slipped him a ten-pound note.

'Och, Miss, there's no need,' he assured her, but pocketed it anyway.

'Nevertheless, have a pint and a wee dram for Tam.'

'I will that.' He tested the door one last time and then left. 'Thanks again.'

Tor smiled at Halley. 'There was no need for that. Mikey is employed by the estate.'

'I know, but this is my bothy now, not the estate's. Sorry, that came out sharper than intended.' She smiled to take the sting out of her words and then changed the subject. 'I'm saving a couple of Scottish ten-pound notes to have framed as a souvenir for my parents. Mary Somerville is featured on the new notes.'

'Should I know who she is?'

'You should.' She wagged a finger at him, playfully. 'She's the twentieth-century Scottish scientist and astronomer after whom Somerville College, Oxford, is named. There's a drawing of a midge cluster and 'moon diagram' taken from her book 'Mechanism of the heavens', featured on the note. However, it can only be seen under UV light. What?' she asked, laughing at the way he was regarding her.

'Midge cluster, eh? You're passionate about your subject, aren't you?'

'I am,' she nodded, 'I'm passionate about a lot of things, actually.' Her reply sounded innocent enough but the way it was said and the unconsciously coquettish look which accompanied it, made Tor's heart beat faster.

Time to rein in these dangerous feelings . . .

'Do you remember my asking you: *Doesn't Scottish blood beat thickly in your veins? Don't you feel as though part of you belongs here?* And you said –'

'*'fraid not*. That was wrong of me. In my defence, it was the day of Tam's funeral; I was jet lagged, bereaved, disorientated and hardly thinking straight. If my reply disappointed you, I'm sorry.'

'Time to set the record straight. I'm the one who should apologise. I was out of order asking that question on such a day.'

'So why did you? Ask it I mean.'

'I don't know. You were getting under my skin and I was searching for reasons to dislike you.'

'Wow.' She looked surprised at his directness, blushed and traced round a knot on the pine table with her nail. A bloom of colour swept across her cheeks and Tor was reminded how he'd spent the previous night tossing and turning in Tam's narrow bed, unable to sleep. Nothing to do with the burglary or the bed, but everything to do with Halley Dunbar sleeping only feet away, separated by a thin wall.

So thin that he could almost hear her breathing. Or had that been his fevered imagination? Either way, he'd be keeping that information strictly on a need-to-know basis.

He walked to the sink, filling the bowl with water, relying on an air of detachment to conceal that she was becoming a daily fix of a drug he couldn't imagine living without. Swishing the bubbles, he reminded himself that she'd be leaving in under a week and, despite owning this bothy, would probably never return.

'Tor? Are you okay?'

Apart from acting like a moonstruck calf, you mean, he felt like asking? Instead, he came back with, 'Sorry; miles away.' Wiping soapy hands on a towel he turned to face her.

'Ask me that question again.' Her expression was serious and the soft light in her grey eyes affected him more than he cared to admit.

Gamely, he repeated the question: '*Don't you feel as though part of you belongs here?*'

This time, Halley answered without pausing for thought. 'Yes, I do. Staying here, even for the briefest time, has affected me in ways I couldn't have predicted. For the first time in years, I feel that there's more to life than academic success. That has been a driving force for so-o-o long. Now I'm beginning to wonder if it's enough. Sure, I have a fulfilling life in Hawaii which is precious to me. However, renewing my friendship with Rowan, becoming re-acquainted with Monty, getting to know Lexie and Bryce and remembering my love of the Scottish landscape –

yes – even the weather, has reminded me that I am a Dunbar. Through and through.' She tapped her breastbone for emphasis, running out of breath after that passionate declaration.

Tor allowed her a moment to recover and then encouraged her to continue. 'Go on.'

'Scottish blood does beat thickly through my veins, although I've been at pains to deny it.'

He was profoundly moved by that but hid it behind a quirky smile. 'And, tell me, Doctor Dunbar, does your affection for the land and its people extend as far as my mother and Bunce?'

'It does not.'

He had one last question, although he knew that asking it might destroy the fragile rapport growing between them. 'Lysander?'

There was a pause, followed by an unequivocal look. 'Though I do feel a certain sympathy for his wife, Suzie, no. Trying to start a family and having no success must be hard on her; on them. However, believe me when I say that there is no connection between me and your brother other than summer days spent playing on the beach with Rowan and other children.'

That was her second speech of the morning and having delivered it, she turned away, leaving him to speculate why she found the subject of Suzie and Lysander's childless state so emotional. He recalled the conversation he'd had with Lexie four days ago.

Why hasn't she married and had children of her own?

None of your damned business, he told himself, remembering Lexie's reply: *I could ask the same of you. You're both driven personalities with little time for romance or the stuff we ordinary mortals consider the norm: marriage, children, a house in the suburbs . . . Halley has her own reasons for deciding that all of the above isn't for her.*

Shaking his head to dislodge the thought he reached under the sink for the meteorite. It was heavier than he remembered so he set it down on the table. Good, it gave him an opportunity to change the subject. Halley seemed to welcome the distraction, too. She touched the meteorite and examined it.

'Why didn't you ask your factor to take this over to Lexie's, too?'

'A – I don't trust him. And B- I'm aware that the meteorite is valuable financially and scientifically. You've mentioned donating it to the Kelvin Grove Museum. If you allow me, I'll keep it at my place until you return next year or send over instructions what you intend doing with it.'

Until you return next year . . .

'Of course,' she agreed. 'I did wonder if it'd make it through customs. The last thing I want is to have it seized and it sit on the back shelf of some dusty cupboard for years to come.'

'Good point.'

'Okay.' All at once she was very brisk. 'I'll shove a few necessities to tide me over the next couple of days into a rucksack and then we can get going.' Her tone made plain that she wasn't entirely sure that moving in with him, even temporarily, was a good idea. Tor watched her disappear into her bedroom and, remembering last night's kiss, acknowledged that she was probably right.

Chapter Twenty-nine

Tor's Land Rover was parked outside and, once they climbed in and belted up, Halley enjoyed splashing through the waves on the way to Tor's Airstream – *Beag air bheag*. The waves skooshing up the side of the Land Rover, the milky blue sky and pale-yellow sun created such a beautiful image that she began to relax and to forget, momentarily, about losing Tam's tin.

'What does *Beag air bheag* mean?'

'Little by little,' Tor replied. Halley frowned, wondering why he'd chosen that name for his highland hideaway. She'd ask him later, perhaps when conversation stalled in the Airstream. 'Lexie christened it *The Zeppelin*, deciding that Airstream didn't quite fit its futuristic shape.'

'I see.' Deciding that he was in a contemplative frame of mind, Halley said no more.

'Here we are,' Tor announced, rounding a bend on the shore taking care to avoid huge slabs of grey and white striped rocks thrusting up through the silver sands. 'And here she is.'

His stainless-steel Airstream came into view and Halley let out a gasp of astonishment at its skilful conversion. The whole structure was raised on two sturdy legs front and back to minimise risk of potential flooding and the front and rear walls had been replaced by fantastical windows shaped like a dragonfly's eye. Through the front one, Halley spotted a large desk and chair and imagined Tor sitting there watching the sun set over the beach at Arisaig. Six metal steps led to a small deck area which gave access to the side entrance of *Beag air bheag*. Immediately behind the dragonfly window the metal flue of a wood burning stove was visible and Halley was relieved to learn that she wouldn't freeze to death during her stay.

Least of your problems a little voice whispered, recalling last night's kiss before consigning it to the back of her mind. Roping it off, much as the police rope off a crime scene with tape. Only, instead of 'Crime Scene. Do Not Cross', it read – cross this line at your emotional peril. Much safer to concentrate on the architectural details of Tor's home she decided, smiling for the first time that morning.

'Come on, you can put the coffee on while I get the wood burner going.' Stiff-legged Tor climbed down from the Land Rover, opened the boot and removed the meteorite. 'Can you carry your holdall?'

Halley fetched her luggage and followed him up the steps to the side door of the Airstream, pausing to look across the Sound of Rum and south towards Arisaig. Tor opened the door and stepped inside, inviting her to follow.

'Wow,' she said, dropping her luggage at her feet and turning towards Tor with a shining face. 'May I?'

'Sure, go ahead; explore. It won't take long.' Grinning self-deprecatingly and putting the meteorite on his desk, he closed the door behind them. Halley walked past the desk and the wood burner towards the middle of the Airstream, the kitchen area and a queen-sized bed. She stood by the bed admiring the stainless-steel pine clad walls and ceiling, the porthole windows providing a breath-taking view across the Sound. Trying not to be too obvious or acting like she'd never been alone with a man, she looked for another bed. There wasn't one. The roped-off area of her brain went into hyper drive and, as she wondered about sleeping arrangements, a shiver ran thorough her.

As if capable of reading her mind Tor, having lit the wood burner, followed her through the open doorway to the kitchen area. '*Beag* can easily accommodate two adults. This sofa converts into a bed. I'll sleep there and you can have the bed.'

She measured the bed against Tor's six-foot-three frame. 'Oh, but its tiny' she protested, 'You'll hardly fit on it.'

'I'll be fine,' he dismissed her concern. 'The queen-sized bed has curtains which can be drawn round it, like this.' He demonstrated exactly how they worked. 'Very private. You can see the Milky Way through the portholes to the side of the bed. I thought you might like to sleep there and enjoy the view.'

'At the risk of repeating myself and sounding like an over excited teenager, *Wow.*'

'There's a seating area and another bay window at the far end of the Airstream. Should you want a shower, there's a bathroom, tiny but fully functioning.' He walked over to a curved stainless-steel door and slid it open to reveal an electric shower, heated towel rail, loo and washbasin.

After the trials and tribulations of the last twenty-four hours Halley started to relax. As he showed her round the Airstream, she gained the impression of a man proud of what he'd achieved. A former soldier who'd been through a great deal but was going out of his way to make her feel at home. Biting her bottom lip to prevent herself from coming out with another juvenile 'Wow', which in no way summed up what she was really feeling, Halley walked to the end of the Airstream. Not only to check out the second dragonfly window and cosy seating area but to hide the fact that she felt completely overwhelmed with emotion as Tor showed her round his inner sanctum.

His safe place.

Letting out a shaky gasp she wiped unbidden tears away with the sleeve of her coat. Tor must have heard her sniff because he was at her side with a box of tissues, wordlessly, pulling out a couple and handing them to her.

'So- sorry,' she gulped, 'I – oh, God.' Conversation being beyond her, she reached for the box, pulling out more tissues to cover her embarrassment.

'No need to say another word. I'll make the coffee. Take off your coat, kick back, enjoy the view, look around. Whatever. I'll join you in a couple of minutes.' He smiled and pulled off his beanie, throwing it and his coat on the pull-out bed. Halley did as she was told and although looking round the Airstream didn't take long it was exactly what she needed to gain mastery over her emotions. Pushing the soggy tissues up her sleeve, she felt chastened that she'd entertained the crazy notion Tor would jump her bones once her guard was down.

Jump her bones? Where had she dredged that up from? Now she'd split an infinitive; she really was on a downward slope. That made her smile and, finally following orders, enjoyed the view. Her breathing and heart rate returned to normal and she knew they'd be able to peacefully coexist until the problem of the bothy's door was sorted out. Smiling, she turned to face him, eager to let him know she was comfortable with the idea of staying in *Beag air bheag*.

Perhaps, here, she'd be able to relax – *little by little*.

'Coffee's on its way.' To demonstrate she was back to her usual calm, collected self, Halley joined Tor in the galley kitchen by the curved, central island. 'One more thing, this side of the central island lifts up and pulls out to form a table which rests on two legs, like so.'

'Everything in its place and a place for everything,' she laughed, the last of the tension slipping away. Looking underneath the 'table' she discovered pots and pans neatly stacked in ascending order. 'Base Camp Basra,' she joked. Then, remembering his injuries, realised her comment was insensitive. 'Oh, Tor, I'm sorry.' She put her hand over her mouth to stop any more tactless words escaping.

Tor put her at ease with one of his smiles. 'You're right. I do like to live in an orderly environment, put it down to army training. Unlike Monty's day, officers have to share a batman, if there's one available. It isn't that officers aren't capable of looking after themselves, their uniforms and so on, it's more a case of us having better things to do with our time.'

'Such as?' Halley picked up the coffee mug he pushed towards her, her hand steady and breathing back under control.

'Organising and overseeing troops, demonstrating leadership, assessing dangerous situations and responding accordingly.' He rattled through the catechism of his previous role in the Scots Guards. Then his face clouded over as he was taken back to the moment when the IED's went up. He gave himself a shake, searched in a cupboard for a packet of biscuits and when he turned to face her his emotions were back under control. 'Think of a batman as a military PA rather than a servant. They learn from their officer and tend to promote quickly or deliberately keep the job long term, because they like it so much.'

'Like Tam.'

'Like Tam,' he agreed. He clinked his coffee mug against hers in salute.

'Now,' she said briskly, feeling suddenly, inexplicably happy and upbeat. 'Tonight, I will be your bat (wo)man,' she laughed. 'I'll make the dinner, wash up afterwards and, if it's a cold, clear night, we can spend some of it stargazing using the telescope I spied on your desk.'

'I should have hidden it. Not quite what you're used to.'

'Size isn't everything.'

There was a 'freeze frame' moment and then they burst out laughing at her choice of words. It was the first time Halley had seen or heard Tor laugh so openly and uproariously and she liked it.

'I have stuff to sort out,' Tor said. 'Phone calls needing to be returned, that sort of thing. Make yourself at home.' He headed for the desk at the front of the Airstream, still laughing at her discomfiture.

'Well done,' Halley said sotte voce. 'Classic Dunbar, simply classic.'

However, she grinned as she collected their mugs, put them in the tiny sink and then got down on her knees to root through the under-the-counter fridge to see what she could find to make for dinner.

Chapter Thirty

It was dark by five o'clock although there was a thread of light on the horizon where the sun sank below the sea. Thanks to the wood burner and top-quality insulation, the Airstream was warm as toast and the soft lighting provided the ambiance needed for Halley to recover from the shock of the burglary. The very word made Tor's forehead wrinkle in consternation as he wondered who was behind the break in and why the telescope, orrery and clock hadn't been taken. Despite the plausible explanations he had given to calm Halley's fears, things simply didn't add up.

Was the plan to frighten her so much that she'd hightail it back to Hawaii without a backward glance? If so, who was behind it? He pushed the thought aside and watched from the chair by his desk as Halley stripped off her fleece, put her hair up in a scrunchy and set about preparing a simple meal of spaghetti bolognaise.

Swivelling his chair slowly from side-to-side, enjoying the heat pulsing out from the wood burner and having Halley in *Beag air bheag*, he relaxed, watching as she turned sheets of kitchen roll into improvised napkins and placed knives, forks and spoons on top. Then, reaching for the open shelves behind the central unit, she brought down wine glasses and tumblers and put those on the table, too. Tor couldn't help his eyes straying to the curve of her bottom in her skinny jeans and admiring how the denim accentuated her long, slim legs.

He reined himself in, those were dangerous thoughts and quite inappropriate.

It had been a long time since the Airstream had benefitted from a woman's touch. Other than Lexie, and occasionally Bryce, he rarely welcomed visitors to *Beag air bheag*. This was his safe space and he hoped that once Halley recovered from the trauma of losing Tam's tin, she'd start to feel the calming vibe he'd taken such lengths to create. Another shake of his head. That assumed she'd be staying for longer than the day or so it took to make the bothy secure. It was time to apply the brakes to his wild imaginings. Placing his hands on his thighs, he pushed himself up from the chair and onto his feet. Pausing to gain balance and avoid putting undo strain on his wasted leg muscles, he cursed as familiar pain travelled the length of his injured limb.

'Sorry about the lack of napkins and candles.' He walked over to her, trying hard to ensure his limp wasn't too obvious. Jings – she was really getting under his skin; he didn't usually bother hiding his disability. 'Your observation earlier was spot on.'

'Which one?'

'Base Camp Basra.'

She turned to him with a serious face. 'I hope I didn't speak out of turn. Is that where you were stationed, when . . .'

'When my Vallon Man stepped on an IEP and triggered a chain reaction?'

'Vallon Man?'

'Yes. A bright young corporal whose job it was to sweep the ground in front of us with a Vallon detector. But,' he took a deep breath and then stalled.

'But?' she prompted gently.

'My cocky second lieutenant, ignoring the warning cries of the corporal and our experienced sergeant, walked straight into the minefield and set off a daisy-chain of IED's.'

Her hand went up to her mouth, her eyes widening in horror. 'Daisy-chain?'

'Yes, an innocent sounding name for a chain of linked IED's.'

She took a step towards him as though, instinctively, she wanted to comfort him but held back. 'Go on,' she urged, perching on a bar stool.

'I was blown off my feet and backwards onto the roadway. I lay there quite some time, I think, I can't be sure as everything appeared to slow down. Unable to move, I heard everything through my headset: men screaming, shouting, garbled messages calling for reinforcements. All against a backbeat of explosions and gunshots.'

'I'm sorry, I shouldn't have probed.'

'No, it's fine. I can't deny what happened. That would be wrong and disrespectful to the men who lost their lives. My therapist encourages me to deal with flashbacks.' Reaching out, he picked up the bottle of red wine she'd left to breathe and poured them both a glass, trying to forget that 'claret' was the soldiers' nickname for blood. 'Slainte Mhath.'

'Slainte,' she replied, touching the rim of his glass with hers. 'Base Camp Basra?' she prompted, evidently wanting to know more. Perhaps in an attempt to understand where he was coming from? He hoped so. Now they'd stopped side-stepping each other he found her easy to talk to and . . . He looked deep into his glass of red wine and made a promise to himself that he wouldn't kiss her, no matter how much he wanted to.

That was a different kind of danger.

'Actually, it happened in Sangin, Helmand Province. But war is nothing new, look.' Walking over to a small bookcase he picked out a battered copy of Homer's *Odyssey*. 'Monty sent this over to me while I was in hospital awaiting skin grafts. It was his personal copy which travelled with him while he was in the army. He maintains that Odysseus suffered PTSD after the Trojan wars and his ten-year odyssey was his way of making himself whole before returning home.'

'What did Tam think?'

'He thought it was *a load of mince*, to use his words, and sent me The Broons and Our Wullie annuals as a counterbalance.'

'Yes, I can imagine that. Tam had no time for psychobabble, deep thinking or internal angst. Homer's Odyssey, indeed!' She smiled at the thought of her no-nonsense great-uncle. She sobered and Tor guessed that her thoughts had returned to Tam's missing medals.

'He'd hate you to be upset over the loss of the tin. He'd probably say: *Och, the tin's gone, lassie, dinnae fash yerself.*'

'You're right, he would. And if I might make a personal observation, Major Strachan, you have a very convincing Scottish accent.'

'That's thanks to our Nanny who was my mother's cousin.'

'Why did your mother employ a cousin as nanny rather than hire one from a top agency? Sorry,' she held up her hands, 'none of my business.'

'Probably because she didn't want anyone outside of the family to know too much about the castle and the open nature of her and Monty's marriage. If you get my drift.'

'I see.' Halley blushed, as if she was being too inquisitive about matters which, although public knowledge, really were none of her business. 'Did she get on with Tam? Your nanny, I mean.'

'God, yes. They were a right pair when they got together, talking about life in Glasgow and the Ayrshire coast, *going doon the watter* on paddle steamers like the Waverley when they were kids, celebrating the Glasgow Fair holidays, going dancing at Barrowland. That annoyed Mother no end, she prefers not to reference her family's humble roots.'

'I can imagine.'

'Nanny Nesbit, or Cousin Nancy as we called her, had a broad Glaswegian accent which we picked up because we spent more time with her than Mother. I am told that I had a fine Central Belt accent until I attended prep school. Then I was sent to boarding school, where I learned to talk like an English gentleman.' He pulled a comical face and Halley laughed.

'What became of her?'

'When Lexie went off to school, Cousin Nancy declared the heilans too tame for her and returned to Ayr where she still lives. She would have come to Tam's funeral but is too frail to travel these days.'

'That's a great story,' Halley declared, sipping her wine.

Tor raised his glass. 'Tam and Monty and Cousin Nancy.'

Halley repeated the toast and then changed the subject. moving the conversation along. 'You mentioned The Broons and Oor Wullie. There's a statue of Oor Wullie next to the V and A in Dundee and a full-size bronze replica of Desperate Dan and Minnie the Minx on the street towards the centre of town. I managed to pay them a visit during my stay. I longed to be Minnie when I was wee and as you say, Tam loved those comics. He used to save them for when I came to stay each summer, until –'

'Until?'

'Until I – no longer came.'

'I see.'

The elephant in the room raised its trunk and waved at them, demanding that Halley open up and tell him everything. However, she was either unwilling or unable to do so and so he had to accept that. Her silence on the subject, however, troubled him.

'It was a combination of Homer's Odyssey and D C Thompson comics which kept me sane during nights when the pain meant I couldn't sleep. Anyway, enough of that.' He gave himself a shake. 'We should make the most of the peace and quiet. Lexie won't be able to keep away once she knows you're here and will probably visit at first light.'

He laughed and Halley joined in.

'I love Lexie. I'm going to miss her and Rowan when I head back ho–' She stopped herself from saying *home* and substituted it with, 'Hawaii.' If there were others she would miss, she didn't elaborate, and Tor didn't push. 'I've had my leave extended, courtesy of the university, chopped-in my ticket on line and bought a new one. I have a few days left and one last thing to do before I return to Hawaii.'

Tor's heart sank when he thought ahead to the days when the bothy would lie empty, she'd be in front of her telescope and he'd be back to his pointless day to day existence. Hiding his feelings, he asked a less dangerous question.

'When might that be?' His mouth was dry after asking that leading question so he took a long drink of sparkling water. Halley walked round to the other side of the unit, drained the spaghetti, added butter and tomato puree and gave it a good stir.

'I want to be in Morar on Remembrance Sunday to lay a wreath at the war memorial in Tam's memory. The woman who handles Rowan's floral tributes is making it for me. Then I'll pack and head for the hills.' She pulled a wry face. 'Quite literally. The Haleakalā Observatory is above three thousand metres in altitude. Oh, I think I covered that topic the other night. Boring, sorry.'

'No. I like to hear about your life in Hawaii.'

'Hungry?' she asked, moving the conversation along.

'Yes, starving,' he replied. She put spaghetti in two large bowls, topped it with bolognaise sauce and finished off with grated parmesan. 'Allow me, Doctor Dunbar,' Tor pulled out a barstool so she could sit at the table.

'Thank you, kind sir,' she responded as he shook out her kitchen roll napkin and laid it across her knees. They laughed, clinked glasses and started eating, leaving the elephant wondering when the topic would raise its ugly head again.

Chapter Thirty-one

Halley put the tray on the table and walked over to the dragonfly window.

'I've said this before, but it's worth repeating . . . this would be a fabulous location for a Dark Sky Park, it has everything: clear view of the milky way and planets, International Space Station bang on cue, zero light pollution and, depending on the time of year, meteor showers by the bucketload.'

'All it lacks is a knowledgeable astronomer to tell us exactly what we're looking at.' He joined her at the window before asking his next question. 'You don't happen to know of a knowledgeable astronomer looking for a new position, do you?'

''fraid not,' she replied. Momentarily distracted by the reflection of them standing together, heads almost touching, she forgot to look at the stars.

'What can you see?' Tor's breath grazed the back of her neck with the lightest of touches. She gave a reflexive shiver, surreptitiously touching her nape to offset the sensation. Did he have to stand so close? She needed a distraction, something to stop her heightened senses remembering the kiss they'd shared and how much she longed to repeat it.

Conveniently, Tor provided it. Moving away from the window he went through to the other end of the Airstream, returning with their coats. 'It's a bit spur of the moment, however I might not have a Doctor of Astrophysics at my disposal any time soon. So, I thought I'd make the most of you.' His sentence seemed deliberately provocative and caused a new quiver of awareness to traverse from the crown of her head to her fleece-lined boots. She glanced up at him through her eyelashes, wondering if he had chosen his words to have that effect.

'You can't afford me,' she said, raising her head and sending him an unconsciously coquettish look.

'We'll see about that,' he laughed, holding out her coat so she could slip her arms in the sleeves. 'Although, to be fair, I don't require payment for your stay in Beag air Beag, so I think it would be in the spirit of the thing if you gave me a guided tour of the cosmos for free.'

'Quid pro quo?'

'Exactly. Unless you're not up to the task.'

'Course I'm up for it. I'd be pretty poor at my job if I turned down the chance to observe stars against such a fabulously dark sky. But what about . . .' she gestured towards the coffee and cheesecake.

'We can microwave the coffee on our return or, better still, have a wee dram to warm us up.

'Really?' Halley's teasing smile concealed that she considered the idea of a 'wee dram' somewhat ill advised. Already slightly squiffy after two large glasses of red wine she was feeling uncharacteristically flirtatious. A tot of single malt might push her over the edge, make her do something dangerous, like . . .

Live a little?

Tor gave her no time for further thought. 'Halley? Coat?'

'Hm? Oh, thanks.'

Casting caution to the wind she zipped up her brand-new parka with its fur lined hood, drew hat and gloves out of the pocket and put them on. Tor let them out of the Airstream via a door leading to a high bank accessed by a metal drawbridge. He crossed the bridge and waited for Halley, holding his hand out towards her.

Halley regarded the drawbridge and made a joke. 'Is this to repel boarders, or mainly Lexie?'

Tor laughed. 'Got it in one. Mind you, once Lexie sets her mind on something she won't be put off.' That Halley could believe. 'Take care, the ground is very uneven.'

Intent on proving she wasn't in her dotage, Halley ignored his extended hand, missed her footing and slipped on the muddy ground. Tor put his arm out to catch her and this time she grabbed it like a lifeline. Effortlessly, he hauled her to her feet, pulling her against his chest and holding her there, in no apparent rush to release her.

Thinking as one, Halley raised her face as Tor brought his mouth down on hers. The kiss trumped the tentative kisses they'd already shared. It was passionate, soft and tender yet full of promise. Halley clutched at his coat, drawing him closer, lengthening and extending the kiss as though her life – their lives – depended on it. It was dark behind her closed eyelids, but she knew that if the International Space Station were to suddenly appear through the green shimmer of the Northern Lights and land on the beach to the accompaniment of the music of the spheres, she would ignore it.

Nothing mattered in that moment as much as kissing Tor Strachan and having the kiss returned with interest. She shifted in his arms, her foot slipped on the muddy bank once more, pulling them apart and the kiss ended. They stood transfixed in the darkness while constellations and stars wheeled overhead, their breaths mingling and coalescing in the frosty air. Then the world righted itself and they drew apart, aware that, in less than a week, Halley would be on a plane to Hawaii and all this would seem like a dream.

'Halley, I'm sorry.'

'Don't be. I'm not.'

'I should have known better.'

'Does it get any better than this?'

'You know what I mean.'

Halley released a breath. 'Sadly, I do.'

'Let's go,' he said.

'Where?'

'Back to the Airstream. Our coffee will be getting cold.' He appeared to have himself under control, although his voice was husky and his hands warm.

'We wouldn't want that, would we?'

'Cold coffee? No way,' he laughed at her feeble joke.

'We can save the stargazing for another time.'

Time that we don't have -

'Of course, we can'

'Come on; I'll try hard not to slip.'

'Give me your hand and . . .'

Halley shook her head to show that she had her emotions under control too and the moment of madness had passed. Holding hands might lead them to stray into dangerous territory.

'I can manage.'

Tor had no answer to that. He simply walked behind her across the drawbridge to ensure her safety and they entered the Airstream. To break the spell which had fallen over them, Halley stripped off her coat and gloves, picked up the two mugs and headed for the microwave, returning with the warmed-up coffee. She handed one to Tor who was sitting in the bucket chair staring out into the darkness, his expression unfathomable.

She sat down with her drink and, for the first time since entering the Airstream, felt awkward in his presence.

Tor was the first to speak. 'You're still wearing your bobble hat,' he smiled, showing that the world was righting itself.

'I am?' She reached up with her right hand and pulled it off. He must think her an idiot, so unused to being kissed that her brain was addled. Time to put him straight and to reset the terms of their relationship, the first rule being – no more kisses.

Tor, seemingly as anxious to get things back on an even footing, opened with: 'So, what does the future hold for Doctor Halley Dunbar?'

Halley took a gulp of her coffee, glancing down at the pudding neither of them seemed to want. 'I've received notification that I've been seconded to the NASA team in Baltimore.' She paused and looked directly at him. Outwardly, he looked impressed, even if he probably had no idea what that meant.

'NASA, eh?'

'Yes. The James Webb telescope will monitor the atmosphere of distant planets and send data back. I've been appointed to the team whose job it is to interpret that data.' It was truly exciting, an experience she could hardly imagine. Yet, in reality, her heart sank at the thought of leaving Lochaber and Tor Strachan. A highland laird and a buttoned-up scientist who'd become pregnant after a summer romance with his half-brother. How could that possibly work?

'Beam me up, Scotty. Little Green Men? That kind of thing?' She took the light-hearted reference at face value, knowing he wasn't trying to denigrate her achievement. That, like her, he was trying to forget that earth-shattering kiss and steer them on to safer ground. 'I'm not sure what that all means but your enthusiasm is contagious.'

Halley smiled; she hadn't realised how skilful she was at hiding her inner turmoil. Shifting the focus away from herself, she asked: 'What about you?'

He sighed, his expression darkening. 'Marry – sooner rather than later, to one of the prospective brides Mother parades before me with mind numbing regularity. Provide an heir and a spare to keep the line going and take over some day in the future. However, I can't live in the toxic atmosphere up at the Big Hoose. I feel suffocated up there and need a breathing space; somewhere to call my own. That's why I had the Airstream converted, even Mother wouldn't dare to drop in uninvited.'

'So, I'm lucky to be staying here as your guest?' she joked, trying to lighten the atmosphere.

'Very.' He smiled but there was a desolation behind his eyes which suggested that, although he'd come a long way since being airlifted home from Helmand Province, he still had many miles to travel. 'You, Doctor Dunbar, have a standing invitation to stay in my Airstream any time you like.'

'Then I am honoured.' Standing, she executed a little curtsey. 'However, you're only saying that because you know I'll probably never take you up on that offer.'

'How's that?'

'I'll be back in Hawaii before I know it and then it'll be – same old-same old.'

'You'll return next summer, though?'

'The jury's out on that one.' She laughed to take the sting out of her words and Tor nodded, evidently understanding that she, too, had unresolved issues.

'I totally get that. If only I could make my mother understand that I can't get married until I've dealt with the baggage I brought back from Afghanistan. It wouldn't be fair to any woman crazy enough to take me on, let alone marry me.'

Halley looked at him covertly. Did he really not know what a catch he was, in spite of all the so-called baggage he believed he was carrying?

'I think you're being unnecessarily hard on yourself, Major Strachan.' Her use of his former military rank made him smile.

Then he sobered. 'In my head I'm still 'me' but physically I'm a different person. I left Sangin but it travelled home with me. Men died on my watch. I can't forgive myself for that.'

'We all need to forgive ourselves for mistakes we've made when our judgement was impaired, or decisions we've made when not in possession of the facts.' She thought back to Lysander and how cleverly he'd kept her in the dark about being engaged.

'I can't imagine you making the wrong decisions? You seem so confident, so self-possessed.' What would he think if he knew the truth?

'We all have demons to confront, secrets we'd rather not share. But that's life, isn't it?'

'I – I suppose you're right. All I know is that when I'm with you I can almost believe there's a light at the end of the tunnel.' He glanced at his watch and changed the subject. 'You have the first shower while I set up the pull-out bed.'

'It still feels wrong to have your bed when . . .'

Tor didn't give her the chance to finish. 'Sometimes, things can be wrong but feel oh so right.' With that he put their mugs and abandoned cheesecake back on the tray and walked through to the kitchen.

Was he referring to the kiss they'd exchanged out there in the freezing cold? She guessed that he was as confused as she was. Making a vow not to add to the tally of kisses no matter how much she longed to, Halley fetched her rucksack and headed for the shower.

Chapter Thirty-two

Halley was awoken by Tor shouting in the darkness followed by a large crash. Drawing back the curtains on her bed she stumbled through the doorway, half asleep, to find him lying on the floor and muttering incoherently. Knowing it was dangerous to wake someone from a deep sleep (or was that sleep walking?) and worried that he might accidently lash out, she called his name.

'Tor. Tor, wake up.' No response. 'It's Halley, you're having a bad dream.' She prodded him with her bare foot a couple of times and then stood back. Eventually, after what seemed like an age, Tor took a couple of shuddering breaths, put his arm over his eyes and surfaced from his troubling dream. Thinking it was safe to step over him, Halley crossed the floor and switched on the light over the cooker.

'Wha– ? Halley?'

'You were having a night –' She stopped herself from saying the word in case it drew him back into his bad dream. 'You fell out of bed. I told you it was too short,' she attempted a feeble joke. 'Have you broken anything?'

'No. I'm okay. The only thing hurt is my pride.'

Halley was glad that he was able to laugh about lying on the floor and dug a little deeper. 'Were you back in Sangin?' Getting to his knees with difficulty, Tor eventually sat on the edge of the pull-out bed with his head in his hands.

'In truth, I'm always there; it's like I've never left.' Halley's heart gave an empathetic squeeze and she took in a deep breath.

'Come on, you can't sleep on that bed. It's only fit for a Hobbit, and we both know it.' She held out her hand and he took it. 'Plenty of room on my bed.' She hoped that he registered she'd said *on*, and not *in*.

'Are you sure?'

'Perfectly sure.' Halley wasn't exactly certain what she was offering or if Tor realised that she'd be sharing the bed, but she was overwhelmed by the need to comfort him. Picking up the pillows from the pull-out bed she carried them through to her sleeping quarters. He followed and stood by while she remade the bed, plumping the pillows and fitting them alongside hers. 'I'll just put out the light,' she said, heading back to the kitchen, 'Wait there,' she pointed to an exact spot on the floor.

Tor did as she instructed, evidently still half-dazed with sleep and too groggy to argue.

Halley looked over at him from the cooker as she switched out the light. She guessed he usually slept naked and that his 'pyjamas', consisting of a pair of shorts and a faded t-shirt, had been hastily thrown on because she was his guest. Not that it mattered; she felt perfectly comfortable being alone in the Airstream with him. How many other men could she say that of? Her only concern was that her hormones appeared to have developed a will of their own, emboldening her and making her act in an uncharacteristically reckless fashion.

Re-joining him by the bed, she climbed on to it. Custom-built to fit the space, it was raised higher than a normal bed in order to escape any drafts entering the Airstream. Drawing up the large patchwork quilt folded at its foot, she lifted a corner and invited Tor to hop in. He hesitated, evidently weighing up the pros and cons of their new sleeping arrangement before joining her under the quilt. They lay side by side in the darkness, ramrod straight, neither speaking or touching until their heartbeats slowed and they relaxed.

As Tor had mentioned, the Milky Way could be seen through the portholes on Halley's side of the Airstream, a streak of paler light in the dark highland sky. That was familiar, calming and encouraged Halley to break the silence.

'Want to tell me what the dream was about?'

Tor let out a long breath before answering. 'It's always the same.

We're being shot at from all sides as we try to evacuate the wounded through a labyrinth of booby-trapped alleyways.'

'Go on,' she encouraged.

'There's a series of explosions as IED's are triggered. Then smoke, confusion, the smell of homemade explosives, cheap but effective. Next thing, I'm being loaded on a stretcher and put in the back of an army Land Rover and a medic – a nurse, is fitting a saline drip and giving me a shot of morphine. Later, she told me that the only way she knew I was still alive was every time we went over a bump I gasped in pain and squeezed her hand.'

'Oh, Tor,' Halley said, a lump forming in her throat. In the dim light she turned on her side to face him, hoping he couldn't see the tears in her eyes. However, his eyes were closed as he rewound the video in his head, reliving every distressing moment. Instinctively, she reached for his hand and held it, encouraging him to continue.

'The injuries were bad enough but the loss of connection with my team when I was back home, hurt more. I felt that I'd let them down. I still do.' He turned to face her, their noses almost touching, his breath warm on her cheek and smelling of toothpaste. 'Can you understand that?'

'I think so.' She wondered if that team included the nurse who'd travelled back to the camp with him under enemy fire. As if reading her mind, he continued, his voice roughened with emotion.

'This might seem a strange thing to say,' he took a shuddering breath, 'but there's a kind of love, soldiers in a war zone share. It makes us brave when we're together but smashes us to pieces when we're alone and apart.'

'Almost like belonging to the same clan?'

'Exactly. I guess I should know all about that.' He laughed at his own feeble joke.

'Like you and that nurse?' she had to ask.

'Like me and that nurse,' he confirmed. 'We met up a few times at the rehabilitation centre when she was on leave, but it wasn't the same. My fault entirely.' He gave a huff of annoyance at his inability to make the relationship work.

'A different time, a different place?' she questioned, referring to the rehabilitation facility.

'Too different, to be honest. Our connection had been severed.' Now it was Halley's turn to nod in understanding. 'Apart from Tam, Monty and my therapist, you're the first person I've opened up to about that moment in Helmand. Now Tam's gone, Monty's grieving and I feel that I can't burden him with any more at the moment.'

'I understand.'

She wanted to say *you can tell me anything, don't hold back,* but felt that might be a step too far.

'Then there's the women mother lines up, like prize fillies, expecting me to choose one and get married ASAP. Like a bizarre version of Blind Date. How could I marry one of them, any of them? How could I make a potential bride understand what's going on, in here?' Releasing her hand, he tapped his forehead.

'If she loved you, she'd have a damn good try.'

'She would?'

'I would.' The words slipped out with such vehemence before she could stop them. Now it was her turn to groan, realising that she must seem every inch the scheming hussy his mother painted her.

Tor laughed. 'Don't worry, I understand. It's the nature of the confessional. Nothing said or done here will go further than the stainless-steel walls of the Airstream.' They both rolled over on to their backs, stared at the pine clad roof above them and the awkward moment passed. 'You're a great listener.'

'I'm glad you think so.'

During the next drawn-out minutes, neither spoke. Tor didn't say: 'your turn', but she gained the distinct impression that he was waiting for her to unburden herself. To reveal what had kept her away from Lochaber all these years. However, she wasn't prepared to do that, she'd kept her secret this long and it was going to stay that way.

As they lay in the darkness, not moving, not touching, Halley totted up the days left before she headed to Inverness and caught the plane to Heathrow. An exact re-enactment of the moment when, on her way home, she'd miscarried Lysander Strachan's child. How could she possibly share that information with Tor who was not only twice the man Lysander would ever be, but also his brother?

Better to keep it to herself for another twenty years, if not forever. No matter how she told the story or how sympathetically Tor Strachan listened, it could only end badly.

Next morning, around seven thirty there was a loud rapping on the Airstream's door.

Last night, following their heart-to-heart, Halley had found it difficult to sleep. After tossing and turning, thumping the pillows into shape, huffing and puffing and getting up to go to the loo (twice) – a tricky manoeuvre which involved climbing over Tor, he'd turned on his side and pulled her into his warm body to still her restlessness. Halley had been too shocked to protest. However, upon discovering that she liked being spooned by Tor Strachan, she'd sighed, settled into the embrace and wrapped her free arm around him. After that, their breathing had slowed, the warmth radiating from each other made their eyes heavy as their bodies connected emotionally and physically in the dark.

Loathe to break the spell but knowing that the person knocking at the door wouldn't go away, Halley disentangled herself from Tor's limbs and tried to sit up. Evidently missing the physical contact, Tor muttered something incomprehensible and pulled Halley back into his arms in an attempt to shut out the urgent rapping. Aware that it wouldn't do for whoever was knocking at the door to find them twined together, like lovers, Halley shook him in an attempt to wake him.

'Tor. Tor,' she whispered, trying to untangle herself. 'Someone's at the door.'

'Hm? No, it can't be; it isn't time yet.'

Time for *what*, she wasn't exactly sure but she managed to wriggle free and was sitting up in bed when Frank Bunce entered the Airstream. Without asking or waiting for permission, he switched on the desk lamp and then stood at the foot of the bed taking in every detail. Halley's tousled hair, flushed cheeks and rucked up night dress, Tor's breathing as he surfaced from sleep and how relaxed they were in each other's arms. Details he would no doubt embellish when he reported back to base later that morning.

'Good morning, Doctor Dunbar,' he greeted smoothly, 'sorry to disturb you and the Major.' He leered at Halley, although apart from opening up and seeking comfort from each other nothing untoward had happened between her and Tor last night. 'We have a wee bit of a crisis this morning.' He brought out his phone and for one ghastly moment Halley thought he was going to take a photo of them in bed. Again, doubtless to be shared with Lady Strachan and anyone else who cared to see it.

'A crisis?' Straightening her nightdress and aware that being found in Tor's bed was a gift Bunce could only have dreamed of, she gave Tor a none-too-gentle dig in the ribs.

'Yes. Monty's developed a chest infection and it's been decided that he should give the Remembrance Sunday service a miss. Which means that Tor will have to stand in for him.'

Bunce's voice and Halley's dig in the ribs had the desired effect, Tor surfaced from sleep and was now fully awake. Pushing himself up on his elbows, he glanced towards the foot of the bed and saw Bunce. 'What the bloody hell are you doing here?'

Bunce repeated what he'd told Halley and held out his phone. 'The signal's really bad and we couldn't get through. Lady Strachan wants you up at the castle to go over the arrangements and sent me down to fetch you.'

'I bet she did,' Tor growled. 'Okay, you've fulfilled your mission, now get the hell out of here. Inform my mother that I'll join her and Monty as soon as I can.' He looked at Halley and frowned, as if wondering how she came to be in his bed.

Bunce gave a mocking little half-bow. 'Of course, Major Strachan. I'm sure you have things to attend to.' His snide remark and ingratiating half-smile suggested that those 'things' involved Halley and a continuation of the sexual gymnastics he believed to have taken place last night.

Tor swung his legs out of the bed and perched on its edge. Bunce lingered at the foot of the bed until Tor's inimical stare made it plain that he'd outstayed his welcome.

'Was there something else?'

'No. I'll see that everything's ready for you to drive over to Morar churchyard.' He made himself sound important, as though the castle and the estate wouldn't function without him.

'That shouldn't take long. Everything's in place, I checked with Monty and the Minister yesterday. The Minister and the British Legion do all the hard work, it's only a case of my standing in for Monty at the cemetery, so don't make a drama out of this.'

Bunce nodded, made for the door and then paused, giving Halley a final, appraising look. 'Will Doctor Dunbar be attending the service alongside the family?'

'You don't need to worry about that,' Tor replied in a tone that discouraged further discussion. Finally getting the message, Bunce left them and once the sound of his utility vehicle roaring up the road towards the castle was heard, Halley let out a sigh of relief.

'Bugger,' was Tor's succinct comment.

'Quite,' Halley replied.

'He's such a clype, and will make it his business to let Mother know that we spent the night together.'

'A clype.'

'An old Scots word for an informer or a grass. Not that I'm bothered about what Mother, or anyone else thinks, I want you to know that.' Tor touched her face and his passionate look brought fire to her cheeks. 'But we can do without Bunce's innuendoes and mother's histrionics when she finds out. Damn. Today should be all about remembering the servicemen and women who've given their lives for their country – unlike Bunce and his ilk. Monty should have ejected him from his position as factor years ago but because of his relationship with my mother and Monty's relationship with Tam, he turned a blind eye to it. You've worked out that he's Lexie and Lysander's father?'

Halley nodded, feeling desperately sorry that Tor felt the need to explain the relationship, today of all days. 'I figured it out for myself, seeing you all standing together at Tam's wake and the familial resemblance between Bunce and your half-siblings. They look nothing like you and Monty.'

Tor stood up, suddenly pensive. 'This will be my first Remembrance Service since leaving the army, I don't want anything to detract from that.' He looked anxious and Halley wanted to make things better.

'I'll make breakfast while you try and contact Monty to find out how poorly he's feeling.'

'Thanks. I'll get the wood burner going so the Airstream's nice and warm for when we return. After breakfast, I'll drive you over to the bothy where you can get ready for the service in Morar churchyard and the laying of wreaths. Are you okay to walk up to the stable yard and travel in with Lexie and Bryce? I'll have to take Mother in my car, sort things out with Monty and . . .'

His voice trailed off and his eyes clouded over and it was clear that his mind was in another place. Halley's heart sank as the feeling of togetherness they'd shared last night evaporated, replaced by a kind of melancholy.

'Of course, I'm a big girl and can sort myself out.'

'Of that I have no doubt.' Evidently regaining his sense of perspective, he grinned and focused his attention on her. 'I have the scars to prove it, right?'

'You remember that,' Halley said, walking away and turning on lights to push back the November gloom. Getting the message, Tor coaxed the wood burner back to life with firelighters, kindling and lumps of coal. She watched as he used the side of the desk to haul himself back on his feet, the scar on the inside of his right thigh clearly visible below the bottom edge of his makeshift pyjama bottoms.

'Bring Tam's glengarry and carry it in lieu of his missing medals. And, Halley,' he sent her a fierce look.

'Yes?'

'If I don't have time to talk to you later this morning it's because I'll be occupied with standing in for Monty at the churchyard. Please don't read anything more into it. Last night was the first decent night's sleep I've had since coming back home and that's thanks in no small part to you. You let me ramble on, listened without judgement and allowed me to spend last night in your bed.' He gave her an ardent look, his eyes resting on her long legs which her shortie nightdress didn't quite hide.

'I'm a good listener,' she dismissed his praise.

'You're much more than that,' he said, bending his head towards her.

Halley wanted to kiss him so much but knowing that one of them had to apply the brakes she moved away from him. 'Sausages?' she asked.

'Sausages?' he looked bemused.

'Yes, sausages. Or, if you fancy the Full Scottish, I'm quite happy to make it for you, for us. Something tells me it's going to be a very long day.'

'Ain't that the truth,' he replied. Then, taking his lead from her, he headed for the shower.

Chapter Thirty-three

Halley closed the bothy door behind her, secure in the knowledge that the carpenter had done his best to make it safe. She'd be fine moving back and if she felt in the least bit anxious all she had to do was summon the cavalry: Tor, Bryce and Lexie. That was the easy bit. First, she had to persuade Tor that her decision to return to the bothy was a sound one as she suspected he'd do his best to deter her.

But what alternative did she have?

Last night had been all about them comforting each other and she was glad Tor had opened up to her. Sharing a bed with him, albeit it innocently, was undeniably seductive but how many nights could they lie together and not take it to the next level?

How many nights?

Therein lay the problem.

In a few days she'd be flying back to Hawaii and her secondment to NASA. It was a dream come true but it came at a price. That price was her burgeoning relationship with Tor Strachan which wouldn't work long distance. Added to which, Tor was an honourable man and once he learned of her and Lysander's shared history there would be no chance of them forming a relationship. Ever. Better she moved back in to her bothy and stayed there until she left, saving them heartache and misery.

Tor had enough to cope with without her adding to it.

Setting her lips in a determined line she resolved that nothing Tor could do or say would make her change her mind. Had her family been in the room they would have recognised the signs that 'the lady was not for turning', and not even attempt to dissuade her. That being decided, she quickly changed into her warmest clothes, headed for the stable yard to collect her car and drive over to the Remembrance Day service in Morar.

Once in the stable yard Halley sat in her hire car and, after turning the engine over a couple of times, acknowledged that the battery was flat. Getting out, she looked around for a member of staff who might have a set of jump leads and could charge her battery enough to get her going. However, the yard was empty and so she headed over to the workshops to see if she could find someone there. Again, no one in sight, and she guessed they'd all headed to the church in Morar for the service; at this rate she'd miss it.

She gave a groan of despair and was about to leave when raised voices across the yard made her pull back and wait.

'Tor, I love you, but you're a bloody idiot.'

'Sorry that you feel that way, mother,' was Tor's calm reply.

'You've made a complete fool of yourself over this-this-girl.'

'Woman,' he corrected.

'Well, I suppose you'd know more about that, having shared her bed last night.'

Halley's cheeks burned. Evidently, Lady Strachan wasn't one to mince her words, especially when it came to her son and heir.

'Is that why you sent Bunce down to the Airstream on the pretext of informing me that Monty isn't well enough to attend the service?'

'Why on earth would you think that?'

'You tell me.'

'I'll tell you something, the Dunbar *girl*,' she stressed the word, 'has had her eye on you from the moment she returned to Glen Annanacross. She wants to be the next Lady Strachan, mark my words.'

'I'll bear that in mind. However, I think you've got it wrong. Halley has been offered a fantastic career opportunity; one she'd be a fool to turn down in exchange for the doubtful honour of marrying an ex-soldier with PTSD and injuries which will take several operations to put right.'

'If that's how you feel, why did you sleep with her?'

'I don't think this is an appropriate conversation for us to be having.'

Halley squinted through the opening in the workshop door and saw Tor standing by her car. Clearly, he was so annoyed by his mother's interrogation that he hadn't noticed her car or that she wasn't on her way to the church.

'What if she becomes pregnant?'

'We're grownups. Do you imagine that either of us would allow that to happen?'

'You might not, but she wouldn't be the first girl – excuse me, woman, to trap a man into marriage.'

'I'm not going to listen to this. Get in the Range Rover or we'll be late for the ceremony.' Walking round to the passenger's side he opened the door, but his mother was in no hurry to leave.

'As for your father, no one is fooled by this alleged chest infection, least of all me. He didn't want to attend the ceremony because Tam-bloody-Dunbar won't be there and he'd probably let himself, and all the Strachans, down by *greetin' like wean*, when they play the last post.' She spoke in an exaggerated faux-Glaswegian accent which her father's money and elocution lessons had eliminated.

'I'm sure that no-one will be surprised that Father isn't there.'

'You're right. Unfortunately, everyone in Lochaber knows our business so they'll draw their own conclusions by his absence. Will she be there?'

'I'm assuming you're referring to Halley?'

'Who else? Don't worry, I won't make a scene.' Halley was relieved to hear that and released a pent-up breath. 'You know,' his mother paused, one foot half inside the Range Rover, 'you sleeping with the Dunbar girl could play to our advantage.'

'How so?'

'She's a tough little cookie; the burglary hasn't sent her scurrying back to Honolulu – or wherever she hails from. Get her on side and maybe she'll sell the bothy to us?'

'I don't think so; it now belongings to her family and has strong associations with Tam and her summer holidays spent in Lochaber. I don't know why you're so obsessed about it, we have properties on the estate worth more than the bothy.'

His mother tutted at his lack of understanding. 'That wretched little shed was where your father and Dunbar spent most of their time, everyone knows that. It's a source of shame, humiliation and embarrassment to me.'

Tor looked as though he'd like to say more, maybe even broach the subject of her relationship with Frank Bunce. Instead, he said: 'If it makes you happy, I'll ask Halley what her family plan to do with the bothy and ask for first refusal should they think of selling it.'

'That'd be something. And, as I say, maybe your sleeping with her can be played to our advantage. You can catch more flies with honey than vinegar.'

'Get in the car,' he repeated, openly struggling to keep his temper.

'Certainly, Tor.' This time his mother smiled and did as she was told.

Halley watched Tor reverse the Range Rover out of the yard. She walked over to the open doorway and stood there, knowing he would see her in the driver's mirror as he drove away. He'd fought their corner and for that she was glad. However, it was plain that there was no place for her on the Glen Annanacross estate, which made her decision to leave in a couple of days easier to bear.

By the time Halley reached the Kilchuimein Cemetery everyone was there: the Strachans, the minister from Morar church, representatives from the Royal British Legion and locals – including Rowan and her feckless cousin, Jim-Boab. Halley hung back, standing by of one of the low walls which led, via a path, to a stonework arch with a wrought iron gate. From her vantage point she could see cast bronze plaques commemorating those killed in the two World Wars, one on either side of the arch.

Was it sacrilege that her eyes swept the crowd for a glimpse of Tor? Was it wrong to admit that honouring the dead made her acutely aware of being alive, of making every second of every day count? There was no time for further thought as Rowan, bearing the wreath ordered in Uncle Tam's memory, joined her.

'Halley, where have you been? I've been looking for you.'

'My hire car took exception to last night's frost and wouldn't start. I ran the battery flat trying and had to ask one of the estate staff to give it a boost using jump leads. I thought I was going to miss everything.'

'I thought something like that might have happened. Here, put your wreath with the others. I hope you're pleased with the result – nothing too funereal, the flowers in the colours of Tam's favourite team, Glasgow Rangers.' She handed the wreath to Halley and they walked towards the wrought iron gate underneath the stonework arch and placed it there.

'Have I missed the Last Post?'

'You have, but stand over here with me, the piper is about to play the *Flowers of the Forest*. Tam has played at the service for more years than I can remember. Perhaps that's why Monty's stayed away? Too emotional. That's Lexie's theory, at least.'

At the mention of her name Lexie joined them. The three women linked arms together as the piper played the lament commemorating the flower of Scottish manhood killed at the Battle of Flodden. The tune was so poignant and reminiscent of Tam, that Halley dashed tears away and took a deep breath to maintain her composure.

Coming to the end of the lament, the piper tucked his pipes under his arm and walked away from the memorial. Servicemen attending the ceremony saluted one last time and the crowd dispersed. Tor drew Lady Strachan away from Lysander and Bunce and walked her back to the waiting vehicle. Then he glanced over at Halley and he sent her a half-smile while his mother glared at her.

Was it wrong to think how incredibly sexy he looked in his Crombie overcoat, grey trousers, white shirt, regimental tie and beret, complete with badge, set at a jaunty angle? Well, if it was, Halley was going straight to hell because as he walked towards her it felt as though her heart would leap out of her chest. The winter sun touched the medals pinned on his left breast and touched his hair, burnishing its copper threads to gold. Halley was reminded of the photo she'd seen on the Wall of Ancestors of him tanned, brimming with good health and leaning against the giant wheel of an army vehicle.

God, but it was going to be hard leaving this man behind and returning to a world of sunshine, blue skies and warm breezes smelling of Coconut, Papaya, and Plumeria. She closed her eyes and exhaled, when she opened them, Tor was standing at her side. Lexie and Rowan, aware of everything that had happened in the Airstream, thanks to Bunce and the castle tom-toms, grinned and gave her the thumbs up.

Hiding her smile, Halley turned to face Tor.

'You heard?' he asked, cutting to the chase. 'In the stable yard, I mean.'

'I heard. Thanks for saying what you did.'

'I could do no less. And I'd do more if you let me.' Halley looked at him, wondering what he meant. 'Mother can be very . . .'

'She certainly can,' Halley agreed and smiled to let him know that anything his mother said couldn't hurt her. 'You're her pride and joy, it's only natural that she should want the best for you.'

'You are the best,' he said.

Halley felt her throat tighten and the tears she'd shed for Tam and all the Flowers of the Forest, welled up again. She could think of nothing more to say so she simply smiled a watery smile.

'Thanks for that. And, further to your mother wondering if I – we'd – sell the salmon bothy, you can tell her that there's not a cat in hell's chance of that ever happening.'

'I don't want you to sell it. I want it to call you home every summer and . . .'

His mother, obviously not pleased to be kept waiting on the sidelines, especially by Tam's great-niece, tooted the horn and made *wind up your conversation* gestures to Tor.

'I think you're being summoned.'

'For the love of Mike,' Tor said in exasperation and then turned his back on his mother. 'Look, Mother is having friends, cronies and some of the most boring people in Lochaber over to the castle for lunch.'

'I'm assuming my invitation got lost in the post?' Halley raised her eyebrow.

'I wish mine had,' Tor groaned. He drew Halley into an embrace, not caring who saw them. 'Please, come back to the Airstream tonight, we have things to discuss.'

'Tor, really, I'm not sure that's a good idea.'

'Please. For me?' Halley's sigh acknowledged that resistance was futile. Holding her at arm's length, he grinned. 'I'll sleep in the Hobbit bed if it makes you happier.'

'I think we both know that won't happen,' was Halley's dry response.

Again, the rude tooting of the horn. This time Lexie went over to speak to their mother and Tor bent his head and kissed Halley on the mouth 'Later,' he said against her lips before pulling back.

'Later,' she agreed, not sure how the night would unfold but knowing that Tor was right; there were things to discuss. He left her, climbed into the Range Rover and drove back to the castle.

'Hey, girlfriend,' Lexie and Rowan joined Halley. 'Word on the street – well, the Silver Sands of Morar, is that you and Tor spent the night together. Is that true?'

'What do you think?'

'I think that Mother's in serious danger of having a coronary at the thought of it. I saw the humongous kiss you just exchanged so . . .'

'You really are a hopeless romantic, aren't you?'

'She is where you and Tor are concerned,' Rowan put in, laughing. 'I'm guessing that you and Bryce are going up to the Big Hoose for lunch, Lexie? In that case, Halley, if you can put up with Jim-Boab's inane chatter, drive back with me to Mallaig and I'll make us dinner.'

'Sounds like a plan.'

'Oh no, you guys, I'm stuck playing *daughter of the house* while you two have all the fun.' Lexie glanced over at Lysander who had attended the ceremony without Suzie. 'While my esteemed brother gets to act *pillock of the house*, a role he was born for. He wasn't going to attend the ceremony but Tor's operating a three-line whip, leaving Ly no room for manoeuvre.'

'A case of: turn up or else,' Rowan added.

'Does Suzie not attend these events?' Halley asked, aware that Lysander had been watching her from the sidelines ever since Tor had kissed her so publicly. She stared right back at him and he had, at least, the grace to look down at his boots. What she did was no business of his.

'Poor Suzie. She's completed another course of IVF treatment, but no luck. It's left her physically and emotionally drained. I think they'll try one more course and then accept the hand fate has dealt them. Lysander is an idiot but he's my brother and I feel desperately sorry for them both. Mother doesn't help, of course, banging on about there being no heir to continue the Strachan name. Like we're the bloody royal family, or something. Tor might come the goods in a year or two but Bryce and I have no intention of ever having children.'

'Never is a long time,' Halley said and Rowan nodded wisely.

Letting out a long breath she looked over at Lysander Strachan and wondered what her two friends would think if they knew the truth about their former relationship. Not that she had any intention of sharing with them or anyone else. If she was good at one thing, it was keeping her counsel.

'So – dinner tonight. What do you have in mind?'

'Pizza from the Co-op,' Rowan said. 'There's a deal on at the moment which includes oven chips and a tub of Ben and Jerry's finest for five pounds.'

'Food of the gods,' Lexie said, adopting a doleful expression. 'I've got to sit through at least five courses making polite conversation with Mother's ancient friends. Monty, citing his chest infection, will have dinner in his room.' Her expression implied that Monty's illness was diplomatic rather than symptomatic. 'The only person there worth talking to is Tor. It's going to be a lo-o-ng day.'

'Poor little rich girl, off you go,' Rowan laughed, waving her away. 'Halley and I promise not to have any fun. If we find that happening, we'll ask Jim-Boab to tell us about the time he had a trial for Fraserburgh Football Club. That'll take the smiles off our faces.'

'Don't discuss what went down at the Airstream last night until we're all together. I want to know everything. Chapter and verse.' She stood on the path as Rowan and Halley walked towards their respective cars. 'Promise?' she called after them but received no reply. Then: 'Come on Bryce, best smiles. Let's get this ordeal over with and then you can get back to dealing with that dead otter deposited on our doorstep this morning.

After one last wistful look she linked her arm through his and they headed back to their car.

Chapter Thirty-four

It was late when Halley returned from Mallaig and a hard frost was setting in. She was smiling because the dinner shared with Rowan, Jim-Boab and the parrot had been unintentionally hilarious. Every time Jim-Boab spoke, Polly had said loud and clear: *Jim-Boab, stop.* In the end, Rowan had taken pity on her hapless cousin, covered Polly's cage with a cloth and moved her into the sitting room while they finished eating.

Halley was going to miss Rowan, Lexie and all the others she'd become reacquainted with during her short stay. As for Tor . . . no, she wouldn't go there, not yet. She simply couldn't. Climbing out of the car she blipped it, hoping the battery would stay sufficiently charged to take her back to Inverness in three days' time.

Three days.

Was that all she had left?

She glanced up at the night sky, automatically pinpointing constellations and planets before taking the steps down to the beach. Was it her imagination, or could she really see the Aurora Borealis – the Northern Lights? They could be quite spectacular this time of year and seeing them before returning home was on her bucket list. Then she remembered, her telescope was in Lexie's bedroom so she'd have to observe them with the naked eye and try to capture their beauty on her iPhone.

Not ideal, but better than nothing. She hurried through the rose gardens then stopped dead in her tracks. How strange, the lights above the beach were fluorescent blue, not the soft colours of the aurora and were too low in the sky. What's more, they were oscillating in a regular manner, not shifting and changing with the solar wind as the ethereal Merry Dancers were meant to. Her brain kicked up a notch and she realised that the flashing lights had nothing to do with the aurora but everything to do with the two fire engines parked on the beach.

She blinked as her confused senses realised her bothy was on fire. Gripping the marine rope banister for support, she hurried down the steps to the beach.

Tor and the firefighters were beaten back by flames as the tinder-dry building burned before their eyes. The flames, heat and crackling as the roof caved in triggered familiar memories, transporting him back to Sangin and the day he'd nearly lost his life. In spite of feeling sick with anxiety he was all set to rush into the bothy in search of Halley, but knew he wouldn't get past the firemen directing their hoses on the roof and interior in an attempt to bring the fire under control.

'Stand down, Tor,' Lysander said, seemingly able to read his mind and pulling him back by the coat tail. 'Your heroic qualities are not in doubt, but, time out buddy; you don't have to be a bloody hero every second of the day. The firefighters have it covered and I'm sure that Halley, had she been in there would have made it out long before the fire took hold.'

'I'm not being a bloody hero, as you put it. And you don't know she's safe. Anyway, what are the three of you,' he nodded at Bunce and Souter who were standing either side of his brother, 'doing here?'

Lysander sent him a haughty look. 'One of the staff saw the flames, called the Emergency Services and then informed Monty and Frank. They in turn called me.' He spoke as if, during Tor's absence after Sangin, it was not unusual for the staff to consult him. That he was the heir to *Creag na h-Iolaire*, not Tor.

'Really?'

'Really.'

'Help me to convince Major Strachan,' Lysander said to Bunce, using Tor's rank ironically, 'that he doesn't have to rush into the burning building and rescue his lady love.'

That was a snarky remark too far and Tor rounded on him. 'You really are a total arse, Lysander.' He regarded Bunce with a caustic look which said: *same goes for you.*

'Thanks for that.' Lysander appeared unruffled by his show of animosity. 'I wouldn't worry about Halley, she has an instinct for self-preservation.' Before he had time to expand on the subject, the fire chief, evidently fearing that the Calor Gas tank to the rear of the building was about to blow, ordered everyone back to the shoreline.

Left with no alternative but to let the professionals get on with it, Tor stood with the waves washing over his boots, clenching and unclenching his fists. Lysander was right, there was no need for him to act the bloody hero, or to be in charge one-hundred percent of the time.

'Everyone – move even further back,' the chief ordered a second time. 'You're in the way and making a bad situation worse.' They did as they were told, sparks rising into the sky and the heat keeping the frost at bay.

Standing on the beach Tor remembered the good times he, Monty and Tam had shared in the bothy, especially after his return from the rehabilitation centre when he'd been at a low ebb. Those conversations had saved him, helping him deal with the mental scars he'd brought home from Helmand. Its destruction would be another body blow for Monty and he was worried how much more his father could take.

The bothy had been his sanctuary, too, mostly from his mother. *She* would doubtless be delighted to learn of the fire, each dancing flame eradicating Tam's memory and Halley's ownership of the building. After all, who would return each year to stand over a pile of scorched timbers and rake through the rubble to see if anything could be salvaged? Tor's heart sank. There would be nothing to draw Halley back to Glen Annanacross each summer. The link between the Dunbars and the Strachans, not to mention the burgeoning relationship between himself and Halley, would be severed forever.

Or was he reading too much into them sharing a bed last night?

His earlier upbeat mood as he'd waited for Halley's return and the thought of spending another night or two in the Airstream evaporated. Lysander's words wormed their way into his brain: *I wouldn't worry about Halley she has an instinct for self-preservation.*

What did he mean by that?

His earlier reservations about Halley and Lysander's past relationship returned and he wondered if he'd been right to dismiss them. As he'd grown to know Halley better, he couldn't imagine her forming a relationship with his brother, now or in the past. She was worth twenty of him and better than that. There was no time for further speculation as Lexie and Bryce rocked up, driving their ancient Land Rover along the beach and skidding to a halt by the nearest fire tender. Lexie was out of the vehicle in seconds, ringing her hands in distress.

'Bryce was in his workshop, saw the flames and the fire engine's blue lights as they drove past and alerted me. Where's Halley? Is she safe?' asked Lexie.

'That's the thousand-dollar question,' was Tor's faltering answer. 'I just don't know.'

'No one knows,' Lysander said. 'I've had to prevent Tor from acting the caped crusader and entering the building in search of her. Which is quite funny when you think of it; didn't we used to call the salmon bothy the Bat Cave when we were kids?'

Tor wasn't given the chance to respond as Lexie pushed Lysander in the chest with the flat of her hands. 'Shut-the-front-door,' she said, in lieu of a suitable expletive. 'Now's not the time for your so-called jokes, Lysander. Nothing about this is remotely funny.'

'I stand corrected, Miss Strachan. Gawd,' he drawled, 'you two have really lost your sense of humour. Take a chill pill, why don't you?'

At that juncture Bunce re-joined them and pointed to the path up from the beach to the rose gardens. 'You can relax, Tor. Looks like Doctor Dunbar has survived to fight another day.' Tor wasn't sure what he meant by that but choose to let it pass.

'Halley . . .' Lexie rushed forward, meeting Halley at the foot of the steps 'We were so worried – we thought . . .' She glanced over her shoulder at the others standing on the shoreline and then at the burning building.

'I was over at Rowan's.'

Lexie nodded, smacking her forehead. 'Of course, I'd forgotten.'

Tor, casting all pretence aside walked up to Halley, took her in his arms and held her as though he would never let her go. 'I thought you were in there. I tried to go in, but the firefighters kept pulling me back. Thank God you're safe.' His clipped sentences revealed the extent of his anxiety. 'If anything had happened to you, I – I don't know what I'd do.'

'Ever the knight in shining armour,' Lysander said in a loud aside, as he and Bunce shared a look.

'I'm sorry to have caused you so much anxiety,' Halley said, remaining in his arms and reaching up to kiss him. 'But . . . oh, Tor. Tam's bothy, my bothy. It's almost too much to bear after the funeral, the break-in and everything. I suppose all my possessions have gone up in smoke, too?'

'It's lucky that we moved the telescope, orrery and wag-at-the-wall clock over to the Dower House.' Lexie ticked the items off on her fingers.

'You're safe, that's the main thing,' Tor added, his voice roughened by the smoke and how close he'd come to losing her.

'Yes, I'm safe.' Turning, Halley stood with her back to him, his arms wrapped around her. 'What now?' she asked, letting out a long breath.

Tor seized his opportunity. 'You can stay at the Airstream until you leave for Inverness in two days' time.'

'Three,' she corrected, frowning as she gave the idea some thought.

'Three days, even better.' He was worried that he was coming across as controlling, manoeuvring her towards a situation she wasn't quite ready for. That was the last thing he wanted. 'Your call, naturally.' He detected her hesitation and sensed she was moving away from him. As if she was already mentally preparing herself to leave Lochaber behind.

At that moment the fire chief approached them. 'Nothing more to do here tonight other than damp down the building and keep an eye on that Calor Gas tank. You're all welcome to stay around but there's no need. Leave it to us. I'll call in and see Sir Monty tomorrow.'

'Actually,' Halley disentangled herself from Tor's arms, took a step back and addressed the Fire Chief directly. 'It's my bothy and half acre of land and I don't want to bother Sir Monty with it. I'm going home in a few days' time. After that, maybe you could liaise with Major Strachan over what's to be done?'

All three of them looked at the burned-out bothy and he nodded. 'Major Strachan? Of course. Nae bother.'

'Do you have any idea how the fire started?' Halley asked.

'No. Once it's safe to return to the scene we'll go through looking for clues. My best guess is an electrical fault, it's an old building, after all. No one's been hurt or injured, that's the main thing. I'll liaise with the major, and he can feed back to you.' Tor was glad that he had a genuine reason for staying in touch with Halley once she left. Although, it felt as if he was clutching at straws and his heart sank. The chief half-turned away from Halley and then changed his mind. 'I knew Tam well, through the British Legion in Mallaig. I'm sorry that this has happened so soon after his funeral.' Turning on his heel, he directed his attention on supervising the damping down of the building.

'Thank you,' Halley and Tor said simultaneously to his retreating figure.

'Pinkie-to-pinkie?' Tor suggested, trying to lighten the mood and to raise Halley's spirits.

'Pinkie-to-pinkie,' she repeated, although it was clear she was a thousand light years away. Tellingly, she didn't link pinkies with him this time.

'Well, that's that,' Bunce said, rubbing his hands together and seemingly bringing the matter to a close. 'If you need anything, Doctor Dunbar, you know where to find me.' He walked off, followed by Lysander, Souter and the estate staff.

'I'm guessing hell will freeze over and the camels come skating home before that happens, right?' Bryce surprised them all by expressing an opinion. This time, Halley smiled and Lexie put her arm round her waist.

'Well said, Bryce. Now, Halley, don't worry, I have loads of unwanted clothes in my bedroom at the castle. Meet me there tomorrow around ten o'clock, we'll soon find some things to tide you over.'

'Thanks, Lexie.' Halley and Tor exchanged a look but kept their expressions neutral. Lexie was a pixie compared to Halley and it would be a miracle if any of her things fitted.

'Come on, Lex, drama's over.' Bryce led her away. 'The otter left on our doorstep this morning is beginning to look a bit ripe. I'd better deal with it before I come to bed.'

'Such a romantic,' Lexie added rolling her eyes, but her love for Bryce was obvious.

Tor and Halley smiled and, there being nothing else for it, made their way to Tor's Land Rover parked further along the beach.

Chapter Thirty-five

Returning to *Beag air bheag* felt like coming home.

Its name, summed up Halley's feelings. Little by little she was falling in love with this place and the man who lived there.

She'd remained silent as Tor drove along the beach, spending time wondering why she was taking the burning down of the bothy and the tin of medals disappearance so calmly, stoically almost. In the end, she'd concluded that neither had belonged to her, not really, and that made it difficult to feel ownership of them. By the same token, all that had happened over the last three weeks felt equally unreal. As though she was experiencing everything at warp speed which, in turn, made it difficult to make sense of the funeral, wake, becoming re-acquainted with Rowan, getting to know Lexie and . . .

She sucked in a great breath – falling in love with Tor Strachan.

There, she'd admitted it.

She wasn't a great one for astrology but in that moment felt the contrary nature of her star sign, Pisces, keenly. Part of her longed for her time in Lochaber to never end while another part of her wanted to return home.

To normal life.

She forced herself to accept that nothing could come of her feelings for Tor Strachan. From day one she'd been bracing herself for a confrontation between Tor and his brother which would result in her cover being blown. Once Tor learned that she'd slept with Lysander, become pregnant and miscarried their child, he'd want nothing more to do with her.

Of that she was quite certain.

The idea of him thinking badly of her, possibly despising her for falling for Lysander's lies and false promises and imagining herself the princess in the tower destined to live happily ever after, was more than she could bear.

Her throat tightened and tears pricked her eyes. She'd be leaving soon and with a bit of luck would take her secret with her. She need never see Lysander Strachan again or be reminded of what a fool she'd been. When – if – she did return in the distant future, Tor would be married, have several children and be laird in his own right.

And that would be that.

So why did her heart shatter into a thousand tiny pieces at the thought of him in another woman's arms? Looking at her with all the love he had stored up inside him, just waiting for the right woman to come along. Sadly, that would never be her. Her head was so full of contradictions and what ifs, she felt dizzy and confused.

Before the fire, it had been her intention to return to her bothy and stay there until she left for Inverness. During dinner at Rowan's, even as she'd been laughing over Polly's antics, she'd been thinking of ways of breaking her decision to Tor. Now it had been taken out of her hands and they were to spend another night together. Events were spiralling out of her control and heading inexorably towards her and Tor becoming lovers.

And, much as she might desire that with every fibre of her being, she couldn't let it happen. Did that make her seem cold-hearted, detached, too analytical and not swept away by the passion poets wrote about? She hoped not; but she had to stay cool, detached. She'd kept her secret safe and wasn't about to reveal all in the closing days of her so-called holiday.

Look where losing control had taken her in the past.

Putting her head in her hands, she groaned. Tor parked the Land Rover and was immediately concerned. 'Halley? You, okay?'

'Fine. Just thinking. My luck appears to be running out, first the medals and now this.'

He paused at the top of the steps leading to the side door of the

Airstream. 'You have to make the most of the hand fate has dealt you, make your own luck,' he said, letting them in to the Airstream. 'Sorry if that sounds like something you'd find written inside a Christmas cracker. I lucked-out in Afghanistan but it's down to me to make the best of things.' He indicated his injured leg. 'But you know all that.'

'Yes, I do,' Halley replied stripping off her coat. She threw it on the bed, sat on one of the bar stools and stared across the counter at the two-burner hob as though it was the most fascinating sight in the world. She chewed her bottom lip, wondering how to keep the conversation going yet steer it away from topics she would rather not discuss.

'You're quiet,' Tor said, and then laughed. 'That was a ridiculous thing to say, of course you're quiet, another link with your and Tam's past has gone up in smoke. No pun intended. Okay, the words are coming out all wrong; I'll shut up and let you do the talking.'

'No, it's all right really. It's hard to always say the right thing. I get it.'

He wiped imaginary sweat off his brow. 'In that case, I'll put the lights on while you move down to the far end of the Airstream and count the stars. In case any have gone missing.'

She laughed as she slid off the bar stool. 'Quite the romantic, aren't you?'

'Given the chance.' He removed her coat from the bed and ushered her towards the far end of the Airstream. 'I'll make us something to drink. Name your poison: tea, coffee, hot chocolate, wine?'

'Brandy-laced hot chocolate would hit the spot.'

'Bien sur. I take it madam requires cream, marshmallow and sprinkles?'

'I do,' she grinned, slipping into the easy way of talking they had.

'That's a pity because I don't have any of those things.' She laughed and this time her laughter was entirely genuine. Tor joined in, releasing the tension they were both feeling.

'In that case, it's only fair to warn you that I'll be leaving a one-star review on Trip Advisor.'

'Is there nothing I can do to persuade you to turn it into a four star?

'Such as?'

They were on perilous ground and knew it. Flirty dialogue came easily to them but it would be foolish to let it get out of control. She caught Tor's expression before he had time to hide it. He was thinking the same dangerous thoughts: mounting desire, a bed made for two, aware that time was running out. They were taking great pains to hide their true feelings, only too aware where this could lead.

Perhaps, once the fire brigade had made the bothy safe, they could turn the hoses on them, douse flames of an entirely different nature and prevent a more catastrophic conflagration. It was such an absurd thought that she laughed out loud.

'What?'

'Oh, nothing. Nothing sensible that is.' And, she really had to think and act sensibly, didn't she?

Tor sent her a puzzled look before continuing. 'I brought a mountain of roast beef and several bottles of champagne back from lunch. I could make you an open sandwich, something I'm very good at, if I do say so myself.'

'I'm guessing that's a skill you didn't learn in the army?'

Safer ground. Good.

'You guess right. As a teenager I was constantly raiding the castle kitchen when the staff had gone to bed. When I hit puberty, I shot up like a weed, developing hollow legs and a hunger that couldn't be satisfied.'

Halley swallowed hard, aware of another hunger which had nothing to do with hollow legs, puberty or an insatiable appetite, but everything to do with the tantalising thought of spending another night together in the Airstream. When Tor returned with two hot chocolates made from shop-bought sachets, her hands had stopped shaking and she was able to look at him with something approaching her customary cool.

'Well?' he asked.

'Well, what?'

'The hot chocolate. Have I earned that other star?'

She took a sip. 'Would you settle for a three star?'

'How about three point five?'

'Sorry, I don't deal in decimals,' she laughed at his crestfallen expression. 'And, to be fair, it isn't the best hot chocolate I've ever tasted.'

'Take pity on a poor ex-soldier?'

'Very well, seeing as it's Remembrance Sunday, I'll up it to three point five.' They drank the reconstituted hot chocolate without further comment, staring out at the stars wheeling over the Airstream. Then Halley broke the silence. 'What are your thoughts about the fire and the burglary. Do you think they're connected in some way?'

'In what way?'

'As if someone wants to scare me into leaving Glen Annanacross.'

'You're leaving in any case, aren't you? So, what would be the point?'

Halley swirled the mug in her hands, trying to dislodge the sludge at the bottom. 'That's true. Unless . . .'

'Go on.'

'Unless they want to make sure I never return.'

He was thoughtful for a moment then looked at her with such a depth of feeling that her heart skipped a beat and her stomach lurched, as if she was descending in a very fast lift. 'Which rules me out.'

'It – it does?'

'You know it does. I have no desire to see you get on that plane to Heathrow.'

No other word or sentiments seeming appropriate, she stammered out his name. 'Tor, I –'

'You're like no other woman I've ever known.' He cut across her. 'You make me feel like my former self, the Tor Strachan equipped to take on the world. From the moment we met, somewhat inauspiciously I have to admit, I've woken each morning trying to engineer ways of meeting you that appeared genuine and purposeful, rather than contrived. You've given me hope that the feelings of dread and foreboding which have haunted me since leaving rehabilitation are finally lifting.' He looked over at her, as if waiting for some sign that she felt the same.

'Am I allowed to confess that I spend most of my time looking out of the bothy window hoping I'd see your Land Rover on the beach?'

'Is that so?'

'It is so,' she grinned, her cheeks burning at how uncharacteristically abandoned she was acting.

'So, what happens next?'

'In what respect?' She needed him to be crystal clear; unambiguous.

'Sleeping arrangements. Last night, sharing a bed and confidences seemed enough. Tonight, however, I'm not so sure, but it's your call.' Cocking an eyebrow, he regarded her quizzically, leaving Halley torn between what her heart wanted and what her head told her was out of the question.

'How about you have your own bed, I have the Hobbit bed and we take it from there?'

Clearly, not the answer he was hoping for. 'You're probably right.'

'Okay,' Halley got to her feet. 'I'll take a shower and then make up the bed.'

'Fine. Take your time. The night is cold but clear and a walk along the beach is just what I need.'

Halley smiled at him, silently acknowledging that not every man would accept the sleeping arrangements with such good grace. She longed to be abandoned, spontaneous but remembered where that led before and hoped that, like Tor's walk on the beach, time alone would convince her that she'd made the right decision.

Walking to the coat rack, Tor fetched his cromack and a powerful torch. After sending Halley a longing look, he left the Airstream. There being nothing else for it, Halley headed for a shower, which she hoped would clear her mind and enable her to act with a degree of common sense and an instinct for self-preservation.

Chapter Thirty-six

Halley climbed onto the Hobbit bed, was soon asleep and didn't hear Tor returning to the Airstream. When she woke up some time later and glanced over at his bed, she could see his shape in the dim light of the desk lamp: long, lean and oh, so desirable. Reaching for her phone she checked the time: three o'clock. Not quite the witching hour but the time when she usually woke up for a drink or a trip to the bathroom.

Unsurprisingly, now she was awake, she found it impossible to get back to sleep. She tried reciting the periodic table in her head, a failsafe which usually sent her to sleep in minutes. Tonight however, she was too aware of Tor's restlessness, irregular breathing and muttered half-sentences. Plainly, he was having a rough night. She longed to climb in beside him, press her body against him and comfort him. Wanted it so badly that she considered it worth the risk of their losing control and becoming lovers.

The thought was a tantalising one, underscored with worry, doubt and whatifs.

If they travelled that road and Tor found out afterwards about her relationship with Lysander, he was sure to revise his opinion of her. Lying in the darkness she acknowledged how much she valued his respect and her own sense of self-worth – which had taken years to rebuild after her summer romance with Lysander.

Punching her pillow into shape, she flipped onto her back, willing Tor to settle, allowing her to dismiss the strong pull of sexual attraction and get back to sleep. Instead, his muttering grew louder and he gave a distressed cry which pierced her to the core. Then he called out a name and issued a stark command – *stop,* followed by more incoherent words. Aware there would be no turning back, Halley left her makeshift bed and was at his side in a flash.

Tor had thrown off the duvet and his pyjama shorts had ridden up to reveal the jagged wound on his thigh. How she longed to reach out, kiss the scar and soothe him to sleep before returning to her narrow bunk. Or, better still, get in beside him. She stood in the darkness, weighing up the consequence of that action. Momentarily, desire overruled good judgment and she thought: *What's stopping you, Halley? Tam's bothy has burned to the ground, his tin has been stolen. Clearly, someone wants you gone. Maybe it's time to stop overthinking this and live a little.*

She whispered his name. No response. 'Tor, wake up.' He was still deep in sleep when she traced along the line of his scar with gentle fingers. That made him stir and he groaned, but in a totally different register.

'Wha'?' he asked, groggily.

'It's me, Halley.'

'Get in,' he said, holding back the corner of the duvet. 'I'm cold, warm me up.' Aware that he was still half asleep, Halley did as he instructed, pulling the duvet over them. Tor's limbs were cold and she twined hers around them to transfer heat from her body to his, almost managing to convince herself that this was a medical emergency and if she didn't work fast hypothermia would set in.

The thought was so ludicrous, she smiled. Her smile vanished and she gave a gasp as Tor, clearly not realising where he was, pulled her into his arms and buried his face in her neck. 'You smell nice,' he said, then dropped into a deep, untroubled sleep.

There being nothing else for it, Halley pressed closer to him, leaving doubts, uncertainties and misgivings for morning.

Tor awoke at first light, wondering where the hell he was. He felt rested, having had his best night's sleep in, say, a hundred years. The last thing he remembered was returning from his head-clearing walk to find Halley asleep. He didn't know how he'd curbed the instinct to pick her up and carry her over to his bed. Yet, here she was, not only in his bed but in his arms. How had that happened? He had pins and needles from her head resting on his shoulder but dared not move in case she woke and ran screaming along the beach away from him.

Then he smiled at the preposterousness of the thought and the unlikeliness of the idea. He'd never come across a woman so cool, calm and collected even though he suspected it was a front for a deeply passionate and, at times, dangerously impulsive nature. She'd probably wake up, assess the situation and offer to make breakfast before strolling over to the castle to collect some clothes as arranged.

However, anything which delayed the moment when Halley returned to Inverness was fine by him. The thought of her leaving, possibly never to return, filled him with dread. He frowned; how could he have fallen for her so irrevocably in less than eighteen days? What could he say to stop her leaving? He wanted her to stay for every selfish reason he could name and the idea of not seeing her again was tearing him apart.

However, he acknowledged she was destined for greater things and that held him back from declaring himself. The clock was ticking and he – they – had to make the most of the time left. Halley stirred and so he pushed her hair off her face, kissed her gently and removed his arm.

'Good morning. Correct me if I'm wrong, but I don't remember you being in my bed when I fell asleep last night?'

'I wasn't.'

'Yet, here you are.'

'Here I am.' She shifted into a more comfortable position and he flexed his fingers to restore the flow of blood.

'After everything we decided last night, I thought . . .'

She swept that aside. 'You were having a bad dream and looked freezing cold so I hopped in to warm you up. It was an act of kindness, really.'

He couldn't see her expression but guessed she was smiling.

'You succeeded. And, if I might get personal so early in the morning,' now it was his turn to smile, 'waking up with you in my bed is the greatest feeling in the world. I've had the best night's sleep in months, lying next to you is better than all the drugs I brought back from the rehabilitation centre.'

'I'm hoping that's a compliment,' she said, snuggling closer, her breath warm on his skin.

'You'd better believe it, Doctor Dunbar.'

After some time, Tor propped himself up on his elbow and looked down on her. 'Your call, Halley. Do you want to stay here or should I do the gentlemanly thing and move onto the put-me-up? While I'm still able, that is. I should warn you that I'm feeling distinctly un-monk-like this morning and can't guarantee my good behaviour.'

'Un-monk-like?' she gurgled, clearly unfazed by his warning. 'Is that even a thing?'

'I believe it is. However, what happens next is down to you.'

Halley's long, slow breath acknowledged the fact. She turned on her side so that they lay nose to nose, shuffled closer and then kissed him on the lips. Tor returned the kiss, taking his time, they had the whole morning before them and making love to Halley was something he wanted to savour. The only barrier was their clothing and so he removed his t-shirt, tentatively pushed up her nightdress and encircled her breast. In that moment, they were so physically and sexually attuned that a bolt of desire shot through them, making them gasp in unison, forcing them to arch their backs to counter the muscle spasm.

Every instinct Tor possessed urged him to make this woman his, but he wanted to slow down, keep things tentative and unrushed. Flipping onto his back he removed his hand from Halley's breast and drew her into the crook of his arm. He was surprised when she replaced his hand, mutely letting him know that she wanted this as much as he did. Unable to resist, he started kissing her again and things soon became very heated.

Yet, he pulled back, hesitating before taking this to the next level. Halley's twenty-year absence from Glen Annanacross bothered him, every instinct he possessed telling him that unless they were honest with each other this relationship was doomed to failure. He was wondering how to broach the subject when Halley provided him with an 'in'.

'I saw the scar on your leg while you were sleeping. I didn't realise you were so badly injured.'

'Mostly shrapnel from the IED, it missed my femoral artery by centimetres,' he said, matter-of-factly. 'I was lucky, luckier than those men in my squad who didn't make it home. If the shrapnel had been any closer, I would have bled out and Lysander would've taken my place as Monty's heir.'

'Which would suit him and your mother just fine,' she commented with surprising vehemence. 'Monty, not so much.' Then, seemingly thinking she'd spoken out of turn, she changed the subject. 'I touched your scar; that's probably what woke you. Then I climbed in beside you.'

It all sounded so reasonable, innocent even. Tor edged closer and kissed her with such passion they were soon breathless. When they drew apart, he felt confident enough to move the conversation forward. 'You know the thing about scars?'

'Don't think I do.'

'Some, like the scar on my thigh, are a physical reminder of a day which changed my life forever. Others are hidden so cleverly that none can see them, but they're there and have to be confronted, dealt with. Otherwise, they fester as surely as physical scars and ruin our lives.' He felt her stiffen, as if she realised what he was alluding to. 'Do you understand what I'm saying?'

'I think so,' she said, quietly and then moved away from him.

Having come this far, he had to continue even though it could ruin things between them. 'We're each scarred in our own different ways. Believing we've let down people who mattered to us; depended on us. In my case, my men and in your case,' he took a leap of faith, 'Tam.'

'Tam,' she repeated.

'I know that your staying away from Lochaber cut him to the quick, although he never said so. Twenty years is a long time not to see someone who means a lot to you.'

'I – I loved Tam and Lochaber, but it's not that simple.' She bit her lip but said no more. Suspecting that being in each other's arms was too intimate for this conversation and desperate not to come across as controlling or pressurising, Tor provided a breathing space.

Rolling to the end of the bed he reached for his jeans and t-shirt and put them on.

'I sense you're holding back; don't you trust me?' he asked, without turning round. 'Won't you tell me the real reason you've stayed away? Unless we're honest with each other I can't see this – us – working out.'

'Do you want it to work out?' she asked in a quiet voice.

'You know I do and I'm sensing you feel the same.' He moved off the bed to sit by the desk. Halley drew the duvet up to her chin as though for comfort, sitting cross-legged on the bed.

Then she spoke quietly, without drama.

'There was a boy, more of a man, really.' Her voice was husky, as though the words drew her back to a place she was reluctant to visit. 'I'd finished my A levels, came to stay with Tam as per usual. I wanted to meet up with old friends, kick back and have some fun before heading for MIT in America, providing I got the grades, that is.'

'I'm guessing that wasn't in doubt?' He smiled at her, encouragingly.

She nodded without any false modesty. 'It was a foregone conclusion I'd win the scholarship, the first step towards my career.'

Despite the double glazing, cold air found its way through the dragonfly windows at the front of the Airstream. Tor went over to the wood burner, started it up and then perched on the end of the Hobbit bed, giving Halley time to get the facts straight in her head. Reluctant to break her train of thought, he remained silent until she took up the story again.

'It was a summer romance.' She seemed cast down, as though the memory wasn't a happy one.

A summer romance? That didn't sound so bad, he could cope with that. He had no right to sit in judgement, he'd had his fair share of romances, love affairs, relationships, some of which had ended in acrimony and bitterness. He simply wanted to learn the truth so they could move forward with no secrets.

'I'm listening,' he prompted when she stalled.

She gave herself a shake. 'He,' she did not reveal his name, 'was at a loose end and we spent the summer together. It's as simple as that. I thought myself in love; fell hook, line and sinker for his lies before finding out that he'd been economical with the truth, hidden stuff from me. If I'd known the full facts, I would never have . . .'

He didn't want to hear her say: *had sex with him.* The words sounded stark, even in his head. Halley sighed, as though it was a relief to finally unburden herself.

'Go on,' he encouraged, sensing there was more. He hoped she knew he wouldn't judge her, no matter what she revealed.

Taking a gulp, she continued. 'Although I didn't know at the time, there was a fiancée waiting in the wings. Date set for the wedding, honeymoon booked, the whole shebang. She was on a gap year with Raleigh International, undertaking good works in the developing world.' She let the duvet fall to her waist and wrapped her arms around herself.

Tor wanted to comfort her, promise her that nothing could shake his faith in her. But he knew it was important to let her to tell the story at her own pace.

'At his insistence, I – we – kept our relationship secret. He said it was more romantic that way, the two of us pretending we were just friends when in reality we were l-lovers. If Tam had known he would have grabbed him by the throat, given him the "Gorbals Kiss",' she smiled, referring to the slang for a headbutt, 'thrown him in the loch and left him to sink.'

'Tam was a wee toughie, right enough,' Tor said, 'and had probably dished out more than a few of those in his time.' He was glad they had Tam's memory to unite them and remember happier times.

Halley carried on, as though eager to get to the end of her story. 'It was Rowan who opened my eyes, told me everything, figuring it was in my best interests to know the truth; what he was really like.'

'You must have been devastated.'

'Worse than that, I felt a bloody fool, falling for his lies and false promises. I'd even contemplated not taking up my place at university, staying in Glen Annanacross and living happily ever after; marrying him. I didn't realise that wasn't on offer. Idiot.' She smacked herself on the forehead.

Tor, unable to listen to her story and remain aloof, walked over, sat on the side of the larger bed, reaching for her hands. 'We've all been there, done stupid things when we were young and impressionable, don't beat yourself up.'

Nodding, Halley began twisting the corner of the duvet into a knot, looking past him as though that summer was playing out before her like a movie. 'When I learned the truth, I had to get away. Fortunately, Rowan is the kind of person who'll take secrets to the grave – no pun intended. We cooked up a story about my having to leave Lochaber for America sooner than expected and everyone accepted it.'

'So, Rowan knew everything?'

'Not everything. Just that I needed to put as much distance between me and my – my stupidity as I could.' She stopped twisting the duvet cover and sent him a straight look, mutely telling him there was more to come. That look pierced him to the core and his breath caught in his throat. 'Long story short? I discovered I was pregnant, confirmed it with a test I bought at the pharmacy at Heathrow. I miscarried almost as soon as I landed in New York. I concealed it from my parents, telling them I was staying with a friend and would join them later. I checked into the nearest ER, got sorted out and no one was any the wiser. Until now.'

Her bottom lip quivered as she relived the moment. Tor climbed on to the bed, and pulled her into his arms. 'Don't cry, Halley, I can stand anything but your distress. It's all over now.' And he meant it, something about the way her eyes were lambent with tears made him want to search out the love rat who'd let her down and . . . but he couldn't, because it would mean betraying her trust.

Then he frowned, if the boy – man – who'd unknowingly fathered her child had married and possibly left Lochaber, then surely, she had no reason to stay away? Halley supplied him with the answer.

'I couldn't return because I knew I'd see him, bump into him accidently and – somehow, I don't know how, he'd find out what'd happened and I'd feel a bigger fool. Or worse, Tam would learn what'd happened and end up facing a murder rap.' Although she made a joke of it, her expression was deadly serious. 'I stayed away because it was easier living in a place where no one knew about *Creag na h-lolaire,* its people, and what a fool I'd been.'

'*He* was the fool, not you,' Tor asserted. He was relieved she'd been honest with him and given up her secret, but something niggled. He kissed her once, passionately, and then, walked into the kitchen, deciding that coffee, possibly with a wee drap of something in it, was necessary. 'I'll make breakfast and then you can meet Lexie up at the castle and we'll take it from there. Cool?'

'Cool,' she responded, looking happy to have unburdened herself. 'What shall we do for the rest of the day?'

'I'm sure we'll think of something.' A weak but sassy smile replaced her worried look.

'You could be right,' Tor laughed, making for the fridge. He began laying things out on the counter top, happy that their relationship was able to move forward, leaving him free to figure out how this would work with his being in Scotland and Halley in Hawaii. Once, he'd been decisive, a man of action. Now, it took him longer to process thoughts, make sense of even simple things and arrange them in logical order.

He switched on the kettle and stood staring into space as something gnawed away at his happiness. She'd said: "it was easier living in a place where no one knew about *Creag na h-lolaire* and its people." Shouldn't that have been: *Glen Annanacross* and its people? Thanks to his mother's draconian rule about 'family' mixing with local children, Halley would never have been invited up to the castle, or anywhere near it.

Something else struck him, too.

Halley had referred to Operation Raleigh, but he couldn't think of any local man whose fiancée would have had the necessary financial clout, let alone the opportunity, to take a gap year in those days. In fact, he only knew of himself, Lysander, Bryce, Suzie and a few others from aristocratic families on nearby estates would have regarded a gap year as a rite of passage. Bryce, he dismissed out of hand; he wasn't the type and was too young for the purposes of this exercise.

Which left Lysander and Suzie.

He vaguely remembered there being a hiccup before their wedding.

Something his mother and Suzie's parents had been keen to resolve and gloss over, bringing the wedding forward by a couple of months. He'd been in Iraq at the time and had no interest in domestic matters, regarding Lysander and most of his contemporaries as over-privileged and in need of army discipline.

He took down a couple of mugs, spooned coffee into them and set the kettle to boil. Glancing over at Halley sitting cross-legged in his bed looking tousled, sexy and very, very desirable made him want to join her. He didn't need to know everything about Halley in order to love her. If she considered it important, she would have revealed the name of the man/boy who had got her pregnant. Let her keep her secret and let him be happy with that. He must have taken longer making the coffee than he realised because she called over to him.

'Toast? Coffee? The Full Scottish? Get a move on Major Strachan, I need to check the bothy this morning, see if the police have any leads on who stole Tam's tin and pick up fresh clothes from Lexie,' Halley called over, unaware of the track his mind was running on.

The kettle boiled and switched itself off a third time.

It was no good; if their relationship was to go the distance, he *had* to know the identity of her former lover. Walking over to the bed he whispered the name which was going round and round in his head.

Lysander.

His half-brother.

Only he would have had the time, opportunity and complete lack of moral compass to pursue someone as naive as Halley while his fiancée was overseas. However, it didn't add up and he hoped he'd got it wrong. Every time he'd seen them together Halley had made it quite plain her distaste for Lysander, that she regarded him as a waste of space. Then there was biology to consider; Lysander and Suzie had been trying for a family for several years, without any luck. He didn't know the ins and outs of their fertility problems and didn't want to – but if Lysander had fathered Halley's child, then . . .

He frowned, waiting for the brain fog to clear, to make sense of what she had told him.

Clearly, he couldn't leave it there, so blurted out –

'Was it Lysander?'

'Was *what* Lysander? Oh, you mean . . . If it was, would it make a difference?' Her warning look, advised him not to pursue this line of questioning.

Having come this far, he had to press on. 'Make a difference? I think it would.'

By which token he meant that he'd have to get his head round the idea that she and Lysander had been lovers, deal with it and move on. His feelings for her wouldn't change, he knew that. However, his mind was in turmoil, his thoughts confused and disordered. He couldn't think straight with her lying there looking beautiful and desirable, the woman he wanted to marry and to spend the rest of his life with.

Damn Lysander and his black, conniving heart, damn him to hell!

He needed to take a deep breath, think carefully before he said something which couldn't be called back.

His safe place beckoned, offering him time and space to work this out. Grabbing his coat, he headed for the door and the beach.

'Where are you going?' Halley asked, panicked.

'I – I need time to think, sort things out; order my thoughts . . .'

Before he had time to finish, she cut in with: 'This is why I've kept this a secret. No one knows the anguish I've suffered, how it's weighed me down. I've told you everything, held nothing back. I haven't asked for details of your love affairs because it isn't important. This is about us, here and now. If you don't understand that, there's no future for us.'

She looked over at him dry-eyed but he suspected tears weren't far away, his soul was in torment knowing he was the cause of those tears. All he had to do was take off his coat, throw it on a chair, forget about Lysander and the unholy mess he'd created. His mind was befuddled, he felt dizzy, disorientated and it was as much as he could do to walk away from the bed without stumbling.

All he needed was half an hour walking the beach, after which he would return and make everything right.

'I – I – I'm sorry. I need to . . .'

The words wouldn't come, at least, not the right ones. He couldn't think straight, let alone marshal his thoughts into some kind of order. There being nothing else for it, after one last aching look at Halley, he left the Airstream and made his way across the silver sands.

Chapter Thirty-seven

Ashes, soot and pieces of scorched paper settled on Halley's hair like sinister confetti as she stood before what remained of Tam's bothy. The damage was much worse than she'd imagined and although the firefighters had done their best, there was little of Tam's old home left. This, coupled with Tor's reaction to the 'great reveal', was almost too much to bear.

The burned-out building was a metaphor for her life, a reminder that dredging up the past and revealing secrets always ended badly. Dashing away tears, she hitched her handbag over her shoulder and climbed the wooden steps to the castle, glad of the rope banister, because her limbs felt as if they had weights attached.

When she reached the stable yard her hire car was waiting. Disarming the alarm, she opened the boot and removed a pair of wellingtons Rowan had loaned her, placing them by an old mounting block. She'd drop Rowan and Lexie a text once she was in Inverness and explain why she'd left without saying goodbye.

It was strange, she reflected, how her mind was able to focus on trivial matters like Rowan's wellingtons and composing text messages, but couldn't make sense of what had happened in the Airstream. One moment she and Tor were about to become lovers and the next – pouf – everything turned on its head. Tor had made it plain that he was shocked and distressed by her confession and needed to put space between them.

Now it was her turn. Her passport, tickets and the deeds to the salmon bothy were in her handbag, she had no luggage and so there was nothing to prevent her from driving straight to Inverness.

Taking one last look around the stable yard, ancient castle and rose gardens she experienced a pang of longing so sharp she found it difficult to breathe. When, at last, she was able to take a steadying breath it turned into a great sob which acknowledged what she had lost.

How could she have been so stupid as to tell Tor the whole story? It would have been more sensible to save the last part until their relationship was strong enough to deal with the fall out. Whispering his name, she climbed into the car, slipped it into gear and gunned the engine before tears made driving impossible. She was just about to reverse out of the yard when the door was yanked open. Her heart gave a glad leap, believing it was Tor telling her not to be such a hothead, to return to the Airstream so they could talk things through.

Instead, it was Lexie with two bags of clothing.

'What's all this? I thought we'd arranged to meet later?' She waggled the bags. 'I'm a bit early but I thought I'd pop in and see how Monty was after the bothy going up in flames.'

'We did, we had,' Halley stumbled over the words. 'Arrange to meet, I mean. I'm sorry, Lexie, I have to go.'

'Go? Go where? I don't understand, you have at least another day left.'

'I – I did, I do, but,' she couldn't find the words to explain what had happened.

'Come over to the kitchen and sit down for a few minutes. You're upset; tell Auntie Lexie everything.' She grabbed hold of Halley's arm and dragged her out of the car with surprising strength.

'I c-can't talk about it.' Tears formed, hot, heavy drops that ran down her cheeks and soaked into the collar of her shirt.

'It must be something bad if it's affecting you like this. Is it Tor? I thought you were getting on so well.' Halley nodded, unable to speak.

'We were, but the p-past caught up with us. As I knew it would.'

'The past? I don't know what that means but I do know that nothing's worth you and Tor breaking up. You're made for each other.'

Halley smiled for the first time since leaving the Airstream.

'Breaking up' made them sound like teenagers. 'We haven't broken up; no promises, commitments or guarantees were made or exchanged.'

'That sounds very businesslike,' Lexie said, perplexed. 'We're talking about love here, true love; not bean counting. Nothing else matters. Come on, let's go down to the Airstream and sort this out.'

'You make it appear as though banging our heads together will put everything right.'

'It will. Believe me. You've wrought a change in Tor during the short time you've been here. It's been almost like having the old Tor back; please don't leave and spoil everything.'

'I was about to leave in any c-case,' Halley said, hardening her heart with difficulty.

'Yes, but not like this. Never like this.'

'I'm sorry, Lexie. Don't make this more difficult for me.'

'You will return, won't you?' Now it was her turn to dash away the tears. 'You've been like a sister to me, the sister I never had. We've been quite a gang these last few weeks: you, Tor, Rowan, Bryce and me. You don't know how that feels, coming from a dysfunctional family.' Her eyes widened as realisation dawned and she took a deep breath before continuing. 'This is about Lysander, isn't it? About what happened between you all those summers ago.'

'How do you know about that? Did Rowan tell you?'

'I worked it out for myself, I'm not the airhead everyone takes me for. You left, Suzie was dragged home and they were married ASAP. It doesn't take a genius to figure it out, especially with Ly's track record. Please, Halley, don't let that feck-wit ruin what you and Tor have.'

'You don't understand. When I told Tor everything,' she skipped over the little white lie, 'he couldn't look at me. He got dressed and left the Airstream.

'No, no, you've got it all wrong. Tor's PTSD makes processing thoughts and dealing with stuff a hundred times more difficult. If he left the Airstream, it was because he needed to find headspace, time to get his thoughts in order, separate the wheat from the chaff. Please, cut him some slack, allow him time to think his way through whatever's happened between you.'

This was a new Lexie, mature, sensible and acting like an adult. There was no doubting she loved her brother and cared for his welfare. Halley's, too, for that matter.

'There's more, stuff I can't share with you; things I took a risk sharing with Tor.' Sighing she dried the last of her tears and stiffened her resolve, closing her mind to how he must feel about her, now he knew every detail of her relationship with Lysander. 'I have to go home, I have a job and a life there. Look upon my early departure as my simply shaving a few days off my holiday.'

Some holiday! It'd been an emotional rollercoaster from start to finish.

'I'm not sure you're doing the right thing.'

'It's a long haul back to Hawaii, that'll give me ample time to assess how I feel about Tor, about everything.' She zoned out, remembering the last time she'd flown from Inverness to the States. 'Once I'm home, I'll get back in touch and we'll take it from there.'

She made it sound so simple, matter-of-fact, but Lexie's face crumpled as reality hit her. 'You won't be back, will you? And I'll have to explain to Tor and Rowan how I tried to make you see sense, but you wouldn't listen. They won't believe that I tried – at least, not hard enough. Here,' she handed the two bags of clothing to Halley, 'you'll need these.'

'Thank you.' Halley put the bags of clothing on the back seat and slid back into the car. She wanted to give Lexie a farewell hug but knew it would be too emotional for both of them. Climbing into the car she completed her manoeuvre and reversed out of the yard. When she looked back via the driver's mirror, Lexie had crossed the yard and was making her way towards the rose gardens and the beach. No doubt in search of Tor to ask what the bloody hell had gone wrong.

Hardening her heart, Halley headed for the open road and the long journey to Hawaii, a place which no longer felt like home. Home was here in Lochaber even if it was a burned-out shell of a bothy.

Home would always be where Tor was, even if he didn't want her.

Chapter Thirty-eight

Halley opened the zoom call with: *Hau'oli makahiki hou*. Rowan came back with '*Lang May yer Lum Reek*' and Lexie added: *Bliadhna Mhath Ùr*. Then all three raised their glasses and welcomed in the new year.

'I can hazard a pretty good guess at *Bliadhna Mhath Ùr*, but what *Lang May Yer Lum Reek* means I have no idea.'

Halley hid her emotion at seeing Rowan and Lexie for the first time in almost two months behind a throwaway remark but couldn't disguise the catch in her voice. She'd turned down several requests for a *zoomie*, fearing that once she saw them on screen, she'd fall to pieces. However, she'd had time to prepare herself for tonight's call and, apart from an initial wobble, was ready to discover what had been happening in Lochaber in her absence.

Rowan laughed. 'It means may you always have enough fuel to light a fire, warm your chimney and make it smoke – or reek. Something to do with prosperity, I think; Tam would have known.' She raised her glass: 'Tam.'

'Tam,' the others echoed.

'I'm glad you suggested this get together, Rowan. But, wouldn't you rather be welcoming the new year with your nearest and dearest?' Halley crossed her fingers, hoping they'd say no.

'Families, schm-amilies,' Lexie retorted. 'We saw in the New Year with them six hours ago. Besides, we aren't in the mood for celebration when our bestie's thousands of miles away in Baltimore. How did *your* family react to the news you wouldn't be home for Christmas and Hogmanay?'

'Badly. Dad wanted me to give a PowerPoint presentation to the Caledonian Society about my trip to Scotland, but I didn't feel up to it. Apart from which, I signed up for the graveyard shift weeks ago, knowing everyone would want to be with their families over the holiday period. Whereas, I –' she drew in a shuddering breath, unable to finish the sentence. 'Fortunately, my parents are so thrilled with my being at NASA they'll forgive me anything,' she added.

'Spotted any little green men through your telescope, recently?' Lexie asked, in an obvious attempt to inject a little humour into the call.

'Not recently.' Halley laughed, trying to respond in kind. 'However, I could be one of the first to see an image of a single star, and . . .' Recognising the glazed look of two individuals whose interest in astronomy was minimal, she stopped mid-sentence.

'Neither of us has been to bed,' Rowan changed the subject. 'I saw the New Year in with Bryce at the Dower House and Lexie joined us after slipping away from Lady Strachan's Hogmanay Ball. Which, according to the honourable Miss Strachan here, was a bizarre version of Love Island.' They laughed, and although Halley joined in, her heart gave an anxious lurch. Lady Strachan was nothing if not determined and it could only be a matter of time before Tor fetched the Strachan heirloom engagement ring out of the bank vault and slipped it on an aristocratic finger.

The thought made her mouth go dry and a pain lodge itself in the middle of her chest. Keeping her features neutral, she asked the million-dollar question. 'Apart from that, how are things?'

'The roads have been impassable for almost a week but the council managed to clear them in time for Hogmanay.'

Lexie laughed. 'Rowan Ferguson, that has to be the single most boring sentence you've ever uttered. That isn't what Halley meant and you know it.'

'I was trying to be diplomatic,' Rowan said in her defence. 'Actually, Halley, it's been a busy few weeks, thanks to Tor. That's what we want to share with you.'

'Tor?' Halley's heart rate increased at the mention of his name.

'You remember him, don't you? Tall, blond, the man you walked out on –'

'Lexie, we talked about this, and what did we say?' Coming over all 'Brown Owl', Rowan glared at the screen.

'*Don't mention Tor until Halley does*,' Lexie repeated dutifully. 'And she just did, didn't she? I can't stand by and watch two people I love screw up their lives due to a misunderstanding.'

Misunderstanding? Halley said under her breath.

'Yes. Misunderstanding. I might be slightly squiffy but there's nothing wrong with my hearing.' Lexie wagged her finger at the screen. 'You shouldn't have walked out on Tor, you should have given him a chance to return from the beach, allowed him to share his feelings and . . .'

Rowan leapt to Halley's defence. 'To be fair, Lexie, it was wrong of Tor to expect Halley to wait for him dutifully in the Airstream with no explanation, expect her to understand the mental and physical effects of PTSD, to give him time to get everything straight in his head.' She took a deep breath, knowing this wasn't what Lexie wanted to hear. 'In my opinion, it was too big an ask.'

Too big an ask.

Halley loved Rowan for fighting her corner. Lexie was the founding member of the Tor Strachan Fan Club and, although she loved Halley, in her eyes Tor could do no wrong. The words hung in the air, putting pressure on Halley to explain what had sent him into a tailspin that morning. The two women already knew too much about her and Lysander's shared history and she was determined they would never learn the whole story. Evidently, Tor felt the same and had kept his counsel and, for that, she was grateful. Not that she expected anything different; no matter how badly things had ended between them, she would trust him with her life.

'How are things up at the castle?' she asked, returning to her original question.

'Difficult,' Rowan began with her usual diplomacy.

Lexie, however, set about bringing Halley up to date. 'The shit's hit the fan and spread over a wide area. Right, Rowan?'

Rowan winced at Lexie's graphic language but nodded. 'Souter's been evicted from his caravan on the beach.'

'Tor's doing,' Lexie interjected. Rowan sent her a look which willed her to hold her wheesht and let her do the talking.

'Tor decided to check out Souter's military career and drew a blank. Turns out Souter has never been in the army and had invented that to trade on Monty's sympathy for a soldier down on his luck. Once Tor learned how he'd conned Monty, conned them all, he evicted Souter off the estate –'

'But only after finding Souter accommodation in Fort William, paying two month's rent in advance and sending him on his way with enough money to tide him over until he finds a job.' So typical of Tor, Halley reflected, and more than the little weasel deserved. 'The best is yet to come; Tor found out Souter is distantly related to Frank Bunce. That's how he ended up in Lochaber in the first place.'

'But doesn't that mean . . .' Plainly, Lexie hadn't worked out that, if Souter was Bunce's distant cousin, he was also related to her and Lysander. Knowing that Lexie was sensitive about not being one-hundred-percent Strachan, Halley decided it was better not to draw attention to it.

Rowan carried on with the story. 'Bunce was using Souter to poach *Creag na h-Iolaire*'s game, salmon, birds' eggs, red diesel and anything else he could lay his thieving hands on. Then he sold everything on and, we believe, shared the proceeds with Bunce.'

'Bunce, doesn't need the money as he's paid well over the odds as factor and Mother bankrolls him, too.' Lexie pulled a face. 'However, he couldn't resist being part of Souter's money-making scheme. And, as we all know, he'll do anything to get one over on Tor and Monty.'

Rowan took a sip of champagne, 'Tor suspects Lysander of somehow being implicated in Bunce and Souter's schemes. Not to make money, obvs, but to cause mischief.'

'Something he excels at,' Lexie said and then added. 'I see Tor as the Norse god, Thor, and Lysander as his less-than-trustworthy half-brother, Loki.' Although she was putting a brave face on it, Halley knew Lexie wasn't happy claiming kinship with two schemers like Bunce and

Lysander, not to mention Souter. A meddling triumvirate who would do anything to discredit Tor and anyone associated with him.

'I don't suppose my tin has turned up?' Halley asked, changing the subject. The other two shook their heads and sent her a sympathetic look.

'With the snow and everything Tor hasn't had the chance to have Souter's caravan removed. However, we aren't holding out much hope of finding any swag there. Everything will have passed through the hands of a fence by now.'

'And the fire?' Halley asked. Bunce and Souter were a couple of chancers but she couldn't believe they'd deliberately set out to cause her harm.

'Tor can't get to the bottom of that. We're putting it down to an electrical fault and leaving it there. Souter's gone, Bunce has been given a warning and if it wasn't for his relationship with my mother, he would have been sent packing, too. Typically, Lysander has distanced himself from everything. The worm.'

Halley sat back in her chair and released a long breath, unaware that she'd been leaning forward as though, somehow, she could pass through the screen and transport herself to Lochaber. She welcomed Rowan and Lexie's revelations but all she wanted to know about was Tor: if he'd forgiven her for running out on him, if tonight's Highland Ball had resulted in him finding a wife.

Her heart sank and ever-present tears threatened to overwhelm her, rendering speech impossible. Much as she loved talking to Rowan and Lexie, she needed time to process everything. The irony of the situation hit her; isn't that exactly what Tor had wanted the morning she'd walked out on him? Time to figure it all out? Ever astute, Rowan picked up on her conflicting thoughts and gave her a way out.

'You must be tired, Halley. You've had a long shift, followed by tonight's revelations. Let's end this call but arrange another for a week or so?'

'Sounds like a plan,' Lexie added, pulling a woebegone face. 'We miss you, darling Halley. Promise you'll come back and sort everything out between you and Tor. Or, would you rather he zoomed you next time instead of us?'

'No!' Halley replied, vehemently. 'Please, stop pushing me into doing something I'll regret! I know you mean well, Lexie, but you don't know the whole story. We've broken the ice with this zoom call, let's leave it there for now. Yes?' She looked directly at Rowan, knowing she could rely on her support.

'Of course, Halley. That's fine with us. You set up the next meeting when you're ready and forward the link to us. We'll be there for you. Won't we Lexie?'

'For sure.'

'Goodbye.' Halley smiled and ended the call before her emotions overcame her. Then she sat at her desk staring at the computer screen. What did she care about Lysander, Bunce, Souter and their schemes? All she wanted, was to know was that Tor didn't hate her and that, maybe, there was a way back for her; for them. Closing the lid of her MacBook she switched off her desk lamp and sat in the darkness.

'Oh, Tor,' she said, her heart breaking. 'How can things ever be right between us?' There being no answer, she finished her glass of champagne, hoping the alcohol would numb her senses and help her to sleep. And, should she dream, she wouldn't dream of Tor Strachan, the man she loved but couldn't have.

'I've been thinking,' Halley said next time they zoomed each other.

'Thinking is good; thinking means you're moving on.' Lexie and Rowan were in the Dower House and sharing a computer screen. Halley grinned as Rowan dug Lexie in the ribs.

'What have you been thinking?' Rowan asked.

'I have some holiday due in March and I'm thinking about going to Padua.'

'Padua, Italy?'

'The same. Tam and I had planned to visit Giotto's fresco cycle in the Scrovegni Chapel. Giotto represented the Star of Bethlehem as a long-tailed, fiery comet in the nativity fresco. He painted it in 1305, four years after the comet's appearance, so it would have been fresh in his mind. Somehow, that held a resonance for Tam, possibly because I was born in 1986, the last time the comet appeared.' Her voice tailed away as she thought of the times she and Tam had discussed visiting the chapel. She didn't mention the airline tickets and the hotel reservations she'd discovered in the tin because it was too painful. 'I want to be there for my birthday on the eleventh of March; to keep faith with Tam.'

'It's a bloody long way from Baltimore to Padua,' Lexie observed.

'Agreed. But, sometimes, you just have to go for it.'

'Here's an idea. Why don't Rowan and I fly over to Padua and meet you there?' Lexie's eyes were bright with excitement.

'Sorry to be a damp squib,' Rowan interjected. 'That weekend I'm booked on a course on Asian funerals in Edinburgh.'

'Do you have many of those?' Halley asked, interestedly.

'More than you might think. So, no can do.'

'I won't go without you, Ro; we're the three musketeers, remember? All for one and one for all. Hopefully we can all be together this summer when Halley returns to collect her telescope and other stuff. Unless she plans staying away for another twenty years?' She sent Halley a look, begging to be contradicted.

'Well, that's sorted then.' Rowan shifted in her seat, not giving Halley a chance to respond. Then she changed the subject. 'Go on, Lex, share our other piece of news with Halley.'

'News?' Halley repeated, her stomach giving an anxious lurch. Please God, don't let it be anything to do with Tor.

'Suzie's pregnant.'

'Oh.' Halley wasn't sure how she felt about this. In her mind, her miscarriage and Suzie and Lysander's fertility problems were somehow linked. And, over the years she'd wondered if she'd be able to carry a baby full term. It was madness to think that way, of course, but she couldn't help it. 'I'm thrilled for them,' she said, truthfully.

'There's more. Suzie, quite sensibly in my opinion, has insisted that she and Ly move out of the castle and into a property on her parents' estate.'

'Lysander wanted to move into the Dower House and had no qualms about evicting Lexie and Bryce,' Rowan said, quietly outraged. 'However, Suzie found an unexpected ally in Tor who said that she'd be better off near her mother once the baby's born.'

'He's right, of course, my mother wouldn't be able to resist meddling and interfering. It's what she does,' Lexie said, bitterly.

'And, because of the whole Bunce/Souter/Lysander business, the majority of which Tor has kept from mother, Ly has little choice but to do what Suzie wants.'

'Who knew Suzie has a backbone of steel?' Lexie laughed. 'Yay. Go Suzie.'

'Looks like we're all moving on,' Halley observed, feeling suddenly out of the loop. 'My secondment to NASA ends after I return from Padua. I must admit, I've enjoyed being part of the bigger picture, astrologically speaking.' She didn't add that immersing herself in work had helped with feelings of displacement and loneliness. 'I have a review next week and I'm hoping they might ask me to stay on. Watch this space.' She had meant to deliver the last sentence in an upbeat manner but it hadn't come out like that.

Then the kitchen timer went off and Rowan glanced at her watch.

'Time to put the Yorkshires in the oven, Lex. Sorry, Halley, we'll have to cut this call short, or dinner will be ruined. Good news about your job, though.'

'Go; make dinner.' Her response hid how alone she felt in her rented accommodation.

Then, unintentionally, Lexie made things worse. 'Tor's joining us for lunch. He can't believe I'm capable of producing something edible, even under Rowan's supervision. According to him, one of Bryce's Wild Sporrans would taste better than anything I'm capable of cooking.' They all laughed, then she sobered and added. 'I wish you could be here, too, Halley.'

Rowan appeared to zone out of the conversation, looking as though she had other things on her mind. Then, snapping out of her reverie, winked across the miles at Halley. 'Brotherly love, eh?'

'Absolutely. Have fun, ladies; I can smell the beef cooking from here.' Halley ended the call and, as had become her habit, sat looking at the blank screen until her eyes ached. Then, picking up her phone she ordered a takeaway from the nearest vegetarian restaurant knowing that, while it satisfied her appetite, it wouldn't feed her soul.

Only reconciliation with Tor Strachan could accomplish that, which was about as likely as Lexie being taken on as commis chef at the Gleneagles Hotel.

Chapter Thirty-nine

Halley stood before Giotto's fresco in the Scrovegni Chapel. A group of tourists joined her and, not wanting to appear as if she was taking a free ride, she hung back. However, the tour guide beckoned her forward.

'Please, Signora, you are on your own? Join us. This is the last tour of the day and the chapel will be closing soon.'

'Grazie,' she said, adding 'thank you, very much' to the other tourists.

'English?' the guide asked.

Smiling, Halley corrected him: 'Scottish.' How Tor would love to hear her proclaim her heritage, loud and proud.

'Ah, Scozzese,' he nodded and then returned to the fresco. 'As you can see in The Adoration of the Magi, Italian artist and architect Giotto di Bondone has represented Halley's comet as the Star of Bethlehem. This fresco is considered one of the greatest masterpieces of western art. Note his use of ultramarine for the background and a vivid palate of colours which would have cost his patron a small fortune to source them from all corners of the Mediterranean and import via Venice.'

Halley didn't have to look, she knew the fresco by heart: the camels with their horse-like heads, the sloping eyes and white faces of the Holy family, magi and angel. The wooden shelter representing the stable where Jesus was born. And, above their heads, the blood-orange comet with its blazing tail.

'Tam,' she whispered, 'how you would have loved this.' As the other tourists moved on to the next panel, she took one last look at the fresco. Sensing another tourist standing behind her, she waited, not wanting to ruin the moment for them. After a few minutes, she gathered her things together and prepared to leave.

''scusi, Signora,' a deep voice said, 'I think this belongs to you.'

'I'm sorry; what?' She glanced down at the tourist's outstretched hand. Nestled in its palm was a brooch shaped like a flattened triangle, edged with semi-precious stones representing shooting stars.

Tam's brooch!

The last time she'd seen it, it'd been laid out on a yellow duster on the kitchen table in the bothy. 'Wait? How do you come to have this?' She turned round, demanding an explanation.

Her attention was caught by the tourist's signet ring depicting a leaping stag with a thistle in its mouth and the motto: *Non Timeo Sed Caveo*. Her breath caught in her throat and she gave a sob of disbelief believing that, longing to see Tor Strachan, she'd somehow conjured up his presence.

In that moment, the level-headed scientist who only believed in the quantifiable and measurable, was superseded by a woman whose heart had been broken and was prepared to accept anything – magic included – if it reunited her with the man she loved. She raised her head and beheld the face she'd spent every waking hour thinking about since she'd left Lochaber.

A face she truly believed she'd never see again.

'T- or,' she tried to speak, but her heart was full. Her breath came in gasps and her heart rate quickened. Black dots swam before her eyes and she felt as if she might faint. Tor put his arm round her waist and held her fast.

'Steady the Buffs,' he laughed softly, voice husky and eyes as vivid as the cobalt Giotto had used in his fresco. 'Don't you want the brooch? In that case, I'll take it and go.' He started to walk away from Halley but she gained control of her emotions, shot forward and blocked his exit.

No way was he walking out on her again.

'I'll take what's mine,' was her reply. 'The brooch and you, Major Strachan.'

Then she threw herself into his arms, hugging him so fiercely that she imagined she heard a rib crack. Not to be outdone, Tor tilted her face and kissed her on the mouth long and hard. Then he put one arm around her shoulder, the other round her waist and held her close until they'd both recovered from the kiss.

'Let's get out of here. Italians love a lover, but I think kissing you in this sacred place might prove too much, even for them. No, don't say another word, we have a lot to discuss and I know the perfect place. Trattoria San Pietro, about a five-minute walk from here.'

Halley wanted to say that she'd walk a thousand miles over burning coals to be with him, to be allowed to explain her actions that morning when she'd confessed everything and then walked out on him.

'Trattoria? Great, I'm starving.' She hid her tumultuous feelings behind a throw away remark. 'I was going to light a candle for Tam, but . . .'

'We can do that tomorrow. He'd understand.'

Tomorrow? That meant he saw a future for them. Halley's breath caught in her throat and she found it difficult to speak. Tor was right; Tam would understand. Holding Tam's brooch firmly in her hand she matched her steps to Tor's, left the chapel behind and headed for the Trattoria San Pietro.

Tor ordered a delicious Cabernet from Veneto to accompany their antipasti. 'To us,' he toasted, holding up his glass. 'Chin-chin.'

'Slainte Mhath,' she replied, spreading her napkin on the table and placing the brooch on it. 'My mind's buzzing; the brooch, where did you find it?'

'It's a long story.'

'I have all night.'

'We have the rest of our lives,' Tor affirmed, linking their fingers and then raising her hand and kissing it. However, Halley was in no mood to be distracted, even if the sound of his voice, his touch and the passionate look he sent her made butterflies turn cartwheels in her stomach.

'First things first; how did you know I'd be here?'

'Rowan and Lexie.'

'But you wouldn't have known the exact time I'd visit the fresco.'

'I've been sitting in the chapel since first light, not daring to leave my post in case I missed you.'

'As befits a soldier,' she laughed, her heart filled with love. 'Now I know why Lexie seemed fixated on knowing my exact itinerary for today.'

'It took all of Rowan and Bryce's powers to convince Lexie that she didn't need to come along, to supervise me, to ensure nothing went wrong. Lexie,' he toasted his sister and Halley followed suit, clinking their glasses together.

'Back to the brooch,' she said, determined not to be sidetracked.

'You know that Souter has been thrown off the estate?'

'Yes; and Lysander and Suzie have moved out.'

'A case of Lysander jumping before he was pushed. He's persona non grata and no longer welcome in the castle, for obvious reasons. Even Mother acknowledged that.' Tor sent her a straight look, plainly designed to reassure her that Lysander's leaving had nothing to do with their joint past, but everything to do with his mischief making. 'You know he's related to Bunce and Geordie Souter?'

Halley nodded. 'A distant cousin, I believe?'

'Exactly.'

'The brooch? Tell me more, please.'

'Brooches, plural, actually. Tam's tin has turned up, contents intact.'

'Where? How?' Conversation stopped as their antipasti plates were removed.

'When we dragged Souter's caravan off the beach, we discovered a pit below the caravan concealing a cache of stolen goods. Souter had constructed a false floor in the van which gave him access to his swag, something no one knew about. Even Bunce.'

'Jings,' Halley said, using one of Tam's favourite expressions.

'There's more.'

'Go on.'

'This brooch,' he picked it up and polished it on his sleeve. 'I hope you don't mind; I've had it valued by one of mother's antique dealers who specialises in brooches, jewellery and medals. Drum roll,' he beat out a tattoo on the table, 'he believes it to be 'house of Faberge'. Although not designed by the great man himself.'

'That's something Tam had always dreamed of finding. His dream has come true.' Halley's voice snagged, 'Oh, Tor.'

'I know.' Tor placed the brooch on the table and reached for Halley's hands. 'Talking about dreams coming true, I've dreamed of this moment since you walked out on me last November. When you told me about your miscarriage, I should have supported you. I'm not excusing my behaviour but I needed time and space to figure it out. I expected you to know that, somehow. That was wrong of me and I am deeply, desperately sorry.'

'Lexie has kind've explained . . .'

'It was my place to explain. I shouldn't have expected you to understand how PTSD affects ex-servicemen, how it's affected me. I'm luckier than most and know it. However, since I returned from rehabilitation, everyone's been pussyfooting round me, taking care not to upset me, in case . . .'

She squeezed his hand. 'It's okay; I get it. Equally, I shouldn't have stormed off and driven to Inverness like a mad woman. When Lexie explained things to me in the stable yard, I should have got out of the car, returned to the Airstream to wait for your return. Talked things through, together. Although, to tell you the honest truth, I was scared.'

'What? Scared of me?'

'Not of you, of my feelings. The idea of falling in love with someone I couldn't have.'

'Why would you think you couldn't have me?'

She sent him a little smile. 'Highland laird meets astrophysicist; they fall in love but live thousands of miles apart. How could that work?'

'We could make it work.'

Halley's forehead wrinkled in concentration as she considered the obstacles in their path and tried to dismiss them. 'We could?'

'Of course. Whoa . . . rewind. Did you say: 'fall in love?'

'Isn't that what's happened? Against all the odds?'

'I'm not sure about 'odds', I'll settle for 'inauspicious beginning'. Maybe more romances should start with the heroine knocking the hero out stone cold with half a tree!'

'Only after he'd rugby-tackled her to the ground and pushed her face into the sand.'

'The Silver Sands of Morar, if you please. Almost an UNESCO World Heritage Site.' They both laughed, their eyes dancing, hormones skooshing through their blood at warp speed. Relief showed on their faces that, in spite of everything that had happened, there was a way forward.

Turning his hand over and raking her nail across his palm, Halley sent Tor a teasing look. After that, he seemed to find it hard to concentrate. 'Mind you, being knocked out by a branch will be a mere scratch compared to what will happen if I don't report back to Rowan, Lexie and, yes, even Bryce, telling them I've sorted out the unbelievable mess I created.' He frowned. 'I have made a mess of things, haven't I?'

'We both have. However, by coming here, with the brooch and your explanation, you've made everything right. At least, right for now.' She didn't want to spoil the mood but there were things which still needed to be sorted out. Tor's thoughtful expression showed he thought so too. However, that was all for the future, tonight was about finishing off what they'd started four months ago in the Airstream and finding a way forward.

'Signore, Signora, primo piatto, risotto ai funghi.' The waiter placed two plates of risotto in front of Tor and Halley, accompanied by a bowl of grated parmesan cheese with a professional flourish.

'Grazie,' Tor said.

'Prego, Signore; buon appetito.' After topping up their wine glasses he walked away. Tor looked down at their risotto and then let out a long breath, as though he'd reached a momentous decision.

'Would the patron be offended if we asked for the bill and left?'

'Probably. However, if there's one thing Italians understand, it's *amore.*' Standing, she slipped on her coat and hooked her handbag over her shoulder. After the angst of the last few months everything seemed to be going their way and she wasn't about to allow a plate of rice and mushrooms spoil that. 'Go; pay the bill and leave a large tip.'

Tor walked over to the desk and explained in halting Italian that they were leaving, nothing to do with the food but everything to do with the moment. The patron smiled, accepted his card payment and, after leaving a large tip as instructed, Tor joined Halley at the door.

They walked on to Via San Pietro whereupon Tor drew Halley into his arms and kissed her, leaving them both breathless and wanting more, much more.

'Your place or mine?' He asked, grinning.

'I'm staying in an airbnb with faulty plumbing and a rock-hard single bed. Can you do better than that?'

'I believe I can.'

Putting his arm round her shoulder, he led her towards Parcheggio Prandina where he'd left his hired car. With each footstep Halley's cares and worries slipped away. She let out a pent-up breath, squeezed Tor's hand and stood on tiptoes to kiss the sensitive spot just below his jaw, Tor shivered and she sent him a wicked, teasing smile. He'd better get used to it, she'd been yearning for this moment and wasn't going to let him out of her sight until she'd kissed every square inch of him.

She giggled, prompting Tor to ask: 'What's amused you, Doctor Dunbar?'

'You'll find out soon enough, Major Strachan.'

'Something nice?'

'Better than nice,' she replied.

'I'll hold you to that.'

'I'd expect nothing less,' she smiled. Her teasing laugh acknowledged that tonight was the beginning of something wonderful. And, if there were obstacles ahead, they'd overcome them together as lovers and best friends; and spend the rest of their lives doing so.

Chapter Forty

Six months later, Halley walked down the wooden steps to the beach where Tam's bothy had previously stood. She had one hand on Tor's shoulder while the other gripped the rope banister for balance. Tor had insisted on her wearing a blindfold so nothing would spoil the surprise.

'Surprise?' Halley had echoed. 'There's nothing else in this world I want or need.'

'That's what I expected you to say.' Tor laughed, leading the way to ensure she didn't fall down the steps.

After their honeymoon in Hawaii and tour of the south pacific they'd settled into life in the Airstream, two lovers enjoying the privacy it afforded. They had no desire to move into the castle, to be near his mother with her endless reproving, disappointed looks which made it plain that, in marrying, they'd shattered her dreams and broken her heart.

'She'll get over it,' Tor had said to Halley. 'Or she won't. The choice is hers.'

Halley shook the thought out of her head and concentrated on where she placed her feet instead. She knew exactly how many steps there were leading to the beach and counted each one as they descended. When she set foot on the penultimate tread, the long-drawn-out drone as a piper blew air into his bags was heard. Then Monymusk, the Regimental charge of the Argylls, filled her ears.

'What?' She asked, laughing. 'Are we going into battle or having a highland fling?'

'A bit of both,' was Tor's enigmatic reply. Halley laughed; Tor's so-called wee surprises were never less than spectacular. 'You can remove the blindfold now,' he said, as they stood on the sands. Halley did as he instructed, blinking in the sunlight, unable to believe the sight before her.

She gasped in surprise. 'Tor – I don't believe it! How, did you . . .'

'Now you know why I've kept you away from this end of the beach since we returned from honeymoon.'

'I thought it was because the burned out remains of the bothy made me sad, not because . . .'

'. . . because I've rebuilt Tam's bothy?'

She threw her arms around his neck, hugging him with all her might. 'But how, when?' she stammered.

'Bryce and I worked on the project together and, while we were on honeymoon, he oversaw its completion. What d'you think?'

'What do I think? Oh, Tor . . .' She placed hands over her heart and sent him a loving look. Then she noticed the people gathered on the beach drinking champagne and eating barbequed food.

So *that's* why she kept imagining she could smell steak cooking as she descended to the beach!

'There's more,' Tor said, beckoning Lexie forward.

She handed Halley a large pair of scissors, then Bryce, Rowan and Monty escorted her over to the porch while the piper changed his tune from Monymusk to: *I Love a Lassie*, another of Tam's favourites. Then Halley saw the large red ribbon wrapped round the bothy's porch, ending in a bow. However, the most amazing thing of all was the plaque over the front door proclaiming it:

Tam's Place.

'A new name,' Tor said, 'for a new beginning. Go on, mo chridhe, do the honours.'

Halley cut the ribbon and walked into the porch. Unable to resist, she pushed open the front door and saw, not rickety sale room bargains so beloved by Tam, but an up-to-the minute kitchen and living room combo any airbnb would be proud of.

Puzzled but delighted, she walked back to the beach. 'Are we going to live here now?' she asked Tor. He shook his head. 'With your permission, I'd like to turn Tam's bothy into an airbnb for the families of veterans suffering from PTSD. Offer them a safe place to stay, free of charge; a sanctuary of peace and quiet where they can forget the trauma of war and rebuild their lives. What do you think, Hal?

She took a deep breath. 'I think I couldn't love you more than I do at this moment, no matter how hard I tried. This is perfect, you are perfect; thank you. Thank you everyone,' she waved to the assembled guests.

Lexie sidled up, grinning in her usual irrepressible manner. 'We took a risk and got it ready without your say-so because we hoped you'd agree to Tor's proposal. You can change the interior, or anything else if you wish, but the first family is arriving in a few days' time to stay for two weeks.'

'I wouldn't change a thing. What are your thoughts, Monty?' Halley asked her new father-in-law who was leaning heavily on his cromack concentrating on not spilling a drop of champagne.

He pulled a large paisley handkerchief out of the pocket of his padded jacket blew his nose noisily and wiped away his tears. 'To quote darling Tam, I think it's simply braw.'

'You once said, that here was the perfect place for a Dark Sky Park, Halley. Something to think about in the future, maybe?' Tor suggested.

'We should make the most of having an in-house astrophysicist to help with the project,' Rowan said, slipping her arm through Halley's and handing her a glass of champagne.

'A toast,' Monty said, 'Tam's Place.'

'Tam's Place,' they repeated, raising their glasses towards the new bothy.

No one noticed that Halley didn't sip her champagne but simply nursed the glass in her hand, looking over at her husband, her heart full of love and her happiness complete.

She let out a long, slow breath feeling suddenly very tired. She had her own news to share but that could wait until tomorrow. Tonight, was for remembering the past and for looking forward to a bright future.

'Oh look, here it is,' Bryce said, pointing heavenwards.

Bang on cue the International Space Station passed overhead, Halley's comet in miniature, putting its seal on what promised to be a very happy future for Tor, Halley and everyone who loved them.

About the Author

Finalist – Romantic Novelists' Association
Indie Champion 2021 and 2022

A message from Lizzie

Hi everyone and thank you for reading Dark, Highland Skies. Writing it has kept me going through the pandemic and beyond and I hope you enjoy it. I've already started writing #8 (title to be revealed!) and hope to finish it as soon as I can.

Writing can be a very lonely occupation as the author shuts herself away from the world to get those all-important words down on the page. Luckily, I have friends who spur me on, read my rough drafts and make insightful comments when I hit a plotting problem. They are: Jessie, Joan, Jan, June and Jo. Not to forget Miss Wrafter (editor and proof reader) Maggie frae Fife, Maisie of the Glen, mother-in-law, Betty and brilliant beta reader, La Diva, Isabella.

I'm often asked where my ideas come from and I always reply: *everywhere*. I have one of those minds which absorbs information, files it away and downloads it onto the page when needed – aided by the internet, natch. Luckily, I spend time in magical, mystical Scotland each summer and, when I'm there, the writing and ideas just flow.

Once again, I owe an enormous debt to Sarah Houldcroft of Goldcrest Books who has worked with me on all of my novels and Gail Bradley who designed the cover for and who will be helping me to re-design the covers for my other five novels.

A word about the swearing parrot. When I taught at Inglehurst Infants in the mid-eighties a teacher inherited a parrot from an undertaker (seriously). Much to her consternation, every time the phone rang, the parrot said: 'There's another poor bugger gone'. See what I mean about filing information away? You never know when these snippets will come in handy.

And, last but not least, I must mention my uncles who had such an influence on me as I was growing up in Scotland: James, John, Alex, Joseph, young Tommy and Archie. But, most of all, great-uncle Tommy who was the sweetest, kindest and most supportive uncle a girl could wish for and the inspiration for Uncle Tam in this novel.

PS – if you've enjoyed, please leave a review on Amazon as they make a real difference to my sales and to me, as an author. Thank you.

Lizzie – February 14th 2023

www.facebook.com/LizzieLambwriter

www.instagram.com/lizzielambwriter

www.lizzielamb.co.uk

More Books from Lizzie

Harper's Highland Fling

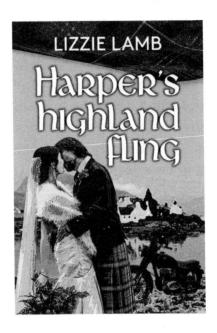

Take a crazy road trip to the highlands of Scotland from the comfort of your armchair.

After a gruelling academic year, head teacher Harper MacDonald is looking forward to a summer holiday trekking in Nepal. However, her plans are scuppered when her wayward niece, Ariel, leaves a note announcing that she's running away with a boy called Pen. The only clue to their whereabouts is a footnote: I'll be in Scotland. Cue a case of mistaken identity when Harper confronts the boy's father – Rocco Penhaligon, and accuses him of cradle snatching her niece and ruining her future. At loggerheads, Harper and Rocco set off in hot pursuit of the teenagers, but the canny youngsters are always one step ahead. And, in a neat twist, it is the adults who end up in trouble, not the savvy teenagers.

Some reviews for Harper's Highland Fling

'A thrilling, entrancing, full on romantic adventure. Hang onto your hat, it's a 5 Star trip all the way!'

'Fasten your seatbelt for the road trip of your life! It's going to be a bumpy ride!'

'Another smart, funny, romantic read from Lizzie Lamb.'

'An exciting armchair road trip to Bonnie Scotland, a gripping romance and a set of characters you're not going to let go. Lizzie Lamb is back!'

'Written with Lizzie's customary blend of warmth, wit and 'will they, won't they' drama. Her best romance yet. I loved it!'

'The humour in this book had me laughing out loud as it was just "my cup of tea". I love Lizzie's style of writing and this is the second book I have read by her and have another 2 on my kindle waiting to be enjoyed'

Tall Dark and Kilted

A contemporary romance set in the highlands of Scotland –
Can Fliss tame the Monarch of the Glen?

Fliss Bagshawe longs for a passport out of Pimlico where she works as a holistic therapist. After attending a party in Notting Hill she loses her job and with it the dream of being her own boss. She's offered the chance to take over a failing therapy centre, but there's a catch. The centre lies five hundred miles north in Wester Ross, Scotland.

Fliss's romantic view of the highlands populated by Men in Kilts is shattered when she has an upclose and personal encounter with the Laird of Kinloch Mara, Ruairi Urquhart. He's determined to pull the plug on the business, bring his eccentric family to heel and eject undesirables from his estate – starting with Fliss. Facing the dole queue once more Fliss resolves to make sexy, infuriating Ruairi revise his unflattering opinion of her, turn the therapy centre around and sort out his dysfunctional family. Can Fliss tame the Monarch of the Glen and find the happiness she deserves?

Some reviews for Tall, Dark and Kilted

'This story is full of romantic Scottish themes; Kilts, bagpipes, scenery, Gaelic whisperings, Clan Urquhart tartans and Strathspey reels. Definitely an enjoyable read.'

'I really couldn't put it down. Makes me want to buy my hubby a kilt.' 'No complications just a relaxing story that drags you in to the end. Quite sad to finish it.'

'You won't be disappointed ladies and men, you could learn a thing or two.'

'I truly enjoyed this book. I stumbled across it on Twitter. I was looking for a light read. However, I had trouble putting this one down.

'If you like your heroes strong, dark, gorgeous and commanding with a vulnerable streak and a passionate nature, or if you just want to know what a sexy Scottish laird wears under his kilt, grab this book and prepare to fall in love.'

Girl in the Castle

A Girl. A Castle, A Hot Laird and Family secrets

Her academic career in tatters, Dr Henriette Bruar needs somewhere to lay low, plan her comeback and restore her tarnished reputation. Fate takes her to a remote Scottish castle to auction the contents of an ancient library to pay the laird's mounting debts.

The family are in deep mourning over a tragedy which happened years before, resulting in a toxic relationship between the laird and his son, Keir MacKenzie. Cue a phantom piper, a lost Jacobite treasure, and a cast of characters who – with Henri's help, encourage the MacKenzies to confront the past and move on. However – will the Girl in the Castle be able to return to university once her task is completed, and leave gorgeous, sexy Keir MacKenzie behind?

Some reviews for Girl in the Castle

'It was the first paragraph that did it. A ghostly lament, images of an ancient Scottish castle above a loch, swirling mists and – yes – the word Sassenachs. Hey, I'm a huge fan of Outlander. How could I resist?'

'Lizzie must have done hours of research to get the facts right and they fit into the book beautifully. There's also a bit of paranormal activity too, buried treasure and of course, lots of her trademark humour.'

'One of Lizzie Lamb's big strengths is her descriptive settings; the history and Gaelic references she includes add such sparkle and authenticity to the story.'

'I was totally hooked from the moment the heroine, Henriette, stepped off the train & walked into the swirling mists & the great adventure awaiting her.'

'I wonder how many people are inspired to visit Scotland after reading one of Lizzie Lamb's books? I bet quite a few ...'

'Girl in the Castle is a lovely, escapist romantic read which is expertly executed by this talented writer.'

Scotch on the Rocks

Family secrets, second chance love and romance in the Highlands of Scotland

Ishabel Stuart is at the crossroads of her life. Her wealthy industrialist father has died unexpectedly, leaving her a half-share in a ruined whisky distillery and the task of scattering his ashes on a Munro. After discovering her fiancé playing away from home, she cancels their lavish Christmas wedding at St Giles Cathedral, Edinburgh and heads for the only place she feels safe – Eilean na Sgairbh, a windswept island on Scotland's west coast – where the cormorants outnumber the inhabitants, ten to one.

When she arrives at her family home – now a bed and breakfast managed by her left-wing, firebrand Aunt Esme, she finds a guest in situ – Brodie. Issy longs for peace and the chance to lick her wounds, but gorgeous, sexy American, Brodie, turns her world upside down. In spite of her vow to steer clear of men, she grows to rely on Brodie. However, she suspects him of having an ulterior motive for staying at her aunt's B&B on remote Cormorant Island. Having been let down twice by the men in her life, will it be third time lucky for Issy? Is it wise to trust a man she knows nothing about – a man who presents her with more questions than answers? As for Aunt Esme, she has secrets of her own.

Some reviews for Scotch on the Rocks

'A cracking book that stays with you long after you have finished.'

'I like the way she weaves 'older characters' into the story; how love isn't just for the young.'

'Lots of romance, humour, quirky secondary characters and a mad parrot. I was kept engaged, right up to the last page.'

'A five-star romance from a five-star romantic novelist.'

'A delight to read. Loved the Scottish'ism and the bits of history and the evocative imagery of a highland castle. Oh, and the hero completely rocked.'

Take Me, I'm Yours

A Wisconsin love story: an uplifting small-town romance

India Buchanan plans to set up an English-Style bed and breakfast establishment in her great-aunt's home, MacFarlane's Landing, Wisconsin. But she's reckoned without opposition from Logan MacFarlane whose family once owned her aunt's house and now want it back.

MacFarlane is in no mood to be denied. His grandfather's living on borrowed time and Logan has vowed to ensure the old man sees out his days in their former home. India's great-aunt has other ideas and has threatened to burn the house to the ground before she lets a MacFarlane set foot in it. There's a story here. One the family elders aren't prepared to share. When India finds herself in Logan's debt, her feelings towards him change. However, the past casts a long shadow and events conspire to deny them the love and happiness they both deserve. Can India and Logan's love overcome all odds? Or is history about to repeat itself?

Some reviews for Take Me, I'm Yours

'Yet again Lizzie Lamb has written a thoroughly enjoyable book, crackling with sparks and humour as well as painting a wonderful image of rural Wisconsin.'

'Ladies take note – Logan MacFarlane is yet another incredibly hot hero. India Buchanan is just the sort of woman needed to challenge him and from their first meeting the chemistry is buzzing.'

'The dialogue is witty, warm and deft and the cocktail of love, dating and passion is deliciously handled. That the reader is kept on tenterhooks to the end is the mark of a captivating writer who weaves unexpected patterns.'

'The immensely well fleshed out characters and great dialogue, glides you through this wonderful tale as the story unfolds with the all-important help of some well-crafted background characters.'

Boot Camp Bride

Romance and Intrigue on the Norfolk marshes

Take an up-for-anything rookie reporter. Add a world-weary photojournalist. Put them together . . . light the blue touch paper and stand well back!

Posing as a bride-to-be, Charlee Montague goes undercover at a boot camp for brides in Norfolk to photograph supermodel Anastasia Markova looking less than perfect. At Charlee's side and posing as her fiancé, is Rafael Ffinch award winning photographer and survivor of a kidnap attempt in Colombia. He's in no mood to cut inexperienced Charlee any slack and has made it plain that once the investigation is over, their partnership – and fake engagement – will be terminated, too. Soon Charlee has more questions than answers. What's the real reason behind Ffinch's interest in the boot camp? How is it connected to his kidnap in Colombia? In setting out to uncover the truth, Charlee puts herself in danger ... As the investigation draws to a close, she wonders if she'll be able to hand back the engagement ring and walk away from Rafa without a backward glance.

Some reviews for Boot Camp Bride

'Boot Camp Bride is an intriguing romantic romp across the marshes of Norfolk with the naive but enthusiastic Charlee and deliciously sexy and terribly capable leading man, Rafa.'

'Loved it.'

'Another sparkling read, full of passion and laughter, but with a sinister undertone that keeps you turning the pages.'

'A definitely great read, as was Lizzie's Debut book, Tall Dark & Kilted... roll on book 3!'

'That good I read it twice!'

'The dialogue between the two main characters, rookie journalist Charlee Montague, and world-weary photographer, Rafael Ffinch is brilliant and full of repartee.'

Printed in Great Britain
by Amazon

25955926R00192